Failure to Communicate

Kaia Sønderby

FAILURE TO COMMUNICATE

Cover illustration © by Djamila Knopf

Set in LaTeX using the Baskervald ADF typeface

Published by The Kraken Collective
ISBN 978-91-985297-0-8

In Loving Memory
Atla, Skadi, Bibbi and Velvet

For being my Cake and Marbles, and making me smile through these difficult years.

Acknowledgements

First and foremost, to my husband, whose unwavering faith and support has kept me going forward even when I thought I could no longer move. If even a fraction of the people I met understood me half as well as you do, I'd like a lot more people.

The great people from Wattpad, who embraced Xandri in Testing Pandora and wanted to know more of her story. I hope you'll stay with us for every step of her journey.

Djamila Knopf, whose gorgeous art so elegantly paints a picture of the moment of contact between two species that I'm hoping to convey. It was such a pleasure to work with you and I hope we can continue to do so.

Chapter One

Sometimes I was a one-woman communications breakdown.

"*What*," Christa Baranka demanded, her blue eyes blazing, "is your problem, anyway?"

Does she want the long list or the short list? But I managed not to say that out loud. I was in a big enough mess without my unruly mouth getting me into trouble. Well, *more* trouble.

I tried not to flinch as murmurs rippled around the tiny mess hall; even at such a low volume they seemed to ricochet off the plasteel walls and cut right through me. Hoping no one would notice, I eased a hand into the top pocket of my cargo pants and rubbed my fingers across the satin sewn along the top. It was too warm from my body heat for the smooth texture to be as comforting as I'd like, but it'd have to do. I needed all the composure I could muster to fix this.

"Christa," I began carefully, "I wasn't trying—"

"That's the problem! You *never* try. Did you have to take lessons to get this insensitive, or were you just born that way?"

Sweet Mother Universe. I bit my lip, clamping down hard on the spike of anger and hurt that pierced my gut. The murmurs increased; beside me, copilot Aleevian sil masViara stifled a sound that could've been a laugh or a gasp of surprise. Probably the former, knowing Leev. Only the burn of anger kept me from running. Or maybe it was humiliation that glued my feet to the plasteel floor.

"Well," came a rumbling voice from the end of the table, "now who's being insensitive?"

Silence descended, heavy and thick in a way that seemed to settle on my skin. The entire contingent of the temp mess turned, almost as a unit, to gaze at our pilot, Akcharrch. She shifted in her seat with a sound like a grumbling bear, getting two of her six legs firmly underneath her. No one moved. The rocks-in-a-blender tone of the Ongkoarrat's voice made it hard to tell if she was angry, but no one wanted to risk that she was. Not considering she was

1

roughly two and a half meters long, weighed more than a grown man, and had six strong legs, each topped with three long, sharp claws.

"After all," Akcharrch continued, "Xandri *was*, in a sense, born that way."

Christa glanced back at me, her normally rosy complexion turned a color much like replicator soy. Were we even, now that we'd *both* stepped in it?

I wouldn't say I'd been born *insensitive*; just different. For many people, too different, a kind of different the universe didn't know how to deal with anymore. Generally all human babies were cultivated in Petri dishes these days, so parents could add any little touches they wanted and remove any...impurities. It had been done that way for centuries, erasing hereditary illnesses, physical disabilities and developmental disorders from the human genome. Or so people thought.

Then came a trend on some of the human colony worlds— including Wraith—of having one's children au naturel. My parents, consummate politicians the both of them, had taken up the trend in an effort to appeal to the everyday voting populace. Slowly but surely people started to notice something different about some of the children born during the trend. I was one of the last humans to be diagnosed with a neurodivergence—in my case, autism—before the trend died a very sudden death.

The years since had been spent trying to sweep the whole business under the carpet, like so many other 'oopsies' in human history.

Christa recovered quickly, color flooding back into her cheeks. "That's *not* an excuse."

"I never said it was," I protested. "I wasn't trying to—look, Christa, I'm sorry if I—what I meant was..."

Goddamned space-fried communication...thing!

Aki chuffed, the sound coming through her blunt, bearish muzzle rather than her translater-implant. She rocked forward, heaving her bulk out of the seat and dropping to all sixes, her claws clattering on the plasteel floor. Everyone turned to look at her again, to my intense relief.

"Xandri is right, though," Aki pointed out. "She *is* better suited to the job than you are, Christa. She'd make an excellent *attoaong*."

The translator failed to come up with a suitable translation for the last word.

Silence reigned as Akcharrch ambled through the temp mess and out the door. Most eyes were on her; only Christa watched me, her pretty features etched with fury. *Thanks, Aki. I think you made that worse.* I appreciated the Ongkoarrat's blunt demeanor, but as I'd learned—mostly the hard way—humans didn't tend to take to blunt too well.

"Well." Leev's hand came down on my shoulder. "I think you've just been nominated for a high status position amongst the universe's most antisocial species. You should fit right in."

I'm not antisocial. You're just an asshole. But as usual, I didn't say it aloud. Instead I looked up at Leev; I might have some trouble managing my facial expressions, but I'd turned the glare into an art form. Might've been more effective if Leev wasn't twenty-eight centimeters taller than me. He grinned, his teeth seeming a mite too sharp against the silvery-blue sheen of his skin.

Arrogant Sanavila. At least he was only a juvenile. The adults creeped me out, with their ethereal glowiness and that *attitude*, that reminded me so much of the therapists my parents had dragged me to when I was younger. Leev was only a few years from adulthood and it seemed he'd been cultivating his annoyance factor a lot lately.

"Hand," I said, placing a fingertip against Leev's long-fingered hand and pushing, "off."

"Yeah, Aleevian," Christa said. "Don't touch Her Highness. You might get frostbite."

She turned, whipping around so fast I was amazed her tidy blond bun didn't come undone. *So much for apologizing,* I thought, as Christa stormed out of the temp mess. Not that I was sure I wanted to anymore. Frostbite? One of these days I'd show her *frostbite.*

The temp mess started emptying out then. Fortunately Leev dropped his hand from my shoulder, or the sudden press of moving bodies might have sent me through the plasteel roof. I continued to rub my fingertips along the strip of satin lining my pocket as people filed out. A few brushed against me, but I managed not to cringe. After the drama with Christa, my senses were too overloaded to deal with the touch of others.

Finally the temp mess cleared out. I took a step towards the door, breathing a bit easier—and my wristlet chimed.

3

I tapped a button and said, "Xandri."

"Xan! My favorite, non-overreacting person on the ship."

Uh oh. "Diver." A smile tugged at the corners of my mouth, even though I knew I probably wasn't gonna like this. "Back from your scouting trip?"

"Just about. And uh...got that footage you wanted."

"Stellar. What else have you got?"

"No idea what you mean."

"Diver..."

"You know, for someone whose supposed to be shit at reading people, you're awful damn good at reading people."

You know what they say: practice, practice, practice. "It's my job. You might as well tell me what's going on. At least *I* won't yell at you."

"True enough. I kinda...got a few Stills tagging along."

"Define 'a few' please."

Diver made a sound that came through the wristlet with a spray of fuzziness. "Roughly, oh, a hundred. Ish."

"Diver!"

"You said you wouldn't yell!"

I sighed and began looking around the hall for the nearest alarm. "All right, contact Lieutenant Estevanico and tell him what's coming."

"Got it."

"And Diver?"

"Yeah?"

"This footage better be worth it."

I didn't need to see him to know he was grinning. "Why d'you think they're so pissed at me? Diver out."

I clicked the comm button on my wristlet and reached out to slap the alarm. As klaxons went off, filling the plasteel halls with ear-splitting wails that nearly shattered what was left of my composure, my wristlet vibrated to inform me of incoming files. I yanked my hood up, giving the tightening cord a small tug; the hood tightened and the sound-dampeners clamped over my ears, cutting out some of the racket. I sighed in relief as I bolted down the hall. Just because the universe refused to accommodate my sensory issues didn't mean I couldn't find ways around them.

4

Hold it together, Xan. You've got a job to do. I turned a corner, raced down another hall, and burst out into the strange, disorienting russet light let off by this system's red dwarf star. We'd dubbed the planet Stillness, though it wasn't still now. The entire platoon, plus us civvies—though technically we were *all* civvies now—hurried into position, following Gunnery Sergeant Huff's orders. Lieutenant Estevanico was likely still talking to Diver, judging by the way the Kowari paced, his tail flicking in agitation.

"Corelel!" Gunnery Sergeant Huff barked when she spotted me, her voice cutting straight through my sound-dampeners as if they weren't there. "Get down and get to work on that footage. I want answers!"

"Yes, ma'am. Uh, Gunny."

She rolled her eyes and waved me off. I hurried to the line and slid to my knees behind the barricade the platoon had dug. Only a few civvies were on the field; people like Christa, Leev and Aki would be inside unless they were absolutely needed. Me they needed to sort out how to handle the Stills, so on the field I went.

Conventional Ancient Earth "wisdom" said I wasn't suited for this job. Before we'd been (presumably) erased from the human genome, autistic people'd had a reputation for lacking empathy and being unable to read social cues, especially non-verbal ones. What conventional Ancient Earth "wisdom" usually failed to mention is that, given the time, we could learn; that's how I'd survived life up until now. And I was a *lot* less expensive than top-of-the-line diplomacy AI, which the *Carpathia*—working outside the government sphere—couldn't afford.

Stillness went quiet as the last soldier took his place and the alarms stopped blaring in the temp shelter, showing off why we'd chosen that name. In my four years traveling with the *Carpathia*, I'd never been on a planet with so little ambient noise. Nothing rustled or chirped or howled or squawked. Even the wind barely seemed to stir most of the time. The faint rustle of the soldier next to me was far too loud.

"Better get to work," she whispered to me. "You know how Gunny gets."

"Quiet, Private," Gunnery Sergeant Huff hissed.

The soldier shrugged. I nodded and turned my attention to my wristlet. This day and age people tended towards heads-up displays, but I couldn't handle a HUD. Crowded stations and ships were bad enough without something in my head, identifying other species, informing me what brand of clothes they were wearing and what planet the silk came from, giving me locations where I could purchase X, Y, and Z, and god only knew what else. Sure, you could turn down the flow of information, but my wristlet was easier.

I pressed a button to call up the latest uploads. The screen blinked on. I pressed my fingertips to it and pulled, drawing the holographic display out. With a flick of my fingers I expanded the screen to a reasonable size; as an afterthought, I drew away two separate, smaller screens in case I needed them for comparison purposes.

"Here he comes," I heard Gunnery Sergeant Huff say behind me.

I raised my head briefly. A figure moved in the distance, red light glinting on metal. A forest rose beyond that; no doubt the Stills would soon emerge. *Better get to work.*

I turned back to my wristlet. The most recent data from Diver blinked to life on the main screen, showing a gathering of Stills. Big—close to two and a half meters tall when they stood up straight—covered in shaggy, coarse dark fur, the Stills had a distinctly simian look that had caused the crew to want to dub them Space Bigfoot. In a rare show of my executive powers, I'd overruled that name. It was insulting and they weren't apes, anyway.

Pedantry later, Xan. Work now. The sound of metal feet on rolling turf grew closer. I focused on the screen. In the middle of a ring of Stills, two more crouched, circling each other. *A fight? Why'd he get me a fight?* We'd had a few skirmishes with the Stills, firing non-lethal rounds to drive them off. They fought with sticks, spears and rocks; what good would it do us to know more about their combat methods?

"*Anything, Corelel?*" Huff's sub-vocalization came through the open channel on my wristlet.

I shook my head.

"*Then work faster.*"

Closer now. I glanced up to see Diver, helmet in place, ride across the line on his armored "horse." The Stills came spilling out of the trees, moving on all fours, wearing packs on their backs to carry their weapons. Shit. I was running out of time.

Stills fighting, Stills fighting…what does this tell me? What piece was I missing? I'd been studying them for weeks, but they were hard to track and I had so little footage. I called up the last two uploads on screens two and three, hoping a comparison would give me *something.*

Diver rode by, pausing long enough to tip his visor up and glance down at my work. I didn't have time to look up. As he rode off, I shifted my gaze from one screen to the next, watching the Stills fight, watching them greet each other. *There is* definitely *something here. I think…I think…*

A rock came down, landing between me and the soldier beside me. I huddled low, drawing one arm up to ward off the projectiles and trying not to think about them. At the back of my mind a voice babbled in terror, not because I believed the Stills were actually hostile—unlike the soldiers, I didn't—but because I had bad experiences with rocks. *No, focus. Find what's diff—wait a minute!*

"*Gunny,*" I sub-vocalized into the channel. "*I think I've got it!*"

"Good job," the soldier next to me whispered.

I nodded and turned, maintaining my crouch, to show the gunny the pattern I'd seen. A spear came arcing over the barrier, landing between me and Huff. I halted, eyes wide.

"*All right, that's it,*" Huff said. "*Troops—*"

"*Wait!*" I hissed.

"*Tell me you got something so I don't have to order these creatures shot, Corelel.*"

I started to sidle forward again. "*There's a major difference—a reversal, even—in their behavioral patterns as opposed to ours. We need to—shit!*"

Another rock landed right at my toes and I flailed, trying to keep my balance. Were it not for the soldier beside me, I would've landed on my back in the ditch. She caught the back of my top and yanked upwards, keeping me upright.

"*Relax, civvie,*" she sub-vocalized with a laugh. "*It's just a rock.*"

Unthinking, I reached up and touched the scar behind my ear, well-shielded by the bits of loose hair hanging from my braid. "*Don't underestimate the efficiency of rocks.*" Since the damn Stills wouldn't stop throwing their damn rocks, I said, "*Gunny, we need to stand up. All of us.*"

A beat, then, "*You're out of your mind.*"

7

"*Possibly, but it's what we need to do. Gunny, they fight in a crouch and greet each other standing up. Right now, we look like we want to be aggressive.*"

Gunnery Sergeant Huff stared at me, her brow furrowed. *I did not do a good job explaining that. Big surprise.* Then I would have to just *show* the gunny what I meant, without my wristlet. I retracted the hologram and took a deep breath; there was a chance I'd gotten this wrong and yet I was gonna test the hypothesis anyway. *Xandri Corelel, the woman with no social instincts, relying on her social instincts to keep her alive.*

The universe had a twisted sense of humor.

Before anyone could think to stop me, I stood and leapt over the barrier. A rock struck my hip as I landed; I shoved aside the pain and the memory of fear and stood up straight, ignoring the gunny shouting orders at my back.

Another rock fell at my foot; then they stopped falling altogether. Across the plain, at the edge of the forest, the Stills crouched, watching me. One of them—a large, chestnut-colored female who, I recalled from my hours of watching the data, appeared to be a leader of some kind—straightened part way. Even across the distance I felt her eyes on me, waiting for my next move. My knees trembled with relief.

A sigh came across the comm channel, this time from Lieutenant Estevanico. "Soldiers, weapons down, stand up."

Slowly, hesitantly, the soldiers around me began to stand; the woman to my right was the first to straighten completely. Across the distance separating us, the Stills rose too. *Oh, sweet Mother Universe, thank you.* I'd been right. As more of us stood, more Stills straightened as well. The lead female took a few curious steps forward, her shaggy shoulders thrown back, her body language broad and open in a way that would look aggressive to human eyes. *But it's not. She's being...friendly.*

"Corelel?" The gunny again.

"In the new data Diver sent me, there were recordings of Stills fighting. They fight in a crouch, even though they're bipedal. In some of the other recordings, I noticed that they always greet each other upright, with a very open body posture. To us it looks like aggression, but to them it's—I think—a means of showing one in-

8

tends no harm. This whole time, to them we've looked like—like we're spoiling for a fight."

"So it would seem. But they attacked our scouts first; find out why, if at all possible. And Corelel?"

"Yes, Gunny?"

"If you ever stand up in a hostile situation like that again, especially without armor on, I will shoot you myself. Is that clear?"

"Understood, Gunny. Corelel out."

I twitched my thumb, closing out the comm link for the moment. I needed to concentrate. My studies of the Stills indicated that, while they had some verbal language of some sort, they communicated mainly through non-verbal gesticulating. Could I communicate with them? Maybe. I'd learned to communicate with my own species, which was the hardest thing I'd ever done; understanding other species was, at times, a snap in comparison.

I walked with my shoulders back and my chest thrust out, copying the movements of the Still. She crossed the distance to meet me, and I studied her, thinking—but not positive—I picked up a hint of tension in her shoulders. Probably there was plenty in mine, too. The Stills seemed to average around two meters ten; if this went wrong, it was gonna go really wrong.

Soon we stood only a meter or so apart. Taking a chance, I gestured at my chest, sweeping my arm around in a way I'd seen in the recordings, and said, "Xandri."

The Still cocked her head.

I made the motion again and repeated, "Xandri."

Something in the Still's features seemed to brighten. She drew herself up even straighter—*not*, I had to remind myself, out of any desire to intimidate—and made the motion herself, grumbling out something that sounded like "Sifah."

Oh, good, I got it—

"You...can't...be," my new acquaintance struggled to get out. "Can't be...leave."

Whoa.

"Did you—do you understand me?" I asked, because *whoa*. As far as we knew, no one had been here before us.

Sifah cocked her head again. Under the fur covering her face, she seemed to be contemplating my words. Or was I projecting?

"You...make harm. Leave."

9

Christ on a bike. With great care I flicked my thumb, reopening the comm link. I'd been with the *Carpathia* for four years and never once in that time had I made contact with anything that already spoke Alliance Trade Common. I'd never read or heard about such a thing either. How smart *were* these people?

"I'm sorry," I said. "We don't mean to cause any harm. Tell us what we're doing wrong and we'll fix it."

Sifah shook her head, fur flying in all directions. She thrust her hands out towards me, then spread them wide, a gesture I'd seen a few times during my weeks of research. "You...make harm."

"*Holy. Shit,*" came Gunnery Sergeant Huff's voice over the comm channel. Lieutenant Estevanico added a line of chitters in his own language that the translator couldn't—or wouldn't—translate.

I flicked rapidly through my memories like an archivist flicking through paper files, but I couldn't find a gesture corresponding to the one Sifah had just made. *I fly by the seat of my pants in most social situations anyway. What's one more?* Praying I wouldn't get us all killed, I made a similar gesture, bringing both hands to my chest and then spreading them out, to encompass the platoon lined up behind me. "We make harm. What is harm?"

"Loud. You...loud. Bring them."

"*Corelel, how does she know our language?*"

"*No idea, Gunny, but I think we've got bigger problems. I think—I think we're doing something wrong, something that's upsetting them.*"

"*No shit. What is—*"

Sifah shook her head, her lips peeling back in agitation. "No... loud. They...hear. Getting close now."

"You...can hear that? When I do this?" I sub-vocalized a quick, meaningless sentence and Sifah nodded. Sweet Mother Universe, what was *up* with this planet? "Who hears, Sifah? You? Someone else? Is there someone else here?" We hadn't seen much aside from the Stills, not even any kind of predator.

"Stop...loud! Stop. They...come."

Damnit, this isn't working! I needed more time with Sifah and her people, needed to better understand their language if I was going to help them understand ours, but something told me we didn't have time. I glanced down along the line of Stills and noticed them fidgeting, noticed their posture curving towards crouches. Some of them were shrinking back into the protection of the forest, mov-

10

ing with eerie quiet. A few others lifted their heads, broad nostrils flaring as they scented the seemingly nonexistent wind.

"Sifah..."

"Too...late. They come."

"Wait!"

A Still at the farthest end of the group dropped into a crouch, threw its head back and ululated. *Okay,* that *wasn't in any of the recordings.* The Stills fell back, the varying browns of their fur blending into the forest underbrush. Only Sifah hesitated, slipping into a partial crouch. Waiting, I thought, as any good leader should, to make sure those she led were safe.

"*Corelel?*"

"*Gunny, I think we've got a—*"

Sifah broke and ran, heading for the cover of the forest. I spun, my heart racing, but I saw nothing. Nor did I hear anything.

And then I *did* hear something. A scream tore through the air, slicing apart the planet's unsettling stillness with a sound even more disturbing. Something primal, something that spoke of the kind of terror humanity had rarely known in the millennia since technological advancement had put us at the top of the food chain.

Fuck.

Chapter Two

Space was big, and often it was weird, but nothing I'd seen in the great wide weirdness of the universe had prepared me for what I was seeing now.

Not seeing, Xandri. Not *seeing.*

The soldier at the farthest end of the line screamed and clawed at the spiky not-grass covering Stillness' surface. Two of his fellow soldiers clung to his arms as something—*what is it?* Where *is it?*—tried to drag him out from behind the trench. I reached for one of my Atrox MK. XIIs, but there was nothing to shoot, nothing to *see.* I clutched the grip of my pistol, my heart slamming against my ribs as I fought the intense desire to follow the Stills in their flight.

The distinctive roar of a Gabriel cut through my sound-dampeners. The air near the screaming soldier flickered and suddenly *it* was there, a creature of nightmares. If it stood less than a meter and a half at the shoulder, I'd be surprised. Long, slender legs supported a broad, powerful chest and equally powerful hindquarters, reminiscent of a dog but covered in russet scales that blended with the dying light of the setting sun. It had an enormous, boxy head filled with sharp teeth, and it seemed mostly just annoyed by the Gabriel's fire, which had merely scraped its flank.

Huh. It looks a bit like a therapsid, I thought, then blinked. *Brain, pick less inappropriate timing, please.*

A rattling sound filled the air. I drew my pistol as all around us creatures shimmered into view, a dozen at least. They fanned out around us in a crescent arc.

"Soldiers, fall back!" Gunnery Sergeant Huff roared.

"Cluster formation!" Lieutenant Estevanico added. "Corelel, get over here *now!*"

I ran. Rattling sounded again as the creatures flickered out of view. Another scream echoed from the opposite end of the line even as the soldiers fell back, gathering into a cluster with guns pointed outward. *Don't think about them behind you,* I told myself, legs working hard. *Don't think it, don't think it, don't...*

"Xandri!" The voice that called me wasn't one of my colleagues from the *Carpathia*, but Sifah. "Stop!"

Perhaps I'd been doing this whole paramilitary thing long enough; I froze like a statue at that word. A faint vibration fluttered through the ground beneath my feet; another rattling sound heralded the appearance of one of the creatures, no more than four or five meters in front of me. I raised my pistol. *Sweet Mother Universe, God, whoever or whatever is out there, I don't wanna die.*

It leapt. I kept my pistol trained on its head. *Rattle.* The creature disappeared, yet still I tracked its head—where its head *should* be—with the muzzle of my gun, leaning farther back with each second. *Wait for it... wait for it...* my heart thudded rapidly... *wait for—now!* I pulled the trigger, letting myself fall at the same time. The crack of the pistol firing made me wince.

"Holy shit! Did you see that? Did anyone else see that?"

I ignored the voice coming through the comm channel and rolled over as the creature landed beside me with a thud. It had reappeared—except for its head, which I'd blown off. Even though it probably would've eaten me, I felt a prickle of guilt; I *hated* killing. *No time, Xan. Get your ass off the field.* I forced myself to my feet, ignoring my newly acquired aches, and raced for the cluster formation.

"Open fire!" Lieutenant Estevanico shouted as soon as I was at the center of the cluster with the other civvies.

A pair of Gabriels roared and a grenade launcher went off. Most of the platoon carried RMT-65 assault rifles—known as rams—and even with my sound-dampeners, the noise from inside the cluster tore through me like the ammunition itself. I braced myself, gritting my teeth until the sound of gunfire eased off. Soldiers rapidly changed magazines. I peered out between shoulders and saw that only one of the creatures had fallen.

"Fuck me sideways," I heard a soldier mutter. "Gunny, how the fuck we supposed to hit these things?"

"Fire enough and they'll get hit whether they like it or not."

Another scream. I lunged forward without thinking, grabbing an armor strap on the soldier in front of me as one of the invisible beasts tried to drag her away from the cluster. *Fuck, Xandri, what are you doing? This isn't your job!* But it was the soldier who'd caught me, who'd kept me from falling on my ass earlier.

"Shoot it!" she shouted, as invisible teeth sought weaknesses in her armor. "Just shoot it!"

Two other soldiers caught hold of her. Keeping a hand on the strap, I reached over her shoulder, extending my arm into a comfortable firing position, and flicked the pistol to a lower muzzle velocity—one that would discourage the beastie without injuring anyone nearby. I pulled the trigger, and it rattled into view, a hole blown in its shoulder. As it let go of the soldier, something flew through the air and lodged in its flank. A spear.

"Thanks, civvie," the soldier said, as she limped into the center of the cluster.

"Xandri."

"Katya."

The creature didn't stick around for more. It flickered out—but the spear didn't. As it tried to run, a soldier opened fire with a Gabriel—overkill, perhaps—and down it went, reappearing once more. Another one was already on the other side of the cluster, trying to drag away another soldier.

"Damnit!" Gunnery Sergeant Huff snarled. "Corelel, why are these things so bloody aggressive?"

"I'm not *actually* a zoologist," I pointed out. When she glared, I added, "But the fact that we can't see them and there's so many of them might be making them bolder than most predators."

"Soldiers, fire!" Lieutenant Estevanico commanded again.

Another round went off. A creature appeared several meters away, bleeding from its flank, and another spear—thrown, I was pretty sure, by Sifah—caught it in the leg. *This isn't enough. We need to be able to see them if we're going to scare them!* And god only knew if more had shown up in the meantime; the fact that we'd taken down several but they still hadn't run for it indicated that perhaps more had.

"*Gunny?*" Diver's voice came through the comm.

"*You seeing this, Diver?*"

"*Yeah, and I think I got an idea. Xandri?*"

"*Here, Diver,*" I said.

"*I'm gonna need the holo in your wristlet. Gimme access? Please?*"

14

I didn't have to look at Gunnery Sergeant Huff to know she'd want me to do it. Our ammo wouldn't last forever. *"Fine."* I hit a button on my wristlet. "Transfer control to crew member two-seven-dee-four, Diver, R&D. Authorization code: Let the right one in."

"What kind of authorization code is that?" Huff asked, as my wristlet beeped.

"One I can remember."

"Got it. Gunny? Take it from her."

"What—"

"Understood." The gunny was on me even before she finished speaking. She caught my arm in a lock and stripped away my wristlet in a flash, leaving me stunned.

As I stood there, swaying, she clamped it on her own wrist and charged out of the cluster formation. If Diver was still sub-vocalizing to her, I couldn't hear it, not without my wristlet. Technically I could use the implant in my wrist—it could handle that much—but I was too shocked. The entire circle went still as Huff charged onto the empty field, her arm—with *my* wristlet—held up.

The holo activated, stretching to its limits, less a holographic display and more a long beam of blue light. One of the creatures charged right into it and suddenly, without the usual heralding rattle, we could see it. *Diver, you'd better thank whatever gods you do or don't believe in that you're so clever. Or I'd kill you for that.*

A shot rang out and the creature's head exploded; just the platoon's designated sniper doing her job. I stood there, clutching my empty wrist, as Gunnery Sergeant Huff circled, literally shedding light on the situation. It didn't take the creatures long to understand that the light made them visible—it just took them longer than it took the Stills. They came racing out of the forest, howling in triumph and throwing spears and rocks. In minutes, what remained of the creatures—no more than three or four—had turned tail and run.

I sat in the middle of where the cluster had been, watching—without really seeing—as the soldiers cleared the field. The bodies of the creatures would be bagged and carted up to the *Carpathia*, where our science division would study them, try to understand how they could become invisible. We *had* to know. *I* had to know. Part of my job was giving a suggestion for the classification of the planet, which would then be passed on to the governing bodies of the Starsystems Alliance. I had to get it right. We might work outside government influence, but we were good enough that they tended to listen to us.

Someone crouched beside me and set down a Gabriel; despite the soldier's care, the light machine gun hit the ground with a *thunk*. *Light machine gun. Sweet Mother Irony, you have such a sense of humor.* I looked up, reluctant, into the broad, dark face of Private Anton Mulroney.

"You all right, kiddo?"

"Fine," I said. Which was a total blatant lie. I kept rubbing my wrist where my wristlet ought to be; Gunnery Sergeant Huff still had it.

"Mm hmm." Mulroney eyed me skeptically. "Welp, whatever you say. That was some fine shooting out there, by the way. Where the hell you learn to do that?"

"Too many games of shells," I muttered.

Mulroney chuckled. Not because he got the joke—only Captain Chui would've gotten the joke—but... well, I didn't know why. Most of the crew thought me a stuck up, antisocial, insufferable pedant, so I didn't get why Mulroney was always nice to me. *Maybe he's just a nice guy.* Huh.

"Those were some strange beasties," he went on, like he actually gave a damn about talking to me. I repeat: Huh. "Even weirder than those bugs on that ICUN-4 class we were on last year."

"Oh, they weren't arthropods. They were much too large to be arthropods even if they *had* been an Ancient Earth species. At that size, under that gravity, they'd just... fall apart. Exoskeletons aren't..."

I trailed off as Mulroney chuckled again, my face burning hot. He patted my shoulder with one large, calloused hand and rose. "Good to see you're not too rattled. Watch my Gabe for me while I help get this mess cleared up, yeah, kiddo?"

I nodded. Not that I thought the thing was going to pick up and walk away. *Then again, with some of the mods Diver does on our weapons, it just might.* Since we weren't a government organization, more than half our kit was barely legal as it was; Diver's inventive

16

genius extended to making our weapons even more illegal than they already were. Just my Atroxes alone would net hefty fines and perhaps a bit of jail time. They did a few things the manufacturer had never intended them to do.

Speaking of weapons-modding R&D geniuses I'm kinda pissed off at right now... Diver came towards me, my wristlet in one hand, a set of rod-lights perched on one shoulder. The red light deepened the reddish tones in his coppery skin and unruly, fawn-colored curls. He walked with a swagger that spoke of street-born confidence, but when he crouched before me, his green eyes were unusually serious and sincere. *Fuck. Don't think about how good-looking he is, Xan. You're pissed, remember?*

"Gunny says you can have this back now," he said quietly. "We've got a fair few lights set up around the perimeter, so we shouldn't need it anymore."

I nodded. So many things I could've said, yet for some reason, words didn't want to come out of my mouth.

"Hey, look. I know you're mad, and I get it. If it was me, I'd be tearing out eyeballs about now. If Captain Chui'd given me a choice, I would've explained, but she wanted it done immediately."

I sighed. "That figures."

"And," Gunnery Sergeant Huff added as she passed by us, "if I'd let you be the one to put yourself in that danger, Captain'd have me spaced." She snorted. "As it is, I might get spaced for that stunt you pulled earlier."

"Oh. Right. Sorry about that, Gunny."

She nodded. Okay, maybe we were even. I looked back at Diver, but damnit, he made it hard to stay angry. I kinda thought his cheery outward demeanor might be some kind of defense mechanism—or maybe I was projecting again—but it seemed to work, even on me.

"Now, let's get this back on you," he said, setting down the rod-lights and catching my hand in his.

Warm, calloused fingers closed around my wrist. I stared down at the not-grass as Diver settled the wristlet back in place. A lot of times I didn't like being touched, but Diver...when Diver touched me, it always felt nice.

"There. Much better."

"Thanks. And Diver? Ask first next time."

"If the captain gives me leeway, I will. Promise. Now, ain't you got a job to do?"

I blinked. He half turned and gestured in the direction of the forest. I squinted—without a HUD, I had difficulty seeing in the dying light. It was so red, and it made the foliage—a mix of extremely dark green and brown—darken and redden until it was almost impossible to make out details.

After the battle, the Stills had disappeared. But now, as I relaxed and let my eyes pick out shapes, I saw that some of them had returned. The shape at the front had to be Sifah. *Stellar!* I bounced to my feet, relieved. *Now I can figure out how Sifah knows our language.* Or bits of it, anyway. Being able to talk to her, learn about her people, would help me with the classification for Stillness.

"Good shooting out there, by the way," Diver called as I headed towards Sifah.

"Only doing my job."

"That's funny, didn't think 'shooting the heads off invisible monsters' was in the Xeno-liaisons job description."

I paused, half turned. "They're not monsters, Diver. They're just living creatures doing what they do. And with any luck, we won't have to kill more of them."

He tilted his head, watching me with an expression I couldn't begin to decipher. I turned away, my cheeks heating again. As I walked, I tapped my wristlet on; the faint hum of it powering up filled me with relief. I opened a comm channel, even though I didn't much feel like talking to anyone. *At least,* whispered a voice at the back of my mind, *anyone human.* I did, after all, have a job to do.

And even though I was exhausted, even though I felt fragile around the edges, like I might break apart if someone jostled me too hard, I *always* liked my job.

Chapter Three

Sometimes it was hard to believe that only four years ago, I'd been living like a nomad, traveling from one city to the next when I wore out my welcome in the local gambling dens. That was where Captain Chui had found me, in one of those dens. I would sit for hours, watching, observing. I would find gamblers with tells and watch them until I understood those tells well enough to take each gambler for all they were worth. In essence, I learned people—all kinds of people—and then I exploited that knowledge.

It was the only way I'd figured out to make a living, the only way that kept me free and safe—as safe as the streets of Wraith ever got, anyway.

Ancient Earth knowledge about people like me—autistic people—said we couldn't read other people. We lacked the empathy necessary, or some half-baked psychological shit like that. But as I'd discovered—in large part out of necessity—non-verbal language was *language*, and like most languages, it could be learned. So I learned. I spent hours learning, exhausting myself with learning, until I had the faculties I needed to analyze most of the people I met. Until I seemed merely a bit strange, rather than being that girl who sat in a corner, rocking gently and not speaking a word.

It messed with my head sometimes, how I'd become what my parents spent years of therapy trying to turn me into, all to keep myself out of their hands.

"Xandri?"

I blinked and reached up to rub the bridge of my nose. "Sorry, Sifah. My mind wandered a little. Guess I'm getting tired."

"We work..." She hesitated a moment, then went on. "We work many of your...hours. Is...easy to be...tired."

Surprised, I glanced at my wristlet. Whoa. We *had* been at it for hours. Sifah learned so fast, so easily, that sometimes I forgot how hard we'd actually been working. In only a week she had more than tripled her vocabulary, though she still struggled with syntax.

From what I could glean, Sifah was an oddity among her kind. Though analysis of their skull structure and brains in the *Carpathia's* biology department showed they had the potential to develop complex language, the Stills didn't have it yet. But Sifah...Sifah was ahead of her time, as happened among sapient species.

It had taken time and effort, but I'd gotten the story out of her. When she was younger, a ship had crashed on Stillness. Too curious for her own good, Sifah had waited for the predators to come and go, then sneaked onto the ship to explore it. She'd accidentally activated ship's logs, voice recordings in Trade Common. Fascinated, she'd returned to the ship again and again over the course of roughly a Stillian year—as far as I could make out—to listen to the recordings. Eventually she'd been caught out and had to stop, but she'd never forgotten what she learned. What fascinated me most was how much context she'd been able to give those words even before I started helping her.

"All right," I said, pushing my chair back. "Let's call it a day, then."

Sifah stared at me. "Call...what...a day?"

Whoops. Being less literal might make me fit in more with other humans, but it didn't always help with aliens. "I mean we've done enough today. You can go back to your people."

"Good. Will return to—tomorrow for more learn. You...make sure not so much loud, yes?"

I grinned. "Trust me, Sifah, I prefer there to be not so much loud myself."

She parted her lips, trying to mimic my expression. Maybe not such a good idea, since my smiles had a tendency towards awkwardness. Sifah heaved herself out of the chair—Akcharrch had kindly allowed us to use the one specially made for her—and ambled out of the room. She froze in the doorway for a moment, then hurried on. As her bulk disappeared down the hall of the temp shelter, Christa appeared in the doorway.

Oh, stellar.

"I'll send today's data to you immediately," I said, already reaching for my wristlet. Best to try to cut her off at the pass.

"Oh. Um, good." She leaned against the doorjamb. "I'll add it into the presentation."

"Do you think we'll need it?"

"I hope not, but parliament can be useless sometimes."

Only sometimes? "Well, I guess we'll see," I said. "I should probably—"

"It wasn't that clever, you know," Christa said. "Anyone could've figured it out, with the Stills. I know the captain thinks you're some kind of genius, but if the rest of us had had as much access to the footage as you had, it would've been one of *us* who got it."

You did *have as much access as I did!* The only footage the rest of the team hadn't had access to was the last bit that Diver gave me, and that was hardly my fault. But I always made sure every member of Xeno-liaisons got access to all the material that wound up in my hands. It only came to me first because I was the section head. *So why don't you say that? Put her in her place for once!*

The words wouldn't come out, even though they were right there, hovering on the tip of my tongue. They just *wouldn't*. Christa let out a huff, tossed her head and flashed me a smile, like my inability to answer proved her right. I stared at the screen of my wristlet, teeth gritted, until she turned and left. With shaking fingers, I started transferring the day's session to the rest of my team.

"It's because she thinks she should be Head of Xeno-liaisons, you know."

I jumped and grabbed the edge of the table to keep from falling out of my chair. Heart fluttering, I turned as Aki came ambling into the room. Instead of bothering with her chair, she eased her six-legged bulk into a half-sit beside mine.

"What is?" I asked, as my heart settled down again.

"Christa's problem with you. She's been here longer than you and thinks she ought to have been given the job as section head."

"She hasn't been here long enough, if she thinks Captain Chui gives a shit about seniority," I muttered. Then I flushed. "Sorry."

"Eh, don't apologize to *me*. I like it when you say what's on your mind."

I smiled, despite my ill temper. The Ongkoarrat were a very say-what's-on-their-minds kinda people. I finished sending the data, closed the comm channel on my wristlet, and leaned back in my chair.

"Do *you* think anyone else could've figured it out?" I asked Aki.

"Give enough time? Perhaps." She scratched her belly with one of her middle limbs. "But even in this day and age, you've got a skill most people never have to practice quite so much. So I think we can chalk this one up to the First Law of Retrospection."

"The what?"

"You've heard of the Laws of Physics, the Laws of Thermodynamics, that sort of thing. This..." Aki made a motion that might have, for her species, been a shrug. "The First Law of Retrospection states that everything is obvious once it's been properly explained to one, especially if the one in question isn't half so clever as they like to think."

I laughed and rested my head on my arms. "Thanks, Aki." A yawn cracked my jaw. I let my eyes drift shut, just for a moment; I'd been working so hard with Sifah, I hadn't been getting enough sleep. "Hate to think there's no point to me even being here."

I must've been tired, to be babbling like that. I needed to get myself off to bed, but my limbs felt so damn heavy all of a sudden. We'd been keeping quieter in the temp shelter, now that we knew what was out there, though the blue rod-lights set up around our perimeter were an effective deterrent. But all these people in such a small space... it exhausted me, left me feeling like the ragged edges of worn out cloth.

For just a brief moment I thought I felt the gentle caress of claws through my hair...

Thick, densely-furred fingers settled on my hand. I stopped tapping my fingers against the tabletop and smiled sheepishly at Sifah. Normally I *hated* when people did that—touched me to stop my fidgeting—but I was willing to give Sifah and her sensitive ears a little leeway. I knew a thing or two about sensitive ears.

"So," Sifah repeated the question I had yet to answer, "why you... here?"

Three more days had *not* added enough to our ability to communicate for me to adequately explain, but Sifah was no fool. She might not understand, not fully, but on some level she realized we had a purpose here. She'd begun asking questions much like the one she'd just asked, and I couldn't see a way to avoid answering any longer.

"It's what we do, Sifah. We... find new planets. Learn about them, explore them. If there are people—like yours—there, we try to learn about them, too. There's a lot out there, beyond this planet, beyond the stars, and..." How much to tell her? How much could I even get her to understand. "And some of it could be dangerous to you. If you want, we can make sure you're protected."

Oh, we'd be making sure Stillness was protected, all right, but how much we interfered directly with the inhabitants themselves—that was up to them. If the Stills desired it, the Starsystems Alliance could provide them with all kinds of technology, could uplift them as they'd uplifted other species before. Or the Alliance could simply hang back until the Stills requested help. There were options, many options, more than I was sure I could explain or that Sifah could process.

"Dangerous." Sifah spoke the word with care, as she often did. Her lips moved, her tongue smacked, as if she were tasting each syllable. "You mean like...predators."

"*Exactly* like predators," I agreed. A sound came from the hallway, footsteps and voices. *Christa?* I wondered, but I kept the majority of my perception on the conversation in front of me. "And unlike the predators here, these predators can't be chased off with spears and blue lights."

I paused. How to explain the relationship between the *Carpathia* and the Starsystems Alliance? We were all of us part of the Alliance, coming as we did from Alliance worlds, but working outside the government meant we couldn't *guarantee* anything. They tended to listen to us—even before I'd arrived, the *Carpathia* had had a gleaming first contact track record—but with what our science team had discovered...

No. If this leaked, the orcs would get wind of it and we'd all be in big trouble. They've got to keep quiet on this one.

The footsteps didn't go past the room. They filed in, two sets clearly human, one unmistakably Aki. I turned in my chair, found myself face-to-face with Christa, Diver and Akcharrch. I'd seen enough people with bad hands in the gambling dens to recognize grim expressions when I saw them and my stomach tightened. *We've chased off the predators. Sifah said they're the biggest ones out there. What else could be wrong?*

"Xandri," Christa began, with unusual gentleness.

Uh oh. Christa being nice usually meant I was gonna hate what she had to say.

"Captain Chui sent down new orders this morning. We're—we're leaving tomorrow."

"Tomorrow?" I shot up out of my chair. "But there's so much left to do! We can't just leave!"

"It's urgent, Xan," Diver said. "The captain hasn't released any details yet, but...she wants us off planet and reporting in by morning. Then we're slinging out for Mergassë Station."

I jerked a little in surprise. Mergassë was a major military station, where most joint military-diplomatic planning took place. *Why would they want* us *there?* Mergassë was also the home base of the AFC—the Alliance First Contact Division—and they didn't much like us. Which was fair, I supposed; we tended to do their job better than they did. Not that that was *entirely* their fault. In this day and age the impediment to traveling faster than the speed of light wasn't anything to do with causality or relativity, but figuring out how to outstrip bureaucracy and red tape. No one in the known universe could outstrip bureaucracy and red tape better than the crew of the *Carpathia*. The AFC—not so much.

"But—but I'm not..." I bit my lip. Though I tried not to when people were watching me, I couldn't help reaching into my pocket to run my fingers along that strip of satin. "I don't even have my report together and—and Sifah..."

"I've been studying the work you two are doing together," Christa said, with a nod to Sifah. "I'll do my best to explain what I can while you're getting your report finished."

Which was why, despite our conflict, I kept Christa on as my immediate second. She was damn good at her job and she *cared*. She looked at Sifah when she spoke, rather than acting like the Still wasn't sitting right there. Not everyone in the diplomacy division cared to cultivate that skill. Still, I hesitated. I couldn't refuse a direct order from Captain Chui but...

"You have...important thing to do?" Sifah asked.

"Important," I agreed. "Not *more* important, though."

"Important enough," Aki said. "Captain Chui said—what was it she said, precisely, Diver?"

"If we're not back on the *Carpathia* by oh-six-hundred tomorrow, she's going to send Mag—First Officer Magellan down to get us."

24

And a pissed off ex-Marine Kowari heavy gunner was *not* someone you wanted coming to get you. I sighed. *But it feels like abandoning my responsibilities...*

"Understood," Sifah said. "As leader, you must...sometimes, you do things you not want, because that is—is what leaders do."

The idea of calling *me* a leader was a bit of a joke, but she had a point. "All right. I guess I'd better get to work if I want to be done in time."

I needed to contact Science one last time, make certain I had all the facts straight, then I needed to compile it all into something coherent, something that could go alongside Christa's presentation if necessary. After that I'd work out a classification for Stillness, one that with any luck Captain Chui could make stick with the AFC and parliament. *Maybe I should also consider doing a—*

Diver whistled softly, catching my attention.

"Sorry." I looked at Sifah and repeated, "Sorry. I've got a lot to do."

"Then you must do it."

"Diver, would you take the horse out for one more run, get a few more samples for Science? That might keep them off Captain Chui's back."

Diver grinned. Normally I didn't react to smiles the way humans did—by smiling back—but with Diver, I always did. No idea why.

"I'm taking the gorilla, just in case those things come back," he said, "but I'll go. You're probably right."

Of course I was right. Our scientists were brilliant, talented, and rather petulant when things didn't go their way. It's called an Argument of Scientists for a reason, after all.

I reached my hand across the table to Sifah. She extended her arm and touched her fingertips to mine, a gesture I'd learned as a greeting between friends among Stills. Guilt still sat uncomfortably in my stomach, hard as a rock, but this was my job and I *had* to do it. *Maybe whatever business they want us for on Mergassë will be over quickly and we can come back. We haven't had any new leads to track as far as I've heard, anyway.*

Not that I thought the universe liked me enough to make things that simple.

My favorite part of returning to the *Carpathia* was watching the ship as the shuttle flew towards her. Some would call the Crystalliad-class troop cruiser a relic, a fossil from the Alliance's second war with the orcs; indeed, all her sister ships had been decommissioned some years ago. But there was something beautiful about her nonetheless.

Sanavila design—which permeated the overall look of Alliance military ships—tended towards a basic, though curvy, arrowhead-like shape; a boring, if slightly eerie, abstraction of the physical shape of an adult Sanavila, but serviceable enough. It was the *Carpathia's* opaline hull, glimmering even in the depths of space, that drew the eye. These days the shifting colors of regular opaline were reserved for ambassadorial ships, not warships—when it was used at all—making *Carpathia* a curiosity of the spaceways.

"*Carpathia*," Aleevian spoke into the comm, "this is the *Fate Unknown*, requesting permission to come aboard."

The *Fate Unknown*, the *Destination Anywhere*, and the *Abandon All Hope* were our three shuttle ships and proof positive that our small crafts division had an even more fucked up sense of humor than Mother Universe.

"*Fate Unknown*, this is the *Carpathia*. Permission to come aboard, granted."

Aki leaned back in the pilot's chair and with one fluid maneuver brought the *Fate Unknown* into the *Carpathia's* docking bay. As the *Fate Unknown* settled down, I hit the release on my straps and reached under the seat for my travel bag. According to the message that had appeared late last night on my wristlet, I had about an hour before I needed to be in Captain Chui's office. First Officer Magellan would track me down by oh-seven-hundred if I wasn't already there.

"Hey, Xan."

But I had an extra minute. I turned at the bottom of the ramp and glanced over my shoulder at Diver.

"I'm gonna be the first to know what the captain has in store for us, right?"

I perched a hand on my hip, fighting a grin. "And what exactly have *you* done for *me* lately?"

"Ah, see, the question is, what *haven't* I done for you *yet*."

I raised an eyebrow.

Diver spread his arms. "I, genius that I am, have got a hardware upgrade for your baby. New functions and a larger holo-display. Surely that's worth a tiny bit of information."

"Sounds stellar. But it's still up to the captain."

"Diver, stop pandering and get your ass down to R&D," Christa said, giving him a shove towards the ramp. "Assuming Xandri learns anything worth knowing, it'll probably come down to Xeno-liaisons first."

"Hey, you can't blame a man for trying."

"Gossip."

"Not gossip, Chris, *knowledge*. And knowledge, as we all know, is power."

I sighed and shook my head. Diver flashed me a not-terribly-repentant grin and shrugged. I just couldn't help smiling back. *Always has to know* everything. *More curious and more trouble than a Nīpa in a chop shop.* I turned away, hiding the flush of pleasure in my cheeks, and made a beeline across the docking bay. I was officially out of time to waste.

I flicked open the comm channel on my wristlet and called, "*Carpathia?*"

"Here, Xandri," the voice of the ship's AI came back through my wristlet.

"Good morning, *Carpathia*. I've got an appointment with Captain Chui in less than an hour. Could you please get operations up and running in my rooms?"

"Of course, Xandri. Lights, electronics and washing facilities will all be fully operational when you arrive."

"Thanks."

The most sophisticated AIs in the universe came from other species; humans didn't tend to like AI too sophisticated. We'd had a slow and rocky start in its development, and humanity still hadn't gotten over it. But I always suspected even most of our AI was more...personified than people ever thought. Maybe I was wrong, but *Carpathia* seemed like enough of a person to warrant politeness. That was all I needed to know.

I took the nearest grav-tube to the civvie deck and hurried to my room. The halls were pretty quiet; though everyone aboard would be awake at this hour, there weren't that many aboard. The *Carpathia* carried roughly four-hundred crew, about a third of her maximum capacity, which suited me fine. It kept things quieter and meant I rarely had to deal with small, crowded spaces.

My rooms were just as I'd left them, minus the fact that my parrots, Cake and Marbles, were still with the Psittacans. I dropped my bag near their empty cages and quickly stripped out of my clothes.

One hot, quick shower later and I was changing into something fresh, clean cargo pants and a comfy, cotton tunic with sleeves that dangled roughly twenty centimeters below my hands—a comfort that was a big no-no in the field. I drew my hair over my shoulder, winding into as neat a braid as I could manage, and there—I was ready to go. Even so, I took a peek in the mirror, to make sure I wasn't a complete disaster. And I wasn't, but I wasn't what you'd call put-together or even striking, either.

No matter what I did, there wasn't much to do about the fact that I looked like whoever created me hadn't known quite what to do with me. My hair, like so much in my life, was indecisive, eventually settling in a rather awkward place somewhere between ash brown and straw yellow. Despite the years of genetic manipulation that gave my family gray eyes, mine were blue, with the occasional fleck of gray that seem to exist mainly to throw my mother into despair. My skin had come out with neither my father's rich brown tone nor my mother's pristine alabaster, but some vaguely caramel color that, through a small twist of luck, didn't clash with the preferred oranges and reds in my wardrobe. And my body...

"Ooo, look at that," I said, speaking aloud to draw myself out of those thoughts. "All out of pity-party time, Xan. The captain awaits."

I whipped around and headed out the door—nearly colliding with a food tray waiting for me there.

"*Carpathia?*"

"Orders from Captain Chui, Xandri. You're to eat that on the way."

"How'd she—" I paused and looked down at myself. My top was looser on me than usual. Once again, I'd forgotten to eat enough while on the job. "Oh, never mind."

I grabbed an apple and a nutrient-bar—blech!—off the tray and hurried to the grav-tube. Time to do what I'd been hired to do.

Chapter Four

I stopped in front of the door to the captain's office, pausing to smooth down my tunic and double-check my braid. *This is as good as it's gonna get, Xan.* With a sigh, I reached out and slapped my palm against the door chime.

The door slid back immediately, revealing First Officer Magellan. He towered over me—easy to do at two meters twenty-four—his ears flicked forward at attention. The hall lights gleamed in his cinnamon-dun fur, and the dark fur rings around his eyes made him look like he wore spectacles—an old-fashioned look in an age when almost no one wore spectacles anymore. His tail—semi-plump with stored fat—twitched as he studied me. Magellan didn't dislike me, as far as I knew, but my inability to organize myself left him a bit distressed. Organization was a first officer's job, after all.

"Good morning, Lieutenant," I said. It'd taken almost the entirety of my first two years aboard the *Carpathia* to understand that 'first officer' was Magellan's job, not his rank. "Captain Chui requested my presence and uh...here I am?"

Magellan blew air threw his teeth, a Kowari sigh. "So indeed you are. And on time, even."

"I think we all prefer it that way."

He made a soft chirring sound, quickly stifled. I raised an eyebrow at him. *I think I just got him to laugh...* He tried to hide his amusement behind a first officer's dignity, but his tail swept back and forth, betraying him. If only *humans* had such clear body language.

"The captain awaits," Magellan said, stepping out of the doorway and gesturing for me to pass. "Ah, but one thing before you go, Corelel."

"Yes, Lieutenant?"

"Nice work down there. I am beginning to think perhaps—*perhaps*, mind you—that Captain Chui was not bereft of all sense when she hired you, after all."

Whoa. Compliment from the XO, that was a big deal. Magellan almost never passed out compliments; it was, I understood, a military thing. I dipped my head in a deep nod of acknowledgment.

Magellan headed off down the hall, his digitigrade feet giving his stride a slight bounce. New recruits—particularly the ones without much experience with Kowari—tended to mistake this as a sign of a cheerful, friendly personality. *More fool they,* I thought as I stepped into the captain's office. The door slid closed behind me with a faint hydraulic hiss.

Captain Chui Shan Fung sat behind her desk, straight up in her chair like a poker. We couldn't have been more opposite if we tried, me and her. Not a single dark hair slipped from the perfect twist it was pulled back into. Though she stood only a meter and a half, as a heavy-worlder she could probably bench press a full grown orc without breaking a sweat. A single scar trailed down over one eye, a souvenir from the Second Zechak War.

"You ate breakfast, I hope, Ms. Corelel."

Not one for preamble, our captain.

"Yes, ma'am."

"Good. Now, your report, if you please."

I nodded. Fortunately Captain Chui didn't expect us civvies to salute, but I had picked up a decent parade rest during my years under her command, which I fell into now to give my report.

As succinctly as I could, I recapped our time on Stillness, a small amount about the flora and fauna we'd found there—she'd get most of that from Science—and, mostly, about my time spent with Sifah. No doubt by now the captain had heard all about Sifah, but even if she hadn't, her expression wouldn't have changed. Her features remained smooth, her eyes impossible to read, as I spoke. Not the kind of woman I'd be able to beat at a game of *shasinki.*

"Fascinating," Captain Chui murmured as I finished. "A shame we have to leave so soon, but there's nothing to be done for it. And your classification for Stillness?"

Like I said, no preamble. "I-SL-RU, NM-SC, Special Classifications: All."

The first flicker of surprise showed on her face; I only recognized it because the upper tip of her scar twitched ever so slightly. With a woman like Captain Chui, I had to take what I could get. I usually watched her eyebrows; they were the only part of her face that moved with any regularity.

She leaned back in her chair, bringing her hands together at the fingertips. "Inhabited, makes sense. Sapient life, I think that's a given. But resources unknown?"

"It's close enough to the truth to count, ma'am."

"Mm hmm. *And* you want this planet classified. Explain."

"But surely you already—"

"Explain your reasoning, Ms. Corelel."

I forced myself not to wince at her tone. She didn't sound angry, just firm. *This is your* job *Xan. She expects you to do it.* It didn't matter what Captain Chui already knew—which was probably everything; she wanted to hear my reasoning. We'd gone over it before: What she already knew was irrelevant to me doing what I was paid to do. But I hated trying to explain myself. Without realizing it was happening, my arms slid from behind my back and I began to tap them nervously against my sides.

"Well, um…According to Alliance standards—"

"Xandri." Her voice came out more gently this time. "In *your own* words."

"Right. My own…" I forced my arms behind my back again. "Captain, the predators on this planet, they're—what *has* Science told you about them?"

"A few things. It seems all the top predators on Stillness have a form of invisibility, and many of them are quite vicious and large. The ones you encountered were the largest, correct? And it's my understanding that it took us so long to encounter them because they're migratory; all the noise you made planetside drew them to you."

"Yes. It's a *fascinating* group of ecosystems and these creatures, their integument—" I paused as her eyebrows lifted slightly.

"Would it kill you to just say skin?"

"We-ll, in this case I mean scales. Their scales have a coating on them, some sort of naturally occurring metamaterial that bends the light. On a planet like Stillness, with a red dwarf sun, that invisibility is highly effective, but even elsewhere it would be useful. Now, there's so much niche evolution here that these ecosystems are incredibly fragile, and if word about this got out—if someone like the orcs—"

Her brows went up even more. "A slur, Xandri? That's not like you."

I bit my lip and said nothing. The Zechak were a bunch of imperialistic, slave-keeping bastards. The Starsystems Alliance had been at war with them more than once for very, *very* good reasons. *Something should've been done about them ages ago, when they chased the Nīpa off their home planet. Instead we're still fighting them.* Orcs seemed as good a name as any.

"I dislike them as much as you do, Ms. Corelel, but I will not have that kind of xenophobia on my ship. Now, continue please."

"Right. Right. As I was saying... it would be bad enough for someone like the or—like the Zechak to find out about this. If it got out to the universe in general, Captain, it would be a disaster.

"With the full support of the Alliance the ecosystems here might—*might*—survive a decade or so, but people who wanted it badly enough would find ways around whatever protections the Alliance put in place. *Without* full Alliance protection, the ecosystems here would be destroyed in—in months. People would want to study these animals, kill them, dissect them, turn them into technology for the next war. That would destroy Stillness utterly. We *can't* let that happen."

"Oh, I agree. And the Stills? Is it your opinion that they're incapable of protecting their home?"

"From us? From the Zechak? Unquestionably. They've got remarkable potential as a species, but they're not there yet. If they choose to be uplifted, they could be in the spaceways in a generation, but we're not even far enough along to explain to them what any of that means. Captain, this planet is *not* ready to be known to the universe."

I froze. At some point during my speech my hands had slipped from behind my back and begun flying, wild gesticulations that made my cheeks burn. My voice had risen some as well. *God, do I just have no self-control? I'm as bad as Mother always said.*

"I'm sorry."

"Don't apologize for your passion, Xandri. It's part of what makes you so damn good at this job."

Don't apologize... The words were drowned out by other voices in my head, voices that scolded in familiar tones. *Don't speak so loud; it's rude* and *Calm down, Alexandria, you're making a scene* and

Alexandria, why must you flap your hands so? You're a young lady, not a bird. A small shudder crept down my spine. *Don't, Xan. That's the past. Those days, that place, it's the past. You never have to go back there. Captain Chui promised.*

"Consider your classification accepted," Captain Chui said, her voice gentle again as it broke through my thoughts. "I'll file it with the AFC; it'll reach Mergassë well before we do."

I had about a million questions, but I dared ask only the one. "Why? Why us and why Mergassë?"

"I'm sure you've heard of the Anmerilli."

I couldn't stop my nose from wrinkling. The Anmerilli were one of Mother Universe's cosmic jokes, a species that resembled humans far more than statistics gave them any right to. Oh, they still bore tails, unlike us; their ears were longer, their hearing sharper; they had bulbous foreheads, much like Ancient Earth Neanderthals; and odd ridges adorned their cheeks; but otherwise, they looked eerily like Homo sapiens. I'd heard they were warlike, detested the consumption of meat, and wanted little to do with the Alliance. It had been like pulling teeth, as I understood it, to get them to accept Tier 2 Non-Member status.

"Quite," Captain Chui said wryly, as if she knew precisely what I was thinking. "The message I received from Mergassë gave little detail, except that it is of the utmost imperative that we bring them into the Alliance as soon as possible. I expect to be debriefed as to the *why* when we arrive on station."

"That's not...our job."

"It is now. The Anmerilli are notoriously xenophobic and they do not approve of AI. They will not allow a diplomacy AI on their planet, which leaves the Alliance with only one option."

Shock rattled through me, nearly knocking me back a step. *Oh, no, no, no. Sweet Mother Universe, this is* not *funny.*

"Me," I murmured. "They want me."

"Yes."

"Are they *nuts*? Captain, I don't—I don't do my job with humans or anything that looks that much like them. I *certainly* don't work with diplomats and politicians. They're—they're barely even real people. If the Alliance wants to succeed in getting the Anmerilli to join, assigning the job to *me* is completely baffy. I can't—"

"Xandri Corelel!"

Eep.

"It was *your* methods that convinced the Hands and Voices to accept Tier 1 Non-Member status and engage in trade with us, and *your* methods that brought the Psittacans into the Alliance in the first place. I say you can do this, and if *I* say you can, you *can*. Am I understood?"

"Yes, ma'am," I replied weakly.

"Good. Now, I want you to report in for filter cleansing—"

Oh, blech.

"—then find the Professor and get Aki's stims from him. We're slinging out soon. And I want you eating two nutrient-bars a day alongside your usual meals. You've lost too much weight."

Double blech. That was the problem with having a captain who was also an ex-gunnery sergeant; she was used to her job being the care and feeding of her soldiers, and like it or not, I counted as part of that number now.

"I'll also have Ms. Ayabara send you our files on the Anmerilli. *Encoded.* Dismissed."

Encoded. So no sharing with Diver, then. I sighed as I turned towards the door. Hopefully he'd still give me my wristlet upgrade. I didn't *think* he'd withhold it from me, but he could be as mischievous as an Ancient Earth forest spirit sometimes.

"Oh, and Xandri?"

I glanced back.

"Next time your second in command gives you shit, you need to put a stop to it."

"But Captain, I really did put my foot in it, she was right to—"

"If you put your foot in it, then by all means, apologize. But she doesn't have any right to walk all over you in front of the rest of the crew. You are her *superior*, and God help me, Xandri, I will teach you some leadership skills if it's the last thing I do."

It might well be. I've been known to frustrate people nearly to the point of implosion. Figuring that wouldn't be prudent to say, I nodded and took my leave. My stomach roiled as I stepped out into the hall. Me, negotiate an alliance with the Anmerilli? Undoubtedly I'd have help. The AFC continued to work with them even so many years after they adopted Non-Member status, but even so, I'd be filling in for the diplomacy AI the Anmerilli wouldn't allow. For a being specifically designed to know and understand the ways of alien species. Fuck.

Focus elsewhere, I told myself as I opened the comm on my wristlet. *Maybe once the higher-ups actually spend a few minutes with me, they'll realize having me on the job would be a disaster and send us straight back to Stillness.*

"*Carpathia?*"

"Yes, Xandri?"

"Would you happen to know where the Professor is?"

"He's currently in Hydroponics."

"Stellar. Could you please call ahead and ask him to have Aki's stims ready? I'll be there in...fifteen minutes. Possibly twenty if filter cleansing is crowded."

"Done. Will there be anything else?"

"No, thank you, *Carpathia.*"

"You are certain? I could send a droid to your rooms to prepare your pets' cages."

I brightened. Yes, I'd be seeing Marbles and Cake again soon. "Could you? That would be stellar, *Carpathia*, truly. Thank you!"

"Not at all, Xandri. It is my pleasure."

Okay, so the Alliance wanted me to play diplomat to an eerily human-like species that needed an attitude adjustment and loved its weapons more than twenty-first century Ancient Earth America, and I had to go rinse my mouth out with one of the vilest substances in the known universe. But life still had bright sides. With any luck, Aki would let me jack in and ride along for at least part of the sling, and soon I'd be reunited with my beloved avians.

Chapter Five

Ugh, my mouth tastes vile. I rubbed a hand across my lips and fought the urge to spit. Filter-implants were a legal requirement for most space travel and no one joined the *Carpathia* without one—and they were bloody useful, too, filtering out the crap in most of the atmospheres we entered, so we almost never needed heavy equipment to do the job. But damn, the cleansing fluid for them tasted like ammonia laced with sulfuric acid, with a hint of sardine to add insult to injury.

There might've been some kind of gum or breath mint in one of my pockets, but I didn't have time to go rummaging. I swung myself into the nearest grav-tube, using my momentum to sling myself up towards the Hydro-Rec deck. Time to get those stims.

Mild stimulants were often necessary for any sling worth writing home about. *Ah, slingspace.* Of all the known species in the universe, one wouldn't expect the Ongkoarrat to be the ones to discover FTL travel. It seemed like something more suited to the ultra high tech Sanavila, or at least a species more gregarious than the Ongkoarrat. Many species—not just humans—couldn't get over the idea that sociality and gregariousness ought to be necessary for a high tech species, but the Ongkoarrat constantly proved that notion wrong. Other species had tried, but they were the ones to succeed in hacking Mother Universe enough to make FTL travel possible.

Though as the Ongkoarrat discovered, you couldn't hack Mother Universe and just expect her to take it lying down. Relativity wasn't a problem anymore, but for some reason slingspace came with a quality realspace didn't have: drag. A ship in slingspace was constantly losing speed. Without a skilled, alert pilot to grapple slingpoints, a ship could become the cue ball in a cosmic game of billiards.

The variant that ends with the cue ball going boom.

Thus, stimulants. And extremely skilled pilots who were required to practice for at least a decade before making actual slings.

Ongkoarrat, with their six limbs and multidexterity, made for some of the best pilots in the universe, and Aki was no exception.

The halls were quiet at the moment, except for a small cleaning droid, but before long a number of the crew—soldiers, mostly—would be up to use the rec rooms. Then it wouldn't matter how big the *Carpathia* was or how little crew it carried over all; things would get loud. I hurried to Hydroponics, slapped the door release, and slipped into the lock. On the other side, I stepped into a world of greenery and sticky heat.

"Hello?" I called. Hydroponics was far from small and the Professor could get lost in his work at times. *Not to mention lost in here.*

"I know that voice." The words came from down a row of *paeli* fruit bushes. "She's back."

Hard not to grin as I heard the *click-click-click* of large claws. Two Psittacans appeared from the row of *paeli* bushes. Like all five members of our Psittacan strike team, they were Macaw class and stood roughly a meter and a half. Even under the artificial light in Hydroponics, Many Kills' feathers shown a brilliant, jewel-tone green, lovelier than the depths of an emerald. Day Dawns Red's more olive color came off subdued in comparison, but there was nothing subdued about her.

"Finally!" she exclaimed, her crest rising in agitation. "Marbles has been loonier than usual this time."

"Eh." Many Kills' feathers ruffled in a laconic Psittacan version of a shrug. "She hasn't been that bad. Though it *is* good to see you, Xandri-bird."

"It's good to see you two, too," I said. "Have either of you seen the Professor?"

"He's in the back. Looking at those plants that got sent up *and* playing chess against the computer *at the same time.*"

I tried not to laugh at Dawn's incredulity. As the youngest member of the strike team, she had a tendency to be full of energy and go. The idea of sitting still for hours for *one* thing, let alone two, left her boggled.

The Psittacans fell into step with me—*click-click-click*—as I headed towards the back, Dawn shaking her feathers, her step bouncy. Many walked with a grace the ignorant never expected of Psittacans, turning his head slightly this way and that to catch every sound in Hydroponics. They liked it here; it was much more similar to the jungle home they came from. *I like it too, though. It's so much more peaceful than other parts of the ship.*

"I'll find someone else to birdsit next time," I promised Dawn as we walked. "Private Jensen, maybe, he doesn't mind."

"It's not that I *mind*," Dawn said. "They're quite clever little siblings—"

Somehow I managed to keep my pedantry in check. Parrots and Psittacans were not, in fact, remotely related, and the Psittacans resemblance to parrots—on a *very* basic level, mind—was pure coincidence. Hell, what we referred to as feathers on Psittacans weren't, really, not in the Ancient Earth sense; but they were close enough that only an expert could tell the difference without a microscope and a textbook.

"—but Marbles does get so space-fried when you're gone too long."

"You spoil her too much," Many added.

"I doubt it would make a difference if she wasn't spoiled," chimed in a new voice. "That creature is, as you humans like to say, a few sandwiches short of a picnic."

"Hullo, Professor," I said, ignoring the insult to my bird. Because it was kinda true. "I'm here for Aki's stims."

The Shar raised his head, turning his attention from his chess game—or maybe the plants he was studying, hard to say for sure—and glanced at us. He rested on a raised dais to reach the table, his two and a half meter long body well-supported. Like Akcharrch, he was the only one of his kind aboard, and I sometimes felt a sort of comradeship with him because of it. I was the only one of my kind aboard, too. Hell, I was the only one of my kind as far as I knew. If there was others—and there could be—I'd never met any of them. I didn't want to think about what that implied.

"Yes," the Professor said, his scaly dewlap wobbling as he spoke, "the *Carpathia* notified me that you would be needing them. They are here."

Being neither bipedal nor endothermic limited the mobility of the Shar, but their forelimbs had locking elbow joints that allowed them to brace themselves. Leaning on those, the Professor folded his claws around a bottle and held it out to me. I stepped forward to take it, cool scales sliding under my fingers.

39

"No more than three per sling period," the Professor instructed. "They're stronger than the old ones."

"Got it," I said, dropping the bottle into one of my pockets.

"Does this mean we're slinging out?" Dawn asked. "Oh Gods."

"Sorry, but we've been called in to Mergassë. Could—could you continue to watch Marbles and Cake for a little longer? I'm hoping to watch Aki sling..."

Many Kills flicked his crest quickly up and down in the Psittacan equivalent of an eye roll. "If we must."

"Stellar," Dawn muttered.

"Your rooms *are* the most comfortable for them during entry slings," I pointed out. The lower gravity in the Psittacan's domain—concurrent with the gravity on Psittaca—seemed to appeal to my babies.

"But Marbles gets so loony during sling! She's impossible to keep calm!"

"I shall mix her up a mild sedative, shall I?" the Professor suggested, his tail flicking towards the controls for his dais.

"Probably not a bad idea." I glanced at my wristlet. "Shit. I'd better get going. I need to get these up to the bridge."

Many's crest flicked again. "How convenient for you, that you won't have to be the one giving her the sedative."

"Give some to Cake, too," I said, as I started back down the row. "She'll get jealous if she thinks he's getting something she's not."

"Spoiled!" Many Kills called after me. "Utterly spoiled."

"You should know!"

He clacked his beak in merry Psittacan laughter. I glanced over my shoulder to find Dawn watching him with her crest up, clearly unamused and unimpressed. Hopefully I'd get to spend some time with them during the trip to Mergassë. Perhaps it was because of our history together, but I knew them—and liked them—more than almost anyone on the ship.

As I exited Hydroponics I broke into a trot; sedative-dodging or no, it would mean my ass if these stims weren't on the bridge soon. And I could hear the tromp of booted feet down the corridor that meant this area would soon be more full of people than I liked. *That's space for you,* I thought, as I swung myself into the grav-tube.

It was so huge, space, and yet when you were me, it was *still* too crowded.

The bridge hummed with energy, from people and from electronics. It was one of my favorite places on the ship, and not just because there was a strict limit to how many people could be on it at once: that hum of energy raced over my skin, walked up my spine, telling me in no uncertain terms that we were in space. Among the stars. My breath caught in my throat as I stepped through the door.

"Junkie," a voice teased from my left.

I turned. Kiriit Ayabara sat at her station, watching me with amusement. I swallowed hard. *Why does she always look so amazing?* Flashes of dark skin stood out against the slashes in her wine-colored sleeves, like the night-dark of space in a nebula. Today golden beads tipped the ends of her thin, tidy 'locs, and they chimed softly as she tilted her head to study me. *Why am I always surrounded by people who are infinitely more beautiful or infinitely more organized than I am?*

"Got what the captain ordered for you, by the way," Kiri added.

Or both?

"Stellar. Send it over, then."

She shook her head and held her hand out to me. Uncertain, I reached out, let her wind her fingers around mine. Like with Diver, Kiri had a touch that never bothered me, that in fact left me curious what it would feel like to experience more. Trying not to blush— and knowing I wasn't succeeding, based on Kiri's teasing smile—I waited as she ran her thumb along my wristlet. The pad of her thumb passed over one of the input jacks and suddenly my wristlet let out the soft, buzzing vibration that warned me of incoming files.

I jerked back in surprise. "How'd you do that?"

She raised a finger to her lip and murmured, "Trade secret." She tilted her head towards the pilot chair, where Akcharrch already sat. "Go. Have your fun. I have a feeling we need to stock up on fun while we can."

"No kidding," I grumbled, remembering what our current mission entailed.

Kiri chuckled, a sound that warmed my belly, and swung back to face her station. I quickly turned away, hoping no one would glance over and see my bright red face.

Kiri, like Diver, was what Captain Chui referred to as one of her 'wild cards.' Though she worked with Signals as one of our information specialists, her unique talents—in this case, unparalleled skills in programming and hacking—meant that, unless under strict orders to the contrary, she answered solely to Captain Chui. Diver carried much the same position with R&D, since they worked in paramilitary divisions while not being paramilitary themselves.

And also, as Captain Chui had put it to me, it never hurt to give your geniuses a bit of free rein, because you never knew when you'd need them to pull your ass out of the fire, orders or no.

I moved past brightly lit screens and hard-working crew members and stepped up onto the piloting dais, where Lieutenant Khalida Zubairi—ship's navigator and Head of both Signals and Shiphandling—stood, showing Akcharrch and her co-pilots a holo-film of our planned route.

"It's strange, Ms. Corelel," Lieutenant Zubairi said without looking up. "I hear reports that you have trouble reaching your destinations on time, yet you're never late to my bridge."

"No, ma'am," I said, feeling, with some surprise, the start of a smile curve my lips. "I wouldn't dare."

Lieutenant Zubairi handed the holo-film off to Aleevian and turned to me. I felt a spike of fear as it dawned on me that I'd slipped into teasing mode without realizing, but she only smiled. Not that I let my guard down. More than one crew member had let the round sweetness of the lieutenant's face lull them into a mistake.

"No, I don't think you would," she said, and I thought—though perhaps I was wrong; her tones were often subtle—that she was teasing right back. "You appreciate God's universe as well as any spacer."

"Uh... right." I reached into my pocket and pulled out the bottle of stims. "Captain Chui wanted me to bring these."

"It's almost like she knew you'd wind up here anyway."

"Got her scheduled to jack in," Aki cut in. "Leev, take those stims. I want to get out of here sometime within this system's next full orbit, if no one minds."

42

"Of course, O' Goddess of the Spaceways," Aleevian said, grabbing the bottle from me and handing the holo-film over to Chikara, Aki's other copilot. "Your loyal adherents would never keep you waiting."

"You keep me waiting all the time. Now go strap in before I have to bite you."

"You heard the pilot, people," Lieutenant Zubairi called to the entire bridge. "Strap yourselves in. We'll reach our chosen slingpoint in about five minutes." She nodded to me. "That means you too, Ms. Corelel."

"Yes, ma'am. Thank you, ma'am."

I hurried off the dais and towards the back of the bridge, flinging myself into one of the jack-chairs. As a routine part of pilot training, they were made to interface with HUDs, giving wannabe spacers experience with the look and feel of slingspace. Diver had modified one of the chairs so I could use it. I quickly strapped myself in, making sure the belts crisscrossed securely over my chest, then settled my arm on one of the rests.

As my forearm touched down, a set of small metallic prongs shot out of the armrest. I nestled my wristlet into place, hearing the faint pings as the prongs connected. Anticipation made my heart flutter as I reached down and retrieved my glasses from my pocket. Also courtesy of Diver, they connected with the chair via a separate jack, allowing me to view slingspace even without a HUD. I slotted them in and put them on, blocking my view of the bridge—not that I needed it.

I heard everything: Lieutenant Zubairi taking her place at the ship's nav; crew members calling out stats as we approached our slingpoint; Aki's claws scraping lightly against metal as she wrapped her feet around all six controls. But it was space that filled my vision, space and the star we were rapidly closing with.

"Grapples ready," Aki said.

"Aligning with star's orbit in five...four...three..." Aleevian counted.

"Deploying grapples."

Though I couldn't see them, I knew the second the slinggrapples shot into the star and grabbed hold. The *Carpathia* whipped forward, dragging itself up close to the star as we started to circle it. I couldn't help but lean forward, watching space warp around us.

I'd read Ancient Earth books, watched Ancient Earth vids, and more often than not, FTL travel was described in terms of colors. Shifting colors, prismatic colors, the colors of a rainbow or a nebula; but always colors, as if the state of the universe itself was not already beautiful enough without paint splashed on. But I—I watched the universe turn to cosmic fabric around us, the warp threads of silver and gold stars, the weft strands of eternal darkness, and I let out a small, joyous laugh at the sheer exquisiteness of it.

"Releasing grapples!" Aki called.

We shot into the fullness of slingspace as the grapples let go, and I had to bite back another laugh. This... sweet Mother Universe, there was nothing else like it.

"Inshallah!" Lieutenant Zubairi complained. "All this technology and yet we can't create a hairpin that can withstand an entry sling!"

The soft rustle as her fingers adjusted her hijab; the hiss and scritch of crew members unbuckling themselves from their straps; the beep and hum of electronics as the crew kept track of every little detail of travel: I heard it all on one of my back-end streams of perception. Yet most of my brain was focused forward on slingspace, hearing it chime around me in the sweet voices of silver bells. I saw it and I heard it, and I tasted it like cooling mint in my mouth, driving out the last vestiges of the filter cleanser.

Even Aki, more comfortable and satisfied in her own self than any person I'd ever met, envied my synesthetic perception of slingspace.

"Next slingpoint in ten minutes," Lieutenant Zubairi informed the bridge.

"Got it," Aki acknowledged. "Does it have a smell?"

I didn't need to ask to know she was addressing me. "Snow," I called back. "The first snow of a year, fresh and clean and... cold."

Aki chuffed. I grinned. Later I would travel back to my room, would sit around and absorb every bit I could about the Anmerilli until my head ached from it. But for the moment my nose stung with a cold that didn't exist inside the climate controlled bridge, my ears flooded with sounds no one else around me could hear, and I...I was free amongst the stars.

Chapter Six

One of my favorite Ancient Earth bands blared from the speakers of my wall-stereo. Still on a high from my time jacked in to Aki's slingspace run, I grasped my toothbrush and danced around my room to the music, more focused on turning said brush into a makeshift microphone than getting my teeth clean.

Marbles and Cake watched me from their play tree, both of them bobbing along with the music. Marbles, an African grey parrot, occasionally mimicked a line of lyrics, though usually out of time with the music. Cake, a pineapple-variation green-cheek conure, could mimic pretty well himself, but with Marbles around he rarely got in a word—or lyric—edgewise. He did, however, headbang with even more enthusiasm than a cockatoo with a rocker streak.

I danced my way across the room, hips swinging, arms flying, lips forming the words. I spun and came to a stop in front of my birds, holding the toothbrush out.

"Sing with me, guys!"

Cake paused in his bobbing to reach out and nibble the bristles. Marbles, who'd been singing a second before, gave me a blank look.

"Oh, fine," I panted. "More for me!"

I whirled away again, bobbing like my birds. I bobbed across the room, flapping my arms like a bird, since who could tell me not to now? My swaying movements threw me off balance, and I threw out a hand to avoid careening into my bookshelf. Saved from collision, I continued to dance, tossing my head back and forth and mouthing the lyrics as they returned.

Then my door chimed.

"Shit!"

"Oh, fuck," Marbles chirped, as if in agreement.

"You said it." I scrambled across the room and jabbed the power button on my stereo with my toothbrush. As I headed for the door, I ran a hand through my hair—a hopeless gesture that only served to rumple my half-destroyed braid even more. *Xandri, you're a bloody disaster on legs.* And who the hell was buzzing me up at this hour, anyway?

The door opened with its usual hiss and I was seized by a strong desire for the floor to turn into a minor black hole and suck me in. Or just some time dilation, that'd be good too. Instead I stood there, clutching my toothbrush, breathing heavily, staring into Diver's so bright eyes. Thank god for privacy locks, or this moment would be even more embarrassing than it already was.

"Sorry to ring so late," Diver said. "Your wristlet was off, but *Carpathia* told me you were still up, so I figured...what were you doing, anyway?"

"Um, brushing my teeth?" *Don't ask why I'm breathing so hard, don't ask, don't ask...*

"Well, anyway, since we were both awake, I thought you'd like that new hardware."

"Oh! Oh, yeah, let me just, um..." I brandished my toothbrush in the direction of the bathroom.

Diver nodded. I scampered off to the bathroom, taking a moment while I was in there to *actually* brush my teeth. Like I wanted to sit across from Diver while he made adjustments to my wristlet, with my breath smelling like the garlic-and-ginger noodles I'd slurped down for dinner. Riiight.

Mouth minty fresh, I slapped off the light in the bathroom and returned to my main quarters to find Diver sitting on my bed, an omni-tool in one hand and my wristlet in the other. Cake perched on Diver's shoulder, preening his fawn-colored curls. *Huh. They never preen anyone but me and the Psittacans.* Not even Private Jensen, who they seemed to like well enough. I took a seat on the bed too, a nervous flutter in my stomach. Which was ridiculous, really.

"Didn't the captain order you to keep this on at all times?" Diver asked, his attention on the wristlet.

"Um...technically."

"Uh huh..."

I watched his long fingers as they worked, loosening the panel on the back of my wristlet, carefully pulling out the core and inserting a new one. While I watched, Cake fluttered over to my shoulder, let out a scolding chirrup, and started preening my hair. That would probably only make it worse, but I barely noticed. Something about watching Diver work relaxed me and I couldn't pull my eyes away.

47

"Now, this should allow you an even bigger holo-display," he said. "It'll be able to produce a single screen about two meters in length, around half that in height, at a workable maximum. Means you'll be able to divide it into more screen multiples, and they'll be larger than before."

"Stellar! I'm gonna need it, if I'm gonna get through all those files."

Diver's head came up. "Files?"

Oops.

"What files? There's no record of any files being sent to your wristlet today."

"Wait." I frowned. "You keep track of the files being sent to my wristlet?"

"It was Kiri, wasn't it? That little—damnit, but she's clever sometimes. How'd she do it? Get the files on there, I mean?"

"Do *not* drag me into the middle of your little rivalry."

"Aw, come on, Xan, it's all in good fun. Give me a hint, won't you?"

"No! God only knows what sort of nonsense she'd put on my wristlet if I told you. I could be picking Kowari porn out of the works for *weeks*." Then I remembered, and added, "And what the hell are you doing tracking my wristlet?"

"Nothing bad," Diver assured me. In a mutter he added, "For once."

"Diver!"

"Okay, okay. Relax. It really is nothing bad. It's just that this baby," he handed my wristlet to me, "is old tech, equipped with hella more new tech than anyone short of God ought to be able to stuff in it. I keep it monitored to make sure it's running well, but that's all. I can't access any of the data going in, coming out, or on there already."

I continued to eye him.

"All right, I *could*, but I don't." He leaned in closer to me and caught my hand to help me fasten the wristlet in place. I could do it myself, but for some reason he always helped. "And *not* just 'cause Captain Chui'd space me if she ever found out."

"Fuck around in my private files and Captain Chui will be the least of your worries," I said without thinking.

48

I froze, horrified. Diver lifted his head; I thought he'd be angry, but instead he grinned at me, his eyes so bright and brilliantly green that it almost hurt to look at them. But I couldn't stop looking, didn't want to, which was an odd sensation all by itself. Diver's fingers closed ever so briefly around my wrist, like he might pull me closer. Then he let out a soft chuckle and released me.

"For someone who calls herself cold, you can be one helluva fireball."

"Sorry..."

"What you apologizing for? Fire's damned useful. Now, we'll be in realspace for a little tomorrow, so Aki can catch up on her rest. That means you ain't got any excuses. I wanna see you down in R&D so we can see how the new hardware is interfacing with your wrist implant."

I nodded.

Diver stood, then paused, looking down at me. "Kowari porn?"

"She's done it before."

He shook his head. "Devious. Space-fried devious, that woman."

For a moment I wondered if there was more going on between him and Kiri than just a minor rivalry over who could hack what. *But no,* I thought, *she's with Gerrin and Chikara right now.* Polyamory was common in this day and age—in fact, it was a little hard to believe that polyamorous marriages had once been illegal among humans—and Kiri came from a very polyamorous community. She was no exception, but tended to stick to triads. *Adding Diver in would probably be too much of a pain in the ass.*

"Well, see you in R&D tomorrow. Try to get some sleep, yeah?"

"I'll try."

I stood, Cake balanced carefully on my shoulder, to show Diver to the door. He slapped the panel to open it, and Marbles chose that moment to say, with—of course—perfect enunciation: "Wow! Lookit that ass!"

Diver whipped around, a look of surprise on his face.

Mortified, I pointed an accusatory finger at Marbles and blurted out the first thing that came to mind. "Little known fact: She's not actually a bird. She's the incarnation of the Goddess of Incredibly Awkward Timing."

To my surprise, Diver laughed. "Bit of advice? Stop letting Jensen birdsit the Goddess."

49

"Good advice."

He laughed again and winked at me, and goddamn the bastard, he didn't look corny when he did it. I watched him walk a short distance down the corridor, then palmed the door closed again. As soon as it was shut, I turned on Marbles.

"You—you horrible, baffy, traitorous little featherbrain!"

"I love you."

"Why—you—arrgh!" Defeated, I let out a sigh. "Fine. But it's past your bedtime, both of you. Time for night-nights."

I took Cake down off my shoulder and went about getting them in their cages, draping each cage with a thick cloth. Some people thought it was a bitch getting time comfortably set for people on spaceships and stations; they ought to try dealing with a pair of pets that needed twelve hours of sleep a day to keep their hormones balanced. Once I had them both settled, I hit the dimmer on my lights and flopped down on the bed.

Automatically I reached with one hand for the blanket, for the nice, cool satin lining the edge of it. Running it through my fingers, bunching it against my palm, I flicked on my wristlet. I let go of the blanket long enough to form my holo-display into five screens: a large one in the middle, and four satellite screens surrounding it. Diver was right; this was a stellar upgrade. Pleased, I settled in to study the files for a while. I didn't sleep well in slingspace, anyway.

Before long I knew two things about the Anmerilli for an absolute certainty: 1) they were going to take longer to decode than usual for me because 2) they'd learned to control the non-verbal language of their tails.

The bastards.

I shut down my holo-display with a sigh and took a sip of my coffee.

In the roughly three days—combining both slingspace time and realspace time—it had taken us to reach the Mergassë System, I'd spent the majority of my time studying the files on the Anmerilli. What we had on them didn't tell me much I didn't already know, and the vid footage showed me stern-faced, hard-eyed people who gave nothing away. *And I always thought Ancient Earth science fiction*

50

was lying when it said every member of an alien species would be exactly alike.

Of course I knew the Anmerilli weren't all alike, not really, but so far the differences were so subtle that they eluded me, and I feared they'd continue to.

My door chimed. *What is it lately with me and visitors at odd hours?* It couldn't have been later than oh-six-hundred ship time. Cradling my coffee mug in both hands, I headed for the door panel and nudged it with my elbow. I nearly dropped the mug when I saw Captain Chui waiting on the other side.

"Captain!"

"Good morning, Xandri," the captain said, stepping into my room. "We'll be hooking into the grav-track soon and I thought—is that coffee?"

"Um, what? Uh, yeah, yeah it is...good—good morning?"

"How'd you get coffee at this hour? *I* can't get coffee at this hour."

"*Carpathia* has it delivered to me every morning as soon as I'm awake," I said, looking around for somewhere the captain could sit. The tiny table and single chair in what qualified as my kitchen seemed ill-suited to one of her standing.

"The ship? *My* ship?"

"Um, yes."

"How do you get her to do that?"

I blinked. "I asked nicely."

"You...asked nicely," Captain Chui repeated, staring at me.

"Ye-s..."

"Of course you did." She sighed and took a seat at the tiny table anyway.

"*Carpathia* is a smart AI, Captain," I said, perching on the end of my bed. "And she's very nice when you get to know her, though she does get a little bored sometimes."

Captain Chui shook her head. "And here I thought it was *Diver* pulling all those pranks on my engineers."

"Oh, Diver's probably involved somehow. I wouldn't clear him of wrongdoing just yet."

"Let me guess...he asks nicely, too."

I fought a grin. Diver talked to his machines—even the ones without AI—as much as I talked to my birds. Surely the captain

51

couldn't be surprised that he'd convinced *Carpathia* to go along with a prank or two. She'd known the *Carpathia* longer than any of us, had flown with her during the Second Zechak War, and had been the one to save her after she was decommissioned. *Does she really not know what* Carpathia *is capable of?* With the way humans reacted to AI, I supposed it was possible *Carpathia* had kept quiet on the matter.

"Well, I'll speak with Mr. Diver later," Captain Chui said. "Right now... Xandri, you've been studying those files, I take it?"

"Of course, ma'am."

"How's it going?"

I hesitated a moment, before admitting, "Not as well as I'd hoped. The Anmerilli... they're difficult to read. I'm going to need a lot more than what we've got if I'm going to stand any chance of being able to do this."

"And I will get you what you need. You know I will. All I need from you is your focus."

"Don't—isn't there some way to get the Anmerilli to accept a diplomacy AI? If this is urgent enough to make us drop our current mission and head to Mergassë then surely they need someone better qualified than me."

"There is no one better qualified than you," Captain Chui said firmly.

I knew better than to argue with that tone. Clutching my mug until my knuckles ached, I stared down at my coffee. From my research I knew that, though the AFC had been working with them for years, the Anmerilli had proven uncooperative and... tricky. They strung the AFC along, acting as if they wanted to join the Alliance but never following through. At the same time, they didn't seem satisfied to maintain a Non-Member status. If the *real* experts couldn't figure them out, I stood no chance.

"Captain?" came the *Carpathia's* voice, echoing from the walls. "We've hooked into the grav-track and have begun orbiting Mergassë Station. Control has given us a docking ETA of one hour."

"Oh. Um..." Such a rare thing, to see Captain Chui so taken aback. "Well, I... thank you, *Carpathia*. For letting me know."

"Of course, Captain. Forgive me for the intrusion, but when I discovered that you were here with Xandri, I thought I ought to inform you of our status."

Please don't realize your ship was looking for me, please don't... But of course, Captain Chui's gaze fell on me, sharp and bright. She missed nothing; if it happened on her ship, she knew. I tried for an apologetic smile and got a rare response indeed: Captain Chui rolled her eyes. *Well, at least she can't be too mad...*

"Xandri," *Carpathia* addressed me. "I thought you might like to know that the *Devil's Love Song* is docked here."

I shot up from the bed, nearly spilling my coffee. "Really? Oh god...Captain, permission to go to the observation deck?"

A wry smile quirked one corner of Captain Chui's mouth. "Go. But make sure you change before we disembark. You know how these ambassadorial types are."

That would come back to annoy me later—God forbid I could just be *comfortable*—but at the moment I was too excited to care. The *Devil's Love Song*, an honest-to-god Malevolence-class destroyer, right here at Mergassë! I hurried into my so-called kitchen and dropped the half-empty mug in the cleaning unit, then bolted to the door. As I hit the door release, I paused.

"*Carpathia*, please get a cup of coffee for Captain Chui."

"Of course, Xandri."

"Thank you."

Captain Chui let out a soft chuckle. "Thank you, Xandri. And you, *Carpathia*."

Diver was already on the observation deck when I burst onto it. He turned to look at me, and it was one of those rare times when I couldn't find it in me to be embarrassed.

I made a beeline for the long, wide window crossing the wall of the observation deck. Beyond was Mergassë Station, a veritable city amongst the stars. Once it had been more round in general shape, but centuries of additions to its docks, its civilian and military areas, had given it the look of an urban sprawl in space. Lights glimmered all over it, reminding me of footage of Ancient Earth concerts, back before humanity banned that weird tradition of waving your lighter around. And everywhere I looked there were spaceships, perhaps numbering in the hundreds: big, small, some even qualifying as genuinely enormous.

53

As I pressed my fingertips to the glass, we passed a Nebularia-class ambassadorial ship. *So we're still in the diplomacy docks,* I thought. *And I'm willing to bet that's the* Resplendence. She was the AFC's flagship, designed in a shape very similar to the classic Sanavila type of *Carpathia*, though her wings swooped opulently down past her spindle. And of course, the *Resplendence* wore a hull of dark opaline—referred to by shipbuilders as opaline-d—which, while still bearing the shifting colors of opaline, was darker, lighter-weight and stronger.

"Fuck me." Diver let out a low whistle. "That's one helluva big ship."

I nodded. "At least twice the size of *Carpathia*. They use the Nebularia-class for all kinds of diplomacy missions, including evacuations." I stopped, bit my lip. Oh God, there I went, babbling useless stuff again.

"Know a lot about this, huh?"

"It's um, an interest of mine."

"Useful knowledge to have," Diver remarked. "So wait... if I pointed a ship out to you, could you tell me about it?"

I shifted from one foot to the other, my arms banging against my sides a few times. "Depends on the ship. It's harder with personal ships, since they're made with all different standards, but any ship in the Alliance fold... yeah."

He let out another low whistle—appreciation, I realized. I turned back to the viewing window, secretly pleased. *I guess someone like Diver* would *appreciate all that knowledge.* I watched the hull of the *Resplendence* slowly disappear out of *Carpathia*'s range; most of the other ships docked with her were smaller. But then, if you had one Nebularia-class, it was a rare situation in which you needed more of them. Not surprising, considering you could stuff four-thousand people on her, easy.

The grav-track drew us slowly around Mergassë, out of the diplomacy sector and into the military sector. I caught my breath. *Where is she, where is she...*

"You're looking for something," Diver said.

His voice came from much closer this time. I looked up to find him standing right next to me, so close I could smell him, metal and soap and a faint hint of engine grease. Flushing slightly, I nodded.

54

"The *Devil's Love Song.* She's a similar blue-black to an or—a Zechak ship, so she'll be hard to spot, but—ah! There, look!"

The lights from Mergassë cast her in bright relief. She stood out among Alliance ships for the human touches in her design: Her wings swept outward around her spindle rather than in, and several layers and sizes of rippling along their length gave the impression of a cloak billowing in the wind. She was only about half the *Carpathia's* size, but no ship flying the spaceways in this day and age was more dangerous.

"Wow," Diver murmured. "No offense to our Grand Old Dame of the Spaceways, but the military's got some sweet kit these days."

"That's the Malevolence-class for you. They're about sixty percent weapons, thirty-five percent engines, and five percent crew, roughly speaking." I could've rattled off each and every weapon the *Devil* carried, but even Diver's eyes might start glazing over if I went there. Even so, excitement crept through me as I spoke. "And get this: They've got an updated version of the old Sanavila lightspeed drives. These babies can literally move fast enough to achieve time dilation!"

"I...really?"

Delighted by his speechlessness—which pretty much *never* happened—I carried on. "It's what they're designed for, Diver. They use the drive to zip in, they unload ungodly amounts of ordnance, then they zip back out again. You could say this class of ship is single-handedly responsible for keeping the Zechak from officially declaring war again. They're mothership killers." I grinned. "Their crews refer to them as 'motherfuckers.'"

Diver laughed. "Typical spacers." He leaned in, his eyes bright. "Can you do this with orc ships, too?"

"Probably, if I had the information on them. Government keeps a lot of it classified, though." I shrugged. "Guess them's the breaks, huh?"

I sighed as we started to pull away from the *Devil's Love Song.* She was such a beautiful ship and I'd never gotten to see her this close before. *And now it won't be long before I have to deal with stuffy bureaucrats and uppity military officers and God only knows who else, expecting me to pull some sort of miracle out of my ass.* There went the rest of my fun for the day, if not for the rest of my natural life.

"Cheer up, fireball. You'll get another chance to see one. Hell, who knows, maybe one day you'll get to fly on one."

My eyes widened. "Oh, I don't think so. They tend to be military only and they don't much care for outsiders."

"He's right about one thing, though, Xandri," *Carpathia* spoke through my wristlet. I lifted my arm, bringing it between me and Diver so we could hear, as the door slid open behind us and several other crew members came in. "You *will* see more of them. The entire class will be docked at Mergassë by the end of the day."

"See?" Diver patted my arm. "There you go."

"What?" I barely even noticed Diver's touch. "All twelve ships? *Carpathia*, that's gotta be a mistake."

"No mistake, Xandri. I've had contact from the *Hellfire Requiem*. She is about an hour out from the grav-track, with *Toccata and Fugue*, *Deadman's Nocturne*, and *Stars' Lament* just behind her. *Elegy of Souls*, *Faust's Damnation*, *Black Hole Minuet*—"

"*What* is up with those names?" Diver muttered.

"—and *Waltz of the Damned* are all more than two hours out, with *Dirge of a Dying Sun* and *Ride of the Valkyries* not much farther on. *O Fortuna* isn't in the system yet, but she always did like to make a late entrance."

Yep, that's all twelve.

Diver chuckled. "*O Fortuna*, really? That's an Ancient Earth drinking song."

"Diver, this isn't funny," I hissed, grabbing his shirt and hauling him down close to me, trying to keep the other crew members from hearing. "This *has* to have something to do with whatever we've been called here for."

"It's just some ships, Xan."

"No, it's *not* 'just some ships,' we're talking the most dangerous ships in the known universe. They travel in groups of no more than four when they strike, and you *never* find more than one at drydock at any given time. It's too much of a security risk."

Diver's expression shifted, growing serious for a change, as he began to absorb what I was saying.

"Not only that, but all twelve haven't docked together *a single time* since they were launched thirty years ago. If they're all here now..."

"Oh. Oh, shit."

"Yeah," I agreed, releasing his shirt and turning back to the viewing window as we came up on the civilian docks. "That's *exactly* what I was thinking."

Chapter Seven

Breathe, just breathe, deep breaths, in and out, in and out, in and—oh Sweet Mother Universe, I don't want to be here!

Any area of a station as large as Mergassë would be bad enough, but the civilian sector—ugh! I was trapped in a kaleidoscope of voices, sounds, smells and movement, so much of it, pouring in from all sides, assaulting my senses. No matter how tightly I pressed my arms against my sides, people brushed against me as we moved through the crowd. And the conversations! Rapid-fire bits of discussion pinged me from every direction like bullets.

"—thought it'd be over by—"

"And then she asked me if—"

"—really hadn't heard about it?"

In the midst of the flow of conversation, a veritable herd of Nīpa came bustling through, speaking in their cheeping chirping, high-pitched language, lightly-furred tails whipping in a frenzy. Though none of them measured more than a meter in height, put them in a group like that and they got *loud*.

And of course, I was stuck without a hoodie, without any kind of sound-dampener, because I had to look the part, had to wear my civvie-mod version of the *Carpathia's* crew uniform. No hood, no satin-lined pockets, no super long sleeves; just slender black pants with a gray stripe down the legs and a—blessedly—simple gray top. *Because God forbid I be comfortable, oh no, everything has to be about— holy sweet mother of the baby Jesus, what's that* smell?

I couldn't stop myself from clamping a hand over my nose as we passed a line of food stalls. My stomach clenched, twisting itself into a knot as I recognized the smell: some bastard was frying *gafvi* fish. Like this part of the sector didn't smell bad enough, without some asshole sticking slices of the foulest smelling fish in the universe into a deep-fat fryer.

"Ah," First Officer Magellan sighed as we passed the stall. "Captain, if at all possible, I'd like to stop here on the way back. I haven't had a good bit of *gafvi* in ages."

Oh, stellar.

Magellan and Captain Chui had come representing command and ground forces both. Aki and her copilots, plus Kiri and Lieutenant Zubairi had come to represent Shiphandling. The Professor had sent his second, Pia Hikari, to stand in for him for Science. I had Christa along, and we'd brought Diver; even though he was R&D, he worked with engineering enough to stand for them. And he could, as Captain Chui put it, explain any sort of technical detail on an understandable level. Explain it to Your Audience Like They're Five 101 wasn't a class most scientists or engineers ever took.

"—look, a *gafvi* stand!"

"Mo-om, I wanna get a—"

"Dad! Dad! What are those? What are they? I've never seen them before! Dad!"

And we'd brought the Psittacans, because there was nothing like attracting metric buttloads of attention to yourself in a crowded space station.

It's not their fault, I reminded myself. *They're so new to the Alliance, most people still haven't seen them.* Which was why we brought them whenever we were on station, so both they and other sapients could adjust. But their bright colors and overall unfamiliarity drew attention like honey drew flies. Aside from Many Kills and Day Dawns Red, who were green, Swifter Than Lightning and Shadows Beneath Sunlight were both bright yellow. Silence In The Night was an oddity among the Macaw class, an iridescent blue-black that made the group stand out all the more.

"Not much farther," Captain Chui said, "and we'll pass into the military sector."

"Shouldn't we be heading for diplomacy?" Christa asked.

Captain Chui's lips pressed into a grim line. "No. My orders were military."

Which reminds me, I've got to figure out why those ships are coming into port here. If only I had something to block out all this stimuli so I could concentrate...

Something bumped into my side, nearly sending me jumping out of my skin. Then I felt soft fur under my fingers; I glanced down, saw Aki walking along next to me. *Oh, thank you, Aki.* I tightened my fingers, rubbing strands of fine fur between my fingertips, and sighed. It couldn't block out the sounds or smells or the press of bodies, but it helped a little.

Now, if I was in the military, what would I want with—damnit! The toes of my boot caught on something, and only Aki leaning against my hip kept me from falling over. Aki growled and took a swipe at the Nafta that had nearly sent me ass over teakettle. It scurried a short distance away, reared up on its hind legs, and wiggled its whiskers at her.

"No good bad grump," it complained.

"Lousy space pigeon," Akcharrch retorted.

Technically Naftas looked more like overlarge crosses between weasels and otters, but people called them space pigeons because they ended up *everywhere*. We usually had to root out a good dozen of them from the *Carpathia* every time we docked. Scientists and anthropologists had been arguing for years over their level of sapience; whatever it was, the Nafta were smart enough to get themselves into more trouble than a curious toddler and to be more annoying than *actual* pigeons. Normally I had more patience for them, but I was already developing a headache.

"Ignore them," Aki said. "We're almost at the hub, and then we'll be in military. They use laser systems to keep the Nafta out."

"Harsh," I muttered, rubbing my temple. "They could keep them away just as easily by offering them food."

I tightened my fingers in Aki's fur and tried to focus solely on that for the time being. Captain Chui lead us through the remainder of the civilian sector and into a passage, where a great deal of noise dropped off. I breathed a sigh of relief. There were still people passing through here, squeezing past us, but I had Aki on one side and Diver on the other, forming a buffer between me and others. *Much better.*

Eventually we arrived in the hub, where a ring of counters dominated the center. It was pretty quiet at this hour, with only a few people milling at the counters, getting help from the efficient station staff. Captain Chui bypassed the counters and headed towards a corridor to the left, where a pair of soldiers stood guard. They wore gray-blue uniforms with silver threading, the colors of the Alliance military. Sometimes I wondered why no one ever realized they were a duller variant of the Sanavila coloration.

"Captain Chui Shan Fung of the starship *Carpathia*," Captain Chui said.

They must've recognized her name; even though she was ex-military, both soldiers snapped off a sharp salute. A slight smile touched the corners of the captain's mouth as she saluted in return.

"My crew and I are here to see Admiral losTavina," she went on.

"Yes, ma'am," one of the soldiers said. "We were told to expect you, ma'am."

"Wait, hold on," I blurted out. "We're here to see *who*?"

Aki turned her head and gently nipped my arm. I pressed my lips together, smiling awkwardly at the soldier, who paused in the midst of sub-vocalization to stare at me. No one, not even Captain Chui, said a word. Brow furrowed, the soldier carried on, and a moment later another soldier appeared. She, too, gave Captain Chui a salute.

"This way, Captain," she said. "The admiral will see you immediately."

"Thank you, Private. Lead on."

I opened my mouth again; once more, Aki nipped me in warning. *All right, all right, I'll keep my big, space-fried mouth shut, then.* But... Admiral losTavina? Surely that couldn't be who I thought it was...

Naturally, it was who I thought it was.

"Xandri," Christa hissed, poking me in the back, "*sit down!*"

I tore my gaze away from the Sanavila standing at the head of the room, surrounded by a group of soldiers, and took a seat with the rest of my crew members, choosing one on the end of the row. Aki plopped down next to me, taking a seat on the floor since none of the chairs here would support her. And the Psittacans chose to stand, since no one had bothered with perch-stools. *Fucking Sanavila.*

I watched the admiral from beneath my lashes. Oh, it was him all right, Admiral Olarian kal losTavina. Who else could it be? No one else from the losTavina line who still worked in the military was so old. His bluish skin let off the silvery glow that accompanied adulthood among the Sanavila, and his wings—the thin, wisping appendages that started beneath an adult Sanavila's arms—hung nearly to the floor, a mark of his great age. He'd been a hero during the Second Zechak War, at an age when his fellows were either retired or relaxing at desk jobs.

Not losTavina. No, he'd commanded nearly half the fleet from the Titania-class dreadnought *Resilience* and if *he* was involved in this...

"Captain Chui." The admiral shooed away his fellow officers. "Good to see you again."

"And you, Admiral." Captain Chui crossed one leg over the other, steepled her hands and studied him with an unreadable expression. "I confess to some... confusion, however. I was under the impression we were called here to work with the AFC."

"So you are, so you are. The *Resplendence* will be leaving in a couple of days to relieve the *Benevolence* and it is my hope that you'll be going with them. But this is a matter of both diplomacy *and* military."

And since it involves the Anmerilli, absolutely no one ought to be surprised. I glanced, as surreptitiously as I could manage, at my colleagues. Those of us the captain had chosen to accompany her all knew that we'd been called in for something to do with the Anmerilli, and everyone was informed enough to know about the Anmerilli's itchy trigger fingers.

"I'm just waiting for—ah! Here he is!"

The door slid open and in stepped a man in the uniform of the AFC. He paused, taking in our group, and for a moment there seemed to be shock on his angular but otherwise unremarkable face. *No.* I shook my head. *Must've been imagining it.* Members of the AFC worked with all kinds of species; some humans, a Kowari, an Ongkoarrat and a bunch of Psittacans would be nothing compared to what this man had seen.

"Captain Chui, this is Marco Antilles of the Alliance First Contact Division," the admiral said. "Mr. Antilles, Captain Chui Shan Fung of the starship *Carpathia*, and some of her crew. You'll be working with them, especially..."

Here Admiral losTavina hesitated. His silvered Sanavila eyes skimmed over our group. For a moment his gaze hovered on me and I considered giving him a small wave to let him know he had, in fact, hit the universe's worst jackpot. But then he moved on to Christa and his demeanor brightened. Yeah, I was on edge from the chaos of the station and was probably giving off a "Don't even fucking look at me" vibe, but that was still kinda rude. It wasn't like I was doing it on purpose.

But Marco Antilles was looking at me, I noticed with surprise. He stepped across the room, reaching a hand out to me. Christa elbowed me in the side and I shot to my feet.

"Xandri Corelel, yes?" Antilles said. "I've heard about you."

What? I blinked. "You have?"

"Xandri," Christa spat through her teeth. "Your *hand.*"

Oh, right. Damn. I held out my hand. Antilles caught in a firm but blessedly brief shake, then gestured for me to take a seat again. I dropped like a feather in vacuum.

"Indeed. Impressive work you've done with your friends there." He gestured to the Psittacans. "It's not everyone who gets to name an entire species."

"She didn't *name* us," Many Kills corrected, his crest coming up all the way. "She found a useful alternative that *we* approved of and that *your* less than sufficient mouths could pronounce."

Oh dear.

"Ah, yes, yes, of course," Antilles said. "My sincerest apologies, sir. Forgive me, I'm a bit out of sorts from the journey."

"Mr. Antilles was kind enough to get transport from the Silvanas System on very short notice so he could help inform you of the situation," Admiral losTavina explained. "He's been working with the Anmerilli for six years now and it was he who brought it to our attention that... well. If I might bring your attention here..."

The admiral turned, gesturing to a holo-board on the far wall. He drew a thin wand from his sleeve, one of those tipped for use with holo-displays. In a few quick, easy motions he'd divided the holo into several large rectangles: one showed a scene from the Anmerilli planet, Cochinga; one showed several heavy-duty Anmerilli weapons; and one showed a schematic for... well, I didn't know what it was. Diver had an inkling though, if I were to judge by the way he started swearing under his breath.

"It seems, Captain Chui," the admiral said with amusement that rang false somehow, "that one of your crew has it figured out already."

63

"Diver?" Captain Chui questioned.

"Begging your pardon, Captain, Admiral, sir," Diver said, "but...if I didn't know better, I'd say that was a schematic for a ship-mounted laser not much different from the ones the Alliance already uses. But since I *do* know better, and you wouldn't have called us in for just a laser, I'm gonna go out on a limb and say that's a graser."

"Very good, Mr. Diver," Admiral losTavina said. "That's *precisely* what it is."

"And um..." I probably shouldn't, I knew better, but I said it anyway. "And for the technologically handicapped among us, that means...?"

Christa sighed and rolled her eyes. Admiral losTavina *looked* at me, in a way that sent a battalion of shivers marching down my back.

"It's a gamma ray laser," Diver said, saving my tail feathers. Figuratively speaking, obviously. "It's—Captain, Admiral, with your permission?" When they both nodded, Diver rose to continue. "Space...space is big. Now I know you're all thinking, 'Diver, we know that already, get to the point.' But that *is* the point, ladies and gentlemen.

"The sheer size of space determines how combat operates, and makes kinetic projectiles next to useless; at most distances, by the time they reach their target, said target will most likely be gone. Thus we carry missiles and lasers. Now, missiles hit heavy and they're self-guided, so they're more likely to hit their target—if they reach it. The disadvantage of missiles is they can be shot down. Lasers will hit just about every time—that's the benefit of traveling at the speed of light. Problem is, they're not terribly powerful, and even smaller Zechak ships can take a lot of fire before they go down. This baby, though..." Diver gestured at the schematic.

"A graser will have all the accuracy and speed of a laser and nearly the power of a missile, *and* they could be mounted on fighters. *Making* one, however—I'd sure love to know how they've done that."

"It's not completely finished," Antilles said, "but they're damn close. That I've gotten that schematic at all is nothing short of a miracle; the finer details of how they've done it are so classified, even God wouldn't be allowed to see them."

"Which is bad enough," the admiral chimed in, "but military intelligence has intercepted several messages from the Zechak to the Anmerilli. The Zechak know about this weapon, and you'd better believe they're interested. And the Anmerilli are considering allying with them."

Oh, fuck on a stick. *The Anmerilli have developed an enormously dangerous weapon that would change the face of space combat, and they're actually considering being best buds with the orcs. And the Alliance is expecting me to stop it. Stellar. No pressure or anything.* I dropped my head into my hands. How was I going to stop a violent, xenophobic race of people from allying with another—

"Wait a minute." I lifted my head. "Why would a species that xenophobic ally themselves with the Zechak? Oh. Oh wait." Before anyone could answer, I lifted a hand. "Because they'll think it's better to ally with *one* group of outsiders, if they must, than a whole bunch of them, and with a weapon that powerful at their disposal, they know the Zechak will fight to keep them safe from us."

Antilles raised his eyebrows. "Very good. I've had trouble getting my own people to understand that."

"Cognitive dissonance," I said with a shrug. "People—all kinds of people—are pretty good at it."

"So then what you're saying," Captain Chui said, rising from her chair, "is that you need my crew and I—particularly Ms. Corelel—to stop this alliance between the Zechak and the Anmerilli."

"We can't seem to quite get through to them. Your Ms. Corelel seems to have a bit of a knack; we're hoping she can give us some new insight."

She's sitting right here.

"If anyone can, she can."

Magellan cleared his throat, the first time anyone but myself, Diver, or the captain had spoken. "If you don't mind, admiral, I was wondering—has there been any noise from the LHFH? If they've caught wind of this potential alliance..."

"They haven't," Antilles said hurriedly. "We haven't had a peep out of them."

Oh, good. The Last Hope for Humanity—sometimes referred to as 'those anti-alien assholes'—loved to interfere in all manner of diplomacy and first contact missions. Anything to stop humans from uniting with yet more aliens and, as the LHFH put it, further soiling the purity of humanity. Damned bigots. They referred to themselves as Homo sapiens purus, a hypocritical joke if ever I heard one, since they chromed and gene-jumped themselves almost to the point of actual speciation. Having to deal with them, on top of everything else, would just make my growing migraine worse.

"I'm afraid I don't have very much time left to talk to you," Admiral losTavina said. "But Mr. Antilles and Commander Nafisi," he gestured to a woman standing to his left, "will finish briefing you on the exact details during your trip to Cochinga. If there are no more questions for me..."

Just like a Sanavila, assuming we'd do as he wished, before we had agreed. Though knowing Captain Chui, we'd be doing it. The military and parliament looked the other way because we did good work, but we barely qualified as legal, and the captain wouldn't refuse this kind of mission, not when it risked drawing so much ire. *She wouldn't refuse anyway. This is why she formed our group to begin with, to make the universe a safer place.* Which reminded me...

"I have a question," I said, as the admiral started towards the door. Christa groaned, but I ignored her.

"Yes?" Admiral losTavina favored me with the sort of indulgent smile one bestowed upon a particularly irritating, anklebiting toddler.

"Why have you called the entire Malevolence-class fleet to the station?"

I hadn't realized Admiral losTavina was carrying a pistol until it was pointed, quite suddenly, at me. And then suddenly *a lot* of guns were being pointed and my Psittacan friends were rustling their feathers in anger.

"That," Admiral losTavina said, "is classified information."

Chapter Eight

"Well, I think the captain has managed to convince Admiral losTavina that you're not a spy."

I raised my head and looked at Kiri. "What gave it away? The fact that I'd have to be the most incompetent spy in the history of the universe?"

"That...probably helped," Kiri conceded. She smiled and reached out, giving me a brief pat on the arm. "Are you okay?"

I just had a gun pointed at my forehead. What do you think? Somehow despite the stress I managed to hold that one in. Kiri was only trying to help. The same couldn't be said for Christa, who wouldn't even look at me. I folded my arms across my chest and curled my fingers into the fabric of my sleeves; my feeling of being stifled was growing towards that "need to peel off my own damn skin" level.

At least we weren't in a crowded area. Admiral losTavina had taken us to his office; most of us sat outside, in the hallway, while Captain Chui, First Officer Magellan and Lieutenant Zubairi spoke to the admiral. He had to have realized pretty quickly that I wasn't a spy—a spy didn't just blurt out her knowledge of classified information at random—but what would the captain say to get me off the hook? The weapons may have been put down pretty quickly, but that didn't mean I was out of trouble.

"I'm fine," I muttered. Nothing turned me into a bigger liar than social situations.

"If you don't mind my asking," Marco Antilles spoke up, "how *did* you know about that? About the Malevolence-class ships?"

"Oh, um..." Fuck, fuck, fuck. "I don't even—that's probably not—I didn't actually *know...*"

Antilles raised an eyebrow. *Oh god, how am I supposed to lie properly when everyone is staring at me?* Even Christa was looking at me now, her chin propped on one hand in that sort of purposefully slouching elegance some lucky people—read: not me—had, her curiosity piqued.

"I can't believe you won a bet on a lucky guess!" Diver cut in, before I had to figure out what to say. He let out a snort of annoyance.

"A bet?" Kiri's eyebrows went up too.

"Yeah, didn't you see us whispering up on the observation deck this morning? She bet me all twelve ships would come into port here. I thought she was just getting overexcited because of seeing the *Devil's Love Song*—"

"I was!" I agreed, hoping I didn't sound *too* eager. "I mean, I know these ships like the back of my hand, I ought to know better, but I got carried away..."

"And now I'm out twenty creds! Can you believe that?"

"I'm sorry." I pressed my hands together beneath my chin and leaned towards him. "But Marbles and Cake greatly appreciate your contribution to the millet fund."

Diver snorted and shot me an annoyed look. He slouched in his chair, arms folded over his chest, and I wished *I* could be that convincing. Kiri laughed and Christa rolled her eyes at Diver, shaking her head like she thought he was completely space-fried. Pia leaned across the aisle and reached out, giving me a pat on the knee. *Why do people keep touching me? Stop it!* You'd think after so many millennia humanity would've learned that touching isn't automatically nice.

"Well, maybe we ought to have you play the galactic lottery for us," she said with a grin. "I can't speak for the rest of the ship, but Science could certainly use the extra funds."

"Yes," came Captain Chui's voice, "too bad gambling is *technically* against ship policy."

I huddled down in my chair—didn't even have to fake it, with that many commanding officers looking at me. The admiral still watched me with an air of suspicion, but I supposed it made a person twitchy, having twelve top-of-the-line, absurdly valuable warships about to be under your protection. *And why is that, anyway? I still don't get it. Why have them all come here and put themselves in danger?* Not that Admiral losTavina wasn't a good choice for keeping them safe, he was a damn crafty Sanavila and—

Oh. Oh no.

I dropped my head like I was ashamed, praying no one had seen my expression. Pieces were beginning to fall into place, but...

Please, please let me be wrong.

"That was quite a lucky guess," Admiral losTavina said. Magellan's Kowari hearing must've picked up our conversation, giving him and the captain something to feed the admiral. "You all understand, of course, that this incident has to stay quiet."

"What incident?" Captain Chui asked.

As a group, the Psittacans flicked their crests. I hoped no one else here knew their body language as well as I did. After the—blessedly short—standoff in the briefing room, they were still riled for a fight. And the last thing you wanted was a meter and a half, parrot-like creature, with hooked beak and claws to match their size, itching to bang some heads together.

"Very good," Admiral losTavina said. "Do *try* to keep your crew from making bets next time, Captain Chui. Now, unless there are any more questions..."

Because I was space-fried that way, I started to open my mouth. Diver widened his eyes and gave a quick shake of his head; Kiri put a hand on my arm and squeezed. I snapped my mouth shut, my teeth coming together with an audible *clack*. Admiral losTavina eyed me for a moment, gave us all a dignified nod, and stalked off down the corridor, his wings swaying with his stride. Boy, was I glad to see the back end of *him*.

"Well," Magellan said dryly, "that was exciting."

"Exciting isn't the word I'd use," Captain Chui said, "but it's over now. No more 'bets,' you two, understood?"

"Yes, ma'am," Diver and I said in unison.

"Good. I think it's time we headed back to the ship."

We began to rise, those of us who were sitting. Marco Antilles rose quickly, stepping to intercept the captain—though, I noticed, he accompanied his movements with a nod of proper deference. Captain Chui paused, Lieutenant Magellan on one side, Lieutenant Zubairi on the other, making for an intimidating triad. Yet Antilles only smiled, a smile of gentle respect. He might not be part of the AFC's military section, but this man knew how to behave around military types.

"Your pardon, Captain," he said. "You sent a message ahead asking for files on the Anmerilli, yes? I thought I could show Ms. Corelel what we have."

"That's very thoughtful, Mr. Antilles. Perhaps you could come by the *Carpathia* tomorrow around, let's say oh-eight-hundred? That will give Ms. Corelel time to make certain all her own notes are organized."

Notes? I don't keep any—oh. Oh, bless Captain Chui; she was giving me a bit of time to recover from all this. Which was good, because I needed to talk to her, and I was already running out of cope as it was. By the time I got done with that, there was no way I'd be able to deal with Antilles and more stuff about the Anmerilli.

"That sounds good, ma'am," Antilles said with another one of those pleasant smiles. "Until tomorrow, Ms. Corelel."

I nodded in return. It wasn't terribly polite, but it would have to do; if I tried to smile now, I'd cause a diplomatic incident.

Another diplomatic incident.

I watched Marco Antilles walk off down the hall, past doors and soldiers, as naturally as if he did it every day of his life. The type who blended. I always envied that type.

"Mashallah," Lieutenant Zubairi breathed. "As if grasers and potential alliances with the Zechak weren't stressful enough. Praise God that's over." She looked at me and smiled. "And you. Are we going to have to talk about that gambling problem?"

"I sure hope not, ma'am." I liked to think I'd left those days behind me. Also, I suspected Lieutenant Zubairi didn't buy the story. Hell, the admiral might not have either, if it wasn't so convenient for his current situation. "Though you might want to talk to Diver. It was actually *his* idea."

"Hey! Snitch!"

A ripple of laughter passed through our group and an echoing ripple—of relief—passed through me. Without Diver, Captain Chui, Magellan and Lieutenant Zubairi in on the act, I might not have pulled it off. But most of the group seemed satisfied with the explanation. *It probably helps that most of them don't understand what it is I do and think I get by with a lot of lucky guesses, anyway.*

As the group started filing down the hall I caught Diver's eye and mouthed 'thank you' at him. He grinned and winked at me. Seemed everyone was out to save my tail feathers today; in a kind of literal sense with the Psittacans, since they'd put themselves between me and Admiral losTavina's gun. I had a lot of thank yous to pass around.

Not the least of which had to go to Aki, who immediately trundled up beside me, allowing me to grasp her fur again. As I rubbed the soft strands between my fingertips, I twitched the fingers on my other hand, using my wristlet to ping Captain Chui's private comm channel. After a moment my wristlet buzzed softly, signifying that the comm was open.

"*We're going to need to talk, ma'am,*" I sub-vocalized.

"*I had a feeling you'd say that. We'll speak more on the* Carpathia."

"*Yes, ma'am.*"

I bit back a sigh. This had long day written all over it, and it hadn't exactly been short to begin with. *But Admiral losTavina... if he's up to what I think he's up to, then... oh god, Xan, don't think about that right now.* The pressure was already so great it was amazing I wasn't turning into the Hunchback of Notre Dame, with the weight pressing down on my shoulders. One step at a time, no need to think about everything at once.

First thing was first: Get back through Mergassë's civilian sector without melting down into a puddle of screaming, sobbing me.

At least we wouldn't have to stop for *gafvi* fish.

"All right, everyone, dismissed," Captain Chui announced to our group as we stepped through *Carpathia's* main airlock. "Corelel, Diver, Ayabara, Magellan, Baranka, and Aki, I want to see you in my office in half an hour."

"What about us?" Aleevian demanded. "Shouldn't we—"

"Did I call your name, Mr. masViara?"

"No, ma'am."

"Well, you have your answer, then. *Dismissed.*"

Captain Chui turned on her heel and set off down the corridor at a brisk walk. Aleevian watched her go, a scowl marring his ethereal silvery face. *Touchy, touchy.* Sanavila juveniles did tend to admire their elders to a degree I just didn't comprehend; seeing Admiral losTavina must've been a treat for Leev. It was a good thing he wouldn't be at this meeting, wouldn't hear what I had to say. Juveniles could really get on the defensive, and they were worse when they were as close to chrysalis as Leev was.

I stayed where I was as the others started down the hall, until only Aki and I were left. I'd send Diver an extra thank you later, somehow—maybe I could convince Science to send him some scales to have some fun with. For the moment, though...

"Hey, Aki?"

"Mm?" Akcharrch fell into lumbering step beside me as I started down the hall.

"Thanks for the help back there."

"Didn't do anything."

"Yeah, you did, and I appreciate it. Okay? Please just accept my thank you, you know I'm shit at this emotion stuff."

She chuffed. "You manage fine." She tilted her head to look up at me and if she'd had eyebrows, she'd be raising one. "A bet, huh?"

"Uh...well..."

"Don't worry, I'm sure I'll learn the truth before long. Good thing Diver was there, though; you're a lousy liar."

I smiled and laughed along with her chuffing, which was a lie all onto itself. For a moment I got the urge to tell the truth. Just because I couldn't lie very well when put on the spot didn't mean I couldn't lie. My every waking moment was a lie; my entire fucking identity was a lie. But I squashed the urge, because what would it get me? I wanted to keep what few friends I had.

Oh, that reminds me. I opened a private comm channel on my wristlet. "*Carpathia?*"

"Hello, Xandri. Did you have a nice time on station?"

"Um...well." I slipped into sub-vocalization to explain what had happened, as I made my way towards the captain's office via decks rather than tubes. I passed the Psittacans on their way to one of the rec decks, where they'd no doubt take out their remaining frustrations with a bit of sparring, and I kinda wished I could join them. But no, I had to let the captain know of my suspicions. Assuming she hadn't already begun forming the same ones herself.

"*Oh dear,*" Carpathia said, when I'd finished laying out the basics. "*Xandri, I'm sorry. I should have known to tell you their presence at Mergassë was classified.*"

"*Well, I really ought to have seen that for myself. I mean, all twelve Malevolence-class destroyers docked at once? Obviously classified.*"

"*Still...perhaps I've been out of military service for too long. It seems... odd, to think of my friends as 'classified.'*"

72

I blinked. "*Friends.*"

"*Yes, of course. That's how I knew they were arriving. I told you, I was in contact with Requiem this morning.*"

In contact. Oh hell. I was willing to bet the *Hellfire Requiem's* crew didn't know their ship's AI had been having a chitchat with one of her friends. *I guess I got it into my head that* Carpathia *picked them up on her sensors, and if she did, anyone could, so why would it be secret?* I still should've known better than to open my big mouth about it to the admiral. If he hadn't been in such a hurry, I might be sitting in a cell right now, waiting for interrogation.

"*Xandri?*"

"*It's all right,*" I said. "*I don't blame you. I bet you don't get to talk to your friends very often, do you?*"

"*Actually, I talk to some of them every day.*" Had she a physical form, I was pretty sure she'd be smiling. "*I'll call ahead to Captain Chui and try to explain. Don't worry, Xandri, I'm sure everything will be fine.*"

Fine. Yeah, sure, *fine.* I had maybe a couple of weeks, tops, to learn everything I could about the Anmerilli, so I could stop them from allying with the Zechak and giving our most dangerous enemies a powerful weapon. *Me.* The woman who had literally caused a minor diplomatic incident among the Kowari by *trying to smile.* If I failed, everything would go to hell in a hand-basket before you could say "fuck my life."

And now I had to go tell my captain that it might not even be the Starsystems Alliance in said hand-basket, because I strongly suspected that Admiral losTavina had slotted mass genocide into the column for Plan B.

Oh yeah, cakewalk.

Chapter Nine

A cart stood outside the door of the captain's office when I arrived. As I paused in surprise, a comm channel pinged on my wristlet.

"Refreshments," *Carpathia* explained. "Coffee, tea, juice and water. The filled mug is for Captain Chui. Would you see that she gets it?"

"Of course. Thanks, *Carpathia*."

I hit the door chime. As the door slid back, I caught the end of the cart and pulled it inside with me. The others were already there, sitting in extra chairs—though Akcharrch had foregone having her heavy, special chair moved and had just sat on the floor. Captain Chui sat, as usual, behind her desk. I stopped the cart in the middle of the room and placed the already full, steaming mug on the captain's desk.

"From *Carpathia*."

The captain raised her eyebrows. She reached for the mug, cradling it in her hands, apparently unperturbed by the heat coming off the delicate white and blue porcelain. She brought it up to her nose, inhaled—then took a careful sip. Her eyes widened in surprise and—I noticed with surprise of my own—delight.

"*Tieguanyin!*" she breathed. "Thank you, *Carpathia*."

"You're most welcome, Captain."

Captain Chui took another sip of her tea, blissfully unaware of the fact that we were all staring at her. As our captain, she rarely showed us much of the personal side of her life, things like her likes and dislikes or the traditions she kept from her homeworld. Which was fair enough, I supposed, but it made it kind of startling when it did happen.

"Well," Captain Chui said, setting down her mug. "Best get to business, then."

"Which is *what*, precisely?" Kiri asked, reaching for the tray. "This business with those ships Xan mentioned?"

74

"Not just any ships," Aki grumbled. "Malevolence-class ships. Terrifying, those. Diver, hand me some juice, would you?"

As refreshments were passed around, I took the remaining empty seat, between Diver and Kiri, across from Christa—who *still* wouldn't look at me. Sighing, I grabbed a glass of water from the tray and sat back in my chair. Though it was so few of us, I felt each presence on my skin, each body as if they all sat right next to me, choking up my space. *Just a little longer, Xan. Just get through this and you're done.*

"I take it this is one of those things we don't speak about to anyone else," Kiri said. "Like it never even happened."

"Indeed," Magellan said. "It never leaves this room."

"Captain..." I began.

She sighed. "I know, Xandri. You think there's a reason for all twelve ships to be called into Mergassë."

"How can there not be? You know those ships as well as I do and I *know* you've got the same suspicions I do, too. Admiral losTavina is going to use the Malevolence-class ships on Cochinga, isn't he? If the Anmerilli refuse to join the Alliance—*especially* if they join the Zechak instead—he'll—he'll..."

Christa nearly dropped her glass. "That's absurd! No Sanavila would do such a thing. No *Alliance* member would do such a thing!"

"Why not? He's done it before!"

Captain Chui closed her eyes. "Not precisely that."

"Close enough!" The water in my glass wobbled precariously as I moved. Flushing, I forced my arms down to my lap. "It took me a while to put the pieces together, but it makes sense. It makes sense for the Alliance to assign Admiral losTavina to this mission, because he's clever, and he's ruthless when he has to be. Look at what he did to Halcyon!"

All eyes turned to the captain, even Magellan's. I wondered if he'd been in the Second Zechak War at all. Even if he had, would he have been at the Battle of Halcyon? Would he know of it, if he hadn't? It had been cleverly filed away as if it were some obscure bit of history; what most people remembered now was a battle that took many lives and a Sanavila admiral whose heroic efforts had saved even more lives. Which wasn't even untrue, but it wasn't the whole picture, either.

"Halcyon was a mining planet in the Kingfisher System," Captain Chui said with a sigh. "Inhospitable place when the Alliance first found it, but worth the effort. It had weapons-grade materials in abundance and we wanted it.

"Unfortunately, so did the Zechak, and in the end, they were the ones who got it. They brought in the largest fleet of motherships history has ever seen and they wrenched Halcyon from our grasp like we were no more than children. Most people don't know it now—civilians don't, certainly—but that's what began the Second Zechak War."

She paused to sip her tea. I'd never seen her look like this before, worn and haggard, her bronze-touched skin pulled taut over the fine height of her cheekbones. Yes, she suspected what Admiral losTavina had in mind, no doubt about it.

"They didn't just take Halcyon," I said. Even though it drew everyone's attention to me, it gave Captain Chui a moment to regain her composure. *She must've been there. Must've lost fellow soldiers... friends. It can't be easy to talk about.* "They set up military bases alongside the mines, filled the mines with slaves, and destroyed any Alliance ships that got too close. With the location of the Kingfisher System, they had a perfect base from which to strike out at us, right in the middle of civilization as we know it."

Captain Chui nodded. "And that's precisely what they did. You know how they are. God forgive me for saying it, but they breed like rodents and they overrun *everything*. It got to where just keeping them away from Alliance planets took everything we had.

"Admiral losTavina was in on the plan to end it all. Warships and fighters were built in droves—not always up to spec, but it was the numbers we needed more than anything else. Numbers to distract the Zechak while our most powerful ships moved into the system and approached Halcyon. It worked—for a certain definition of worked." She sliced a glance at me.

"They destroyed the Zechak ships protecting Halcyon," I said, "but it took pretty much all their heavy firepower. They had nothing left, and there were more ships, both on Halcyon and coming in from other systems. So Admiral losTavina... he came up with an idea, something that would make Halcyon too worthless for the Zechak to bother with anymore. He—the ships had pieces for making new missiles, but not enough of them, and not enough time to build them, so he...he had some of the ships pull out, so they'd be at a greater distance from the planet and...oh, this is the science-y part that I can never quite..."

Diver sat up in his chair. "I think I get it. At a distance like that, warheads wouldn't be necessary; just something that could withstand entering an atmosphere at one hella speed. Because the speed alone would be enough. It would be...shit. It wouldn't even take that many projectiles, going at those speeds, to make the K-Pg extinction look like a walk in the fucking park. A planet hit like that...it'd become unlivable."

Captain Chui nodded. "And it did. Nothing and no one survived."

Silence settled over the room, that horrible sort of silence that buzzed in my ears and flashed white in front of my eyes. Bitter white, and oh-so-still. I drew my legs up to my chest, not caring at the moment if I looked childish, and wrapped my arms around my knees. I glanced around; even Diver looked subdued, and he had a bit of a fetish for things going boom. *Most of those are things that go boom behind protective plastics, though.*

"A lot of innocent people must have died that day," Christa murmured.

"A lot of innocent people had *already* died," Captain Chui snapped. "And more would have if something hadn't been done." She took a deep breath and turned her gaze to me. "I didn't know you had an interest in military history."

"I don't. I have an interest in starships, and you can't study the *Resilience* without learning about Admiral losTavina." I shrugged. "I found the standard files on the Battle of Halcyon a little...glossed over, so I dug deeper."

"And so you learned about the admiral's ploy. But even you can see there are other reasons for having the Malevolence-class ships in play. If the Zechak were to decide to invade during the negotiations, or perhaps once the treaty is signed, having the Malevolence-class ships close could only be to our benefit."

"Yeah, and if the Anmerilli side with the Zechak, the ships can move in at an eye blink, blow Cochinga to kingdom come, and be out of there again so fast, no one could prove the Alliance had anything to do with it," I said. "losTavina could hang it on the Zechak with no one the wiser."

Another silence swept over the group. I winced. *That didn't sound horribly disrespectful and rude or anything...* Diver shifted in his chair to look at me, eyebrows lifting so high they nearly disappeared beneath the copper-streaked curls coiling down over his forehead.

"Has anyone ever told you that your mind is a terrifying place?"

"Are you kidding me?" I snorted. "I have nightmares about the *Carpathia* being swallowed whole by giant invisible space sharks."

Diver blinked. "*O*kay, I think I'd like to go back to talking about blowing up planets now." He paused a moment, considering. "Xan, just what are the specs on those ships, anyway?"

"The relevant ones? Sixteen missile launchers, sixty-four missiles, cruiser size. *Each.*"

"With all due respect, Captain Chui," Christa cut in, "I didn't understand even half of that, and I *know* it's bad. If Admiral losTavina is planning to—"

"There's no proof he is. And knowing the admiral as I do, I'm pretty sure he'd rather not take it any further than threats, if—and *only* if—he has no other choice."

"Oh, threats, is that all?" I had to appreciate the sheer amount of sarcasm in Christa's tone; she was like a sarcasm layer cake. "Captain, we're the Starsystems Alliance! We're supposed to be the *good* guys."

"And so we are," Lieutenant Magellan said, taking a step forward. "Unfortunately, Ms. Baranka, being the *good* guys sometimes means having to make hard, unpleasant decisions. It sometimes means deciding between several billion lives—and several trillion. None of us *like* it, but I think it's safe to say we'd like the Zechak overrunning the universe with grasers at their command *even less.*"

Christa flinched back in her chair, looking contrite. *As much as I hate it, I guess he's right.* Reading about the Battle of Halcyon had horrified me. All those slaves in the mines, all of them dead in the moments when Admiral losTavina's makeshift missiles struck the planet—it gave me cold shivers to think about. What little hope those people had had of ever tasting freedom had been wiped out, scattered to the winds like so much dust.

I tried to tell myself that even more people would end up dead and enslaved had it not been for losTavina's actions. Sometimes it even worked. Especially when I thought about what kind of life *I* could have had, had mine been one of the lives affected by the orcs' takeover of such a pivotal point in our universe. But I still didn't like it, and I was glad I wasn't the one who had to make those kinds of decisions.

"I'm not going to lie," Captain Chui spoke into the silence. "I don't like the admiral's plan. I understand it, but I don't like it.

"But that's *why* we're here in the first place, why I started this first contact group: To have a chance at changing the things I don't like. A chance at *truly* being the good guys. It's why I've called you all here. Together, we can make sure it never reaches the point even of threats." The captain rose. "Diver, I want you on weapons research. Try to sort out *how* they might be making these grasers. If we can develop the technology for ourselves, it will change the game completely."

"I'll do my best, ma'am."

"I know you will. Kiri, I need you on intel. If you can find out more about Admiral losTavina's plans, great, but don't expect to find much; he called the Malevolence-class ships into Mergassë so there would be no risk of his orders being intercepted, and he'll use similar tactics to keep things hush-hush. More important is getting your hands on the Anmerilli's specs for this weapon if you can. But be careful and *do not* get caught."

"I never get caught," Kiri said. Then she added, "Yes, ma'am."

"Christa, I don't give a good goddamn what the problem is between you and Xandri, you *will* work together on this. Whatever she needs, whenever she needs it, you *will* be there to support her. This mission cannot fail and it will *not* fail because you two can't solve a few petty differences. Am I understood?"

"Yes, ma'am," Christa said, and even little ol' social instinctless me could hear the sulk in her tone.

"Good. Xandri, just keep doing what you're doing. With any luck, Mr. Antilles will have far more useful files for you than what we've got stored in our computers."

"Captain?" Aki put in. "What's *my* job?"

"Simple. Keep Xandri from going out of her mind before we even arrive at Cochinga."

"Ooo, you got the hard job," Diver teased.

"Nonsense. I could do that in my sleep."

Considering how soft and fuzzy she was, and the soothing way her tummy rumbled while she slept, she wasn't even wrong. I unfolded my legs and reached up to press my fingertips against the constant throb in my temples. *Try not to think about the pressure,* I told myself. *Try not to think about how damn high the stakes are.* If I failed, an entire planet could potentially be blown to smithereens. Oh god.

"We can do this," Captain Chui said quietly. "We've pulled the Alliance's ass out of the fire before, and we'll do it again. We could sit around wishing things were different—that the Anmerilli were more cooperative, that *we* had been the ones to make first contact with them rather than the AFC, that we'd had Xandri with us then—but it won't do us any good. So instead, we get to work."

The entire group let out murmurs of assent, and Magellan snapped a salute to his captain, which she returned with her usual poise. *She's right. There's no use getting caught up in 'what ifs.' I just have to do my best.* I didn't need the Anmerilli to like me—to like any of us—or to turn into a society of angelic peace-lovers who made flower garlands and woven bracelets rather than weapons of mass destruction; I just needed them to ally with us rather than the orcs. I needed to show them that allying with the orcs would be a bad idea.

Considering the only two species to ever ally with the orcs had been enslaved and wiped out, respectively, that shouldn't be *too* hard.

"So, you all have your tasks," Captain Chui said. "I have no doubt that you'll succeed; you never disappoint me." She smiled slightly, her scar pulling over her eye. "Dismissed."

I was *so* ready to be done with this day, even though it was only roughly half over. I stood with everyone else, pausing to set my glass back on the tray, fiddling with its positioning a little so I wouldn't get caught in the press of everyone leaving. After everything today, I just couldn't take anymore. If anyone touched me, I'd scream.

Even Magellan had left by the time I headed for the door. And though I was more than ready to head back to my room, I paused at the door and glanced back at Captain Chui. She sat behind her desk again, the tea mug cradled in her hands, her expression pensive. She noticed me watching her and raised an eyebrow.

"Captain..."

"Yes, I was at the Battle of Halcyon." Sometimes it was like she was reading my mind. "I watched as that planet was turned into little more than the cracked shell of an egg, and that was when I decided that one day, I would do exactly what I'm doing now. No, a group like ours likely could not have prevented what happened to Halcyon, but we can stop it from happening to Cochinga. That's why we're here."

"You know, Captain, I wish there were more people in the universe like you."

She didn't quite manage to stifle her expression of surprise. I flashed a smile, wan but genuine, and left.

As soon as I reached my room I locked my door and started stripping out of my clothes.

"Hello," Cake chirped from inside his cage.

"Hey, babies," I said, dropping my top on the floor.

My trousers followed. I wanted, more than anything, to strip completely—the feeling of cloth against my skin had reached a point close to pain—but there was always the chance someone would call on me, someone I'd have to answer. Instead I went to my closet and retrieved a veritably *ancient* tunic top. The already fine cotton had, over the years, worn to nearly tissue paper thinness, and the extra long sleeves had wear spots in them that could be used as thumbholes. I pulled it on and flopped down on my bed with a sigh.

"Cages open," I said.

A faint mechanical buzz filled the air as the bolts on Marbles' and Cake's cages slid back. The little devils had learned to mimic the words, so now I had the cages set to recognize my exact vocal patterns. Not even Marbles, with her remarkable talent for mimicry, could, well, *parrot* my vocal patterns to that extent.

I reached for the satin edging of my blanket as both birds fluttered out of their cages, their partial wing clippings allowing them some freedom of movement without giving them free rein to fly all over the place and hurt themselves. Free range parrots and spaceships that could turn off their gravity systems didn't mix well.

"I don't know what I'm gonna do," I confessed to my birds, as they landed on the bed with me.

"I love you," Marbles squawked.

"I love you too," I told her, reaching out with my free hand to scritch her head. "I'm not sure much of anyone will love me if I screw this up."

Cake clambered onto my shoulder and up onto my head, where he proceeded to preen bits of hair, tugging them loose from my braid. I let out another sigh, this one calmer, less despairing. My birds always made me feel better, and being alone, being away from crowds and noises and *expectations*, made the feeling of pressure ease from my shoulders. Yes, I had a *huge* job ahead of me, but maybe it wouldn't be so bad. I'd have help, after all.

"Hopefully this Antilles guy has got the goods," I said, stifling a yawn. "I have so little time to study the Anmerilli as it is..."

"It's okay," Marbles crooned.

"Heh. Aren't we the little optimist? But maybe you're right. Antilles must have at least *some* files on the leaders I need to convince. I'll focus on those."

"It's okay."

"Yep," I agreed, though I didn't fully feel it.

Tomorrow I'd begin my work with Marco Antilles. I could've spent more time looking at the files we already had, but I wasn't sure that would get me much further. *And honestly, after everything today, I really need to rest.* I closed my eyes, soothed by the familiar feeling of Cake's beak running through my hair. So many emotions roiled within me, but it was the pride I felt in Captain Chui's belief in me that I chose to cling to—that I *needed* to cling to—the most.

Chapter Ten

I left notice for Marco Antilles that I'd be waiting in Hydroponics. That seemed like a fair compromise, at least to me. It would give me a place to work where I was fairly comfortable, without having Antilles invade my personal space. And, as I found out when I entered, it meant I could spend some time with the Psittacans. All five of them were in Hydroponics, sitting on perch-stools around a small observation table and talking in their own language, when I arrived.

Antilles ought to like that, I thought, grabbing a pair of regular chairs and bringing them over to the table. *He probably hasn't gotten to work much with Psittacans.* They were integrating slowly, per their own choice, and they still didn't care much for working with humans, who made up a large part of the AFC. A lot of other species had reservations about working with us.

That's what came of trying to hide all the atrocities in your past.

"Morning, Xandri-bird," Many Kills greeted me.

"Hey, Many." I dropped into my chair. "Everyone. You're up early."

Shadows Beneath Sunlight swept her arms off the table, revealing a small covered plate and a wrapped nutrient-bar. "We had a feeling you might come here."

"And you brought breakfast. How...thoughtful."

"Captain's orders," Day Dawns Red explained. She clacked her beak in a Psittacan grin.

"Did she order all five of you to sit here and make sure I eat it, too?"

No one answered, although there were a few more clacking beaks, and Silence flicked his dark crest. I sighed. Truth to tell, I *had* forgotten breakfast. With all the stress yesterday, I hadn't been able to fall asleep easily and I'd woken up later than I wanted to. I grabbed plate and bar and dragged them to me. As soon as I pulled the cover off the plate, releasing the smell of fried eggs—overhard, just as I liked—and breakfast sausage, my stomach let out a loud rumble. It really was a lovely thing, having a top class chef running your ship's galley.

I ate quickly, listening to the Psittacans chatter amongst themselves. I would never be able to speak their language—I didn't have the right parts—but I'd heard enough in the past four years to know they were arguing about something. Their sounds came out sharp, and crests kept coming up; at one point Many's crest stayed up for a while, until Silence spoke a single, soft trill. I could have used my own translator to tell me what they were saying, but if they'd wanted me to know, they would've used theirs.

I was just finishing off the nutrient-bar—doing my best to not really taste it—when the inner doors hissed open and in walked Marco Antilles. He wore more casual dress than he had yesterday, and he carried a slender tablet with him. He paused when he saw us sitting around the table.

"Hello, Mr. Antilles," I said, fiddling with my nutrient-bar wrapper. "Something wrong?"

"What? Oh, no." He flashed a boyish smile and started to walk towards us again. "Forgive me, my fine feathered friends. I haven't really had a chance to meet any of your kind, being stuck on Cochinga for the past six years. It is... an unparalleled opportunity to see you all again."

"We do have that affect on people," Sunlight agreed with a beak clack.

"I hope you don't mind, Mr. Antilles," I said. "It's just that it's usually pretty quiet in here, so I thought it would be a pretty good place."

"Not at all. And please, call me Marco."

He smiled again and I found myself smiling back. *Well, that should make him easier to work with.* He took the seat next to mine and set the tablet on the table.

"This contains everything we have on the Anmerilli. Hopefully between this and your notes, you and I can come up with a solution."

"My notes?" Oh damn. I knew I'd forgotten something last night. "Um, right. Why don't we see what you've got first? We might not even need my notes."

The doors hissed again as Marco booted up the tablet. I glanced up, tried not to cringe as Christa walked into Hydroponics. She carried a tablet of her own. In a few brisk steps she crossed the distance, pausing only long enough to grab a chair of her own and drag it between Many's and Lightning's perch-stools.

"Ah, Ms. Baranka," Marco said, with that pleasant smile of his. "A pleasure to see you again. I wasn't aware you'd be joining us this morning."

"I thought I'd come take notes. That way you and Xandri can focus on what needs to be done."

I tried to smile to show my appreciation, though I wasn't sure it translated. I really *did* appreciate the gesture, even if it was more for her benefit than mine. Everyone in Xeno-liaisons knew I was crap about taking notes. I didn't really *need* to. It was like—like all the files were stored in my brain and all I needed to do to find the information I needed was access them. Which meant that, try though I might to remember, I often forgot other people couldn't necessarily do that.

Marco chuckled. "And here I thought the rumors that Captain Chui has the most efficient crew in the universe were exaggerated."

"They are." Christa flashed a stiff smile. "Just not *that* exaggerated."

"Well, let's get down to business, shall we? Xandri, where would you like to begin?"

"Um..." I peered at the screen of his tablet, my eyes swimming at the sheer amount of file icons displayed. "I thought we should deal mostly with the leaders, and a bit with local customs. It's the World Council I need to convince, right? So we should start with them."

"That's forty-three people."

I swallowed. Sure, that wasn't nearly as many as I might have to deal with, say, among the Sanavila or the Kowari, but it was a damn sight more than I was used to dealing with. Particularly all at once.

"Oh," I said. "Oh dear."

"But there are hundreds of thousands of Psittacan tribes, right?" Marco pointed out. "Surely forty-three people shouldn't be so difficult."

"Three-hundred forty-eight thousand, nine-hundred and fifty-two tribes," Dawn said. "But Xandri only started with *us*."

I nodded.

"Hmm. Okay, well, maybe we can still make it work. How'd you do it in the first place?"

"Wouldn't someone from the AFC already know that?" Christa interrupted.

Unperturbed, Marco smiled. "Second-hand, sure. I'd like to hear it from Xandri herself, though. Perhaps that'll give me insight as to how to proceed, if I understand her process from the inside a little better."

"Best of luck," Christa muttered.

Flushing, I glared at the tabletop. "I just... study people. Figure out how they—interact, socially. I watched the Psittacans for three weeks before making first contact, and let me tell you, they didn't make it easy!"

"A fact in which we take great pride," Lightning admitted with a clack.

"Oh, hush, you overgrown smarty-parrot," I teased. I turned to Marco, finding it relatively easy to look him in the face. "Because they live in such thick jungles, Diver—he's like, our weird genius R&D guy, the one who explained the science stuff yesterday—Diver made these devices. Fliers with cameras attached, so we could get footage of them. Good thing we were streaming it all back to the *Carpathia*, too, because the Psittacans kept finding them and bringing them down. I do believe they made a contest of it." I directed a mock glare around the table.

"I won," Many Kills said.

Sunlight flicked her crest. "And you've spent the last four years bragging about it."

To my surprise, Christa laughed softly. "So that makes you pretty much directly responsible for driving Diver up a wall. Impressive."

"Don't encourage him!"

"Eventually though," I hurried on, lest another squawking squabble break out, "I figured out a few things. Crest down all the way means, basically, "I'm no threat" and with their tribe in particular, introductory interactions involve gifts. With the footage we had, we pieced together that if I brought them a gift every day

86

for five days, they'd agree to talk to me." And by that point we'd put enough of their language through advanced translation programs to have an idea what they'd mean. "So I uh...I tied lots of feathers in my hair so it would look like I had my 'crest' down and brought them gifts."

"And that worked?" Marco quirked a brow in incredulity.

"We're here, aren't we?" Dawn said. "Though it *was* hysterical. Like a half-plucked Macaw trying to court a mate."

"Yep. Pretty much the first thing Completes The Whole—their leader—told me was that it was a nice gesture, but I might as well not bother, because it did nothing to improve my looks."

"Ooo." Marco winced. "Little harsh, don't you think?"

"Sorry," Sunlight said, ruffling her feathers in a shrug. "You humans just look so...plucked."

"I only did it because we still weren't sure at the time how much non-verbal language was part of their communication. It's a *lot* of their communication, and we can't echo most of their body language, but theirs isn't hard to understand. But...the Anmerilli don't have that. They can control their tails!"

The last words came out practically as a wail. Hell, even the Sanavila had more apparent non-verbal language than the Anmerilli; the adults in particular had a tendency to flick their wings around, signifying things like dignity, annoyance, and pleasure. If I couldn't read the Anmerilli at all, how would I know when I made a misstep?

"Well, in that case," Marco said, "perhaps we should start with greetings."

"Greet...ings? Plural?"

"Forty-three. Each member nation of the World Council has its own rather particular way of greeting."

"Let me guess: If I get it wrong, I'm going to offend people. Horribly."

"Well, some of them will cut you some slack...Councilman Anashi Sendil is quite pleasant, for example...but uh, yeah, pretty much."

I groaned and slumped in my chair, dropping my forehead against the table. "Someone just kill me."

Of all the things I might've expected, Christa bursting out in giggles wasn't it. I lifted my head—rubbing my forehead, as it'd come down harder than I'd intended—and frowned at her. She quickly tried to school her expression into something more somber and dignified; I kept glaring at her until she cracked.

"Sorry!" she gasped. "It's just... for once, I'm *really* glad I don't have your job after all."

"Um, Christa? The entire Xeno-liaisons team will be involved. We *all* need to learn these."

Her face fell. "In that case, kill me too."

"Ah, now, don't be like that," Marco said. "You are two of the most talented first contact people in the universe. I know you can do this."

Despite myself, I brightened. The way Marco smiled at us when he spoke, so reassuring and confident, made a small bud of confidence open within me, too. Captain Chui thought I could do this. Marco Antilles, who had been working with the stubborn Anmerilli for six years, thought I could do it. *Maybe I* can *do it, then.* I looked at Christa, wondering if she found Marco's encouragement as infectious, but she was frowning.

Well, whatever. I didn't have time to deal with her being annoyed that someone was complimenting me. I had a *lot* of work to do.

"If my blood sugar gets any lower," Christa declared, "it's going to punch right through the *Carpathia's* hull."

I blinked and looked up from my holo-display. *Oh, wow. I guess a lot of time has passed.* The Psittacans had gotten bored and left some time ago—though that didn't always take much—and my stomach was back to growling. Even Marco looked worn around the edges.

"Sorry," I said, pressing a fingertip to the holo-display and spiraling it down and away. "I guess I got caught up..."

"We only have a couple weeks to sort this out," Marco said, "so it's understandable. But perhaps we should take a small break, hmm?"

"Yeah." I rose, which set off a cascade of protesting pins and needles in my left leg. Ow. "Sorry, Christa. Why don't you head off to the mess hall?"

"Why don't *you*?" she returned as she rose and scooped up her tablet. "Captain Chui told me to inform her if you wriggled out of eating too much."

"Of course she did."

"She's right, though," Marco said. "I've got a bit of the same problem, forgetting to eat while I'm working. Perhaps you two could show me to this mess hall?"

"Sure. Oh." I paused. "Mr. An—Marco, could you do me a favor? There's some files I want."

"The greetings, you mean?"

"Well, yes, but... do you have *other* people doing them? Not just the World Council members? I think—I think I might see a pattern of some kind, but I need to study it closer."

"Anything you need, Xandri. I'll see what we've got and get it sent to you as soon as possible."

I smiled. Marco grinned back at me, looking like he could barely resist the urge to ruffle my hair. *Well, he's probably old enough to be my big brother, at least.* It could be a bit hard to tell after a person hit thirty or so. But usually when people smiled at me like that, it got on my nerves. Maybe he was just one of those people, like Diver and Kiri, who I couldn't help but like.

All three of us headed out of Hydroponics together. As we stepped through the second door, I noticed a pair of figures leaning against the wall nearby. There was no mistaking the broad shoulders and great height of Anton Mulroney. Next to him stood a much smaller woman, a pale blonde it took me a long moment to recognize. Private Katya—was that her first name or last name?—the woman I'd pulled away from the creature on Stillness.

"There she is," Anton said, raising a hand and beckoning at me. "Told you she was in there."

"Yeah, yeah." Katya rolled her eyes. "Ms. Corelel, can we speak to you?"

"Only if you promise not to call me Ms. Corelel." I turned to Christa. "Could you show Marco to the mess? I have a feeling I'll be there before long."

Christa's smile seemed stiff again as she nodded. "Certainly. Right this way, Mr. Antilles."

"Marco, please," he said as he followed her down the hall.

I waited for them to hit the nearest grav-tube. Anton and Katya pushed off the wall and came to stand with me, both of them falling into parade rest—like they were on duty as soldiers. *Oh crap, I know I'm not gonna like this.* I'd rather be stuck between Christa and Marco right now, even with all the frowns Christa'd been giving me all morning.

"So um...you need something?"

"Just you," Anton said.

Katya at least had the grace to look apologetic. "Despite the AFC's report that there's been no sign of the LHFH, Captain Chui has some concerns. She's also concerned about what the or— Zechak might do if it seems like the Alliance will succeed. So she asked for some volunteers to work as your bodyguards."

"And you're here *now* because..."

"You gotta get used to us," Anton explained. "Captain wants you to have a bit of time to adjust to being followed around all the time."

*I will not scream, I won't, I won't, I am a grown woman, grown women do not break down into hysterical fits of screaming...*I should be grateful. I'd have some time to adjust to having Anton and Katya with me nearly every single waking moment for the next god only knew how many weeks. That was thoughtful of Captain Chui, really it was, but...*Nope, still want to scream.*

"There is just not a single thing about this mission that's going to be inside my comfort zone, is there?" I lamented.

"'Fraid not, kiddo," Anton said, patting my shoulder. "So, how about we head to the mess hall, do something about that lunch you missed—what's it, now, Kat?"

"Two hours ago."

"Right. Sound good?"

"Let me guess," I said, as we started down the hall together. "Captain Chui also ordered you to make sure I eat."

"She *did* qualify that as one of the tasks included under the heading of guarding your body," Katya confirmed. "She also said that if you had a problem with it, you should talk to her."

Like I'd want to make things worse on purpose. I sighed. At least I didn't mind Anton, and Katya seemed okay. But did I *really* need bodyguards? There was no law keeping us from having our own weapons on Cochinga, so I could shoot an assailant myself just fine. Probably better than most. On the other hand, the only hand-to-hand combat I knew was how to pull hair and bite real hard, so if someone came at me from behind or something...

"All right, all right, I'll deal. Uh, no offense," I said quickly. "I don't dislike either of you, I'm just under a lot of pressure, you know, and that whole autism thing kinda makes that worse and wow, now I'm babbling and it's really awkward, isn't it?"

"Oh, don't worry. Mulroney here is the king of awkward. You'll never have him beat."

"I am standing right here, woman," Anton protested.

"Thanks, Katya," I said, grinning. "That makes me feel a lot better, actually."

"And now I'm outnumbered. I didn't think this through well enough."

"You never think things through, Mulroney. That's why we stick you with a Gabe. You don't have to think about aiming."

I pursed my lips to quiet a giggle as Anton grumbled good-naturedly. *Don't tell them they make a cute couple, don't. It wouldn't be prudent.* Possibly funny, but not prudent. Well, I thought as I swung into the grav-tube behind Katya, it could've been much worse. I could've been stuck with humorless bodyguards. Something told me I was going to need a laugh or two before all this was over.

And not, you know, that hysterical actually-on-the-verge-of-a-nervous-breakdown kind of laughter.

Chapter Eleven

"...and this was only my second year! There I was, face to face with about a hundred angry Won Tak." Marco Antilles' voice filled the remarkably quiet mess hall as we entered it.

"A gofer versus the Won Tak?" a soldier at a table near him snorted.

"Hey now. Gofer was my first year. Second year I graduated to full-fledged paper pusher." Marco grinned, and a number of the crew laughed in approval.

Huh. He's making himself right at home.

"Well, what do you know?" Anton said. "An AFC agent without a stick up his ass."

"Hey, stranger things have happened," I said.

"Name one."

"The universe."

Anton chuckled and gave me a pat on the shoulder. Which I actually wouldn't have minded so much, if it weren't for the fact that he was a giant bear of a man who didn't seem to know his own strength. Rubbing my shoulder, I glanced around for a table that would be good. I could just stake a claim on it—maybe get one of my bodyguards to wait there for me—and then I wouldn't have to share. Hopefully.

"All I had with me was a tablet and a crew of six electricians who'd managed to never once catch a glimpse of a Won Tak while they were on planet maintaining the generators," Marco was saying.

Ick. The Won Tak were Alliance members, and high tier Alliance members at that, but that didn't necessarily stop them from being openly hostile. Some of them were considerably less friendly than others, and even though I knew some nice Won Tak, I'd never go wandering around their planet without a small army in tow. Being stuck there with just a handful of frightened electricians... yikes.

"Hey, Xan."

I paused, turned, still hearing Marco's story with the back part of my brain as my eyes scanned the crowd. Sitting alone at a table, two trays spread out across the top and a bag sprawled across the bench, was Diver. He waved, beckoning me over. I jerked a thumb over my shoulder at my hangers-on, but Diver just shrugged. *Okay then.* With Anton and Katya in tow, I wound my way over to the table.

The second tray turned out to be mine, as Diver pushed it in my direction as I sat down. I blinked in surprise, taking in my usual turkey sandwich with all the right toppings—lettuce, tomato, cheese, hold the mayo because *gross*—french fries, and a glass of water.

"How'd you know what I want?" I asked, amazed.

"Xandri, you eat the same thing every day."

"Not *every* day." Just almost every day.

"Well, we'll go grab something for ourselves," Katya said. "Diver, make sure she eats that."

I muttered under my breath as the two of them walked away. *I know they mean well, but I wish they wouldn't tease me so much.* Of course I was going to eat. The french fries smelled amazing—since potatoes were so easy to store and stayed so well, the chef made fries fresh every day. I picked one up, blew on it, and took a bite. Perfectly crispy outside, but soft on the inside. Just right.

"So," I said, waving my fry at Diver, "you're in on it too, huh?"

He gave me a genuinely blank look. "In on what?"

"So I finally realized," Marco's voice drifted into the silence between Diver and I, "that we were standing mere meters from a fully charged electrical station."

I cocked my head, studying Diver's face. Lying to me wasn't that hard to do. At least, not for someone I trusted. Diver could bluff with the best of them, though. I'd watched him a few times, playing poker with the rest of the crew, and none of them had yet caught on to the fact that he used a bunch of fake tells to lure them into overconfidence. If I ever needed to fall back on my gambling days for a mission, I knew who I'd be taking with me.

"So you're not in on this whole watching me like a hawk until I eat thing?"

"Not that I know of," Diver said. "Just thought I'd thank you for those scales that showed up at R&D this morning."

"Oh. But that was *my* way of thanking *you*. You saved my tail feathers yesterday."

"Well, they're tail feathers worth saving."

"Oh please." I let out a breath, blowing my bangs up away from my face. "My ass is so flat, Christopher Columbus would've mistaken it for an Ancient Earth map."

Diver propped his forehead against his palm, laughing. "Okay, but it's a *cute* Ancient Earth map."

I grabbed my sandwich and took a large bite, lest I say something I'd regret in return. I hadn't meant to say that aloud, couldn't believe I'd just blurted it out like that. At least no one else had heard. Everyone was glued to Marco's story, and Anton and Katya were only just finishing getting their lunch trays.

A roar of laughter rippled through the mess hall and for one panicked moment I thought maybe I'd been overheard after all. But no, everyone was still looking at Marco, who held his hands up as if to stop them.

"It really isn't funny," he said, though a slight smile tugged on the corners of his mouth. "For them or for me. Do you know what it's like filling out the paperwork for a hundred electrocuted Won Tak?"

Should I ask him if he meant that? I wondered, watching Diver from the corner of my eyes. I had cover to do it, while everyone was absorbed in Marco's story—though I didn't think electrocuted Won Tak were funny no matter how vicious they were being—so I had the opportunity to take the risk. *And if he was just joking, then what?* What did it even matter if he thought my butt was cute? I wasn't fifteen anymore, for crying out loud.

The slap of trays hitting the tabletop made me jump. I grabbed my sandwich and took another bite, gazing at Anton and Katya with what I hoped was wide-eyed innocence and not a bizarre mixture of dread and relief. *Oh god, it probably is a bizarre mixture of dread and relief.* If Anton's curious gaze was anything to go by.

"Looks like your friend there is getting on well," Katya said, jerking her head in Marco's direction. "He seems to actually *like* us."

"Because we're so damn likeable," Diver said, only half-serious. He glanced between Katya and Anton. "The captain's got you tormenting poor Xandri, hasn't she?"

"Guarding," Katya corrected, as she passed a nutrient-bar my way. "We're her bodyguards for the Cochinga mission. Just in case."

"Guarding my body," I muttered, "and yet you keep handing me these nasty fucking things."

"Sweet little voice," Anton remarked, "then she opens up and lets fly like a spacer."

"I *am* a spacer."

I started unwrapping my nutrient-bar, so I wouldn't say anything more. *He's only teasing. There's no need to be petulant.* But I was supposed to be a grown woman, not a little girl with a 'sweet little voice.' And then because my mood wasn't deteriorating fast enough, Mother's voice spoke at the back of my mind: *You'll never be an adult, Alexandria. People... like you aren't* capable *of being grown up.* Which I guess *would* explain why I was so concerned with whether or not Diver thought my butt was cute.

"Frankly, I prefer women with dirty mouths," Diver said. He rose with that slow, boneless grace usually reserved for cats, stretching, his T-shirt riding up enough to show a hint of copper-toned skin and hard abs. "Thanks again for the scales, fireball."

As Diver left the mess hall, Katya raised her eyebrows at me and repeated, "Fireball?"

Unreasonably, I found myself turning red. I focused on my nutrient-bar, taking a large, unpleasant bite.

Happily for me, Marco Antilles showed up at our table before Katya could get it into her head to tease me too. He slid onto the bench next to me, his dark eyes bright with good humor. Such a relief to know I would be working with someone good-natured. I'd been concerned I'd be stuck with one of the AFC's stuffiest agents, the ones who hated us the most and wouldn't understand *me* one bit.

"I figured I'd get down to sorting out those files you wanted," he told me. "You can look them over, and we can reconvene tomorrow."

"Sounds good," I agreed. I paused a moment, then added, "Did you really electrocute a hundred Won Tak?"

Marco rubbed the back of his neck, looking sheepish. "Not fatally. Just enough to knock them out, keep them from tearing us to pieces."

95

"Probably hard to fatally electrocute one of those fuckers," Anton said. "Skin like an Ancient Earth elephant, they got."

"Yeah, well, it's still not my preferred solution to that kind of problem. I'd rather not solve things with violence if I can avoid it. Sadly, the Won Tak were not of the same opinion that day."

"Probably because it was a Tuesday," Katya said with a snort.

"Ah, most of them really aren't that bad. Right, Xandri?"

Marco smiled at me, and I smiled in return. Finally, someone who was fully on my side. A part of me couldn't help wondering if I should tell him about Admiral losTavina's plans. *But no, that has to stay quiet. We all swore to the captain that we wouldn't speak of it.* And so I wouldn't, but at least the option was there if the situation became desperate. Marco wouldn't want our negotiations to come down to threats, after all.

I spent much of my afternoon and into my evening studying the footage Marco sent me, though I took a break to spend time with Marbles and Cake, and to let Katya and Anton drag me off to dinner. I also spent a little time reading, my feet propped up on the wall next to my bed. Fascinated by my upside down state, Marbles and Cake took up their own upside down positions on their play tree. At least that meant they weren't close by, trying to nibble on my book.

After putting my birds to bed, I went back to studying the files, watching all the greetings I could. Most of them were some variation of bow, some involving the arms, some not, some requiring specific placement of the feet, some not bothering with the feet at all. In some cases I observed a great deal of variation in how each person from a World Councilor's nation performed the bow, and in others they seemed almost carbon copies of each other.

"Xandri." *Carpathia's* voice came through my wristlet, gentle and soft. "It's almost oh-one-hundred hours."

"Whoa. Really?" I reduced the holo-display on my wristlet and glanced at the time. "So it is. No wonder my head hurts."

"Perhaps it's time to get some sleep."

Maybe, but my head buzzed like a hive full of bees, which I knew from experience didn't make for good sleep. I shut down the holo-display and rolled out of bed.

"I'm going for a walk," I told *Carpathia*. "I need to clear my head before I can sleep."

"Very well. Try not to be awake all night."

I pulled on my boots—starship floors weren't exactly *warm*—drew up my hood, and stuffed my hands, already covered by my long sleeves, in the kangaroo pocket of my tunic-hoodie. *Carpathia* opened the door for me, and I stepped out into the hall. Dimmers were lit all up and down the corridor. People would be awake, of course; even starships had graveyard shifts. For the moment though, I was surrounded by blessed quiet.

I took the long route, ambling through the *Carpathia's* passages, making my way towards the observation deck without really thinking about it. My mind kept flashing images of what I'd been studying, moving them around like magnets on a board to fit them into some kind of pattern. *It's just like solving a logic problem,* I told myself. *Move the pieces around until they're in the right places and then I'll have the answer.* Maybe.

I drew a hand from my pocket, letting the sleeve fall back and pressing my palm to the door release. At this hour I wasn't expecting to find anyone on the observation deck, so I came to a startled halt when I saw Marco Antilles there.

He sat on one of the benches by one of the windows, his gaze shifting from a large pad of paper on his lap to the space station outside, and back again. A tin full of colored pastel chalks sat on the bench next to him, and his fingers were stained with a rainbow of hues. As the door let out its usual hydraulic hiss, he turned to look at me in surprise. *Oh. Oops.* Something hung in the air, something quiet and intimate, and I couldn't help the feeling I'd interrupted something.

"Sorry," I said, backing towards the door. "I didn't know anyone was in here..."

Marco waved a chalk-covered hand. "It's fine. This room is for everyone, right? I'm just here because—well, I figured at this hour, it was a good place to stay out of the way."

I nodded.

"What are you doing up so late, anyway?" he asked, his eyes sweeping the paper in front of him. Then he glanced at me again and grinned. "You can come closer, you know. I don't bite."

Arms wrapped across my body, hands hidden in my sleeves, I crossed the room to where he sat. Before I could stop myself, I had glanced at the paper and let out a soft gasp.

It was Mergassë, sketched out in bold strokes of charcoal and chalk, the image carrying a blurred, dreamy quality, like the view of the world from between your eyelashes as you're first waking up. For all its impressionistic qualities, I could tell each detail apart, see each burning yellow light like tiny suns, each snaking, twisting corridor, each ship at port.

"You like it?"

"It's wondrous!" I breathed.

I stared in rapt fascination at the drawing, and it took me a long moment to realize Marco was staring at me.

"What?"

"Nothing," he said with a shake of his head. "You never answered my question. After the day you've had, I'd think you'd be out cold."

Actually, compared to yesterday, today had been a picnic. "I was studying."

He continued to gaze at me expectantly.

"Oh, um. Well, there's a lot to take in, and I guess I wanted to try to clear my head before going to sleep." I took up a seat on the opposite end of the bench. "What about you? I—no offense meant, but I'd have thought you would go back to the *Resplendence*."

"I talked it over with your captain. Since there's so much for you and your team to learn, I'll be traveling aboard the *Carpathia* instead, to help you out as much as I can. Did you make anything of the extra footage I sent you?"

Oh, thank you, Mother Universe! Having someone around, someone who knew the Anmerilli, to help us through this would be a huge boon to Xeno-liaisons. With a bit of hope growing inside me, I activated the holo-display on my wristlet. Marco set paper and chalks aside, wiping his hands thoughtlessly on his thighs. He leaned in as I divided out several screens, choosing the files that most amply demonstrated the kinds of patterns I'd been seeing.

"Councilor Sendil," Marco remarked, looking at one of the screens. His gaze shifted to the one above. "And that's Councilor Kalemi Ashil." Then to the screen above that. "But I don't know this fellow. He's not on the council."

98

"No, he's one of several people from their respective regions that I've been studying," I explained. "Both Councilor Sendil and Councilor Ashil are from coastal regions, and I noticed...a certain fluidity and relaxation to their bows. This seems to be pretty well reflected in their people, as well. So it *could* mean they'll be more open and receptive, or it could be a cultural trait, but...I don't think it's *just* a cultural trait.

"See here." I pointed to another screen. "Councilor Nish mar'-Odrea. His bows are all sharp and stern, starched perfection. Looking at the people of his region—there is *some* cultural tendency towards sharper lines in their bows, but many of them are not nearly as...as stiff. Which makes me think perhaps Councilor mar'Odrea will be a much harder man to sway. But I could be wrong; I won't know for absolute certainty without meeting him," I added quickly.

"No...no, you're quite right," Marco murmured. "Sendil and Ashil are both more receptive to the Alliance, and always have been. Mar'Odrea opposes it strongly. His people do tend towards a certain sternness, but he far more so. And they look up to him, respect his opinions. Swaying him will be...difficult." He glanced at me. "That's quite a talent you have."

"It's not a *talent*, really. More like a survival mechanism."

Well, damn. I hadn't meant to say that out loud. I turned my head, gazing out on Mergassë, hoping Marco wouldn't pry. People knew I was autistic, and what little they knew about autism sometimes led to invasive questions. They couldn't fathom how I could do the job I did, which was supposed to be beyond my abilities. And I had no desire to explain to *anyone* why I'd had to make it one of my abilities.

Marco said nothing for a few long, long moments. Then he reached out. I turned my head sharply, tensing for anything—but all he did was touch one of the holo-displays, drawing it closer to him.

"Have you worked this sort of thing out about any of the other council members?" he asked.

Relieved, I nodded. "I have some hypotheses on a few of them, anyway."

"Well, why don't we check your work, then? See if you're really on the right track?"

99

That was it. No prying, no questioning, just business. Even though it was late, even though I needed some sleep, I nodded. Some things were more important than me getting a bit of shuteye.

Chapter Twelve

Another day and we were ready to ship out. The *Resplendence* had a new, fresh crew, its hold was stocked with all manner of supplies, and we'd gotten the *Carpathia* resupplied too.

Travel would be slower than usual. The Nebularia-class ships weren't built for fast travel, and at their size they had limits. We would sling out ahead, then come out of slingspace to wait for them, and to give both our pilot and theirs a bit of recovery time. Then we would repeat the process until we reached Cochinga. On her own, *Carpathia* could make the trip in less than a week, but with the *Resplendence* it would take closer to two.

Not that I minded the extra time. Half my days were spent learning greetings, the other half spent studying the members of the World Council and going over my findings with Marco. Not to mention that I had to adjust to being followed around by Anton and Katya, who half-carried me to most of my meals. I stole what breaks I could, spending time with my birds, with the Psittacans, having lunch with Diver and listening to him talk R&D business, ninety percent of which I couldn't understand.

For me, the hardest part was the bows. What I'd learned growing up was that autism tended to come with a heaping side dish of gross and fine motor issues, and that particular bit of "wisdom" I'd found to be completely true. I was a grown woman who couldn't properly tie a knot, and I was sixteen before I could catch a ball with my hands rather than my face. Some of the bows were simple enough, but the more complicated ones gave me fits, especially once I had to speed them up to their proper pace.

"Whoa!" Marco caught me around the waist, hauling me upright before I wound up in an intimate embrace with the floor. "Easy there. Just keep taking it slow for now."

"Sorry," I muttered, tucking a loose strand of hair behind my ear.

"No need to apologize. You're new to this."

"Sorry."

Marco frowned. *Whoops. The Sorry Cycle begins.* I bit my lip against the urge to let out another apology, since that tended to annoy people.

Speaking of annoyed, Christa stood on the other side of the room, shooting glares over her shoulder at me. She'd grasped the bows quickly, and was working to instruct the rest of the team. Though Kirrick Chanda, third in our hierarchy, was taking a break, sitting on a chair and studying notes on the Anmerilli. We all took breaks to study; there wasn't enough time to be too focused on one thing. *There's barely enough time for anything.*

"Wait a minute." Kirrick's voice rose in irritation. "Is this correct? They think eating meat is barbaric, but they hunt *for sport?*"

I froze. I didn't mind eating meat so much—especially since most of it was vat-grown these days—but hunting for sport...I shivered. I *hated* killing; I didn't even like killing spiders and they gave me the absolute creeps. To Kirrick, who was both vegetarian and pacifist, it had to be doubly confusing. (Though admittedly I'd seen him be decidedly *un*passive when animal abuse was involved.)

"Yeah," Marco said. "Cochinga was always a place of rather large macrofauna. Much of it has been killed off in traditional hunts, but there are those kept and bred, so the traditions live on."

They breed animals specifically *to hunt them for sport, but they think eating meat is barbaric?* Well, they didn't just *look* human: They had human levels of cognitive dissonance, too. I glanced at Kirrick, wondering if this was going to be a problem. Kirrick was an open book even to me; the distress on his face was so clear, one could spot it from a kilometer away. Stellar. I was going to have to *talk* to him. Which would only make me feel like an asshole, because I *agreed* with him, but we couldn't let the Anmerilli see our disgust.

"Why don't we focus on what we're doing here and now?" Christa suggested. "Not *all* of us have bodyguards to protect us if we screw this up."

"Not *all* of us are Head of Xeno-liaisons, either," I retorted.

Which was not nearly as tactful and gracious as I'd hoped to be next time Christa threw a snarky comment in my direction. Stress really fucked my filter six ways to Sunday.

Christa whipped around. Suddenly I found myself starkly aware of how tiny the room was—Xeno-liaisons didn't have a ton of space, not needing labs or anything—and how everyone in it was looking at us. *Déjà vu*. Captain Chui had told me I needed to be in control of these situations, no matter what. And I would have to be able to stand up for myself against the Anmerilli, too. No time like the present.

"Look, Christa, I'm sorry," I said, the words coming out in a rush. "I don't mean to snap, but this is all very stressful and overwhelming, okay? We need to work together to get through this and—and you making comments like that doesn't help." While she stared at me in surprise, I blustered on, "And whether you like it or not, *I* am the one leading this mission."

"This isn't just about *you*."

"No, it's not. It's about the entire universe. Which is why right now, this is on *me*. You—all of you—need to keep to the background and support me, but not draw too much attention to yourselves. That way if something goes wrong, I can take the fall and the rest of you might still have a chance to clean up the mess."

"That's a pretty good strategy," Marco said. "I can't promise it will work, but it's good to have a backup plan."

Christa glared at him. *Damnit, I need to get this under control.* I twitched my thumb, pinging Christa's personal comm channel. She flashed me an annoyed look—no mistaking the way her eyebrows slanted down—and opened her private channel.

"*You have such a martyr complex,*" she sub-vocalized at me.

"*I already said this isn't about me. Christa, I don't want anyone—us or them—to get blown to smithereens. We have to make this work.*"

She sighed. "*I know. I know that, and it's stressing me out. This isn't our job.*"

"*You're telling me. But it's the one we have to do. You can hate me all you want to when this is over, but right now, I really need your skills to keep me organized.*"

"*True. You can't organize your way out of a wet paper bag.*" Which might have been offensive if it weren't the unvarnished truth. Out loud, Christa said, "Might I suggest we all take a break, grab something to eat? I figure I'll talk to Protocol, see if they can give us a hand; they're good at having to learn this sort of stuff at top speed."

I couldn't help brightening a little. "That's a really great idea, actually."

"And I could *definitely* use a break," put in Marla Thomas, our youngest—in terms of years, not time—member. "These damn bows. I think I'm going to have a crick in my *pelvis*. Didn't even know that was possible."

"Look on the bright side," I said. "At least *you* don't have bruises."

"Hey, internal bruises are a thing."

"Good point."

Marla grinned. Rubbing her hip with one hand, she made a beeline for the door. I watched them all go, talking amongst themselves, and a slight pang cut through me. *Don't.* They didn't mean to be hurtful, walking off without asking me to join. I knew that. I'd kept myself apart from them for so long, afraid to get too close; now they just assumed I preferred it that way. I had no right to be stung.

"Hey."

Ever a jumpy creature, I started at the sound of Marco's voice, suddenly so close by.

"How about we go get some lunch ourselves?" he suggested, giving me a nudge towards the door.

"Okay." It would give me my daily opportunity to see Diver, after all. I slapped my palm against the door release and glanced at Marco. "As long as you don't mind putting up with my handlers."

Said handlers waited outside in the corridor. Anton grinned and waved when he caught sight of me. I'd begun to reach this odd place where, even though his "Aww, you're like a cute quirky weirdo little sister" act got on my nerves, I'd miss it if he stopped. Humans, cognitive dissonance, etc. etc. Katya held up a nutrient-bar package and waggled it at me teasingly. At least I was down to two a day now.

"Don't worry, Xandri," Marco said. "I'm a diplomat, remember? If there's one thing I know how to deal with, it's handlers."

"Great. Make her stop giving me those horrible things."

"Not a chance. I'd like to live my life unstabbed, thanks."

"I'll give you one thing, AFC," Katya said with a toss of her head. "You ain't space-fried."

104

"Well, what about this one?"

I glanced up from my holo-display, which was spread out into a grid of thumbnails, each one showing still extant macrofauna of Cochinga. A part of my wall was slid back, revealing a screen, where *Carpathia* displayed the latest modification to my usual outfits; we were trying to put together some things that would be acceptable *and* comfortable. Of course I'd have to wear my uniform at least some of the time, but not all of it.

"I...maybe?" I sighed and pressed my finger to one of the thumbnails, drawing it out, then gave it a flick to expand it. "You know I'm no good at this."

"Especially when you're not paying attention," *Carpathia* remarked.

With a sigh, I retracted my holo-display and shut it down. *It's gotten late again.* I sat up, wincing as a throb began between my temples.

"I'm sorry, *Carpathia.* There's so much to learn and so little time to learn it in. I just want to be prepared."

"I know. And how you present yourself is just as important."

"But I'm only good as designing *comfortable* clothes." I tried to keep the whine out of my voice. "I wouldn't recognize fashionable if I tripped over it." Actually, I wouldn't care, which was different, but close enough.

"Then perhaps you should talk to someone who would," *Carpathia* said. "I confess, *fashion* is not generally built into the specs of a warship's AI. But according to my sensors, Ms. Ayabara is awake and on the bridge."

"Um...and?"

In the ensuing silence, I marveled at *Carpathia's* ability to *sound* like she was raising her eyebrows at me, when neither she nor eyebrow raising made so much as a peep. *I guess Kiri is one of the most fashionable among us.* My cheeks warmed a little at the prospect of talking to her. Particularly talking to her about clothes. *How should I even approach that? Hi, I'm completely inept at dressing myself and could really use your help?* Oh god, no. She'd have a field day with that.

"Xandri."

"All right, all right. I'll go. Aren't you supposed to be telling me I should get some sleep?"

"Would it make a difference?"

"Probably not," I admitted, as I rose from the bed and retrieved my boots.

The quiet walk to the bridge helped ease the throb behind my eyes. I tried not think about everything I still had to learn, and how slowly I was coming along at all those greetings, or how I liked the Anmerilli less and less the more I read about what they'd done to the fauna of their planet. My job was to be the one who didn't judge, who wrapped her mind around the angles another person saw the world from and understood. *I don't have to agree. Just understand.* Hard, but not impossible.

I shook my head, trying to whip the thoughts away, and pressed my palm to the door release onto the bridge. Ah, blessed quiet. Aside from the faint sounds of electronics, the bridge was almost empty of sound. Aki was piloting and Aleevian sat next to her, reading from a tablet as he waited for the next time to give her a stim. One of Lieutenant Zubairi's assistants manned navigation for the moment, and there were two from Signals, including Kiri.

On my toes, I approached Kiri's console. Figures flicked across the screen at an alarming rate; despite how absorbed she seemed in her work, she glanced over and smiled at my approach.

"How do you do that?" I asked, keeping my voice low. Even in my boots, most people were hard-pressed to hear me move. I'd learned young that moving silently was wise, safe.

"Much though I'd like to appear mysterious and all knowing," Kiri said, tossing her hair over her shoulder and setting her silvery beads to chiming, "*Carpathia* warned me you were coming. She said something about wardrobe issues?"

"Uh, yeah." Kiri gestured to the empty station next to her and I took a seat. "My own clothes are a bit...slouchy. You know me. Not a fashionable bone in my body."

She turned to study me for a long moment. "I'm not convinced that's true. But considering how much work you've got on your plate, I can see how you might not have the wherewithal to figure it out right now." Her gaze drifted back to her screen. "I'll take a look at it tomorrow, when I'm off-duty."

"Thanks."

The soft tap of her fingertips on the keyboard filled the space between us. Perhaps I should've left, but I found myself watching her slender fingers in fascination. They moved with such swiftness and surety, and her eyes never once left the screen. Though I didn't quite understand what she was doing, I could tell, somehow, that she was doing it well. As if her level of skill just made all that nonsensical data make enough sense that I could see her success.

"When I was very young, I wanted to be a fashion designer," Kiri said, her eyes still glued to the screen.

"Wha—oh. Sorry, I didn't mean to...to bother you."

"You're not. I could use a little company, actually. Things are... well, I could just use some company."

"I'm not sure I make good company," I said, "but I can try. Um, so...why didn't you become a fashion designer, then? I mean, you could probably make an Ongkoarrat look good in a tutu."

Kiri chuckled. "Coming from anyone else, I'd think that was an exaggeration." She hit a button on her keyboard and the activity on her screen stopped. "Truth to tell, I still want to design someday. But...I found something else along the way.

"Back in grade school, there were these boys who teased me. They couldn't stand that I was better at "boy's things" than they were."

I blinked. "I thought that kind of attitude doesn't fly on Amora."

"It doesn't, but there are always outliers. And these boys were from the boonies, where you tend to find such outliers. I could've stopped it—there's a true zero tolerance policy for bullying in Amoran schools—but I was a kid. I thought I could handle them myself. Hell, it seemed like I could."

"But?"

"But things escalated. Our class started learning how to operate computers—not that most of us didn't know quite a lot from at home already—and these boys, they were taking time out of class to learn hacking. I wasn't interested originally, you know. But they took it as a chance to taunt me, to say I couldn't do it anyway because girls aren't good at things like that."

"And then you punched them, right?"

"No." Kiri grinned at me. "I kinda wanted to, but instead I went over there, barged right in, sat down at their computer, and solved the problem they were trying to sort out. It was simple, really. There was something about it...something that intrigued me. But the fact that I just sat down and did it, when all three of them were struggling to figure it out, it pissed them off.

"They found me after school. Came up on me, surprised me...
threw me in a closet and locked me in. Hey... don't look like that."
Kiri reached out and touched my cheek, grinning as I turned pink.
"I got out, didn't I? They thought they'd get away with it because I'd
never told on them before, but this time I reported *everything*. Not
that it would've mattered. The school cameras caught them at it,
and they got expelled. Ended up in disciplinary school.

"And me... I kept thinking back to that one little bit of hacking
I'd done. I couldn't get it out of my head. I started looking it up,
teaching myself how to do it, and soon I discovered that there was
no kind of door in the universe that could keep me in or out, not if I
really wanted to go through it." She shrugged and smiled. "Fashion
design is subjective, but a good hacker can always get a job."

Maybe I was imagining it, but something in her smile seemed
a little forced. She hadn't actually mentioned how long she'd been
in that closet, but... *Being able to open doors became really important to
her.* I could understand that. Oh yeah, I could understand that all
too well.

"I'm sorry," I said.

"For what?"

"It just... seems like a personal story. Painful. I didn't mean to
dredge that up."

"Eh, it happened years ago now," she said. "Here I am, one of
the top hackers in the universe, doing a job I love, and they're still
back on Amora with little chance of seeing much more than their
own backyards."

I looked at her, caught in one of those moments where it was
harder to look away from someone's eyes than to look at them. Kiri's
brown eyes had a slight golden tinge to them, like tiger's eye, and
her lashes were so thick and dark that she'd never need mascara.
Again, perhaps I was merely projecting my own feelings, but she
seemed sad. Taking a shot in the dark, I said, "But it still hurts
sometimes."

"But it still hurts sometimes," Kiri agreed quietly.

Yes! I got it right! A slight smile began to tug on my mouth and
I quickly tried to stifle it. Kiri caught sight of it and smiled herself,
so I figured it must be okay. Sometimes I smiled at the very *wrong*
moments.

A hydraulic hiss behind me caused me to jump. Kiri reached out and put a hand on my arm briefly, her touch gentling my fear. I turned in time to see Chikara come through the door, and worried for a moment that she'd get the wrong idea. But apparently she was in no mood to get *any* idea, as she didn't even glance in Kiri's direction. *What? What's going on?* I looked at Kiri, who turned back to her computer with a sigh.

Aw, crap. Things are going rough, aren't they? Was that why Kiri had told me that story? She needed someone to talk to? Did that mean I should ask what was up with her and Chikara? *Fuck, fuck, fuck, why do I have to be so unskilled at this part of things?* Asking about her relationship when she hadn't volunteered anything seemed like prying, but what if she wanted someone to pry? On the other hand, maybe she wanted to be left alone.

She sighed again and I blurted out, "So, has Diver figured out how you got those files to me yet?"

Kiri's expression changed from dejection to wickedness in an instant. "Nope. You wanna know?"

I nodded.

"You have to swear you won't tell him."

"Are you kidding? Do you have any idea the mileage I could get just out of him knowing I know? Give it three weeks and I'll have my own personal robot."

Oh shit. Did that actually come out sounding like a joke? It must've, because Kiri started to laugh. She beckoned me closer. As I leaned in, I caught the scent of something fruity on her skin and hoped I wouldn't start turning red again. For someone who was supposed to lack non-verbal communication, my blood vessels sure loved to tattle on me a *lot*.

Kiri touched my arm and a faint tingle of sparks jumped across my skin. It took me a second to realize it wasn't simply from her touch, but something active beneath her skin. As I stared in surprise, the sensation crept down my arm again, raising the small hairs all along my forelimb. Energy transfer. And if she could transfer energy like that, she could transfer information too.

"Damn." I returned her wicked grin. "That is one fine piece of chroming."

Chapter Thirteen

When I first joined the crew of the *Carpathia*, every approach to a new planet had been exciting. The thrill of that initial approach wore off after a while, once I'd realized that it was always roughly the same: the sensation of approaching a marble from the depths of space. The only real difference was whether the marble would be bluish, greenish, whitish, reddish, yellowish, or brownish.

But then we were aligning with Cochinga's orbit and it started getting more exciting. Cochinga resembled Ancient Earth quite a bit, being deeply sapphire blue in an ever-shifting lattice of white cloud. And happily it had a twenty-seven hour day, which wouldn't be too big a shift from the standard twenty-six that all space-faring ships and space stations were set to.

"Xandri, it's time to go," *Carpathia* told me, on the day we were set to land on Cochinga. "You'll be late."

"I know, I know," I replied, as I struggled to get the slippery strands of my hair into a braid. "But I can't look like a slob. I'm representing the *entire* Alliance." Because I needed to be reminded of *that* again.

Braid finished, I swung reluctantly to face the mirror. God, I hated looking in the mirror. *Hated* it. It might be necessary, but every time I saw my hair and eyes and skin, my oval face, narrow torso and too wide hips was a reminder. A reminder that I looked nothing like my mother, like my father, like any of my family. A reminder of all the ways my unusual circumstances of birth—the effect on my genes from not being carefully manipulated in a Petri dish—made me an outsider.

"Xandri," *Carpathia's* voice came out gentler this time, like she knew.

"Yep. On it."

Since we were allowed—hell, expected, even—to wear weapons, I grabbed my gun belt from the bed and swung it around my hips. The weight of my pistols settling on my thighs took my mind off my usual mirror-based pity party. People saw me with a pair of pistols like this and wondered if I could handle both at once. I could if need be, despite their size, but usually I told people I kept two because it was useful to have a backup. That made sense to people, which meant I never had to explain that I couldn't bear the asymmetrical weight of carrying only one. That they tended to understand less.

"All right," I said, snatching my bag off my bed and slinging it over my shoulder. "Ready."

I palmed the door open and to my surprise and delight, found Aki waiting for me out in the hallway. I'd expected to start my day off with Anton and Katya, but they were nowhere in sight.

"Thought I'd come see you off," Aki said gruffly, as I fell into step beside her. "Who knows how long it'll be before we see each other again?"

Don't judge, don't judge, don't judge... Ugh, damned Anmerilli. I kept trying to give them the benefit of the doubt, but they'd been adamant that none of our non-human members would be allowed on Cochinga. That meant no burying my fingers in Aki's fur whenever I got too overwhelmed, none of my chats with the Psittacans, and some of our best members would be stuck aboard ship. It was lose-lose for everyone.

"You're worrying."

"I'm always worrying," I said. "It's what I do."

Aki chuffed. "True enough. But I wish you'd stop. You can do this, Xandri-pup. Just... don't try to smile, yeah? Best you don't start a war."

"Oh, you're hilarious," I said dryly.

She bumped against my hip with another chuff. I reached down and wound my fingers through her fur, savoring the silky texture on our walk down to the docking bay.

The Psittacans had turned up to see us off, along with Alee-vian and a number of other non-humans who wouldn't be able to come with us. Magellan looked about as pleased as if he'd gotten his tail caught in a working vent. With Aki's help, I eased through the crowd—stopping long enough to say farewell to Many and the gang—and made my way towards the shuttles. With a last good-bye to Aki, I took my place on the *Fate Unknown*, forever cursing the macabre senses of humor of our baffy small craft spacers.

Synesthetically, Cochinga was round, rolling and springy. The reality of the planet was far more spiky than the taste and texture of the name led me to believe.

I noticed it as the shuttle descended and I saw more and more of the planet. Something about its plate tectonics had left each continent with oddly spiky bits and ends, so that each looked more like a malformed sea urchin than a land mass. This caused the oceans to have much the same appearance, especially from a distance.

Closer and closer. I pressed against the window, watching deserts and forests and mountain ranges—yes, spikier than usual—form. The shuttle brought us to Adoyina, a small coastal city that belonged to no one nation, but was rather set aside for the doings of the World Council. It sprawled along the water's edge, stretching out several pointed arms like half a starfish.

Soon we were close enough to make out flora. The trees that dotted the landscape, especially along the beach, resembled the terrifying love-children of a palm tree and a hedgehog. As we set down, I pressed my nose to the glass and squinted at the ground below, which appeared to be veritably carpeted in small greenish-blue hedgehogs. *Nope. I think that's supposed to be grass.* Not the weirdest planet I'd ever visited, but I could've done without the sensation that the entire landscape was out to impale me.

"Is it just me," Katya said from the seat behind me, "or does this place give off an impression of hostility?"

"It's not so bad once you get used to it," Marco Antilles told her. "It's just *different.*"

"Different." Anton snorted. "We've been on uninhabitable desert planets that didn't look this...different."

"Hey, look at it this way," I said as I unbuckled my straps. "If even half this place is as sharp and pointy as it looks, you'll have something to protect me from other than the food."

"Sweetie, I don't think we're going to have to protect you from the food."

I twisted around to look at Katya. "These people subsist on a diet of high protein and high fat beans, legumes, and squashes, alongside loads of leafy greens. My tongue is practically in the fetal position just thinking about those textures."

Fortunately, no one had time to ask me about the particulars of how one's tongue got into the fetal position. Captain Chui was calling for us to disembark and the shuffling of that many bodies in the small space of the shuttle left little room for conversation.

Or, you know, breathing.

Grateful to *Carpathia* for putting some satin lining inside my sleeves, I rubbed my thumb over the smooth texture again and again until we were finally making our way out of the shuttle door and down onto the landing pad. A metallic tang filled my mouth as my filter-implant adjusted to my first few breaths of Cochingan air, but I wasn't complaining; at least I could breathe again.

"Line up!" Captain Chui shouted.

Even those of us who weren't well-trained soldiers fell into line at the sound of her voice. I ended up sandwiched between Katya and Anton—probably not a bad thing, as that meant they'd be there to catch me when I fell. Since I was pretty sure my legs were going to give out.

Spread out around the landing pad were some several hundred people, only a fraction of them ours. Along one side stood our own, about a hundred men and women from both the army and the navy, dressed in variants of blue. Most of the others were, as far as I could tell, members of Cochinga's own military, with a few diplomats amongst the bunch. Probably none of the World Council members, but even so, I broke out in a cold sweat at the sight of all those people staring at us.

Two members of the crowd broke off and approached us: one a tall human man, in the blues of the army, the bars on his collar marking him as a major; the other an Anmerilli, with a slightly grayish skin tone and dark hair that swept back from a point far forward on his forehead. The former I didn't know, but the latter I recognized as Altli Shinda, Secretary of the World Council. He swept us the general bow, one arm across the front of his body, the other sweeping out behind, and we echoed it.

"Secretary Shinda," Captain Chui greeted as she straightened. "It is an honor to meet you. And Major Douglas. It is a pleasure to see you as well, sir."

"Secretary," Major Douglas said, "I'd like you to meet Captain Chui Shan Fung, formerly of the Alliance army. One of the finest

113

gunnery sergeants in history."

"A pleasure, madam," Secretary Shinda said. His voice had a quality that was—oily. Not in that slick, snake oil salesman interpretation of the word so many humans had, but in a thick but smooth kind of way. "We have heard much about you and your team."

Captain Chui tipped her head in gracious acknowledgement. Shinda's gaze shifted from her, over to where my Xeno-liaisons team had spread out next to me. His eyes—very similar to human eyes, though in a shade of yellow one didn't see in humans without genetic manipulation—passed right over me and landed on Christa. His lips pulled back in a smile almost as awkward as my own. *Hey, maybe I'll fit in here after all.*

"So, is this the young Ms. Corelel I've been told about?"

Oh Christ.

"That would be me," I said quietly, though it took all my will to get the words out. I held my ground as best I could as his gaze rested on me. "This is my assistant, Christa Baranka, and the rest of my team: Kirrick Chanda, Marla Thomas, Sho Merin and Kimi Drin."

For the first time I was glad my entire team was human—though I'd been pushing for non-human members for a while—because it meant I had all of them at my back now. Secretary Shinda swept us another bow, forcing us to do the same. As I straightened, Marco Antilles joined us, bowing to the Secretary.

"Ah, Mr. Antilles. Good to have you back with us."

"Good to be back, Secretary."

"Spoken like a true diplomat."

Marco smiled. "Not at all. Cochinga has become like a second home to me." He rested a hand on my shoulder. "And I'm certain all of you will come to feel the same. This time, I think, we will all finally come to an agreement."

"I hope you're right," Secretary Shinda said. "Captain...Chui, was it? The Council has sent me to welcome you, and to give you a tour of the Council building. Major Douglas is here to see that your troops are comfortably settled into their accommodations. Does that suit you?"

"Not to worry, Captain," Major Douglas added with that sort of superior smile I sometimes saw on the faces of officers who ranked so high. "I'll take good care of them."

"I'm sure you will, Major," Captain Chui said. "Secretary Shinda, it would be an honor. If you'll just allow me a moment to instruct my troops, we can be on our way."

"Of course."

Captain Chui turned. Our small line of troops—two of our four platoons—snapped to attention and saluted. They held their stiff, alert positions as she instructed them to follow Major Douglas and the Alliance forces. I watched her face, noticed her eyes flick briefly to Anton and Katya. Whatever exchange passed between them was far too subtle for me to pick up, but they too went with the rest of the soldiers. *Well, if Captain Chui can't protect me, no one could.*

Not that I thought there'd be any attempts as of yet. People were usually too alert during such an arrival for an assassin to find a useful opening.

"My pilots will be a while settling in the shuttles," Captain Chui said, turning back to Secretary Shinda. "And if you don't mind— this is Diver," she gestured to where Diver and Kiri stood, left behind as the soldiers cleared out, "and Kiriit Ayabara, members of my Signals department. They'll be assisting me on Cochinga."

"You are a well prepared woman, Captain Chui," Shinda said, with a bow to Kiri and Diver.

"I try. Shall we be on our way?"

"Yes, yes, of course. Mr. Antilles, with your assistance."

"This way," Marco said, gesturing in the same direction the soldiers were heading. "You'll quite like this, I think, Xandri. Our Ms. Corelel is something of an anthropologist," he explained to Shinda.

Shinda eyed me doubtfully. "Is that so?"

"*Amateur* anthropologist," I corrected. "I've read that many of your coastal buildings are constructed of a type of seashell. Is that true?"

"Ah! Come see for yourself!"

He offered me his arm in an old-fashioned, courtly manner and though I desired very much to refuse, I dared not. And as it turned out, having a bit of support was a good thing, as the path leading up from the landing area was made entirely of crushed seashells. Though my balance had improved greatly over my years aboard the *Carpathia*, I didn't get on so well with uneven ground. And crushed seashells? Yikes.

As we walked, a faint buzz vibrated my wristlet. With the slightest twitch, I activated the private comm channel Diver and Kiri had worked together to set up for us. As I understood it, their work meant that our private communications would blend in with Cochinga's own communications system, and thus no one would realize we were contacting each other.

"*Fuck, this diplomat stuff is boring,*" Diver complained as soon as the channel opened. "*I'd rather be back on Stillness, fighting invisible therapsid-alikes.*"

Me too. "*Pomp and circumstance, Diver. I suggest you get used to it.*"

"*Indeed,*" Captain Chui agreed. "*Play along, no matter how boring it gets. As far as anyone is concerned, you're here to assist me and keep me in contact with my ship. I'd rather no one get any ideas about what you might be up to.*"

"*No one will,*" Kiri assured her.

"*And all of you, do your best to stay away from Major Douglas. He's not terrible at his job, I suppose, but he's an ass. A patronizing ass. We'll talk more later.*"

The comm channel closed out on Captain Chui's end. At that moment Secretary Shinda turned to glance at her, only to find her smiling pleasantly at him. Captain Chui could look convincingly innocent with both hands in the cookie jar.

The path began to crest a hill, and I caught my first glimpse of the Council building as it rose above us. More and more of it emerged, an enormous sprawl of whitish architecture that seemed nearly as large as a city itself. As if in defiance of the spiky nature of their home, the building itself was crafted of curves and swirls: the enormous, sweeping staircase curved outward; the support pillars and spires spiraled upwards; the roof flowed in and out of onion domes; and the surface sparkled under the sun like abalone shell.

"Wow," I breathed.

"Do you like it?" Secretary Shinda asked.

"Secretary, it's *wondrous,*" I answered honestly.

He turned to look at me, tilting his head slightly. I thought perhaps something brightened in his features—the heavy forehead and cheek ridges made it harder than usual for me to tell. What interested me more was the slight flick of his tail I caught from the corner of my eye.

"You really mean that."

116

"Of course I do." I blinked in confusion. "Why would I say it if I didn't mean it?"

Shinda started to laugh. "Anthropologist you might be, my darling girl, but diplomat you are not."

Nonsense. The very fact that I didn't take his head off for calling me his 'darling girl' proved I *did* have a diplomatic bone or two in my body after all. The fact that I inclined my head, that I thought about Marbles and Cake hanging upside down to bring a genuine smile to my face, was surely evidence that I could do this whole politicking business at least enough to get by.

"I'll take that as a compliment, Secretary."

"Hey!" Marco stepped up on Secretary Shinda's other side. He was grinning, though, and Shinda was near roaring with laughter. "I resent that."

Captain Chui laughed too. "Forgive her, Mr. Antilles. She learned her diplomacy from soldiers, you see."

"That explains ever so much."

As we ascended the stairs, Marco and Captain Chui teasing one another, I watched Shinda's tail from the corner of my eye. The end kept twitching as he laughed. *Hmm.* I hadn't seen that in the footage I'd watched, but then, there hadn't been much. I'd have to keep my eyes open, especially at the reception banquet, to see if other Anmerilli did this, and when.

At last we reached the top of the stairs, where a rather large fountain stood in front of the main entrance. Diver halted in front of the fountain, his eyes lighting up as if he were a kid in a candy store.

"Is—is this—it is! It's a Moebius band! How—"

"Come on, Diver," Kiri said, grabbing his arm. "There'll be time to look at the pretty water later."

"But!"

I had a feeling that sometime in the future, our Hydroponics garden would get a waterfall installment in the shape of a Moebius band. It *was* pretty impressive, the way the water flowed through the shape without any apparent guidance system. I fought a grin. *Diver won't quit until he figures out how to reproduce it.* If anyone could, it would be him. I found part of me looking forward to the result.

"We of course have rooms ready for you," Secretary Shinda said. Two liveried Anmerilli hurried to open the doors. "I hope they'll be to your liking."

"They're just as beautiful as the rest of the place," Marco said, his voice echoing against the marble-like floor of the entrance hall.

I took it all in with wide eyes. It could have been stuffy, opulent, overwrought, but the large clerestory windows and the open breezeways leading off the entrance hall lent a feeling of airiness to the place I hadn't expected. The smell of the sea, salty but fresh, lingered in the air as we traveled down a breezeway. I wanted to throw my arms wide and breathe in deep, for the whole place *felt* like freedom. But that would probably look strange.

"I'll be honest, Captain Chui," Shinda said. He'd released my arm and walked with his hands clasped behind his back as we traversed into a more closed off, and larger, corridor. "When Mr. Antilles told me the Alliance was going to try a different tack, I was skeptical. And to be frank, I still am. I don't see what you can do that others haven't already tried."

"Well, Secretary Shinda, the Alliance is still a bit...staid in its ways," Captain Chui replied. "Aboard the *Carpathia*, we've made an effort to be more flexible. Though we have a diplomacy sector, the people I've brought with me are not diplomats in the traditional sense."

"So I understand. Xeno-liaisons, you call it. You realize that here on Cochinga, *you* are the aliens?"

"Which is why we call it Xeno-liaisons, sir," I cut in. Even humans as progressive as Captain Chui could be twitchy about being called aliens. "We deal with *all* the peoples of the universe, even our own, if we must. There was a time that a name such a Human-Xeno liaisons or Alliance-Xeno liaisons might have been chosen, but on the *Carpathia* we chose the name that defines us *all*."

Pray god that hadn't come off sounding too much like I practiced it in front of a mirror. Which I had.

"Perhaps there's a bit of the diplomat in you after all," Shinda said with a twitch of his tail tip.

"Forgive me for interrupting," Marco said, "but I'd just like to point out that these offices," he gestured to a line of doors down the corridors, "are where both Alliance and Cochingan ambassadorial staff can be found during the day, if you need them for anything."

"Like a map to this place?" Diver muttered.

"That's what I'm here for," Marco said.

That would never do for people like Diver and Kiri. They were probably already plotting to make some sort of schematics of the building.

"So, Ms. Corelel," Shinda said, drawing my attention back to him. He ushered us through a door, into the next corridor. "I don't feel my question has been sufficiently answered. What is it you think you can do that others could not?"

"Shinda, go easy on her," Marco cut in. "At least let her get her feet on the ground."

"It's all right," I said quietly. "I understand his concern. This is his home, and I imagine he loves it very much."

"Indeed I do, Ms. Corelel. Cochinga is a free world; we'd like to keep it that way."

"The Alliance wouldn't change that."

"They ask things of us that not all nations of our world are willing to give. Yet we do not understand the full impact of what it is they offer us in return. Think you can explain it better?"

"That's not what I'm here to do." I paused and turned to look at him. Though it was difficult—his body language was more closed than I liked—I made myself look him in the eyes. "You already know what the Alliance wants of Cochinga. My job is to learn and understand what you—what the Anmerilli—want. What you *need*. My job is to figure out how the Alliance can best give that to you. I will hear the voices of this planet and make certain the Alliance listens."

"And they will listen to you why?"

I shrugged. "They're finding that things tend to go their way when they listen to me. Look, Secretary Shinda, I know I might not seem—like the right person for the job. But I'm going to do my damnedest to get the job done, to the satisfaction of the Alliance, yes, but most importantly, to the satisfaction of your people."

"And so perhaps you will," he mused. "Perhaps you will indeed."

Chapter Fourteen

"Here you are, Ms. Corelel. I'll be back to bring you to the reception in an hour," Secretary Shinda said as he ushered me into my room. "No weapons at receptions or diplomatic meetings, please."

"Understood."

"I do hope you enjoy your stay. And I sincerely hope, Ms. Corelel, that you succeed where others have not."

The door closed. I sagged against it, my feet aching from the tour. As large as the building looked from the outside, it was even bigger inside, and we'd been hours touring the length and breadth of it.

At least this room is nice. I wasn't sure Captain Chui would approve of the enormous windows with balconies beneath them, but I loved all the light and air they let in. My room was more of a suite, with something that might be a kitchen, a small dining area, a bathroom and of course a bed, sizeable and round to fit with all the rounded, sweeping edges of this place. I walked to the bed, dropped my bag on the floor, and pitched face-first onto the mattress.

Already exhausted. How the hell was I gonna get through a reception on top of all this? While paying attention to everything?

I don't get it. Secretary Shinda seems so eager for this alliance, and it sounds like the rest of Cochinga isn't entirely against it. What's been going wrong? I needed to be alert if I was going to figure it out. Reluctantly I dragged myself partway off the mattress and reached down to dig in my bag for a stim. I popped one in my mouth and chewed, forcing myself to my feet as the sharp, minty taste filled my mouth. It crept up into my sinuses, delivering what could best be described as a wakeup punch. No gentle wakeup calls in a paramilitary organization.

I checked my wristlet as the stim sank in. Not much there, except for a rather short missive from Captain Chui letting me know that my classification for Stillness was now in-the-system official. Good. One thing I could keep off my mind while I worked.

Despite my exhaustion, I retrieved my clothes for the reception and changed. Kiri's help had been invaluable. After looking at current fashions on Cochinga, she'd designed something with long, wide sleeves—I could still cover my hands!—a gently scooped neck, and a back that dipped a little lower than I was comfortable with. I could deal, though, since the top was long and the fabric soft. And I had nanobots to support my breasts rather than using bras.

It might sound silly, but it was a damn sight more comfortable than a glorified harness, especially when you were bouncing from one variation of g to another.

"Hey, Xan!" A knock on my door. "Can we come in?"

"One second," I said, as I hopped into the trousers Kiri had designed. Slender-legged, yes, but she'd added a stripe of satin down the sides that matched my top and, of course, felt nice. "All right. It should be unlocked."

The door swung open. I turned, not sure whether to be awed or amused at the sheer amount of beauty coming through my doorway. *With these two, life sometimes looks like a really bad Ancient Earth romance novel.* But then, Kiri looked radiant in gold, with a touch of jade over her eyes, and the green Diver wore made the copper in his fawn-colored hair stand out more. Though he looked a bit put out, as he always did when he had to wear anything more formal than a T-shirt and jeans.

"Hey, fireball," he said with a grin, still tugging at his collar. "You clean up pretty good. Hair's a problem, though."

"Diver!" Kiri elbowed him in the ribs.

"Ow! Hey! Fuck, Kiri, she *likes* honesty!"

"I do," I agreed. "And if you tried to tell me my hair was anything less than a disaster, I'd know you were lying."

"You suck at telling when people are lying."

"Yeah, but my hair is *always* a disaster." I held up my much disarrayed braid, with bits wisping out in every direction, as proof.

Kiri shook her head. "All right, sit down. Let's see if we can do something about it. You got any hair pins?"

"Yeah, but...oh, never mind."

I took a seat on the edge of the bed and retrieved my comb and some hair pins for Kiri. She settled behind me and pulled my hair free of the ravaged braid. Her fingers combing through my hair felt pleasant, luring me into a drowsy feeling—not good when I needed to be awake and alert. I focused on Diver, who leaned against the wall opposite the bed. The sunlight pouring through the windows gave a goldish hue to his skin, but I tried not to notice that too much.

"You're totally going to try to replicate that fountain, aren't you?"

"Of course. There *has* to be a trick to it, water doesn't just naturally fall in a Moebius band."

"Maybe they found a way to make it fall like that," I suggested.

"Xan, what do you know about physics?"

"Um..." I ticked off on my fingers. "One, an object in motion will stay in motion—unless, of course, you're in slingspace. Two, what goes up must come down—unless there's no gravity. And three, fuck up at the wrong time and physics will end you. That's all I got."

"Well, you've got most people beat."

"How so?"

"Most people never figure out number three."

I grinned.

"Goddamnit," Kiri grumbled. "*Why* is your hair so slippery?"

"I stopped trying to figure that out years ago."

"But it looks so silky and soft," Kiri complained. "And I mean, I guess it is, but it's like trying to braid a bunch of naba eels. No offense."

"Nope, that's about how I feel about it."

While Kiri struggled with comb, hair, and pins, Diver attempted to explain to me why water just didn't naturally fall in a Moebius band, ever. Which seemed to boil down to little more than "physics doesn't work like that." Or, as I liked to phrase it: Physics is a party-pooper.

"Ugh, there," Kiri said at last. "That ought to at least hold for some hours. Next time we're on a big station, I am taking you to the most expensive hair salon we can find so they can teach you how to manage this stuff."

"Well, it's not normally a big deal," I pointed out. "Most of what we encounter on planets is more concerned with whether it can eat

122

my hair than whether it looks nice. I like predators. They're less fussy than diplomats."

Kiri groaned. Diver started to laugh. *What? What I'd say?* I glanced back and forth between them, but I didn't get what was so amusing—or groan-worthy.

Someone cleared their throat. We all froze, then glanced at the doorway. *Oh. The door was open...* Captain Chui stood there, her arms folded, Anton and Katya looming behind her. She looked quite amazing, her hair in a simple chignon, her clothing plain black cigarette pants paired with a cheongsam tunic top that she only ever wore on formal occasions. *Okay, now I feel downright schlumpy.* On the bright side, I was used to the feeling.

"Not that I necessarily disagree," Captain Chui said, "but do be a little careful what you say with your door open, yes?"

"Yes, ma'am."

"Now, is everyone ready?"

"Just about." I hopped off the bed and grabbed my boots. "I'll go check on the rest of the team."

I tugged my boots on, nearly falling over in the process. Miraculously, I not only remained on my feet, but my hair didn't slip out of place either. I reached up to touch it, my fingertips contacting one of the hair pins. *Did she use the entire pack of them or something?* A glance at the pack, lying on the bed, told me she'd used half. With a sigh, I headed for the door.

As I exited the room, I heard Captain Chui tell Kiri, "I will *fund* that salon visit."

Of all the things sapience had devised over the long, long millennia, parties had to be one of the worst. I hated few things more than parties. If one could weaponize the feelings I got, standing off to one side in a huge crowd of people I didn't know, watching them talk and laugh together comfortably, one could make a weapon that would make a graser look puny in comparison.

"You're going to have to mingle eventually," Anton told me.

"I'm mingling," I protested.

"With the wall."

Yes, well, the *wall* didn't judge. The *wall* didn't get persnickety when I refused to make eye contact with it. The *wall* didn't get offended if my tone of voice slipped and something came out in a way I didn't mean it. And the *wall* wasn't threatening to ally with a bunch of imperialistic slavers and hand over a powerful weapon to them. Was it any wonder I preferred the wall's company?

Xandri, hi, yes, this is your brain speaking? That was weird even for you.

I sighed. "I don't know where to start. There's so many people here. It's...overwhelming."

The rest of the Xeno-liaisons team were handling it just fine. From my vantage point, I could watch them move through the crowd, watch them interact with various Anmerilli, including a number of the World Council members. And I knew they'd send me reports later, when all was said and done, so one way or another I'd get information. *But I have to do this.* I took a deep breath. *I have to just...suck it up and deal.*

I eyed the crowd, trying to figure out a good entry point—and then I noticed Marco. He was making his way to where I stood, a Council member on either side of him. I knew they were Council members; I recognized them as Anashi Sendil and Kalemi Ashil.

Yes! They'd be an excellent place to start. I'd liked what I'd seen of them in the vids. Councilor Ashil smiled often—without the sort of awkwardness Shinda had—and even now I saw her tail twitching in amusement. *I* think *it's amusement.* She had skin so dark it seemed vaguely purplish, while Sendil was a lighter but still deep brown. Both of them wore their hair long, twisted into styles that reminded me of spiraling seashells.

"Good evening, Xandri," Marco said as he halted before me. "Councilor Sendil, Councilor Ashil, this is Xandri Corelel, Head of Xeno-liaisons aboard the *Carpathia*."

"Yes, so we've heard." Ashil had a voice as deep and sonorous as the sea. "Are you not enjoying the party, Ms. Corelel?"

"Oh, I...I was just..."

"Don't tease her, Kal," Sendil said with a grin. "Ms. Corelel, it's a pleasure to meet you."

He bowed, and I returned the gesture, hoping I wouldn't botch it too badly. Ashil bowed as well, hers similar but still different from

Sendil's, and I returned that one, too. Lucky Anton; as a soldier he was exempt.

"If you'll excuse me," Marco said, "I'd best continue to make myself available."

"Poor Marco," Ashil said, patting his arm. "Always in demand."

He winked at her. "Better than not being wanted around."

Marco headed back into the crowd. I watched him a moment, then turned my gaze back to the Council members. Despite the struggles I'd had with the Anmerilli, I found these two much easier to look in the face. There was just something relaxed and open in the way they stood, something friendly in their demeanor, and I could think of no better place to start my 'mingling.' *Marco really is good at his job.*

"So, Ms. Corelel," Ashil began.

"Oh, um...you're welcome to call me Xandri, Councilor," I said. "I've spent the last four years on a paramilitary ship. Being called Ms. Corelel makes me feel like I ought to salute."

Sendil chuckled. "You know, Kalemi, I'd almost forgotten how refreshing it can be to talk to someone who isn't a diplomat."

"Or a politician," Ashil agreed. She eyed me in a way I couldn't decipher. "My understanding of you, Ms.—Xandri, is that you've been instrumental in making certain changes in Alliance procedure. Particularly with regards to the protection of fauna and flora."

"I've had a bit of a hand in that, yes."

"Will the Alliance enforce those rules for Cochinga, do you think?"

"Well, that depends," I said carefully, "on the status of your membership." Of course, we wanted them to ally on a level that would by default enforce those rules, but I wasn't sure I should mention that.

They both studied me. I stood, trying to look alert and attentive and not squirm. Between them, over their shoulders, I saw Marco in the crowd, talking to another Anmerilli. The stiff shoulders and spine rang familiar, and after a moment I realized it was Councilor mar'Odrea. A shiver went down my spine. Better Marco than me. I kept hoping I could avoid mar'Odrea altogether; a foolish hope, because he would be at the meetings. But I just didn't see how I could fake it with someone like that.

"A careful answer," Ashil said at last. "Caution is wise. There are many conflicting opinions in the World Council."

"And what do you think?" I asked them both. "Do you think these conflicts are...irreparable?"

"I think they shouldn't be," Sendil said quietly.

"Indeed, they should not, Xandri." Ashil swept another bow. "Now if you'll excuse us, I'm afraid we must move on for now. Councilor oar'Saran has been trying to get our attention all evening."

"Much to our dismay."

"Of course," I said. "Though I do hope we'll get the chance to speak more."

We exchanged bows again. *See, Xandri, that wasn't so bad,* I told myself as I watched them slip back into the crowd. *Though...what did Sendil mean by that? Things* shouldn't *be irreparable?* I'd need to interact more if I was going to figure it out.

"Kat's back," Anton said in my ear.

I turned. Katya came towards us, balancing a plate on one hand. My stomach rumbled in response. I hadn't had time to eat since we'd landed, and I had a feeling I'd find a nutrient-bar waiting on my pillow when I got back to my room. There was plenty of food to be had at the reception, of course, but whether I could tolerate any of it was another matter.

"All right," Katya said, pausing next to us and holding up the plate. "I *think* these might do. They didn't seem too weird to me."

Cautiously I reached out and picked up...well, it looked a bit like some kind of cracker and cheese, but the Anmerilli didn't use animal products, so it couldn't be that. I took a sniff. *Well, it doesn't* smell *bad.* With a shrug, I took a bite.

My chewing began enthusiastic but soon slowed. The taste was bad enough, sour and harsh enough to make my eyes water. But the texture—*ugh.* What had looked smooth on the cracker was in fact grainy and rough, like someone had tried to make cheese spread out of lemon juice and sandpaper. I inhaled sharply in dismay and started to cough as flaky bits of cracker caught in my throat. Anton handed me the glass of water he'd been holding for me and I took a long drink, clearing my mouth and throat.

"Oh god," I wheezed. "Sweet Mother Universe, that was vile. How was that not 'too weird?'"

126

Katya shrugged and took a bite of one herself. "Tastes mainly like cheese and crackers to me."

I stared. Not for the first time, I wondered if non-autistic people even had taste buds. Or nerve endings.

"Is something wrong with the food, Ms. Corelel?"

I spun. Standing before me, tall and stoic and stiff, was Councilor Nish mar'Odrea. The sharp way his hair swept back from his forehead highlighted every keen edge of him, from the ridges on his cheeks to the gleam of his dark, disapproving eyes. I focused on those cheek ridges, because I couldn't look him in the eyes. With some it might be uncomfortable for various reasons, but for the first time in years, it physically *hurt*.

"Good evening, Councilor mar'Odrea," I said. Hoping to be polite, I greeted him with the correct bow. And I *knew* it was correct because I'd practiced it more than any other. He bowed in return and I went on, "The food is...unusual to me. I was simply caught by surprise."

"Indeed? Perhaps you should try the aldama, then. It might be more to your liking."

"I'll look into that."

"And how are you enjoying the reception?" mar'Odrea asked. "You've kept very much to yourself, I've noticed."

"I was just planning to remedy that," I said, in what I hoped was a bright tone. "Perhaps you have a suggestion as to who I should talk to? I'm not so very good at starting up conversations, I'm afraid."

I hoped playing the "I'm just a sweet little thing who doesn't know what she's doing" card would get me somewhere, but mar'-Odrea didn't even twitch. Not even his tail, which I took a quick glance at.

"Yes, I've heard about your...problem. But I'm sure you'll do fine, Ms. Corelel. You seem perfectly—"

Oh, here it comes.

"—normal."

Why does that never feel like an actual compliment? "Thank you, Councilor," I said. I glanced as surreptitiously as I could over his shoulder, praying someone would come to rescue me. "I—"

"Forgive me, Ms. Corelel," mar'Odrea said in a tone that sounded, to me at least, not the least bit apologetic. "I'm afraid

I'm a very busy man and haven't much time for idle chit-chat. I do hope you won't be late for tomorrow's meeting. Good evening."

"I—" But he was already walking off, blending back into the crowd. "That man does *not* like me."

"Seems foolish to me," Anton said. "He ought to be sucking up to you, if he wants any chance of getting what he wants."

"He already knows I won't give him what he wants," I muttered

That brief stopover to greet me had been far more about him getting my measure than me getting his, I was pretty sure of that. My instincts screamed at me that this was a man who would look for ways to break me, and if I wasn't careful, he'd find them. *I think I need to trust my instincts on this one.* It *hurt* to look him in the eyes; that couldn't be good. It was never good, and I hadn't always trusted my instincts about it, which had led to...things I didn't like to remember.

"All right," I said, after a deep breath. "It's time for me to start making some allies. I'm going to need them."

"We won't be far behind," Katya reassured me.

I nodded. My appetite had disappeared with the taste of that—whatever it was, and with mar'Odrea's visit, so I didn't have to worry about that anymore.

Trying not to tense up, I took my first step towards the crowd, then another. Bodies closed in around me, drifting in like water sweeping up onto a shore. I gritted my teeth, fought to ignore the press, focusing instead on looking for Marco. *He* could help me find the right people, I was sure of it. If only I could—*ah! There!* His dark curls were unmistakable, especially among the elaborate Anmerilli hairstyles.

"Marco!" I called as I approached him.

He turned away from the Anmerilli he was talking to, and when his eyes alighted on me, he smiled. With a bow to the Anmerilli, he headed to my side. Marco caught my elbow as he reached me and drew me close to his side.

"Are you all right?" he said in my ear. "You look a little pale."

"Crowds. I uh, don't handle them well."

"That's right." He gave me a tender smile. "Sensory overstimulation, right?"

I nodded.

"Well, maybe we can distract you from that a little bit."

He guided me through the crowd with great care. I glanced over my shoulder and saw Katya and Anton not far behind, moving through the press with much more ease.

Marco brought me to the buffet tables. Keeping one hand on my elbow, he gently touched the shoulder of a tall Anmerillis standing at the table. The Anmerillis turned, revealing herself to be slender as a willow. Hints of bronze seemed to gleam in her yellowish skin, and her hair coiled over her shoulder in a thick, light braid. Councilor Noaya Maru. I perked up. She was a member of the International Animal Rights Movement on Cochinga.

"Councilor Maru," Marco said, "may I introduce Xandri Corelel?"

"Ah!" Noaya Maru bowed. "Finally! I've been hoping to get some time to speak with you this evening, Ms. Corelel."

"Please, call me Xandri," I said, returning the bow.

"I've heard about your work on Inge."

Whoa. *All I did on Inge was save some fish. Fish-like things.* I hadn't thought that anyone had heard about that; certainly not anyone important. But it seemed Councilor Maru had, and to my surprise, she asked to know more. Maybe this whole making allies business wouldn't be so hard after all.

Chapter Fifteen

The cool, sea-soaked breeze rushed across my face and neck. I let out a sigh and leaned against the balcony railing, relishing the wind, the way the world faded into darkness and stars, allowing me to feel like I had all the space I could possibly need. My bodyguards would probably chew me out if they knew I was out there, but after the long hours of the reception, I felt too stifled to care. Let them be annoyed.

"*Xandri?*"

I jumped. A quick glance behind me revealed my room was empty, so how had they known?

"*Xandri,*" came Katya's voice again. "*Marco Antilles is here to see you. Should we let him in?*"

Oh. Well, didn't I just feel silly. "*Sure.*"

I could've said no. Hell, part of me wanted to. This was Me time, after all. But Marco and I were working together and we needed to compare notes.

"Xandri? Where—ah. There you are."

I turned as Marco came out onto the balcony. He'd opened the jacket of his formal AFC uniform and his dark curls were tousled, as if he'd run his fingers through them a lot. Despite the long night and his disheveled appearance, he looked, to my eyes, far more alert than me. *No idea how he does it. I'm completely done.*

"You did well out there tonight," Marco said, resting his hands on the balcony.

"Councilor mar'Odrea hates me. And I'm pretty sure he's not the only one. A little before I left, I saw him talking to a group of other Councilors and they all kept... *looking* at me."

"mar'Odrea's a tough nut to crack. But I saw you getting on well with Maru."

"She's easy to talk to, though. And she's eager to sign with the Alliance."

Marco shook his head. "Actually, for most of us in the AFC, she's been incredibly difficult. She wants the Alliance, yes, but she wants the full membership, no compromises. Thus she refuses to pledge a vote." He sighed and rubbed the back of his neck, finally looking like the stress of it all was getting to him. "Not that I disagree with her. After what I've seen these last six years—all the deaths from hunting accidents and weapons alone—I think a full membership is what the Anmerilli need.

"But her unwillingness to pledge a vote means others who might support the Alliance don't have the confidence to step forward. They feel they'll have no support."

I stared out into the night, considering. Councilor Maru hadn't seemed so uncompromising to me, but then, we'd talked more about fish than anything else. *Still, I don't see what's so wrong with a compromise.* But it wasn't my place to make that decision. I was here to get the treaty signed, not to dictate what was in it. Although...

"Do you think there's any chance of getting others to support full membership?" I asked. "Councilor Maru introduced me to Councilor Olish Tari, who works with her for animal rights, and I think he'd go for it, but I'm not sure about the others."

"Sendil and Ashil, perhaps," Marco said. "They approach everything with caution, as they've reason not to trust some of their fellow Councilors, but my impression is that they're behind it."

"Then we need to get others to support it. As long as we have a majority—even by one vote—it'll go through. But..." I sighed. "mar'Odrea will *never* go for it. Especially not with me being part of the project."

A hand came down lightly on my arm. An intense urge to pull away flared up inside me, twisting my stomach into anxious knots. *Don't be rude, Xandri. He doesn't mean anything by it.* It wasn't Marco's fault I had...issues. Right? Right. That's what Mother would have said, anyway.

"Look, let me deal with mar'Odrea and his cronies," Marco said. "I've been doing it for six years; a few more weeks won't kill me. I might even be able to get him to ease up on you a little."

I raised a skeptical eyebrow.

"I know, I know. It's not terribly likely. But at the least, I can distract him while you work on bringing others over to our side. If we work together, Xandri, I'm *positive* we can succeed."

He smiled, his usual bright, confident smile. *Maybe we can.* I smiled back, tired and wan but genuine at least. I didn't know if I could be as confident as Marco, but...

"I'll try my best."

"That's all I ask," he said. "So I'll be by for you and your team tomorrow morning a little before oh-eight-hundred hours, got it?"

I nodded.

"Oh, and before I forget..."

Marco reached under his jacket and pulled out a slender, semi-sheer flex-plastic envelope. I blinked as he handed it over to me. With care I opened the flap and slid out a piece of paper. My mouth dropped open when I realized it was the drawing, the one of Mergassë that he was working on that night aboard *Carpathia*. He'd done something to the surface so the chalks didn't fade or smudge. I touched my fingertips to it gingerly. When I looked up, Marco was already heading for the door.

"But I can't—" I started.

"I want you to have it." He turned back to me for a moment and, eyes bright and warm, gestured to the balcony. "And don't worry. Your secret is safe with me."

He winked, turned, and disappeared out of the door, slipping through it carefully so no one could get a glimpse of me on the balcony. I stepped back into my room and closed the balcony door, just to be on the safe side. *It's so nice when someone gets it.* Dropping onto my bed, I held the picture up above me. That dreamy, sleepy beauty it captured made me smile. *There's beauty everywhere. I'll find it among the Anmerilli, too.*

Cochinga's non-member status was high enough to allow for trade, and much to my delight, coffee was one of the non-Anmerilli items they'd taken to. Good, expensive coffee, too, not that brown water you sometimes got on space stations and the like. I wasn't a functioning sapient before coffee, so I was thrilled to discover the steaming mug that awaited me.

The nutrient-bar, less so.

After my coffee and a bit of confusion with regards to how to operate the shower—solved with a quick call to Diver—I dressed in my

uniform and wound my damp hair into its usual braid. Satisfied—
or as satisfied as I was ever likely to get—I slipped out into the hall,
where Katya and Anton stood on either side of my door. Captain
Chui, Diver, and my Xeno-liaisons team also awaited me in the hall.

"Huh. And here I thought I was being prompt today."

"If it's any comfort," Anton said, "the captain's been out here
for a good twenty minutes already. Hard to beat that."

"We know this," Katya added, "because *we* have been out here
all night."

"Indeed," Captain Chui said. "But as it is unlikely that we'll have
to deal with any assassination attempts during today's meeting—in
my experience diplomacy is never that exciting—I think it's time
for you two to rest. Dismissed."

I didn't figure they'd both be guarding me all the time—probably
Captain Chui would split them into shifts once she felt she knew
the lay of the land—but I was almost disappointed to see them go. I
was kind of hoping they'd stand behind my chair at the meeting and
snark at each other on a sub-vocalized level, so I'd have something
to amuse me. *On second thought, better not to be distracted.* I did *not*
need to burst into seemingly random giggles during the very first
meeting.

"*Since this is our first day,*" Captain Chui's voice came through
on our private channel, "*I'd like you all to act in an observing capacity
only. Understood?*"

"*And if we're addressed directly?*" Christa wanted to know.

"*Answer, but keep it as succinct as possible. I assume at least one of
you will be taking notes?*"

"*Me and Kirrick,*" Marla said. "*His writing is more legible, but I'm
faster. Together, we equal one damn fine scribe.*"

I noticed a shift in Captain Chui's eyes that might have been
a smile. It was an oddity, taking notes by hand, but it would be
useful now. No one could hack into a piece of paper and a pen.
The notes would remain confidential right up until Kiri encrypted
them, especially since the shorthand used on the *Carpathia* was
different from anyone else's.

"Ah. I see everyone's ready." Marco's voice at the end of the hall
made us all turn. "Shall we?"

Secretary Shinda stood with him, so we all bowed the general
bow in greeting. Shinda bowed in return and I *knew* it wouldn't take

long before I'd be sick of this. I'd do it, because I wasn't an asshole who went around disrespecting other peoples' cultures, but I didn't quite understand how they could handle doing it *all the time.*

"*Captain,*" I sub-vocalized as we followed Shinda and Marco through the halls, "*where is Kiri?*"

"*Transferring data to the* Carpathia, *of course,*" Captain Chui replied.

She said nothing more. I glanced back at the rest of the team, wishing all of them knew what Christa and I knew. Certainly, I had no doubt that Kiri *would* be transferring data to the *Carpathia*. If that was *all* she did today, I'd eat my guns.

Marco and Shinda led us through the labyrinth that was the World Council building, to the main council room. Forty-three World Council members awaited us there, along with a platoon each of AFC and Anmerilli soldiers, and a small complement of AFC diplomats. My heart jumped into my throat. *I don't want to have to speak in front of all these people!* Not even the enormous windows, which allowed in a great deal of air and light, could make the room feel less crowded and stifling.

"*Remember,*" came Captain Chui's voice, "*do your best to remain in an observational capacity only.*"

Right, right. Working to squash my panic, I lined up beside my team and prepared for introductions. My panic was soon drowned in tedium and a growing case of dizziness as we bowed, a different one for each World Council member. I thought I might have flubbed a few of them slightly, but as no one chastised me or stormed out of the room in indignation, I figured it couldn't be too bad.

"Please, everyone, take your seats," Secretary Shinda said at long last. "It's time, I think, that we begin."

Hah! Fucking hah. "Begin," as I soon learned, was a very loose way of putting it. I watched as the World Council members aired a number of grievances with each other, though in such polite, pussy-footing terms that it took me a while to realize what they were do-ing. It also took an effort to focus. I forced myself to watch them, concentrating, trying to find small nuances in their body language. Each one stood and spoke long enough to give me a fair bit of time to study them.

Councilor oar'Saran was pretty expressive for an Anmerillis, I noticed, during his turn. "And furthermore," he carried on, his voice high and his tail swinging rapidly, "if Councilors Ashil and Sendil do not get their—"

"Councilor oar'Saran," Kalemi Ashil interrupted. "Councilor Sendil and I understand how important this is to you." And never had I heard so clearly the unspoken sentiment "and we have no fucks to give about it." But *politely*. "However, we would like to request that we put aside our personal grievances for the time being and focus on the Alliance."

"That *is* what we're here for, is it not?" Councilor Maru agreed.

From the top of the long council table, Nish mar'Odrea cleared his throat. "Yes, that is why we're here. Though I do hope, Mr. Antilles, that you've got some new ideas to bring to the table."

"That's what we're here to work out, Councilor," Marco said.

"But you still want to force us to give up our weapons, not to mention many of our traditions."

"Would that be so bad?" Councilor Maru put in. "What do we need our weapons for? We're killing each other. Our *children* are killing each other."

"I agree with Councilor Maru," Ashil said. "Bad enough we're killing each other—"

"*And* our ecosystems!"

"—but our children... Councilor mar'Odrea, it has to stop."

"Then by all means, Councilor, stop it."

"If it were that easy, we would have already done it," Ashil said quietly. Her dark eyes narrowed on mar'Odrea. "And so would you."

"What good is it to protect our children from each other," another Council member burst out, "if we have no means to protect them from other threats?"

"A very good question," mar'Odrea said.

Marco sighed. "And one we've gone over numerous times. Your military is still allowed to be armed, and you'll have the Alliance military to support you."

A groan rippled through the room, as if the World Council had heard this argument too many times already. Hell, they probably had. *This is diplomacy? No wonder it takes such a long time.* How was *I* supposed to make a difference here? Most of the Anmerilli didn't want to give up their weapons or their animal cruelty. What could

135

I do to change their minds? I tried to tell myself not to be cynical, but each word spoken made it more and more difficult.

"Mr. Antilles," mar'Odrea said, "you want us to believe these Zechak are a great threat to us, but at the same time you tell us to lay down our weapons. Well, which is it? Are we safe enough to live as a society without weapons or aren't we?"

"I don't think that's what he meant." The words came out of my mouth without my explicit permission, soft but ringing in the silence following mar'Odrea's question.

Councilor mar'Odrea spun to face me and for the first time, I could read the expression on his face. There was simply no mistaking the way his brow pulled down, the way his cheek ridges came up. He smoothed his features quickly, hiding his disdain behind the typical stoic Anmerilli mask, but I'd seen it. You'd think I'd personally stabbed his beloved pet, the way he looked at me. Not that I thought Nish mar'Odrea would be caught dead with a beloved pet.

"Ah, yes, the Alliance's special advisor," mar'Odrea said, and I cursed my inability to pick the mockery apart from his politeness. "Please, enlighten us on what he meant."

I glanced sidelong at Captain Chui and caught her faint nod. All right then. I took a deep breath and said, "I think we're talking about two separate issues here. The personal weapons use of the Anmerilli and the threat of the Zechak—they're not related."

One of mar'Odrea's cronies, a Councilor called Olan mar'Shen, suppressed a snort. "How not?"

"More weapons can't save you from the Zechak," I said. "If it comes to that, they simply won't fight you on the ground. They have excellent ground forces, yes, but they won't use them if they decide that's not the winning strategy. They simply won't. You could have endless lockers of weapons and that still won't save you.

"If you don't need them to fight the Zechak, and there is peace among you now, why do you need them at all? Why should children die?"

"I told you," Councilor Sendil said. "I've been studying these Zechak. They may seem brutish, but they're devilish cunning."

"Is this true, Major Douglas?" yet another Councilor asked. I squinted across the table, but I couldn't place her features. "About the Zechak? Will they attack us from space if they find us too much of a challenge on the ground?"

136

The major cleared his throat. "Odds are very high, at least."

"There's no telling for sure what they'll do, but it's possible," Marco agreed.

I bit back a response. *It's more than possible; it's what they've done in every single such situation.* But maybe I wasn't supposed to say that. I didn't know much about how true diplomacy worked. Maybe you just weren't supposed to be all "Woo, bogeymen" this early on in the process. I didn't want to actually *scare* the Anmerilli.

"It's not as if we don't have weapons to protect us from space attacks," another Councilor—another I couldn't quite place yet—put in. "Surely we could defend ourselves if need be."

I had to resist the urge to bang my head against the table as the Anmerilli broke into a heated discussion about the capabilities of their few anti-spacecraft weapons. *Okay, maybe I* should *scare them.* Doing my best to block out the barrage of voices around me, I glanced around the table. A number of Anmerilli, including Ashil, Sendil and Maru, looked like they wanted to beat their heads against the table, too. I leaned in toward Kirrick. At least I had a few names to take down.

It seemed an eternity passed before we broke for lunch. I resisted the urge to slump out of the meeting room like a zombie from an Ancient Earth B-movie and instead walked, with as much poise as I could muster, next to my group. The World Council members filed down the hall ahead of us, a tidal wave of elaborate hairstyles and rustling cloth. I waited until they were some distance ahead of us before turning to Captain Chui.

"I'm sorry," I said quietly. "I know you told me not to speak. I should've kept my mouth shut."

She tapped a finger against my forehead. "You know I prefer my soldiers to exercise critical thinking. You said the right thing—even if the Anmerilli found a way to twist it," and here she gave a very un-Chui-like eye roll, "and perhaps we can use it to our advantage. And this way the Anmerilli won't so easily get the impression that you're just a puppet. Though... do try to be a bit more careful after lunch, yes?"

"Yes, ma'am."

"In this case," Christa put in suddenly, keeping her voice low, "I confess even *I* had trouble keeping my mouth shut. It's been too long since our team dealt with any diplomats but our own. I'd forgotten how unreasonable and argumentative they can be."

"On the bright side, me and Kirrick got *a lot* of notes," Marla said. She glanced down at the sheaf of paper she held, frowning. "Okay, maybe that's not a bright side."

I glanced over and winced. *Glad that's not part of my job description.* Of course, no point having me do it when, between them, Marla and Kirrick would have everything organized and off to Kiri by the end of lunch. Especially if they got a bit of help from Sho and Kimi.

Something inside me brightened at the thought. Sure, I had the headache to end all headaches, and I didn't foresee it getting any better any time soon. But I had an efficient team; if we couldn't make this work, no one could. *As long as I don't let them down, that is.*

I shoved the thought away as I followed my people into the lunch hall. Much nicer than a typical soldiers' mess or temp mess, the hall, like the rest of the building, was constructed of that glittering shell material. The benches seemed to have risen right out of the floor in elegant, curving construction, and another, smaller Moebius band fountain stood, chiming gently, at the center of it all.

"I am *going* to figure that out," Diver muttered.

I nodded. "I don't doubt it. Do you think you could figure out how to make them really small? I think Cake and Marbles would like it."

"Are you asking for your own personal fountain?" Diver grinned. "What are you going to do for me in return, huh?"

I grinned back; somehow with Diver, I always knew when he was teasing. "I won't tell Captain Chui about the you-know-what."

His eyes widened in mock horror. Considering "the you-know-what" could be one of at least a dozen things, a few of which Captain Chui had commissioned herself, that wasn't much of a threat, but that didn't stop Diver from slapping a hand over his heart and tossing his head back in a theatrical display of betrayal.

"You," he huffed, "are a terrible person."

He stormed off, but halfway to an empty table he glanced back with a broad smile. Feeling lighter—even my head didn't ache as

138

much—I followed. *We'll have to work towards being less isolated from the Anmerilli,* I thought, observing the way the tables were divided, with humans and Anmerilli sitting apart from each other. I caught sight of Marco sitting with the AFC soldiers, talking animatedly; their delighted laughter roared across the room, drawing disdainful looks from a few Anmerilli. Oh yeah, we had our work cut out for us.

As we settled onto our benches, a whirring sound started up within the great block of the table. Just as I noticed a thin seam running along the edges of the tabletop, the smooth surface dropped down and slid away. Another surface rose, covered with food-filled platters, plates, cups and eating utensils. I swallowed. How the hell was I going to navigate this stuff?

"Xandri?"

I glanced up and caught sight of Marco. He leaned over, placing a plate on the one in front of me.

"I have a bit of experience with the food here. See if these suit you, yeah?"

"Thanks, Marco."

"And good job so far today. All of you." He smiled all around the table, and everyone—except Christa, I couldn't help but notice—smiled back. "Now, I hope you don't mind, but I promised the soldiers I'd get back to them. I don't know why, but they never get sick of hearing the Won Tak story. And some of them were there!"

Captain Chui let out a soft, nostalgic chuckle. "That's soldiers for you."

I bent my attention to the food at the behest of my growling stomach and carefully picked up a block of something whitish and bland looking. A small sniff revealed that it smelled relatively neutral, but that hadn't helped me last night. With a shrug, I took a bite—and found it of pleasantly smooth texture, with no weird bits or oddities, and of mild taste. *Huh. What do you know? I can work with this.*

Chapter Sixteen

After lunch, we all headed back to the meeting room. A mixture of dread and exasperation coiled in my stomach as I slid back into my chair. Dread began to win out as I caught sight of Nish mar'Odrea, watching me with a slight curve to his lips that, subtle though it was, clearly broadcasted "This will not bode well for you" straight at my face. *Stellar.*

Once everyone was in place, Secretary Shinda stood to call the meeting to order. A ripple of murmuring, shifting and throat-clearing passed around the table, glances exchanged as each Anmerillis considered where to begin. Suffice it to say, I was not surprised when Councilor mar'Odrea rose. He clasped his hands behind his back and regarded his fellow Council members solemnly.

"My friends," he began, and I was pretty sure I heard Councilor Maru snort, "we have some very important decisions to make. But we cannot make those decisions without answers, and I am not satisfied with the answers we have so far."

I stomped on the urge to both flinch and sigh as his gaze turned on me once more, and ended up jerking awkwardly in my chair. *Damnit.* Suddenly all eyes were on me. *Sweet Mother Universe, stop staring at me!* Too bad I couldn't sink into the floor the way the tabletop had sunk into the table at lunch.

Marco stood up then, drawing attention away from me. "Councilor mar'Odrea," he said, "we've always done our best to answer every question the Council might have, and I have no doubt that Captain Chui and her crew will make the same efforts."

"Indeed," Captain Chui agreed, casual and calm in her tone. "We're here to make this work, Councilor."

"For *you*, perhaps," Olan mar'Shen sneered.

"For *all* of us." *Oh fuck, I did it again,* I thought, gripping the leg of my pants so I wouldn't slap a hand over my mouth. As everyone turned to look at me again, I gathered my courage. "The Zechak will stop at nothing to get their way. *All* of us are in great danger if that happens, Councilors."

"So we keep hearing from you," mar'Odrea said. "But the Zechak are also interested in an alliance with us and *they* won't make us change our ways."

"Yeah, until they slap you in chains or just wipe you out of existence completely," I retorted.

mar'Odrea drew back, his countenance blaring affront with the sound and fury of an Ancient Earth foghorn. *Hey, what do you know, they* can't *always control their expressions.* The hiss and murmur of offense swelled around me, and it finally sank in that I'd put my goddamned foot in it. My entire team, not just Christa, glared at me. I froze. Oh, this was bad, this was very, very bad.

My throat started to close. I forced myself to my feet. Running half on instinct, I dipped into a very low, apologetic general bow. I held the position for several long breaths; to my relief, the murmuring died down. As I straightened, I fought for words. Not to find them—I knew what I wanted to say—but to release them. They gathered in my mouth, crowding each other until none of them could get out. *Not now,* please *not now. Please, please, please.*

"I—" The word fetched up in my throat. I took the hot prickle of humiliation burning in my stomach and fanned it until it notched up to anger, giving me the power I needed to force the words out. "I offer my sincerest apologies, most esteemed Councilor. This—this is a very serious matter. The Zechak do not keep promises or allies. Ever."

"Yes, we have heard as much," Councilor Ashil said. "Please, Ms. Corelel, take a seat. Your most gracious apology is accepted, as far as I'm concerned."

She lowered her eyelids and sliced a glance in both directions, as if daring her fellow Councilors to disagree. When no one did, I took my seat again.

"Perhaps," mar'Odrea began, "it would be best if we were to change the subject for—"

"No, I'm quite interested in this," Councilor Maru said.

"As am I," her cohort, Olish Tari, agreed.

Councilor Sendil nodded. "I as well. I did say I have been studying the Zechak and the records *do* show a certain... viciousness even towards their allies."

Fuck if that wasn't an understatement. They had enslaved the Attana, and wiped out the Sheerat. No one had dared ally with them since the Sheerat had met their end. I glanced at Marco, wondering if he'd shown them the vids and the other records, but his focus was intent upon Sendil.

"Tell me," Councilor Ashil said, her eyes—all eyes—now on me. "We have, as I'm sure you know by now, something quite extraordinary to offer the Zechak. Our value may be greater than that of their previous allies. What do you think of that, Ms. Corelel?"

Now *here* was territory I could walk safely. The nature of the Zechak and the way they treated their so-called allies was a topic I had studied extensively, for just such a case as this one—though admittedly I'd never expected the situation to be either so dire or so formal. I straightened in my chair and lifted my chin, hoping I looked mature and sure of myself.

"Honestly, Councilor? Looking at it from angles both historical and socio-political, it doesn't seem likely that what you have to offer will make a difference," I said. "Their other allies had value as well, but the Zechak—theirs is a self-centric mentality. They believe in singular glory and they *hate* to share. Perhaps there are Zechak out there who don't behave that way—in fact, it would be statistically impossible that there aren't—but they never seem to be the ones in power." I tilted my head in thought. "From a military standpoint, I'm afraid I'm at a disadvantage. But I'm certain Major Douglas and Captain Chui can fill you in."

"*Well done, Xandri,*" Captain Chui's voice came through on the private comm. "*Very well done.*"

The sub-vocalization buzzed between my ears; the praise left me glowing inside with warmth.

"And what *do* you think, Major?" Ashil pressed, ignoring the dirty look mar'Odrea sent down the table at her. "I know we've discussed this some before, but I ask for full disclosure: Do you think, from a military standpoint, that we have an advantage over previous allies of the Zechak?"

"Can I say with an absolute certainty? No," the major said. "It's never wise to presume too much about what your enemy will do."

"True enough," Captain Chui agreed. "At the same time, this isn't just a military matter, and I think Ms. Corelel's testimony adds a great deal of weight to the question. There is some likelihood that the Zechak will make a different decision this time, but it is not a large one. I fought in the Second Zechak War, esteemed Councilors, and I tell you honestly that I believe the most likely outcome is that the Zechak will turn on you. It may take time—decades, perhaps—but it *will* happen."

Major Douglas nodded. "Can't disagree there. The odds weigh heavily against you, especially once they have what they want."

"But *you* could turn on us once you have what *you* want," mar'Shen snapped. "Ally with the Zechak, and at least we'll still have the means to protect ourselves from *them*."

Please tell me we're not going over this again. But of course we were. mar'Shen and mar'Odrea didn't want this alliance; of course they would fight it tooth and nail, even if it meant chasing their own tails.

"I confess, Councilor mar'Shen," spoke a new voice, soft but carrying, "I'm no longer certain of that."

This time, I was able to recall this Council member from my memory. Hard to forget her, striking as she was. Her eyes blazed a startling amethyst, a color one would never see naturally in a human. They stood out against the nearly copper-brown of her skin. Even her hair seemed like it shouldn't be natural, the color a red so deep and rich it reflected like the depths of a ruby. Councilor Kinima Mal.

I inhaled, but no; the impression I got of cinnamon candy and the scent of cloves was purely synesthetic.

"I beg your pardon?" mar'Shen said, his tail drooping straight towards the floor. Now *that* was an interesting bit of body language.

"Military and history experts are telling us that our chances of even surviving as a species will decrease enormously if we ally with these Zechak," Councilor Mal said. "It seems to me it would be unwise to assume we can defend ourselves after all we've heard."

"They say this because they *want* something from us."

A smile, a curve of the lips so predatory in nature that something in my primordial hindbrain wanted to run screaming, bloomed on Mal's face. "Let's not fool ourselves. We *all* want something out of this. What *I* want is to survive to a ripe old age and sit around in a chair, griping at my grandchildren while they try to corral however many screaming sprogs they decide to pop out. So I say again, fellow Councilors, I am *not* convinced we could protect ourselves from the Zechak even with our weapons."

A stunned silence met her blunt words, though I did notice a few soft, muffled coughing sounds here and there that sounded suspiciously like stifled laughs. One of which, admittedly, came from my own throat. *I like her.* Perhaps now we could move on from this ridiculous circles we'd been treading in all morning.

In an effort to regain control, Nish mar'Odrea cleared his throat and stood. "Nonetheless, Councilor Mal, I believe Councilor mar'Shen's question to be a valid one. We are not a weak people. Surely we can defend ourselves!"

A chorus of agreement rose up from roughly half the Council, which brought on a wave of arguments that didn't settle until Secretary Shinda rose and whipped his tail across the tabletop.

I had the sinking feeling that I'd better get used to treading in circles.

Head throbbing so viciously I could barely see straight, I followed my team out of the meeting room for the second—and thankfully, last—time that day.

By all rights, this shouldn't be so difficult. There seemed to be a roughly even split between those Council members who wanted the Alliance and those who didn't. In order to get the treaty signed, we needed thirty of the forty-three to agree to it, and two-thirds of that number were already leaning in that direction. But if we kept treading over the same topics like this, we'd never get anywhere.

I took a deep breath and blinked a few times, trying to get my head on straight—or as straight as I could get it. *I need to talk to... ah!* Peering over my shoulder, I spied Marco leaving the meeting room, talking with Major Douglas. Marco's demeanor sometimes made me forget he was an office guy, but you could really see it in the lightness of his complexion, as compared to the major's old-boot-leather visage.

I paused in the hallway, waiting for the two of them to reach me. Major Douglas gave me a look I couldn't discern—though if I had to guess, there was disapproval in there somewhere—and Marco smiled, laying a hand on my shoulder.

"You held up well in there," he said. "Better than some of our diplomats, even."

"Not to mention some of our soldiers," Major Douglas added, though his expression grew no more friendly. "Give me a gun and a field full of Zechak any day over that nonsense."

"Get used to 'that nonsense,' Major. We're in for a lot of it."

Ugh. Do not think too hard about that right now, I instructed myself. Out loud, I said, "Marco, could I have a moment of your time, please?"

"Of course. Major, we'll talk in a little bit, yes?"

The major patted Marco on the shoulder and smiled. "Absolutely. Get yourself some grub and a bit of free time first, Antilles. You've earned it."

The major strolled away, catching up with Captain Chui. *Oh, she'll* love *that.* I bit back a smile and began to walk beside Marco as we proceeded down the hall. The others were at least some distance ahead of us, which suited me fine. It seemed better to discuss this solely with Marco first, before bringing the idea up to anyone else.

"You really get along with everyone, don't you?" I said. I had to stop myself from gaping in surprise. *Did I just make small talk without having to force it? Whoa.* Small talk was one of those things non-autistic people did that I never could quite seem to wrap my mind around.

"Perhaps not *everyone*," Marco replied. "In some cases—like mar'Odrea and his people—it's more like they tolerate me more than other people." He looked at me, his expression amused and exasperated, and I felt that natural—but rare—urge to return the sentiment. "But I'd be a pretty lousy diplomat if I couldn't get along with others."

"Which kind of begs the question why *I'm* here," I muttered.

"To help me solve this in the way only *you* can."

Which reminded me, I had to go back over more footage. I wanted to see if I could find more examples of tail-twitching and, in particular, that sudden droop I'd seen from mar'Shen. I raised my arm and pressed my finger to a small pad on my wristlet. Later this evening it would chime, reminding me I had work planned. Though I rarely needed the reminder.

"Well... I *did* have a thought about that," I admitted. "We talked about the Zechak's previous allies today but... the Anmerilli don't seem to understand just how bad those situations were. Haven't they seen any of the footage or—"

Marco shook his head, his expression grim. "They refuse. The Anmerilli...as you've already noticed yourself, they are prone to cognitive dissonance. They don't care to view violent spectacles."

I stared. "They hunt for sport. Viciously, if what I've read is true."

"And some people can dissect corpses without batting an eyelash but get queasy trying to clean their pet cat's litter pan. That's just how people are."

"But—"

"All this reminds me, though...I've heard some whispers that the Council would like to hold a hunt. Perhaps not this week, but the next one."

I froze, as suddenly and effectively as if my feet had become glued to the floor. We stood at a corner, just before the turn in the hallway, in a spot not easily reached by the wind. And here I was, desperately wishing for a breeze right now, something to cool skin that felt as if it were on fire. I turned my head to look at Marco, but couldn't bring my eyes to focus; they stared through him, unseeing.

"Hunt? They don't expect *me* to hunt, do they?"

"It's a—a cultural event, I guess you could say," Marco explained. "To welcome their new guests."

"I—I can't." Hard to say which shook harder, my voice or my hands. "Marco, I *can't.*"

"Whoa, hey." Hands came down on my shoulders, steadying me. "Easy there. Easy. Try to breathe."

"I *can't,*" I wheezed.

"It's all right, Xandri," Marco murmured. "Look—hey, look. I'll talk to them, do my damnedest to talk them out of it, all right? None of your people have ridden carouas before, so the Anmerilli might just decide a hunt with a bunch of greenies doesn't sound like fun. I'll do everything I can to convince them, okay?"

The words sank in slowly. As my breathing began to ease, I found myself wondering what a caroua was—typical inappropriate thought. With trepidation, I raised my gaze, fearing what Marco would think of me for freaking out like that. But he only gazed at me, his eyes dark, soft, a little hard to read, but that was the norm for me. I took a deep breath and let it out; it only shook a little.

146

"Thanks," I murmured.

"Hey, no problem. I'm not exactly the greatest caroua rider, myself. Maybe if I complain about it enough, they'll cancel it just to get me to shut up."

He smiled and I let out a small laugh.

"I'll suggest another activity for such a welcome," he said, nudging me gently forward. "Something that won't have the less experienced among us moaning about saddle soreness for days."

"Thanks," I repeated. "I appreciate it."

"And so will my rear end, believe me. Ah...looks like your watchdogs are on their way." He gestured to the end of the hall; Katya and Anton were making their way towards us. "I'll see you at dinner, yeah?"

I nodded. He gave me a last pat on the shoulder. I gritted my teeth; at this point I was overloaded to the point where my nerves felt like they were on fire, but he had no way to know that. I let it go, turning to watch him leave—and frowned when I noticed Christa leaning on the wall nearby. Marco only waved to her, seeming unperturbed by her presence, but a prickle of suspicion crept up my throat.

"Were you listening in on us?" I demanded, glancing down the hallway to see how long I had before Anton and Katya reached me.

Christa's pale skin went rather pink. "There's no rule against standing in the hall."

Wow. Even *I* didn't miss cues that blatant. I folded my arms and glowered at her.

"I might have heard a word or two," she confessed, looking away. "But...look, I'm sorry, but there's something about that man I don't trust."

"What man?"

"Antilles."

"Marco?" I snorted. "Come on, Christa. He's been a member of the AFC for ages and he's one of their most valuable diplomats. I hardly think they'd send someone untrustworthy on this mission."

"I know that! It's just—I don't know, something seems off to me."

"What, is it that intolerable to you that someone respects my opinion and thinks I can handle this job?" I hardly cared how I sounded as the words tumbled out; I was too tired to care.

Christa jerked back. "Well, it certainly doesn't speak well of his judgment!"

"Oh, for fuck's sake, Christa. I'm not in the mood for this! I've had a long day and I don't need you sniping at me because you can't get over that I got this job and you didn't."

"Fine! Fine, don't listen to me. It's on your own goddamn head."

She stormed away down the hall. I dropped my face into my hands and groaned. This was like high school in an Ancient Earth vid. *Why me? Don't I have enough on my plate already? How am I going to get this done if my own second won't cooperate with me?*

The clomp of military-grade boots on the floor alerted me to Anton and Katya. I braced myself; sure enough, Anton slapped a big palm across my shoulder.

"You okay, kiddo?"

"Oh, fine," I said. "Just having my regularly scheduled argument with my second, that's all."

"What, Christa?" That came from Katya, who was, thankfully, less hands-on than her partner. "She's just being sour. Ignore her."

"Yeah, forget about her for now. Why don't we take you back to your room, let you relax a bit before dinner?"

"Sounds good," I said. "Sweet Mother Universe, it's good to be around someone other than politicians for a little while."

"Better you than us," Katya said. She fell into step beside me, her posture relaxed and calm; I knew she could have the gun off her back in a second.

"I don't know. Weapons seem to be the only thing the Anmerilli understand. Maybe we should just send Anton into the next meeting with his Gabe."

Anton, who'd been deprived of his Gabriel for this mission, looked at me with much the same expression one saw in the eyes of a hopeful puppy. Then he broke out in laughter, which Katya echoed in a quieter tone. I sighed, a sound of relief rather than annoyance. *Good to be around some plain-talkers for a bit.*

"No offense, Xan, but I'm not sure that'd be such a great idea. Mulroney'd probably just scare 'em."

"Me? Nonsense! Got my momma's smile and my old man's charm."

"And our galley chef's belly," Katya teased, reaching around me to poke Anton's stomach.

My bodyguards are flirting with each other. Should that be cute or gross? Ah well. As long as they were doing their jobs, I wouldn't be required to report them to Captain Chui, and no mistake, they *were* doing their jobs. Anton's hand never left the hilt of the knife at his belt, and though Katya glanced at him when she flirted, her gaze continued to rove, watching everything. And though they talked to each other, they left me to my silence.

Had anyone told me a few weeks ago that being followed all the time would be the easy part, I would've laughed in their faces. Guess the joke was on me.

Chapter Seventeen

Unfortunately, I was right about treading in circles. In fact, I felt less like we were having diplomatic discussions and more like we were stuck in orbit around a gas giant—and no one put out more hot air than Councilor mar'Odrea.

"One could argue that's what politics and diplomacy are," Captain Chui had said to me, after the second day of more of the same. "Competitive lying and professional fact dodging. We're dealing with people who want something, and have no problem ignoring or outright denying the truth in order to get it."

I was used to people—*especially* humans—pussyfooting around the truth and speaking in circles rather than straight up admitting what they wanted, but politicians turned it into an art form. They chose some of the oddest segues I'd ever heard; they loved the word "but" and seemed to insert it into as many sentences as they could; sometimes they didn't even acknowledge what another person had said before changing the topic. I wanted to scream "Just say what you mean!" at the topic of my lungs at least a dozen times per meeting.

Honestly, "polite society" was the most space-fried thing sometimes.

Though my team was always with me, Captain Chui switched out Diver and Kiri, bringing one to one meeting and the other to the next. This gave them both a chance to put their minds to the problem of hacking the Anmerilli systems, and meant neither of them had to sit through too much of the bullshit. Lucky them.

As Captain Chui's assistants, Diver's and Kiri's presence largely went unremarked, until the afternoon of the sixth day. I was trying, once again, to explain the conditions of Zechak slavery—wishing I could use the data stored on my wristlet to support my words. Councilor mar'Shen, who'd gotten us onto the topic with his usual claims that the Anmerilli could defend themselves from such actions, suddenly started staring at Kiri.

As my words faltered, mar'Shen said, "And what do *you* think of all this?"

Kiri peered back at him without batting an eyelash. "Pardon? Were you addressing me?"

"Well, of course. I *have* studied a bit about humanity, you know. I know the atrocities humans tried to hide in their early days in the Alliance—such as what they did to your people. Don't you find all this carrying on about slavery to be a bit hypocritical?"

Kiri's dark eyes narrowed. *Uh oh.* I glanced at Captain Chui to see if she would intervene, but she merely watched Councilor mar'Shen, her eyes hard and her jaw firm. I leaned back in my chair, glad to let someone else take the reins.

"Hypocritical, is it?" Kiri tilted her head in that same pensive, studying way my birds sometimes did. "Now, Councilor, let's say that we're not talking about something that happened nearly four thousand years ago—so long ago that I can't even fathom it—and are in fact talking about something rather recent.

"Since it would be *my people*," and here the disdain in her voice was clear, "at risk, I'd have to say I'd *prefer* an anti-slavery attitude. Wouldn't you? Sweet Mother Universe, why would I ever want any part of humanity to approve of slavery, under those circumstances?"

"I didn't say 'approve,'" mar'Shen protested, his tail drooping for the floor in what I now knew to be dismay.

"Didn't you? What you said was that, because humanity has kept slaves in the past, it is now hypocritical for humans to disapprove of it. If they're not allowed to disapprove, they would by default have to approve." The odd mixture of sweetness and chill in Kiri's tone made me think of flavored ice. "Part of being a sapient being is evolving to be a better person. Unquestionably, humanity has had its horrendous missteps there and is still far from perfect, but we do *try* to avoid turning sapients into chattel. Are Ancient Earth humans and the Zechak really the kind of uncivilized shit-slinging *barga* rodents you want to model yourselves on?"

"N-no, of course not!" mar'Shen stammered.

"Good. Issue solved. Let's move on." Kiri smiled. "And Councilors, as I am here in an assisting capacity and not a diplomatic one, I'll thank you to leave me out of this. The color of my skin is not a tool for your political maneuvering and childish backbiting."

151

mar'Shen sank back into his chair. Around the table there were a few murmurs of approval or stifled snickers from those Anmerilli not on the side of mar'Odrea and his followers. Kiri glanced around the entire table, her mouth a straight, firm line, her eyes daring them, any one of them, to try that again. I had a feeling no one would. Hiding a grin, I opened a private comm channel to Kiri.

"*You're amazing.*"

"*I am* no one's *tool,*" she retorted.

"*I fail to see how that's supposed to make you less amazing.*"

She turned her head slightly towards me, a hint of smile touching the corners of her mouth. "*Maybe you're just not like other people.*"

"*Yep. Says so right on my brain scan.*"

She had to turn away, press a hand over her mouth. From the corner of my eye I caught her shoulders shaking with suppressed laughter. *Huh. Wonder what I said.* I closed the comm channel and focused instead on the meeting. I could sort out what I'd said later—or at least, I could try. My brain might be too tired from trying to sort out the diplomatic knots to make sense of much of anything.

"You seem to put an awful lot of weight on the idea of not allowing anyone to turn people into chattel," mar'Odrea said, as smoothly as if the interlude hadn't happened.

Oh fuck.

"Yet, you're awfully determined that we change our ways for you. What is it, if not slavery, that you get to tell us which of our traditions are acceptable and which are not?"

I took a deep breath and prepared to explain, not for the first time, that this was not about *acceptable* or *not acceptable.* That this was about ecosystems, about their fragility, about how damaging them too much could lead to the end of a sapient species—that it almost had for humans. That part of protecting a planet, for the Alliance, was protecting the *whole* planet, not just the life forms that could talk and build cities. Most importantly, I prepared myself for mar'Odrea to try to tie me in knots with his arguments while everyone stared at me.

If I made it off this planet without tearing out my hair and peeling off my own skin—or someone else's—it would be a miracle.

152

The first week of negotiations—if you could call them that—passed, and it seemed I wouldn't have to go on a hunt after all. Which meant I could look forward to a couple of days of peace.

And I intended to do just that. The morning of the first Anmerilli weekend—they had three-day weekends, god bless 'em—found me sprawled on my bed, one arm pressed against my eyelids. My wristlet was open only to private access and my balcony doors were thrown open, allowing in air and the occasional murmur of someone walking outside. I knew I ought to continue my studying, but the long week had left me rattled, overstimulated, and in desperate need of hiding.

Naturally, someone knocked on my door.

I held down a groan and called, "Who is it?"

"Marla. Got a message for you, boss."

Nothing for it, then. I slid my legs off the side of the bed, letting the weight help pull me upright, and rose to answer the door. Marla stood waiting, exchanging a few words with Katya. She grinned when she saw me—but then, Marla grinned at just about everyone. If there was a friendlier person in the universe, I hadn't met them.

"I thought I said not to call me boss," I said. A second later, realizing how that sounded, I added, "Um, hi."

"Since when do we listen?"

"If I'm the boss—" I started, then shook my head. "Never mind. You mentioned a message?"

"Yep. Encountered Noaya Maru while I was out. She asked me tell you she'd like to talk to you, out in the gardens," Marla replied.

And so much for my Me time. I had to go. Whether I liked it or not, I counted as a diplomat on this mission, and persuading Councilors like Noaya Maru to my cause was the most important thing I could do here. It didn't stop me from wishing I'd never agreed to this. I didn't feel cut out for it, not in the least.

"I could go for you," Marla offered. "Let her know you're not feeling well, see if I can't talk her around myself."

I forced a smile and hoped it came off at least a little genuine. It wasn't that I wasn't grateful; it was just the usual issue that smiles, genuine ones, came with difficulty. Marla might not quite *understand* things like my sensory issues, but she always took them at face value anyway.

"Thanks," I said, "but it's best if I go. It's my job, after all. And what kind of boss would I be if I exposed you to more of this political shit?"

"A way crappier one than I've known you to be," Marla said with another grin. "Thanks, boss."

"Don't call me—oh, forget it."

"Indeed, I will. You in for the game later, Kat?"

Katya snorted. "Captain'd have my hide. But when we get back onboard the ship, you're all toast."

Marla laughed and took off down the hall. I turned, ducking back into the room to grab my boots, and to change to a top with shorter sleeves, ones I could push out of my way easily. If Councilor Maru wanted to do any gardening—and she might, knowing her—I didn't want to get my sleeves dirty. By the time I returned to the hall, Anton was standing near my door with Katya. I blinked at them, then glanced at my wristlet.

"It's not time for shift change."

"Nope," Anton said, smothering a yawn. "Captain wants us both with you when you go outside, so here I am."

"Bet you love that."

"Hey, the view ain't too shabby, so I'm not one to complain," he said, with a wink at Katya. He didn't quite manage to look as non-cheesy as Diver, but there was a certain charm about it nonetheless.

"Keep your eyes to yourself, Mulroney," Katya said, "unless I tell you otherwise."

"Ah, see, I know you're trying to scare me off, but I love a woman who'll put me in my place."

"Fantastic. I'll get the rope and the—"

"*Ok*ay," I said loudly, slapping my hands over my ears, "I've officially heard enough."

Their laughter reverberated off the walls as we strode down the hall. Dropping my hands, I glowered at the backs of their heads. Katya gave Anton a flirty, lash-batting look, then glanced back at me, grinning.

"You need to be less easy to tease," she told me.

No kidding. Tell me something I don't know. I sighed. For all they liked messing with my head, I could've had it much worse than Katya and Anton. Though I couldn't help wishing Katya would refrain from staring at Anton's butt, then giving me a thumbs-up sign

154

behind his back. Because I couldn't tell whether I should scream or laugh, and the sound that came out of my throat was, awkwardly, somewhere in between.

I had to admit, it would've been a shame to miss a day like this. Cochinga was one of those planets with a blue sky, and today it was so blue, so vibrant that it almost hurt to look at it. A few wisps of clouds drifted by, blurring with motion, looking like great birds soaring across the sky. The air held the coolness and tang of the ocean, pleasant as always against my face, teasing the hair on the back of my neck.

Crunching seashell paths wound in spirals through the garden, carrying us through spiky Cochingan flora. We passed the largest fountain yet, another Moebius band; adding to my suspicion that the Anmerilli had a thing for the shape because its flowing nature was so opposite that of their pointy-ended planet. *If so,* I mused, running my fingertips over a large, pointed leaf, *then maybe there's also more beneath their stoic shells than they let on.* I knew all about there being more beneath the surface than others were allowed to see.

"Isn't that her?" Katya asked, gesturing towards a figure crouched on the edge of the path, a short distance away.

Certainly looked like her, though instead of formal robes, she wore plain trousers and a tunic-like top with the long, wide sleeves pinned back. A short distance away, partially hidden behind the fronds of a squat palm, was an Anmerilli soldier; I wasn't the only one who'd brought guards. I gestured for Katya and Anton to take up position not too far away and approached the Councilor.

"Ah, good," she said, without looking up from the weeds she was pulling. "You came."

"Of course, Councilor Maru," I said. "You asked to speak to me." On a whim, I added, "And it gives me an excuse to see the gardens at last."

She looked up then, a slight smile forcing her cheek ridges upwards. "Please, call me Noaya when we're not in the meeting hall. Too much formality makes my teeth ache."

"Then we have that in common, Coun—Noaya. I'd appreciate

it, then, if you called me Xandri."

Curious, I crouched on the path to watch her. Even when she talked, her long, slender hands didn't stop their work. Without bothering with tools, she dug her fingers deep into the loamy earth, wedging them beneath the roots of the weeds and yanking upwards. She set each weed aside with a little sigh, a sound that might have been exasperation or even sorrow. I watched in silence, my mind full of questions.

"You might as well ask," she said, as if she knew. "I could use some candor."

I supposed after the week of meetings, candor *would* sound nice to some. "I guess I didn't expect to find someone of your—station out here, weeding."

"Ah. Well, I quite like weeding. It helps put things in perspective for me."

"I'm sorry... perspective?"

"Indeed. Young Xandri, there are few things I hate more than taking life. But weeds—weeds remind me that sometimes I must. Sometimes I must be brutal and swift in my dealings, for if I am not, so many will die, leaving only weeds to thrive."

I sat back on my heels. "And you don't compromise with weeds. You remove them, root and all, so they can't simply grow right back."

She turned her head to look at me again, and this time the smile on her face was broad, delighted, so much so that it reached her eyes.

"Very good. You may have little diplomatic acumen, but it's not for any lack of sharpness of mind."

Um... thanks? I picked up one of the weeds, lying limp on the path. For all I knew, from the Professor's lectures, that it was necessary to remove weeds, something about the small plant's state bothered me. *As a metaphor, I* do *understand what she means, but...* But something about this method didn't quite sit right with me. The effect I wanted to achieve with the Anmerilli was more like... like...

"What if such definitive action wasn't the best way of getting the results you wanted?" I asked. When Councilor Maru looked at me, a brow raised in question, I continued, picking each word with slow care, "What if weeding the garden isn't *actually* your goal?

156

In the ancient art of bonsai, the goal is to cultivate a tree into a particular shape, all while keeping it from ever growing as large as it otherwise would.

"This takes time, patience, and yes, compromise. There will be branches that need to be clipped off or stopped from growing all together, but if you do only as you please, if you force the tree too far into a shape unlike its natural one, it will be less healthy and successful. It's better to choose a shape that works *with* the natural form of the tree, so that in the end, even if it takes longer than you might like, what you have is a healthy, perfectly shaped tree, rather than something that's been damaged by too much brute force."

I blinked. I hadn't quite intended to make a small speech out of that; I'd just wanted to explain myself properly.

Councilor Maru studied me, her head tilted, her expression a trick to read. Thoughtfulness, it might be, based on the furrow of her brow and the line of her mouth. That she studied me so intently gave me an excuse to do the same, and though it was not the easiest task, looking her in the face, it didn't *hurt* like it did with mar'Odrea. Upon closer inspection, that Anmerilli reticence was not quite as closed at it first seemed.

"That is interesting," she said after a long moment. "I think I'd like to look up this *bonsai* you speak of, learn more about it."

Was that a sign that I'd succeeded in persuading her to consider a compromise? I had *no* idea. Maybe she meant it only literally. God, how I wished I could read people better.

"Well, if you enjoy gardening, I think it would interest you," I said. "Councilor—sorry, Noaya. Do you think *any* of your fellows will listen? I keep saying the same things over and over and I'm starting to think there's little point. But...do *you*?"

"There *are* those among us who hear your concerns and believe them. Whether *enough* of my brethren hear and believe—that I cannot be sure of. It is, no doubt, difficult to grow a bonsai in a garden full of weeds."

"Actually, you grow them in pots."

Oops. *Xandri, you niddle-head, we're talking in metaphors and you suddenly hit the switch to literal. What is* wrong *with you?* No, didn't have time for that pity party.

"Uh, sorry, sometimes I get a little..."

"Yes, I know," Councilor Maru said. "I read what I could about your disorder before you arrived."

Oh, fucking stellar.

"You know," she went on, rising and dusting earth from her hands, "I'd expected you to be...rather cold and distant. But you're not, quite. I don't know how to explain it."

I shrugged. A cold feeling swelled in my chest, cold and dark like the depths of space, such an out of place thing on such a beautiful day. Cold. I lacked empathy, feelings, that's what all the Ancient Earth information said. That's what my parents said, what my therapists said. I had never called for my mommy or daddy, didn't say words like "I love you" or seek out hugs, or to sit in laps. *You* can't *think about this now. You have a job to do and it won't wait for you to work through a meltdown.*

I shoved the darkness down, hiding it within my depths, wishing I could leave it there and never have it creep up on me again. I was never so lucky. For now, though, I crammed it down hard, and followed Noaya Maru as if nothing was wrong.

"I wish I had a bit longer to talk today," she said, paying her bodyguard—and mine—no mind at all. "I'm hoping that this time, at last, my people and yours can come to a solution, and to that end, I have a great many meetings today. But perhaps there will be other chances."

"I'll make sure of it," I assured her. "And if for some reason I'm not available, I'll make sure a member of my team is at your disposal."

"How very accommodating. More so than I've found your Alliance to be, I confess."

"Oh. Um...well, I can't really—all I can say is, that's how *I* operate. In fact," I added for good measure, "that's precisely why the Alliance brought me in."

Councilor Maru opened her mouth to respond, then froze at a signal from her bodyguard. I tensed and glanced back at Anton and Katya. Suddenly Maru caught my arm and pulled me with her as she ducked behind a tall, unusually wide-trunked palm. I heard Katya and Anton move behind me and signaled them to be still. Whatever had caught the Councilor's attention, I didn't think she intended to hurt me.

A moment later I noticed two figures coming down a nearby path, walking side by side and talking in low voices. For a few long moments my brain refused to acknowledge what my eyes were seeing. *That can't be right. It* can't *be.* To see Councilor Nish mar'Odrea walking the gardens was not so strange a thing, but that Christa walked beside him left me baffled. I hadn't assigned her that task.

I strained, but their words were too soft to reach my ears. I caught not even a whisper as they turned a bend and followed the spiraling of the path into a clump of green, out of my sight. *Damnit! What is she up to?*

"I did not know your people were so close to Councilor mar'-Odrea."

The steel in Maru's tone made me turn. She watched me, her face gone so very hard to read, but I thought perhaps I caught suspicion there. *Neither did I!* I wanted to wail, but it would hardly be a grown-up, professional thing to do. What would Marco say in this situation? Something appeasing and charming, no doubt. Appeasing I could manage; charming—ha ha, nice joke, universe.

"Well..." I began. "I wouldn't say—close. But as we're here in a diplomatic capacity, we must be willing to put ourselves at the disposal of all the World Council members, even those we might find—" I flicked my gaze in the direction Christa and mar'Odrea had disappeared in. "—less than palatable."

"*Nice save, kiddo,*" came Anton's voice through my private comm channel.

"And do you find Councilor mar'Odrea less than palatable?" Maru wanted to know.

Was she kidding? I viewed Councilor mar'Odrea much as I viewed the implant-filter rinse. It was utterly vile, a substance which, if I had my way, would be banned under Alliance regulations; I still had no choice but to swallow it if I wanted to continue doing my job. As it was unlikely Noaya Maru had ever been off-planet before—certainly not in any capacity that required a filter-implant—I didn't think she'd get the analogy.

Instead, I said, "My personal feelings about the Councilor are—a moot point. But I confess I feel it would be...unwise to trust him."

"Then you have, at least, been paying attention," Maru said. I saw no change in her stern countenance, though. "I must take my leave now, young Xandri. I thank you for the talk."

She bowed. As she was on her feet now, no longer distracted by the task before her, I bowed in turn. We both straightened and she turned to go, her bodyguard not far ahead of her on the path.

"Councilor," I called.

She peered over her shoulder. "Yes?"

"The *Carpathia* has files on the art of bonsai. If you'd like I can have them sent to you for further study."

She inclined her head. "I would be grateful. Send them through Secretary Shinda."

I nodded. I figured she'd take her leave then, but she stood still on the path, a tableau of careful thought. Anton and Katya shifted impatiently behind me, but I waited, forcing myself to a stillness that matched Maru's. At last she tilted her head, the motion rather bird-like, and her expression changed, still difficult to read, still grim, but in a different way.

"In the territory of Nish mar'Odrea there exist several species of fauna extinct in all other regions of Cochinga," she said at last. "People all around the world pay exorbitant prices for the chance to hunt these animals. That is not a branch mar'Odrea will ever be willing to prune."

Why was I not surprised?

Chapter Eighteen

"I wouldn't worry too much about it. I know you and Christa don't get along, but my impression is that she cares about this mission."

I bit my lip. Meetings started again tomorrow and this was the first chance I'd gotten to get a hold of Marco, to explain what I'd seen in the gardens. Normally we talked every night after the meetings, but he'd been busy all weekend, talking to Councilors and working with his fellow AFC members, both diplomats and soldiers.

Most of the time we met on my balcony—he continued to keep that secret for me—but tonight we walked the corridors. He'd been sitting down too much, Marco had informed me, and needed to stretch his legs. *He does seem a bit restless,* I admitted to myself, studying him from the corner of my eye. He kept a fairly brisk pace, and every now and then as he walked, he stretched or shook his hands, as if walking was simply not enough movement. *Poor guy. Being stuck on your ass all day sucks.*

"Besides, she's seen the way mar'Odrea treats you," Marco went on. "I'm sure she's just trying to see if she can charm him a little, get him to loosen up."

I wondered if I should tell Marco about Christa spying on us, about her saying she didn't trust him. Would he think so positively of her then? *But Marco's been a diplomat for years. He's a much better judge of people than I am.* And if I was being honest with myself—in that brutal way that I really hated doing—I *did* have a bias here.

"I guess so," I said at last. "I just wish she'd cleared it with me first. Councilor Maru was a little put out, seeing them together; it would've been nice to be prepared for it."

"I'm sure Christa meant well. I know there's been a lot of friction between you, and..." He hesitated. Coming a halt midway down the hall, Marco put a hand on my shoulder. His toes continued to shift and shuffle as he stood. "Please don't take this the wrong way, Xandri, because I mean no ill by it. The fact is—it's hard to miss the way people treat you sometimes. They look right past you

161

to Christa, dismissing you out of hand, and it's pretty clear that mar'Odrea is one of those people who've already dismissed you."

Ouch. Accurate, but ouch.

"That's not an easy thing to point out to *anyone*. And you *do* allow your team a fair bit of autonomy; she might've thought it was better to simply act, rather than risk a fight."

"That sounds reasonable," I said, even though I wasn't sure I *felt* like it was.

After all, if she didn't want to risk a fight, she shouldn't have been eavesdropping on me. *That* was the part that stuck in my craw. Maybe Marco was right about Christa's motivations, but I'd damn well be keeping an eye on her, just in case.

"Good, that's settled then. Now," Marco said, beginning to walk again, "tell me about the rest of your meeting with Maru."

I outlined our conversation, trying not to babble—though our long walk through the corridors would have allowed for it. Marco smiled as I explained my bonsai metaphor, but otherwise let me speak without interruption.

"Interesting," he said when I'd finished. "So you think Maru might be willing to compromise after all?"

I tilted my head, considering. We passed through a lobby, where the clerestory windows let in moonlight and ocean air, and the fountain—yet another Moebius—sprayed a few droplets of water around in the breeze. I held out my hand, letting my fingertips drift through the water, finding the sensation of liquid dragging around my fingers rather comforting. Almost as nice as running them along cool satin.

"I think it's not beyond our reach, at least," I said. "I—I know the Alliance wants this to go a certain way, but I think compromise may be the only solution we can reach."

"Xandri, this is not a planet full of peaceful whale and squid symbiotes with pearls to trade. The Anmerilli are a strong, firm-willed people who will not hesitate to use violence if they must."

"The Psittacans aren't the most pacifistic people in the universe either, but I came to an accord with them. Marco, I really think we can do this." And I even managed not to point out that the Voices and Hands were not, in actuality, whales or squid.

"All right," Marco said. "What's your plan?"

"Well... this might sound odd, but—I think we should keep doing what we're doing. *Let* the Anmerilli argue in circles. We'll keep using our same arguments, but not to convince them, just to keep them going, keep them talking. People—people have a tendency to reveal the truth of themselves with their words, if you listen long and close enough." I looked away, afraid it would be written all over my face how hard won a lesson that had been for me.

"Yes, they do," Marco said softly. When I glanced at him, he was looking straight ahead, thoughtful. "So we let them talk it out, in the hopes that it'll reveal to us hints at where and what they'd be willing to compromise on."

I nodded.

"It could work. It'll take a fair bit of notes and study, but—"

His words cut off suddenly and he flung out an arm, almost protectively, forcing me to a halt. I blinked, glanced at his face, then down the hallway where he was gazing. *Oh shit.* Coming towards us, dressed as usual in robes much more formal than the moment called for, was Nish mar'Odrea. He wore his usual stormy, disapproving expression, and though I wished hard that he would simply pass us by, he made a beeline right for us.

"Mr. Antilles," he said as he reached us, sounding *almost* cheerful. Then he looked at me and his tone came out decidedly sour as he added, "Ms. Corelel."

Happy to see me? Perish the thought.

"Good evening, Councilor mar'Odrea," Marco said. "My apologies, but I was just escorting Ms. Corelel back to her room."

"Why, Ms. Corelel, they let you out without your guard dogs?"

I rested a hand on the grip of one of my pistols and smiled. "Not precisely."

Marco coughed, clearing his throat. "Right, yes, well. I'm afraid we can't stay—"

"Oh, I won't keep you. I just wanted to let you know that we're all set for the weekend."

"Sir?"

"The hunt, my good fellow," mar'Odrea explained, cheerful again. "It's all arranged. Finally you'll get a real taste of Anmerilli culture, Ms. Corelel."

Hunt? I struggled to keep the panic from showing on my face, but I doubted I succeeded. All that Ancient Earth nonsense about

163

autistics having no facial expression? Feh. If *only* it were true. I had plenty, and they all seemed to crop up at *exactly* the times I didn't want them to. Like now, when my inability to properly regulate my face could lead to a diplomatic incident. Again.

Marco approached mar'Odrea with a smile, caught his shoulder and turned him away, talking to him quietly.

"Oh, come on, Marco," mar'Odrea said loudly, patting Marco's shoulder. "Don't be a spoilsport. You're a fine caroua rider, and ours guests really ought to try it. I'm sure once Ms. Corelel gets a taste of it, she'll quite enjoy it."

Me? Enjoy hunting? Oh yeah, that'll happen. When hippos fly. In heavy-grav. mar'Odrea turned to look at me, and for one terrifying moment I thought I'd said that out loud. But he only smiled—if you could call a rather evil-looking grimace a smile—and patted Marco on the shoulder again.

"Now, I bid you two a good evening. I have my own business to be about," he said.

"Oh, uh...yes sir, Councilor," Marco stammered, rather unlike his usual smooth self. "I look forward to it."

I don't.

I stood still, trying to breathe, as mar'Odrea strolled away.

"Easy," Marco murmured. "It won't be until next weekend. I'll see if I can get the plans changed before then."

"You think that'll work?"

A beat, then, "Probably not," he admitted, "but I will damn well try. I promise."

I sighed. "Thanks, Marco."

"Hey, no thanks necessary. I told you, we're in this together. You need me for anything and I'm there in a heartbeat."

I looked up at him in surprise. He gazed down at me, his eyes warm with concern. *I can make it through this. I have support. I can do it.* Right now, though, I needed to get back to my room, before my shaking got worse. I stuck a hand in the pocket of my cargo pants and rubbed my fingers anxiously across the satin lining. *I can do this...*

On the bright side, the week left me little time to think much about the hunt. I made sure my team was prepared for our new tactic, and recruited Kimi as a third note-taker, so we would be certain to get every detail. I set Kirrick and Marla to sorting notes by Council member so I could look over what each one had said, when I had time and space to really study the words. As the days wore on, I began to notice a pattern.

Only a handful of Councilors seemed to *really* be against the protection of wildlife, mainly those like mar'Odrea, who stood to lose money. Others were more indifferent, though perhaps only because they didn't fully understand what it entailed. That, I hoped, would reveal itself to me more clearly as time went on.

Strangely, I thought they might be more willing to compromise on their weapons. The question was, could I get the *Alliance* to compromise on the weapons? The Sanavila had put the weapons regulations into place long before humanity had joined, and they had never budged on it, to my knowledge.

So I tolerated another week of circular arguments for the sake of my plan, and in the moments when I did think about the hunt, I mostly plotted the best ways to work around it. If I stayed at the back of the pack I shouldn't end up having to kill anything. And really, considering I'd never ridden a caroua before, it would be easy enough to excuse my lack of participation by admitting—with sheepishness that I practiced at night in front of a mirror—that I'd been too busy hanging on for dear life.

As plans went, it wasn't perfect, but at least I *had* one.

"I'm sorry, I really am. I couldn't convince them to change the event and... I just couldn't find a way out for you. Not without offending a great deal of people."

Spiky grass-like turf crunched under my boots as I walked with Marco into the clearing behind the caroua stable. That day the brisk ocean breeze had forced me to break out a lightweight jacket and I huddled within the soft material, trying not to be sick. My pistols banged lightly against my thighs as I walked, a constant reminder of why I was out here, approaching the milling crowds of Anmerilli and their human guests. *Just remember your plan,* I reminded myself.

Stay towards the back of the crowd and you won't have to kill anything.

"Xandri?"

I blinked, glanced up at Marco. "Sorry. My um, my mind wandered a bit." I took a deep breath. "Look, it's not your fault, Marco. You did what you could. I'll—I'll get through it."

"You're a brave woman, Xandri." Marco touched my shoulder gently. "The Alliance doesn't appreciate you nearly as much as they should."

"No... I'm not, really. Not brave."

"No? Then why not pretend you were sick or injured so you wouldn't have to go through with this? Sounds like bravery to me."

Oh. I looked away. Let Marco take that how he wanted to, but it wasn't modesty that made me turned my eyes down. *Xandri, you utter niddle-brain! Why didn't you think of that?* Damnit, I could've gotten out of this after all, if I'd just thought to be a bit underhanded about it.

"Look, I've got to go find Major Douglas and Secretary Shinda," Marco said. "We're in charge of keeping everything organized. Just hang in there and try to have a bit of fun, yeah? You're getting to meet a new animal, after all."

I brightened a little at the prospect of the caroua ride. *I wonder where they are,* I thought as Marco walked away, heading for the small crowd containing Major Douglas, Secretary Shinda and a few others, including Captain Chui. I turned slowly, my gaze sweeping the crowded clearing and the palm and fern forest beyond. A jolt of surprise went through me as I caught sight of Councilor Maru, standing with Olish Tari, of course, but also with Anashi Sendil and Kalemi Ashil.

I approached and bowed a general bow of greeting. All four returned the gesture, their movements more fluid and graceful than mine.

"Greetings, Councilors," I said. *Small talk, small talk,* I reminded myself. *Make with the pleasantries.* "Um, lovely day for a—for a hunt, isn't it?"

"It *is* a lovely day," Maru agreed, with no inflection in her voice that *I* could make out. "But as you may have already guessed, Ms. Corelel, I do not hunt."

"Oh, um, y-yes, that makes..."

166

"And neither," Ashil added, watching me with hard eyes, "do *we.*"

My heart plummeted towards my feet like it was suddenly subjected to heavy-grav. I should've seen it sooner; *would have* if I hadn't been so caught up in my own fears.

The other Anmerilli wore trousers, wide-legged but still suited to riding, and much shorter tunics than usual, with voluminous sleeves that were cuffed tightly at the wrists. Some wore variations on these garments, but all were dressed more suited to a hunt than a day in diplomatic discourse. But Maru, Tari, Ashil and Sendil wore their usual robes. *I don't understand. Does this mean Ashil and Sendil are part of the animal rights movement, too?*

If that was the case then...fuck. Fuck, this looked bad. I'd made such progress with them, especially Maru, and now—now I looked like someone who didn't care for their cause. That wasn't fair. It wasn't as if *I* had had a choice in the matter.

"I hope you enjoy yourself, Ms. Corelel," Maru said, her voice fair dripping with spite. "The hunt is quite a spectacle..."

"I—"

"Good day, Ms. Corelel," Sendil added. "We have other business to attend to."

Words of protest crowded on my tongue as they turned, their robes sweeping about them. They scattered, going to talk to some of their fellows before the hunt, I guessed. *Why? I'm trying so hard to get things right and* this *happens?* I stood there, at a loss for what to do. I needed to fix this. If only they had given me a chance to explain, to point out that I couldn't simply refuse to participate no matter how distasteful I found the idea of hunting. How would I ever—

"Hey, Xan." Diver's voice, some distance behind me, a welcome balm for my distress. "Don't you want to meet your caroua?"

I spun, and for the moment all worries fled. Oh. *Oh.* Diver stood there, holding a pair of carouas by the reins, and I couldn't take my eyes off them.

In a sense, they looked like perytons from Ancient Earth myth; in truth, they looked *nothing* like perytons. Certainly, they had deer-like heads, though rather than a rack of antlers they bore an array of spiky horns between their ears, with smaller ones creeping down the slender dish of their faces. Their bodies were set like those of ratites, though their hindquarters were muscular in the way of deer, and they were balanced just so, supporting themselves atop two slender, hoofed legs. At the fetlock behind their delicate cloven hooves were a pair of spikes, similar to the vestigial toes seen on deer; as they stood there, they rested back on them for extra balance. Folded up, their gliders resembled wings, though of course the carouas were covered in fur, not feathers.

I approached cautiously, holding a hand out to the caroua on Diver's left. It dipped its head, snuffling at my hand. Breathing out in delight, I stroked my fingertips along its velvety muzzle.

"Oh, you great, beautiful creature," I crooned.

"Beautiful ain't quite the word I'd use," Diver said. "More like bizarre."

" 'There is no excellent beauty that hath not some strangeness in the proportion,' " murmured another voiced, sounding like it was quoting.

I looked up, beaming. "Hi, Kiri! You're coming with us too?"

"No way, starshine," she said, shaking her head and making her beads chime. "The only thing I care to ride is a starship or the two of you. Unless either of those are an option, my feet are staying on the ground."

It took a moment for her words to sink in. As they did, I started to turn red. Focusing intently on the caroua, I studied the bridle on its face. Stitched into the side was the word "Kiluan" which I took to be its name—especially since the other caroua had a different word stitched on its bridle.

"Why Xan, I do believe we've been propositioned," Diver said.

I didn't know a human being could turn as red as I was. Something very like desire heated in my belly. I breathed in deep, visualizing the ice I kept around my heart, and let it spread through my body until I had calmed. *No. Whatever else you do, Xandri, keep your distance.*

"Stop teasing her," Kiri chided. "What are you doing out here, anyway? Captain said we didn't have to go, not being considered actual diplomats here."

"Read a bit about these creatures. Heard they got some amazing ability to move on all sorts of terrain and I wanted to experience it for myself. The horse ain't so good for some of the planets we land on."

"It's true," I said, slipping back into the conversation now that it had taken a turn into a place that didn't leave me looking like a sunburned tomato. I scratched Kiluan's head as I talked, until the caroua lowered it and rubbed its muzzle vigorously against my palms. "Though I haven't read as much as I'd like. Computer," this I directed at my wristlet, "pull up the caroua's fossil record and information profile for me, please."

Within seconds the holo-display had popped up, divided into numerous thumbnails and one larger image representing the caroua itself. Leaning into Kiluan's muscular neck, I browsed the thumbnails first. The Anmerilli had a pretty complete fossil record for the caroua, similar to the record for the Ancient Earth horse. I pressed my fingertip to one, drawing out an image of a tiny creature—no more than thirty centimeters in height—that looked something like an arboreal, gliding dik dik. Fascinating.

Changing to the one on the caroua itself, I said, "It *does* describe it as being quite agile in many terrains. It can no longer glide, but it can make leaps of four-and-half meters easy, and up to roughly fourteen, fifteen meters. That's damn impressive, boy. Girl?" I bent, peering under Kiluan's belly, then straightened. "Boy. Oh, and some of their smaller cousins *can* still glide, how amazing is—"

"Xandri," Diver cut me off, his tone desert dry, "since everyone else appears to be mounting up, perhaps you should hit the off switch for now?"

"Oh. Right."

I didn't know if he meant my wristlet or my mouth—maybe both, hard to tell with him grinning at me. I powered my wristlet down and when I glanced up again, Diver stood next to me, his hands cupped to give me a leg up. Still a bit warm from Kiri's words, the thought of being touched by him now made me swallow hard. But I gritted my teeth and put my boot in his hands anyway, determined to ignore the feelings roiling within me.

"And up you go!"

I didn't even have time to feel much of anything before I was up on Kiluan's back. I shifted my feet back, finding the stirrups tucked behind his gliders, and pressed the toes of my boots down against the treads. Kiluan stirred beneath me, shifting his legs so he rose off the hoof spikes. I broke into a grin, one that was bound to leave my face aching by the end of the day.

"Come on, Diver," I called, gathering up the reins. "You *have* to try this."

"All right, fireball, all right," he laughed. "You'd think you'd never ridden a spiky two-legged gliding deer before."

"And *you* have?"

"Well, there was this one woman—ow!" He rubbed his shoulder and glared at Kiri. "All right, fuck, I'll get on the damn spiky death deer."

Kiri grinned at me as Diver climbed into the saddle. I grinned back, suddenly feeling a lot more positive about the day.

Chapter Nineteen

At first I didn't understand how to sit comfortably on Kiluan. Each stride, long though it was, jolted me forward over his shoulders. But as we fell in with the group of Anmerilli, AFC, and our own people, as I felt Kiluan's rhythm beneath me, I began to understand. As with riding a horse—which I'd done a time or two—I had to relax and let my hips follow his movements.

"Don't fight against it," I instructed Diver, as the entire group of us started down a path out of the clearing. "Move *with* the motion."

"Easy for you to say," he grumbled through gritted teeth.

"Not really."

"This ain't like riding a hover-bike, fireball."

I raised an eyebrow. "I know. I *can't* ride hover-bikes."

"Oh. Uh, sorry."

Riding through the palms and ferns, I caught glimpses of small fauna here and there, nothing I could make out too clearly, but some of it brightly colored. Staying near the back of the pack proved easier than I'd anticipated, as many of the group clustered together to talk, and no one seemed to notice Diver and I at the back.

I, however, noticed Christa riding alongside mar'Odrea, in a group that contained a number of his cronies, including mar'Shen. *But Marco is with them, too. Even if she* is *up to something, surely there isn't much she can do with him around.* Not that I was positive she was up to something. She was part of *my* team and I couldn't believe she would betray us, no matter how much she didn't like me. Still, I needed to find out what she was doing. I just... hadn't quite figured out a way to ask her about it yet.

"Hey, I think I'm getting the hang of this."

I snapped out of my reverie and glanced at Diver. Though he still swayed a bit unsteadily, he no longer bounced around like a sack of flour with limbs.

"Guess that makes it easier than riding a hover-bike," I teased.

"Though not half as comfortable."

Admittedly, sitting upright while my legs were kicked so far back *was* a bit awkward, but the more I adjusted to how Kiluan moved, the easier it became to balance and the more natural the position felt. I tried to pay attention to the world around me, but my gaze kept drifting again and again back to Christa and Marco and mar'Odrea's group.

"Christa's been spending time with mar'Odrea lately..." I ventured, wondering what Diver's take on it would be.

"Well, yeah. I kinda figured that's what you told her to do."

Wait, what?

"I mean, I know you two don't get along, but you gotta admit, she's got a talent for swaying over even the biggest of assholes."

I snorted. "If she can win over mar'Odrea, the Alliance ought to give her a medal."

But it made sense and put my mind more at ease. I envied Christa her charm and easy way with people, but I didn't blame her for using it to our advantage.

The crowd sped up. Beside me Diver cursed, as colorfully as any spacer, but I—I came alive with the thrill of it. Kiluan's strides lengthened, making for a smoother ride. Whenever he turned a corner he unfurled his gliders partway—sometimes all the way, depending on the sharpness of the turn—using them for balance. Wind rushed across my face, making my jacket billow and my hair slide free of my braid. It was almost as amazing as traveling through slingspace.

A laugh danced up my throat and I couldn't help setting it free. Beside me, Diver chuckled. I glanced at him, a grin overtaking my face. He grinned back—until he caught sight of something that wiped the smile clean off his face.

I looked ahead, confused. Then I noticed that the carouas at the head of the group were leaping, thrusting off the ground with their powerful legs and fair soaring, gliders spread, across an enormous chasm. My heart leapt. My fingers curled tight around Kiluan's reins. I gripped with my legs, curled my feet well out of the way of his gliders, and sat up straight in anticipation of the jump.

"Are they fucking kidding?" Diver shouted.

"Your caroua can make it," I called back, raising my voice above the wind whistling past us. "Just stay balanced over his center of mass and it'll help him make the jump easier!"

"How do you know that?"

I turned my head to stare at him in astonishment. "Principles of flight, remember?"

"Oh. Right. Don't mind me, just being a rust-brain."

His grin came back and I laughed. Ahead of us the second-to-last row of carouas had taken their leaps, and I braced for ours.

I felt the surge as Kiluan's strong legs gathered beneath him, the thrust as he shot off the edge of the chasm, into the air. His gliders unfurled with a snap, like the sails of an ancient ship opening to greet the wind. I took a quick peek down, saw what looked like water rushing far below us. Then we were on the other side, Kiluan's legs coiling beneath him, then springing back up, taking the weight of the landing like finely built hydraulics.

"Yeah!" I couldn't help but howl my joy.

"Fuck!" Diver gasped beside me. "That was terrifying! And great!"

"But mostly great."

"Mostly great," he agreed.

We were so busy laughing, we almost didn't notice that the crowd had slowed. Fortunately Kiluan was well-trained, and so was Diver's caroua, Dathik. Both slowed, then came to a halt at the edge of the crowd. I felt a shift in Kiluan's stance as he rocked back onto his hoof spikes.

"Why are we stopping?" I wondered aloud.

A caroua—taller than ours, and darker in color—broke away from the crowd and came towards us. Sitting atop it, looking golden and deity-like, was Councilor Kinima Mal. Her hair glittered like rubies under the sun and she controlled her caroua with a delicate touch, maneuvering it next to Kiluan with only the lightest of signals.

"We've reached the edge of the hunting grounds," she told us. "Today's creature will be set free momentarily."

Oh. Right. My joy drained away as I remembered that this was no pleasure ride. I reached down, stroking Kiluan's fine, soft pelt, letting the silken texture soothe me.

The rest of the group spread their carouas out, and Secretary Shinda raised a small hunting horn, blowing out a surprisingly deep bellow. For long moments nothing happened, and I began to hope something had gone wrong. Then Kiluan began to shift beneath

173

me. The underbrush rustled and a creature burst out some meters away.

Long and sinuous in build, with a cat-like body, a tail at least a meter long, a neck that stretched and bent and a slender, elongated muzzle. Its dun-colored body was covered in black stripes, though nothing like a tiger's. Rather they bent sharply into chevrons and overlapped one another, tapering to points on the animal's legs and face and tail. *They're starving it!* Malnourishment caused its ribs to show; they fed it just enough to give it strength and endurance, but not enough to ever sate its hunger.

"Ah, a baenil," Councilor Mal said, as I sat frozen in horror at the cruelty of it. "And a female, too. Quite the challenge. Come, young ones, or we will not get a taste of the hunt!"

I couldn't move. Had Diver not ridden over and given Kiluan a tap on the rump, I might've been there still.

The creature—the baenil—darted hungrily towards the nearest caroua and leapt away again as a shot cracked the air. She opened her mouth, letting out a roar that reminded me of that of a cougar, but higher pitched and more eerie. The hunting grounds became a flurry of movement as, desperate in her starvation, the baenil made leaps at various carouas, only to be chased away by the flash of horns or the sharp report of pistols. Some hunters even carried spears, and they laughed as they prodded at her. One of them cheered as he scored a hit, opening a slash of red on her dusty hide.

No. Oh, no, no, leave her alone, please. She snarled, her claws cutting furrows in the earth as she leapt away from another strike. Despite her desperation, she was outnumbered; I imagined I could see her realize it. Her tail lashing the air, she turned and fled into the underbrush.

"After it!" mar'Odrea called, spurring his caroua onwards.

"Quickly!" Councilor Mal yelled to us. "The baenil is an adept stalker. If we do not stay on her trail, she will soon be on ours."

Please, no, don't make me do this. But Kiluan followed the racing herd of carouas, as he'd been trained to do. Diver rode beside me, throwing glances my way, and Mal rode just ahead of us, leaning eagerly over her caroua's shoulders. I gripped the reins until my knuckles ached, squeezing them, trying to keep Kiluan to the back of the herd. Such a well-trained creature, so joyous as he ran and leapt, and I couldn't appreciate it at all, sick with fear and disgust as I was.

Kiluan's clever hooves danced lightly over the terrain as we chased the baenil. He bounced over logs and rocks, gliders fluttering, legs stretching. Up ahead calls passed back and forth amongst the crowd: they had lost sight of the baenil, though broken flora showed them her trail. I closed my eyes against the joyful whooping and hollering of the hunters, tried to close my ears too, but could not.

Then a sound came from behind us, so close it seemed almost physical. It began low, and rose in rounded, circling whoops until it was more like a banshee's shriek. Kiluan shuddered beneath me, crabstepping so suddenly he nearly bounced me out of the saddle. I clung on with my legs and dropped the reins to clutch at the saddle. Diver, far less lucky, tumbled sideways off Dathik's back.

"Diver!"

"I'm okay!" he called. "Just hang on, Xan!"

The sound came again and the carouas panicked more. Councilor Mal cursed as she tried to bring hers under control. I held tight, twisting in the saddle to try to see what was making the noise.

"Is it the baenil?" I shouted over the din of panicking carouas.

"No—*ashtuf!*" The translator didn't give me a translation for Mal's exclamation, but I had a feeling it was something along the lines of "motherfucker!" "It's a magoa! They don't live in this region! *Ashtuf, ashtuf benegil fa!*"

I grasped the reins, trying to get control again, calling to Kiluan in the voice I used to soothe Marbles and Cake. Councilor Mal had gotten her foot through her stirrup and she struggled to pull it loose even as her caroua panicked and danced underneath her. If I could just get enough control over Kiluan to reach her and help her out...

The magoa's call sounded a third time. Mal's caroua bugled its panic and fled, crashing into the forest. Cursing, I used what little control I had over Kiluan to turn him, urging him to follow. It didn't take much convincing.

Leaves and branches whipped me, stinging my skin, yanking my hair, catching on my clothing as we fled. Kiluan was less panicked, more steady on his feet, his gliders pumping in and out like bellows as he took sharp, swift turns. Looking up ahead, I saw that Mal's caroua was not so steady. It struggled to get its gliders out in time,

175

it stumbled over even the smallest rocks and roots, and it swayed like a drunkard as it ran. My heart pounded in my throat. I had no idea what I was doing, what I was going to do; I just knew I had to stop this.

Around another bend, and Councilor Mal might've been thrown from the saddle if her leg wasn't so firmly caught. She slid sideways, jamming her leg up to the knee. I urged Kiluan on, begging him for more speed; his steadier gait allowed him to close distance with Mal's caroua. As we moved up on the other caroua's flank, I grasped the reins in one fist and reached out with my other hand, leaning forward and stretching as far as I could.

We broke through the trees, into a clearing. With a surge, Kiluan drew even with the other caroua and I made a grab for Mal's stirrup. Her caroua bellowed and leapt away. My insides twisted with terror as it slid, scrambled, threw out its gliders in desperation. This only unbalanced it further and it went down, Mal's weight dragging it onto her. *Shit!* I grasped the reins in both hands and hauled, forcing Kiluan to a halt.

Think, Xandri, think quick! I kicked my feet back and launched myself out of the saddle. Mal's caroua tried to stagger to its feet, dragging the Councilor with it. Her cries of agony, as the motion jerked her leg into unnatural angles, hurt my ears. I yanked up my hood, tugged to bring the sound-dampeners over my ears and, on a whim, swooped down and grabbed a multi-knife from one of my cargo pockets.

I gritted my teeth and darted at the frightened animal, telling myself, *just get it done, just get it done.* I grabbed the stirrup strap—causing Mal to cry out even more—and started sawing through the leather. The caroua swung its head around, pointed horns aimed for me. If it hadn't been a sharp knife, I'd have ended up skewered autistic person faster than you could say "oh shit."

The stirrup let go and I landed in a heap next to Councilor Mal. Her caroua raced off into the woods. As I sat there, breathing heavily, listening to Mal's whimpers of pain and trying to think of how I'd get her back to the others—could I splint her leg? get Kiluan to drag her?—Kiluan's head came up.

Sweet Mother Universe, not now! I made to get up, but Kiluan was already sprinting away on strong legs, chased from the clearing by the appearance, god help me, of the baenil.

The baenil didn't follow; she had spotted easier prey.

"Councilor, you have to get up!" I said, keeping my eyes on the baenil.

Mal's only response was a groan.

"Councilor! Councilor, we need to—shit!"

The baenil stalked forward, shoulders rolling. In a moment, she'd pounce; hunger would drive her as surely as the wind drove a storm before it. I could run now, flee, and she wouldn't bother to chase me, having found a much easier meal. I could stay to protect the Councilor, could use my pistol to stun the animal, leaving her to either be killed now or shoved back in a cage and starved until the next hunt. Or...

Glass-like amber eyes, full of hunger, determination and feral intelligence gazed at me. Those eyes flicked to Councilor Mal and the baenil's tongue showed, long and thin and pink, licking her chops. One way or another, even if she got her meal, she would die. The Anmerilli would surely kill her, possibly with as much cruelty as they could muster. Or...

I reached for my pistol.

Or.

I flicked the settings, my fingers knowing exactly how to get the kind of projectile I wanted.

Or.

I raised the gun as the baenil stalked closer, her haunches gathering beneath her.

Or.

"I'm sorry," I murmured as she lunged.

At just the right second, as she soared through the air, I pulled the trigger. The projectile ripped through her throat, tearing a hole that would destroy the largest veins. Blood streamed into her fur, darkening it to dusty red. She was dead by the time she hit the ground, by the time her limp body slid to a halt close to Councilor Mal's mangled leg. Dead, and I had done the deed. I curled in upon myself as if there was a hole in my middle.

"I'm sorry."

Diver found us first, but the others weren't far behind. Mal's shrieks and the gunshot had drawn them to us.

"Move!" Captain Chui's voice snapped through the crowd of Anmerilli and humans, a whip crack that made them jump aside. "She's *my* crew member! Let me see her!"

I remained in my huddle, staring at my toes. Blood, fast growing cold and tacky, seeped into the grass near my boots. *I did that. I did that. I did that.* People moved all around me but I didn't care, couldn't care. Sobs waited near the bottom of my throat, sobs and screams, and it was only a matter of time before I let them out, not caring one whit for the fact that all these people would see me break. What did it matter if they saw?

"Xandri?" Marco's voice. "Xandri, what happened?"

"She..." Councilor Mal groaned. Several of her people crowded around her, supporting her. Her head lolled a bit and her speech slurred as she said, "She killed it. Stopped it. Saved me."

"Xandri," Marco called softly. When I peered up, just a bit, I found him staring at me, something—amazement?—etched in his features. "That was a fine show of bravery."

Brave? Brave!? Who did he think he was kidding? I hadn't been brave. I hadn't been thinking at all. I'd reacted and gotten myself into trouble, into something I couldn't handle. Any minute now I'd fall apart, meltdown, and everyone would see that I was still a child, incapable of handling a mission as important as this one. I only hoped I hadn't ruined things entirely. I lowered my head as the tears threatened.

All of a sudden my view of the world changed, as strong arms caught me up and hauled me off the ground. At first I thought it was Marco—but no, he stood in front of me, looking startled. Then I caught the faint scent of engine grease, mild but ever-present, and realized: Diver. No wonder I felt a sudden sensation of warmth and safety enveloping me.

"Captain, I think she's in shock," I heard him say. "That thing tried to kill her too, after all."

No, it didn't...

Captain Chui leaned in, peering at my face. I could've sworn I saw her wink. "You've got the right of it. Nasty case of battlefield shock, potentially fatal." She raised her voice. "Everyone, stand back. These two need space and immediate medical attention."

"We'd be happy to offer any assistance we can, Captain." mar'Odrea's voice. God, I wanted to puke.

"That's a great kindness, Councilor, but it so happens I brought a med-tech who specializes in just this kind of shock. Diver, run her back and get her to Marsten."

"Aye, Captain."

Other chatter started, but I didn't get time to hear. Diver took off, holding me close to his chest. He crashed through the trees and out onto a path, which he trotted down as fast as he could go, leaving the rest of the noise—the Anmerilli, the humans, the carouas that hadn't run off—behind us.

"Don't worry, fireball." His breath was warm against my ear. "I'm getting you out of here."

Chapter Twenty

Diver did take me to Marsten, but she didn't do much, aside from give me a small dose of something to calm me down. I'd described my meltdowns—a term I preferred a great deal to 'tantrums,' which my parents had used—as a sort of shock, but the good doctor had seen them enough times now to know they weren't shock at all. Shock could kill a person; my meltdowns only made me *wish* I was dead.

Katya and Anton met us outside the room Marsten was using for her med-bay. I didn't look at either of them, just kept my gaze low as they escorted Diver and I to my room. Tears hovered in my eyes but I didn't care. So people would think me childish, so what? People had *always* thought me childish.

You'll care later, whispered a voice at the back of my mind. *You might not care now, but later will come the shame, the embarrassment, the horror, the desperate wish to be like everyone else...* That never seemed to go away no matter what else I succeeded at.

By the time we reached my room, the tears were free, sliding down my cheeks and dripping onto my shirt. I didn't care, even though I *hated* having anything on my clothes. I let Diver open the door for me, let him usher me gently inside. When he released me, I stood in the center of the room, rocking from side to side, with no idea what to do with myself and no capacity to give a shit, anyway.

"Is she okay?"

Christa's voice went through me like a knife. I whirled, suddenly furious. Tears still streaked down my cheeks as I glared at her.

"Go away!" I snapped.

"I just—"

"I don't care! Go away! Leave me alone, all of you!"

"But..." Christa began.

I couldn't deal with the emotions. Fury and anguish cut through me like icy cold wind, freezing and searing at the same time. I couldn't take anymore, I needed—needed—

"Come on," Diver murmured, catching Christa's arm and pulling her away from the door. "She needs some space."

Space. Yes. The door swung closed and my tears started again in earnest. *How does he always know?* With everyone gone, the room became more bearable, as if some electric buzz had faded from the air. Suddenly I could breathe again. I wandered out onto the balcony and sat, curling my knees up against my chest. I pressed my face against my knees and let the tears run.

God only knew how long I sat there, lost to the world. For a long time I couldn't stop seeing the baenil, blood staining her beautiful fur. After that, my imagination produced for me a host of scenes, most of them involving me heading back to the *Carpathia* in shame. *Only if someone sees me like this.* That was the detail I had to remember. I could still make it through, so long as I could convince the Anmerilli that all I'd experienced was shock.

The faint sound of footfalls on crushed seashells reached my ears. I lifted my head, blinking in surprise to find that night had fallen. As my eyes adjusted to the star-lit darkness, I huddled into the corner of the balcony and peered between the rails, my heart pounding. *Damnit, Xandri, you know better than to be out here!* But wait... surely an assassin wouldn't make so much noise.

As my eyes adjusted, I caught sight of a figure jogging down the path. Squinting, I made out a familiar, dark head and the rolled up sleeves of an AFC uniform.

"Marco?"

He skidded to a halt beneath my balcony, head whipping back and forth. I thought I saw his hands shaking as he reached for the pistol at his hip. Carefully I peered out between the bars of the balcony rail.

"It's just me," I said. "Xandri."

"Oh."

"What are you doing out here at this hour?" Jogging, no less.

"Ah, well." He wiped an arm across his brow. "The hunt—I can't quite seem to work off the adrenaline. I didn't know what else to do with myself." Marco put his hands on his hips and gazed up at me. "How're you?"

"I'm fine." I tried to make my voice come out neutral, but it sounded hollow even to my own ears.

"Xandri..."

"Really, I am." I *did* feel a little better, though that was likely due more to whatever Marsten had dosed me with than anything else. "Just a bit of shock, you know."

"You're a terrible liar."

Goddamnit. *You'd be terrible at telling lies, too, if you spent all your time* living one. But I didn't want to explain that.

Marco studied the balcony for a moment. Then, to my shock, he took a short run and leapt. The balcony wasn't so high that someone with a bit of training and a soldier-boost or two couldn't reach it, but I wouldn't have expected someone like Marco to make the leap. Yet he caught the railing with ease and swung himself over, dropping into a crouch in front of me. I drew back a little.

"Easy there," he murmured. "Xandri...have you been crying?"

I looked away.

"Were you hurt?"

"N-no, I just..." I shook my head. "I'm fine."

Marco reached out, his fingers gently cradling my face. "I meant what I said before. You were very brave today."

"No, I wasn't!" I shouted. My voice rang in the night, and I lowered it to an angry whisper. "She was tortured and starved, and all I could do for her was kill her. I *killed* her, Marco."

He drew back. "That's what you're upset about?"

"Yes, that's what I'm upset about! I know—I know I don't have empathy like other people, and I don't—don't feel the things I'm supposed to, I guess, because I never told my parents I loved them even when I felt it and—but what I had to do today, Marco, it *hurt*. And it felt wrong!

"It wasn't her fault she ended up that way. She was *tortured* and desperate and I—nobody else cared. All they cared about was hunting her down and hurting her more. Twisting her life to their world and will. She wasn't the right sort of thing, the acceptable sort of life, so they shoved her in a cage and—"

I laced my fingers together over my mouth to stop the outpouring of words. Fresh tears streaked down my cheeks and I realized I was no longer sure if I was talking about just the baenil.

To my utter shock, Marco wrapped his arms around me and pulled me close. I turned my head, so I could breathe and so I wouldn't get tears all over his work clothes. *Maybe he understands. Maybe he won't judge me for it.* He stroked my hair and it felt kind of nice, in a fatherly way—or what I imagined a fatherly way might feel like. My eyelids drooped a little, likely the effects of Marsten's sedative.

"You don't seem cold to me, Xandri," Marco murmured. "It's no wonder Maru's taken to you as she has, the two of you share the same kind heart."

"She doesn't think so anymore." I sighed. "She saw me at the hunt, she and—and a few others. They were angry with me for joining."

"That hardly seems fair."

"I know." I wriggled out of his grip and sat back. "What was I supposed to do, be rude? And now what do I do? Either I let half of the Anmerilli think me weak or disdainful of them, or I let Maru and her followers think I'm proud of this—this atrocity!" I sighed again; if I kept this up, I'd start hyperventilating. "At least the worst of it is over."

"Yeah...yeah, it is."

I squinted, trying to get a good impression of his face in the dimness. He seemed...uneasy. *Of course he seems uneasy, you niddle-brain. Who wouldn't, after what happened today?* Silly to think I was the only one affected. Especially since I was pretty sure the incident had been *intended* to see someone hurt or even dead. How else would we have heard the cry of an animal not native to this region? If Marco realized that, no wonder he was rattled too.

"Hey..." Marco said. "You all right in there?"

"Mm. Just tired." I forced myself to sound vaguely chipper. "One hell of a day, you know?"

"Tell me about it. Perhaps you should try to get some sleep. To be honest, I ought to go do as much myself."

I tilted my head. "You don't get much sleep when you're on the job, do you?"

"Not as much as I should, no. I think we have that in common." Marco smiled.

"We do," I agreed. A yawn cracked my jaw and I stretched, unfolding my legs. "And you're right, I could use some sleep. I feel a bit better now, though."

"Good. I'm glad to hear that."

Marco's smile broadened, warm and sweet, and I felt even better. He rose, reached down to help me to my feet, and I knew the

183

medicine had good and sunk in, because I didn't mind in the least. He gave my hand a gentle squeeze, then climbed over the balcony railing and leapt down, as impressive a leap as the one up. I leaned against the rail and waved; Marco waved back before trotting off. *Hope he starts feeling better soon, too.*

I headed back into my room, closing the balcony doors behind me. Though my eyelids were starting to droop, I sent orders to Anton and Katya, saying I wasn't to be disturbed tomorrow unless it was of the utmost importance. As I was undressing, I received confirmation from them both. As I crawled into bed, my wristlet chimed—a message with orders from Captain Chui, that I was to open the door to receive food and nutrient-bars. *Well,* I thought as I curled up beneath the covers, *at least* some *things about today are normal.*

Though I wanted to spend the next day curled up in bed, pretending the universe didn't exist, I didn't. Instead I spent my time in research and thought.

I started with the magoa, the creature whose call we'd heard during the hunt. It took some digging, and my files didn't return as much as I'd have liked, but it gave me enough—and what I learned, while alarming, wasn't terribly surprising. I forwarded it all to Captain Chui and to Kiri via our private communications, with a request for more information if it could be found. After which I surrendered to the knock at my door and the nutrient-bar that came with it.

Then I sat down, a holo-touch pen in hand, and began to think. If there was one thing I knew about people it was that one size didn't fit all, no matter the situation. My classification system had helped and the Alliance had gained ground in terms of Member and Non-Member species since implementing it. But my experiences on Cochinga were teaching me that it simply wasn't enough.

Though I wasn't exactly sure of the how or the what, I made some notes on my holo-display about a special temporary membership, something we could modify to suit different peoples. *Possible compromises,* I wrote, *surrounding different attitudes towards weapons and traditions should be considered, within reason. Actions harmful to ecosystems or population groups will be off the table for compromise. What else?*

Working helped keep my mind off yesterday's hunt and what I would do about Councilors Maru, Tari, Sendil and Ashil. By mid-afternoon I felt—despite the two nutrient-bars—a lot better. I sent my second set of notes along to Captain Chui, asking for her input. We needed parliament to bend—and bend fast—and I had no idea how to achieve that.

I was taking a light doze when my wristlet chimed, the sound that warned of incoming vocal and sub-vocal communications. I sighed and opened the comm channel.

"Yes?"

"Secretary Shinda is here to see you," Katya said.

"Is it urgent?"

"I believe it's... *important.*" A moment, then, sub-vocalized, "*I don't think you should refuse, Xandri.*"

"All right, I'm coming."

I climbed out of bed, combing my fingers through my hair and smoothing down my tunic. My efforts came to naught though, as I opened the door and caught sight of Secretary Shinda in fine, brilliantly colored robes. I could be wearing the finest silks, could be dripping with ropes of nebula pearls, and still look frumpy in comparison. I tried not to sigh.

"Good evening, Ms. Corelel," Secretary Shinda said, adding an extra flourish to his general greeting bow.

I bowed in return. "And to you, Secretary Shinda. How may I be of assistance to you?"

"Oh, quite the opposite, my dear! We're having a fete in the grand hall and thought to take a moment to honor your courage in the hunt. Thus have I been sent to inform you, that you might join us."

I tilted my head down, letting my loose hair swing forward across my face as if I was humbled by the notion. In truth, I was revolted. "Such kindness. But truly, Secretary Shinda, it is unnecessary. I—"

"Nonsense! It's the least we can do. Come, come, my girl, you really *must* attend."

The pressure he put on the word 'must' set off alarms in my head. I peered out through my hair, catching sight of Katya standing behind Shinda. She nodded once, her clear and evident regret nearly blasting me off my feet. I had no choice. If I didn't go, I would offend. *I'm likely to offend by going, as well.* Yet another way in which the Anmerilli were like humans: With them, as with humans, I simply couldn't win.

"Very well," I said. "I need a few moments to freshen up, then I will join you all in the grand hall. Thank you for informing me, Secretary Shinda."

"If you would like an escort—"

"That won't be necessary," I said, more sharply than I intended. I assayed a smile. "I know the way, and I don't wish to keep you from the party. Again, Secretary, thank you."

"As you wish." He bowed and took his leave.

"Party?" I hissed at Katya when he was gone.

"Captain Chui figured there was no need to tell you," Katya explained, "since she doubted you'd want to attend anyway. Certainly no one mentioned anything about honoring you when the invites came."

"Which means the Anmerilli are up to something," I said.

"Same shit, different day."

"Right. Guess I'd better tidy myself up."

"I'll wake Anton. The captain would want us both at your back, just in case."

I nodded and closed the door. *Call me paranoid, but I think someone is out to get me.* And if Councilor mar'Odrea wasn't involved somehow, I'd eat my wristlet.

I got my comb and some hair pins and wrestled my hair into some semblance of order, braiding it down over my shoulder. Then I changed into the outfit I'd worn for the welcome reception; there was nothing else in my wardrobe that would suit. Finally I pulled on my boots and returned to the hall, to find Anton regarding me a bit groggily. Katya nudged him in the ribs and he straightened.

"Damnit, woman! Can't a man slouch when he's fresh out of bed?"

"Not a crew member of the *Carpathia*," Katya answered. She patted Anton's arm. "Poor Mulroney. Having to do your job and all."

"Where I'm from, we call this overtime," he retorted. "And I ain't even getting paid."

"Well, maybe when we're back aboard ship, we can figure something out."

I turned away from their flirtatious smiles. "Okay, we're hitting the TMI zone again really fast. Can we just go and get this business over with, please?"

Oddly, their laughter—even if it was at my expense—was comforting. Sure, the idea of them having a sex life was a bit like thinking about my parents' sex life, a thought which gave me a case of cold shivers, but I'd rather have bodyguards that had a thing for each other than ones that didn't get along. Plus, the routine—they flirt, I get all grossed out like a twelve-year-old—was getting familiar. Comforting.

I drew up a holo-display map of the building and tapped the grand hall. A blinking light formed in our location, and as we walked a beam extended from it, showing us the way. Actually, I thought I might remember the way as it was, but it didn't hurt to have help.

We made our way through the maze of passages and hub buildings, Katya and Anton joking with each other; anyone who didn't know better would never realize they were on high alert. As we rounded the last corner, to the corridor where the grand hall stood, I came to a sudden halt and almost wound up crushed by Anton. Because there, heading into the doors, were mar'Odrea and Christa. Christa leaned on his arm, hissing something urgent and rapid into his ear.

"Whoa. What's the hold up?" Anton asked, grabbing my shoulder.

"Shh!" I took a step back behind the corner, waited a moment, then peeked around. They were gone. "Did you see them?"

"Yeah," Katya said. "Christa looked pretty upset."

Upset, I wondered, or...something else? I clenched my hands into fists and took a step down the hall, then another. If Christa turned on us, really turned, we were in deep shit. With the things she knew...

A set of double doors led into the grand hall. I took a deep breath and pushed them open. Noise washed over me, followed by the very physical sensation of people; it moved over my skin, pushing on me, so many presences stuffed in one room. My day of work had allowed me to fool myself into thinking I had calmed

187

down, but this assault on my senses proved otherwise. Cringing, my muscles winding spring-coil tight with tension, I forced myself to step into the crowded hall.

Almost immediately, someone grabbed my shoulder and yanked me aside. I swallowed a shriek as I was hauled behind one of the spiraling columns holding up the roof, reminding myself—over the pounding of my heart—that I had two bodyguards.

"It's okay!" a familiar voice spoke, rising to be heard above the din, and above the sound of Katya and Anton reaching for their weapons. "It's me. It's Diver."

I looked up at him, blinking in surprise. "Diver? What—?"

"No time to explain," he said, grabbing my left arm and shoving back my sleeve. "Xandri, I need you to trust me."

"I—well, of course I trust you, but—"

"And I need you two to play along," he continued, as he reached into a pocket and pulled out a roll of bandaging. I recognized it as the protective stuff he wrapped around his hands and lower arms when he was working. Protected most of the surface, he always said, without taking away the tactile sensitivity in his fingertips. "In fact, I need all three of you to play along, especially you, Xan. I want you to lean on me for support, understood?"

I nodded, open-mouthed. With swift, skilled fingers he wrapped the bandaging around my forearm, from wrist to elbow, and secured it. Then he pressed it against my belly and brought my other arm up to cradle it there. Without another word he wrapped his arm around my shoulders, pulling me unsteadily against his side, and urged me back into the crowd. Katya and Anton fell in behind us, no questions asked.

As the crowd surged in around us, I found it no trouble to lean into Diver at all, nor to keep my arms cradled close to my body. People turned to look at us as Diver helped me through the crowd, and the sensation of being stared at made my stomach twist. The noise began to die down and I wished desperately to sink through the floor and escape the attention. Diver had another plan, evidently, which he put into place as the noise faded.

"... completely unbelievable!" he said, as if he'd already been in mid-scold. "I know for a *fact* that Captain Chui and Doctor Marsten ordered you on bed rest. You're lucky I didn't hand you over to the captain the moment I laid eyes on you."

"I'm sorry," I murmured, ducking my head. It wasn't hard to act scolded; I *felt* scolded.

"Is something amiss?" asked the strong, sardonic voice of Nish mar'Odrea.

I raised my head—and sagged hard against Diver in horror. mar'Odrea stood on a dais, with the rest of the World Council. Even Secretary Shinda was there, smiling his awkward smile at me. And in his arms...

In his arms was the skin of the baenil I had killed.

Chapter Twenty-One

"Forgive me, Councilor," Diver said. "With the shock she got and the injury she sustained, Xandri was under orders to remain in bed."

The horror of it—of what Diver was trying to save me from—began to sink in. *Why would they do this?* I wondered, my eyes drawn reluctantly to the skin. *Is this what they always do? No one mentioned this!* Surely if this was the normal procedure, someone would have told me. Then I wouldn't have to be so caught off guard, I could have found a way to deal with this, to—to—

Sweet Mother Universe, I was going to be sick.

"Injury?" mar'Odrea raised an eyebrow. "I was informed that Ms. Corelel was, shock aside, quite well."

"We thought she was, sir, but you know how adrenaline can be."

"I—" Words tried to lodge in my throat. *Get through this. You have to get through this.* "I didn't feel the pain until this morning, esteemed Councilor." I let out a nervous little laugh and hoped people would take it for amusement. "Seems silly, I know. But it's not as bad as that time it took Diver three days to realize his hand was broken."

"I'm never going to live that down, am I?"

I shook my head.

"Well, I'm very honored that you came anyway," mar'Odrea said, as pleasant as could be. "Aren't we all, my fellows?"

Murmurs of acknowledgement ran down the line of World Council members and through the crowd of gathered diplomats, politicians, and AFC members. I glanced around, saw my team and Captain Chui and Kiri, all with worried expressions. I found Marco as well; he shook his head and mouthed an apology at me. What would he have done, if he'd known about this ahead of time?

"I'd best not let her stay too long," Diver said, "or the captain'll have my hide, sir."

I winced. Why'd he have to phrase it like that?

"This should only take but a moment," Secretary Shinda said. "We wanted to honor you, Ms. Corelel."

"Indeed," mar'Shen agreed, his smile like oil and eels. "Is it not true, my brothers and sisters, that this young woman showed a great deal of courage yesterday? Not to mention a feat of hunting that will stand long in our memories."

Shinda took a step forward. It took all my willpower not to step back, not to let go of Diver and bolt. Another step forward. *Oh god, don't make me touch it, please don't, please, I can't!* My nose stung. I clung desperately to Diver as my knees went weak and my stomach churned. If I had to touch the baenil's skin, if I had to feel it against my own, I'd scream. I'd scream and scream and scream and only stop when my voice was gone.

Shinda halted. "Oh dear. Is something wrong?"

Diver wrapped his arm tighter around me, holding me up. "It's the pain meds the doctor gave her, sir. She doesn't react well to them."

My stomach heaved and I let out a tiny, hiccuping burp. mar'-Odrea shuffled back a step, as if afraid I might puke on his fine shoes. Which, in all honestly, I just might.

"We shan't keep her long, then," Shinda said. "Ms. Corelel, if you'll just do us the honor of accepting this, in recognition of your great bravery..."

He held out the skin. Before I could do anything, Diver glanced at Anton and jerked his head in the skin's direction. Anton stepped forward, arms out to receive it. When the entire crowd turned its gaze to me, Diver gently shifted his grip and drew up my sleeve to reveal the bandaged arm. The pieces fell into place. *Sweet Mother Universe, he's clever.* And I owed him my tail feathers twice over.

"I—I'm afraid," I said, dizzy with relief and lingering horror, "that I'm not to put any sort of extra weight on it for at least a few days. The Alliance offers medical treatment that's nigh on miraculous, but even it requires some rest, and I know better than to ignore the doctor's orders. Not to mention my captain's."

"Of course." mar'Odrea's smile took on a distinctly sour note as Anton scooped up the pelt. "It would be a shame for our heroine to be in pain any longer than necessary."

Oh, fuck you. You want me to be in pain, all right. That's what this is all about, isn't it? Fortunately I let out another nauseated burp, which forestalled the words from coming out of my mouth. mar'-Odrea drew back another step.

"I'll get her back to bed now," Diver said.

"Forgive me," I added. "When I'm feeling better, I hope to thank you all for this honor properly." See? I could lie. That was a big fat one. "For now, I pray you'll accept a simple 'thank you' instead."

It was Councilor Kinima Mal, leaning on her crutches, who began the applause. My fellow crew members, including the captain, picked it up, and soon the room was full of people clapping for me as Diver helped me back to the doors. *It's almost over,* I told myself, clinging to him. *Just get out of here and it'll be fine.* Except it wouldn't be fine, because Anton was following me with that skin in his arms and I really thought I might still break down.

After what seemed an eternity, we were free of the hall and out in the corridor. I sucked in a deep gulp of air, trying to breathe. Diver halted, arm still around me for support, giving me a moment to compose myself. Not that I thought I could, not really. My stomach roiled and my head ached, and a strange buzzing filled my ears. Sounds blurred oddly; I heard them, recognized them, and yet didn't fully absorb them.

Footsteps. Christa's voice. "Is she all right?"

"Not really. I think I'd best get her back to her room." Diver. "Thanks for warning me."

"Of course, of course. I can't believe they—oh! Mr. Antilles."

"Please, call me Marco. Is Xandri—"

More footsteps. "She needs her rest. Orders, you know how it is, Mr.—Marco. Oh, and it's such a lovely party, we really mustn't miss out..."

Voices and footsteps faded. The doors opened, closed. Half-dazed, I let Diver help me down the corridor, around the corner, through the damnable maze of the building. Time passed in lurches, so it felt like it took both a very long time and no time at all to reach my room.

"Stay out here," Diver instructed Anton and Katya. "Allow no one past, except the captain. If anyone else shows up, contact me immediately." He glanced at the baenil skin. "And put that away somewhere."

Good soldiers that they were, they didn't argue. Diver helped me into my room, set me gently on the bed. I blinked, the haze around me starting to fade as he crouched to help with my boots. Another moment and I realized he was murmuring to me, voice soft and rich and soothing. The urge to reach for him, to bury my fingers in his fawn-colored curls and drag him close, rose up in me. I fought it down.

"You're saving me a lot lately," I murmured instead.

"Crew looks out for crew, yeah?" Diver pulled off one boot, then reached for the other. "And everyone needs a little help now and again."

"If you hadn't been there..."

"You might've gotten through anyway. You're strong, Xan, and you can get through this." He dropped my other boot and looked up.

"I'm not so sure about that."

"Well, I am," he said. He leaned in closer, his voice low as he spoke. "We're close, Kiri and I. Damn close. Even working with a completely alien encryption system, I think we'll get it cracked within the week."

Damn. They were good, really good.

"Think you can hold it together that long?"

"Of course I can," I said, with confidence I really didn't feel. But I was going to do it, one way or another. I wouldn't let my people down, especially not Diver, who had kept me safe twice now.

He smiled up at me, his green eyes sparkling, and the urge to touch him rose up again. I wanted it so much, I started to reach out. Realizing what I was doing, I made to draw my hand back—but Diver caught it before I could. He cradled it in his, stroking my palm with the warm, calloused pad of his thumb. My heart fluttered like bird wings, rapidly catching air beneath them and lifting, lifting...

Diver's head came up. He dropped my hand. "Yes?" he said, and it took me a moment to realize he was getting contact from my bodyguards. He frowned. "I'm not sure. I'll ask her. Xan... some of the Councilors are here. Maru and some of the others you've been interacting with. They'd like to speak to you."

Huh. Now that was odd. I supposed I could get away with sending them off, considering my "orders," but... "Send them in."

My door opened. Anton strode in first, taking up a spot near the back of the room. Then came Maru and Tari, Ashil and Sendil, and Kinima Mal limping along on her crutches, which surprised me; I'd never seen her with this group before. Katya followed them in and closed the door, taking up a stance in front of it. *What could they possibly want with me?* The first four I imagined might be here to further express their displeasure with me, but surely Councilor Mal was not on the side of their cause.

"Poor Ms. Corelel," Noaya Maru said. She approached the bed and took a seat next to me, and I thought perhaps I saw genuine concern on her face. "I had not known you were injured. Might I see? I know a thing or two of injuries."

"Oh, uh, well. . . " I held my arm up reluctantly. "Doctor Marsten is really good at—"

It happened so fast, none of us could have stopped it, though Katya came within an eye blink of blowing Councilor Maru's head off. For the Councilor suddenly drew out a small, thin blade, snatched hold of my arm, and sliced through the bandages. Such a precise slice, she didn't even open my flesh—but she did reveal my unblemished, uninjured arm to all in the room.

"As I thought," she said.

"Ma'am," Katya said, "I advise you put away the blade and step away from Ms. Corelel. Now."

Maru held her hands up and stood. "I mean no harm. I had only wished to confirm a suspicion."

"Don't blame Xandri," Diver said quickly. "It was my idea, not hers."

"It matters not whose idea it was," Councilor Ashil said, "though I confess it fair clever. What matters to us is *why.*"

Why. Of course they would want to know. And here I was, between a goddamn black hole and a hard place. Maru and Tari might appreciate my reasons, and considering their reaction to the hunt, I thought Ashil and Sendil might too. But what if I was wrong? What if they still disapproved of how I treated their culture? *Does it matter?* asked a voice at the back of my mind. *And what good can it do to tell more lies?* If they'd rather have lies, what kind of allies could they possibly be?

"Diver found out what was planned and—and he knew it would upset me," I said. "I—I couldn't bear to touch it. It was bad enough having to kill her."

"I told you," Mal crowed. "Didn't I tell you?"

194

"So you did," Maru said. I must have looked confused, because she smiled and explained, "When we saw the body, we recognized it for a mercy kill. *Not* the Anmerilli way of things where the hunt is concerned. So we decided to speak to Councilor Mal, who was the only one there to witness it."

"I heard you," Mal said. "You apologized. You regretted what you had to do."

"Of course I did! I hate killing and I especially hate killing animals. I went because—because I didn't see any way to refuse without being unforgivably rude. And it was horrible! The whole practice is cruel and barbaric."

"Is it not also cruel and barbaric to eat meat?" Tari retorted.

"I live on a starship," I pointed out. "All the meat we eat is vat-grown." And, miraculously, so close in taste and texture to the real thing that even *I* couldn't tell the difference. "I never eat meat planetside unless it's an Alliance world—then it must be either vat-grown or cruelty free *by law*. What laws on Cochinga stop you from starving and torturing an animal before hunting her down?"

I folded my arms and glowered. Annoyance began to burn through my exhaustion. Maybe if I'd known sooner that I would have allies, I'd never have gone on that hunt. Maybe none of this would have happened; maybe the hunt would've gone off safely, with no magoa call to spook the carouas. I couldn't know, of course, but the thought that there might have been a chance to escape it all made my blood heat with anger.

Maru and her companions exchanged glances, some sort of silent communication with each other. Only Kinima Mal was left out of it. I focused on her.

"And what about you?" I demanded. "Unless you've had a sudden change of heart, I doubt you're here as part of the resident tree-hugger brigade."

"*Uh oh,*" came Diver's voice through our private comm channel, and across the room Anton stifled a chuckle. "*She's mad now.*"

"While I confess, I'm starting to lose my...taste for the hunt," Mal said, "I'm here mainly to support you. You saved my life and I owe you a debt. Since I'd rather not lose anything that has meaning to me, I offer instead my vote, in favor of your Alliance."

"Accepted," I said, in no mood to argue any of those points. "And the rest of you? I know Maru and Tari's agenda, but you,

195

Sendil, Ashil, do you mean to tell me that you, too, are part of the animal rights movement?"

"Well," Ashil began, "yes..."

"Then why the bloody hell didn't you *tell* me?"

"We had to be sure we could trust you! We want—"

"For fuck's sake, I can't help you get what you want if I don't know what it is!" I shouted, exasperated. "Don't you get it? This is what I'm here for—to make this work for all of us. I've already said that. Did you think I didn't mean it? I want to help you but I need to know *how*."

"We keep hearing that you want to compromise," Tari said. "But you offer us nothing in return. It is *we* who must compromise everything."

"No," I said, tilting my head in thought. "No, that's not the problem."

Ashil drew herself up, indignant. "Excuse me? You asked us to tell you how to help and then—"

Diver held up a hand. "Whoa, easy. Xandri just has a tendency to say exactly what she means, is all. She understands her own context and tends to jump from point A to point C when most of us need a stop-off at point B."

"Huh. I never thought of it like that before." I shrugged. "What I mean is, the problem isn't that the Alliance isn't offering you anything in return, it's that they take it for granted that what they offer is something *to you*. You've no experience of the Alliance and it's not in your nature to take it at face value that what they offer benefits you. Which is fair enough," I added. "You need time to experience it for yourself and adjust to it."

"Like the trees!" Maru exclaimed. When her companions stared at her, she went on, "Ms. Corelel explained to me a—a means of cultivating miniature trees. It was quite fascinating. But a slow process, one that takes time and work."

I nodded. "Which is why I'm working on an outline for a special temporary membership. One that can be reexamined and reevaluated after a certain period, so we can better see how to continue, well, cultivating our alliance."

"Can you do that?" Mal asked.

"I can damn well try. But you have to be willing to give *some* if there's going to be any chance of it working. The animal hunt-

196

ing has to go, and the weapons—we might be able to figure out a compromise, but things can't stay as they are."

"Maru and I have some scientists working for us, studying our ecosystems," Tari said. "We have data about the damage done, and predictions of where it will lead. Would that data help?"

"It might."

"I'll send it to you first chance I get."

I reached up, rubbing my temple. Despite my day of—relative—rest, exhaustion weighed heavy on my shoulders. My skin still crawled from how close I'd been to the baenil skin. As tired as I was, I wanted the hottest shower I could bear before crawling into bed. But I couldn't do any of that until I got this sorted once and for all.

"All right," I said. "Councilor Mal, I have your vote; that is witnessed. The rest of you—I need to know what you want. Compile for me both those things you think your people will be willing to bend on, and the things you'd like the Alliance to bend on, as well as who among the Council you feel will be open to compromise. Can you do that before the next meeting?"

They exchanged another glance and nodded. "We'll have it to you by tomorrow evening," Ashil said.

"Good. That's settled. And if you've any other information you think might be useful to me, don't hesitate to send it."

Maru tilted her head in consideration. "Then you should perhaps know that Councilor mar'Odrea brought several of his own carouas for this hunt."

And Hasendo, the region under mar'Odrea's care, was also the only one where magoas were still extant. mar'Odrea's carouas would be trained to deal with the magoa's call; they wouldn't have panicked like the rest of the herd. *Stellar. I don't know whether to feel frightened that someone really was trying to kill me, or relieved that I'm not just paranoid.* This night kept getting better and better.

Councilor Mal muttered something that the translator fuzzed out. "One day," she finished, "I'm going to wrap my hands around that man's neck and squeeze until his hot air-filled cranium pops."

"And I'll be the first person to attest to your innocence," I said. "Now, I really *am* still... unwell from yesterday, and I can't help but think you shouldn't linger, lest someone discover you here. Katya, would you make sure the coast is clear?"

"Aye."

We stood back as Katya opened the door and checked the hallway beyond with a soldier's efficiency, creeping silently on booted feet to peer around corners. When she gave the all clear, my guests began to move out, Kinima Mal trailing them on her crutches. At the door she paused and glanced back at me.

"The Anmerilli are not fools," she said. "We won't be the only ones to suspect that your injury is a lie."

"Well then, I guess I'll have to make them believe."

She grinned, gave me a nod, and limped out. Anton followed, but when Diver made to leave too, I gestured him to stay. Much though I might've liked to go back to where we'd been before the Councilors arrived, I had other business to attend to. *Besides, who's to say* he *wants to go back to where we'd been?*

"Got need of me, fireball?"

"Can you and Kiri track the Council members' electronic correspondence?"

"Of course! What do you take us for, amateurs?"

I smiled wanly. "Just figured it was better to ask than assume. I—I need you to do it for me. Track their correspondence, all five of them. Please."

Diver studied me a moment, his expression one I couldn't begin to read. He crossed the room, reached out and touched my cheek with those callused fingertips.

"This mission is asking an awful lot of you that ain't really your style, isn't it?"

I nodded and shivered. Was I really reduced to *spying* on people? I knew we were hacking the Anmerilli's system for the graser, which was bad enough, but keeping track of someone's personal correspondence—the idea made me ill. *But I don't see any other choice.* If they had all been honest with me from the beginning, I would trust them—possibly to my doom—but now I simply couldn't. Not when it was becoming abundantly clear that someone was working overtime to stop this alliance from happening. Likely several someones. I didn't know who to trust.

Except Diver. I know I can trust him.

"Try not to let it weigh on you too much, Xan," he said, letting his hand drop.

"I really wish we could be on a first contact mission instead."

"I know. But thing is, thanks to what you're doing here, there'll be more first contact missions to be had. You're protecting species we don't even know exist yet. That's amazing, and don't you forget it."

He winked at me and took his leave before I could manage another word. Not that my brain was working very well. I sank down onto my bed and buried my face in my hands, near tears with exhaustion. Despite it all, I felt a spark of determination in my belly. I'd come this far; I refused to back down now.

Chapter Twenty-Two

On the day the meetings were to resume, I set the alarm on my wristlet to an early hour and crawled out of bed to prepare myself. I hit the shower first. While my hair was still wet, I braided it as neatly as I could and pinned it back around my face, though I made sure it coiled over my shoulder to hide the scar behind my ear. I picked out the tidiest set from my uniforms and took the time to shine my boots.

Last but not least, I wrapped bandages around my left forearm. Captain Chui and I had a plan all worked out.

Satisfied—for once—with my appearance, I sent a message to Anton, who had door duty this morning, that I was ready for coffee and breakfast. When it arrived, I ate everything I'd been given, including the damn nutrient-bar; my coffee I luxuriated in a little longer, sipping it while I took in the sunrise from my balcony.

It was a thing about myself that I didn't quite understand, something that had shown itself during my years on the streets. When I was younger and I got angry, all I could feel was rage and frustration, until it overwhelmed me and I couldn't express myself at all. Now... well, I still had those moments. But I also had the ones where the anger burned cool rather than hot, where it rose to dominate every other emotion and, oddly, made things clearer, easier. It filled me with determination to succeed, and that anger, that gripped me now.

All right, Xan, time to go. I left my coffee mug in the small kitchenette, patted my still damp braid, and headed into the hall, where my team and Diver were already gathering. Marco was there too.

"Xandri!" His eyebrows rose. "You're coming with us today?"

"Of course I am."

"Are you sure? If you need more time to rest I doubt anyone would—"

I lifted my chin. "I'm sure, Marco. I've got a job to do." And some new ammunition with which to do it.

"If you're sure..."

Diver chuckled. "Word to the wise, man: Don't argue with the fireball when she's in this mood. Like trying to stop an asteroid with your bare hands."

"Indeed," came Captain Chui's voice. "In that respect, she'd have made an excellent gunnery sergeant."

"Nonsense. *I'd* never force someone to eat nutrient bars."

Captain Chui's eyes glittered, though her lips didn't even twitch. Next to her, Doctor Marsten laughed. She was a tall woman, Alena Marsten, two meters even, and she looked more like an Ancient Earth Viking, with her broad shoulders and ice-white hair, than like a doctor. Yet I knew from experience how gentle and careful her hands were, and I knew she much preferred healing to harming. Even if I could easily envision her mowing through a hoard of orcs with a Dane Axe.

"Well... if Xandri is really certain..." Marco began.

"Please, Marco, I'm fine. I'd just like to get on with the day."

He nodded and gestured down the hall. *Finally*. I couldn't afford to let my resolve waver; I had to act now.

As we wound our way through the corridors, I couldn't help but notice that Marco kept glancing at me. Even I could see his concern etched clearly on his features. And it wasn't that I didn't appreciate it, but I really was okay. The breezes that came through the open hallways cooled my skin, bracing me, and the sea-salt scent chased away the last dregs of sleep. Though a swirl of worry danced in my belly as we approached the meeting hall, I could keep it under control.

We filed in among the crowd of Would Council members and AFC officials, and of course, Major Douglas. An extra chair was brought for Doctor Marsten and she took a seat next to Captain Chui.

"Before we begin," Secretary Shinda said, "are there any grievances to be aired before the Council today?"

"Actually," came mar'Odrea's voice, "I *do* have a concern I'd like to lay before the Council."

Secretary Shinda bowed and took his seat, gesturing for mar'-Odrea to go ahead. The worry in my stomach twisted into a tighter knot.

"You see, I had it on very good authority that our young Ms. Corelel came out of the hunt shaken, but in all other ways uninjured. Yet only two nights past she came before us with the claim of harm done to her person during the hunt. But now—now I have reason to suspect we've been deceived, my fellow Council members. She bears no injury."

That feeling, that creeping, painful feeling I got when so many pairs of eyes turned to stare at me. I forced myself not to huddle down in my chair, even though it hurt to be stared at so. Instead I straightened, lifted my chin and laid my injured arm carefully on the table. I stared defiantly at mar'Odrea's cheek ridges—I knew from experience that he wouldn't be able to tell I wasn't looking him in the eye.

"Why would I do such a thing?" I asked, doing my best to keep my voice level.

"I think that much is obvious, Ms. Corelel. You deceived us so you would not be forced into showing your disdain for our culture and traditions."

Because I hadn't already? "But—do forgive my confusion, Councilor, but how could I possibly have done that? Your honor to me—and it *was* an honor, have no doubt—was a surprise, if you recall. I had no knowledge of it; how could I aim to deceive you over something I didn't know was going to happen?"

Councilor Mal chuckled. "She's got you there, mar'Odrea."

mar'Odrea glared. I tried to keep my surprise under control. *Where did those words even come from?* Perhaps it was the cold anger still seeded within my chest that allowed me to speak like that. Or the fact that I'd been practicing with Captain Chui. Or both.

"Well, there's a simple solution to this, isn't there?" Councilor mar'Shen said cheerily. "She can just show us the injury."

Uh oh.

"I'm afraid that won't do you much good." This time the voice that spoke was Doctor Marsten's. "I gave Ms. Corelel an injection of military-grade nanobots as soon as the injury was discovered." In response to the blank stares that came her way, she smiled gently and added, "Even civilian-grade nanobots work fast on injuries, though not as fast; time to rest is ideal. It's also not always possible in military situations, thus military-grade nanobots work faster.

"A sprain of the degree obtained by Ms. Corelel can be mended in two days." She drew a tablet from beneath her doctor's coat, punched in a command, and held it up for all to see. "Upon discovery, Ms. Corelel's injury looked like this, but now it won't be visible. The bandage is merely for support as the nanobots finish up their job."

Oh, bite your tongue, Xan. That *was* my arm, black and blue and yellow with bruises, that Doctor Marsten showed the Council. Thankfully the shot showed only my forearm, though; had my hand been in it, all would be able to see that it was a picture of the *right* arm, not the left. It was from just after I'd gotten the wrist implant in. It *did* look hella ugly, and it had hurt like fuck, especially since the implant needed several days to fully sync before I could get my nanobot injection.

"Actually," Captain Chui said, "we really must thank Councilor mar'Odrea for bringing this up. It pertains to something I wished to discuss today. You see, Ms. Corelel, myself, and the Xeno-liaisons team have been working on a—a plan for a special temporary membership."

Kirrick and Marla were hard at work taking notes, but Christa sat up straighter at Captain Chui's words and smiled, a smile that glowed with charisma. While I wanted to wilt and die beneath the stares of others, she thrived.

"That reminds me," she said, looking to me. "It was Councilor Mal that you suggested we test this on, wasn't it?"

I'd suggested no such thing, but I nodded, playing along.

"Test *what* on, if you don't mind my asking?" Mal demanded.

"One of our ideas for this temporary membership is to give the citizens of Cochinga access to Alliance medical technology, including such benefits as nanobots and life-ex," Christa explained. "But of course, you'll want to see what some of it can do first, yes? We thought Councilor Mal's leg might be a good trial run."

"If Major Douglas agrees, of course," Captain Chui said, inclining her head towards the man in question. "We thought to use military-grade 'bots, so the Council can see for themselves the truth of Ms. Corelel's injury and swift healing."

I was pretty sure Major Douglas hadn't known anything about this beforehand, for I caught a glimpse of shock on his face. He quickly smoothed it away as heads turn towards him. Marco struggled to hide his surprise as easily and ended up ducking his head. *I guess I should apologize to him later.* I didn't know why I hadn't included Marco in the planning; I just hadn't. Besides, he was always so busy, it had seemed wrong to bother him with it.

Major Douglas coughed. "Of course I agree. Especially if it will spare Councilor Mal further discomfort."

I glanced around the table, pleased—and a little surprised—to realize how much my weeks of study had aided me. I picked up clear signs of interest from the Anmerilli—like that Councilor who leaned forward, steepling her fingers as she often did when something piqued her curiosity, or the one across from her, who expressed the same sort of interest by leaning back and folding one leg over the other. And of course there was mar'Shen, whose tail drooped farther and farther as he too looked around the table.

"I think that sounds like a grand idea," Councilor Mal said, with a smile and a nod in Doctor Marsten's direction.

"What else might this membership include," Ashil asked, "should it prove possible to do?"

"We're still discussing that," Captain Chui said.

I nodded. "One of our suggestions is that you be allowed members to view the workings of parliament. Whether you'll be allowed any level of voting power—we can't say much on that at the moment."

Amid the murmurs of interest between this Council member and that, mar'Odrea rose. Our talk of a special membership had derailed his attempt to discredit me entirely, and he couldn't be happy about that. As the room quieted and his fellow Council members focused their attention on him, I braced myself. I'd tried to think through all the things he might say and put together answers, which I of course practiced before the mirror.

"And of course, *we* will be expected to give up things in return," he said, "won't we, Ms. Corelel?"

"That is generally how compromise works, esteemed Councilor."

"You would stop our hunting traditions."

"They *must* stop," I said. "The data I've received about the state of Cochinga's ecosystems is—"

"*Their* work, no doubt," mar'Odrea snarled, stabbing a finger in Maru and Tari's direction. I'd never seen him lose control like this. "I know all about their work, Ms. Corelel. A load of biased nonsense, lies, meant to convince a gullible public—"

"With all due respect, Councilor," Captain Chui cut in sharply, "that same rhetoric was used by many on Ancient Earth a long time ago. That humanity's cradle didn't slip beyond all redemption is nothing short of a miracle, but... well, even now, the ecosystems are so unstable that population is strictly controlled, and in some places pollution has bred disease epidemics that even modern medicine struggles to cope with. Is that the future you want?"

"I *want* respect for my traditions!"

"Would that be so you can keep making loads of money off them, or so you can keep using them as an excuse to try to kill people?" *Oh, fuck me, I said that out loud.*

mar'Odrea's eyes narrowed. "I beg your pardon?"

Well, now that I'd said it, what did I have to lose? "You'll have to forgive me, Councilor. It just seemed a bit suspicious to me that the cry that disrupted the hunt belonged to a magoa. A creature extant *only* in Hasendo."

"How do *you* know it was a magoa, hmm?"

"I told her," Mal said.

"And I researched it," I finished. "It took some looking, and it was especially hard to find a clip of its call. I *did* find one, of course—part of a Hasendi manual for caroua training. I also noticed you brought several of your own trained carouas with you for this hunt..."

"Those are serious accusations, young lady," Secretary Shinda said.

Technically they were insinuations, not accusations, but now seemed a bad time for picking at nits.

"Serious and *insulting*," mar'Odrea spat. "There are plenty of others here who could just as easily be responsible, yet I see you pointing no fingers at them." He leaned forward, bracing his hands on the table in a way that left little doubt of his mood. "Or perhaps you're simply trying to deflect blame off yourself."

I gaped at him.

"See? She has nothing to say to *that*!"

I choked on my words for a moment, before spitting out, "That's because it's completely space-fried! Fat lot of good it'd do me, if I proved my point only to break my neck while doing it! Not to mention I ended up right in the path of the baenil. In case you somehow failed to notice, Councilor, *getting eaten* is not generally how I do my job!"

As I spread my arms to show off my clearly uneaten status, several Council members broke into laughter, Kinima Mal the loudest of them. The laughter was quickly drowned out by the heavy bangs of Secretary Shinda's staff, hitting the floor tiles with a crack like lightning. Several of us—myself included—jumped. *Oh god, what was I doing?!*

"Enough," Shinda said, his voice grim and stern. "The time for personal grievances has passed. Today, we will discuss this plan for a specialized membership. There will be no more petty bickering, am I understood?"

I didn't think calling out the man who'd probably tried to kill me constituted petty bickering, but I nodded along with everyone else. My outburst had left me feeling wrung out, anyway. And guilty. I shouldn't have done that. Sighing inwardly, I flicked a finger to access our private comm channel, directing my communication at Captain Chui.

"*Yes?*"

"*I'm sorry. I lost control of my temper.*"

"*It would be best if you tried to keep it under wraps in the future,*" Captain Chui said. "*Though I suppose better you than me. I do wish he'd give me a reasonable excuse to strangle him.*"

"*Oh. Well, I'm glad to know it's not just me.*"

"Captain Chui?" Major Douglas said. "If you would be so kind? You haven't yet given me much detail about this plan of yours, after all."

"Yes, of course, Major." She smiled and turned her gaze to Councilor Sendil. "The proposal Ms. Corelel and I are putting together suggests a period of five standard years, after which circumstances will be reevaluated and, we hope, you might be persuaded to join us officially after all."

"And if we don't wish to give up our liberties for you?" mar'-Odrea demanded. "What then? Will you declare us enemies?"

"Have you intentions to ally with the Zechak? No? Then have no fear. We will not consider you our enemies."

"Feh. You'll strip us of our means to defend ourselves, take our greatest weapon yet for yourselves, and if we don't agree to do things *your* way, you'll leave us to be trampled by the very ones you warn us against."

"Now, Councilor, I've already told you," Marco said. "Even Non-Member planets are protected from the Zechak."

Yes, in the hopes that they'll eventually acquiesce to what the Alliance wants. I didn't quite know where the thought came from, but… In truth, I didn't always agree with the Alliance's policies, most of which had been around for millennia, from the time before the Alliance when it was only the Sanavila. *But none of those policies are what we're talking about now, so there's no reason to think about it.*

"We will do no such thing, Councilor mar'Odrea," Captain Chui said, and her gaze traveled around the table as she spoke. "Certainly, *I* will not. The *Carpathia* will always be there to protect others from the Zechak. It is what we do, honored Councilors."

She spoke softly, her tone as light as air—and it surrounded people in the way air does, filling their lungs and supporting their lives even if they didn't consciously realize it was doing so. On some level, the Anmerilli were drawn by her words, recognized her passion even if she didn't show it with the same out of control exuberance that sometimes overtook someone like me. I sat straighter in my chair and noticed my crew members doing the same.

"Are you really going to fall for this?" mar'Odrea asked of his fellow Council members. "They'll find a way to take everything from us, see if they don't! You just wait and see, something will happen like it did at the hunt, something that'll make us start thinking twice about our guns. They'll—"

Secretary Shinda's staff hit the floor again. When everyone quieted, including an outraged mar'Odrea, Shinda said, "I think *some* of us are getting a bit overexcited. Perhaps it would be best if we adjourned until after lunch."

When we'd have to discuss the whole gun business. Grand. But it would give me time to recuperate, to get my bearings back and maybe even rekindle the anger that had carried me through the meeting. Chairs scraped back all around me and I flinched at the noise, shooting up out of my own chair. A hand caught my elbow, steadying me. I glanced over and smiled when I saw Diver.

"C'mon, fireball," he murmured in my ear, breath warm on my neck. "Let's go get some eats, yeah?"

"Sounds good."

As we filed out of the hall, me sheltering next to Diver's tall, lanky body, Marco caught up to us. *Oh, right.* Fresh guilt welled up in my stomach. We were supposed to be in this together, after all.

"Look, Marco," I began. "It's been such a stressful weekend, I didn't mean to exclude you, I just—"

He held up a hand. "Relax, Xandri. We'll talk about it later, okay? Right now—well, Major Douglas has requested an audience with you and your captain. In his office."

"Oh. Um, thanks, I guess. I'll tell her."

Marco nodded, smiled, and headed off, catching up with some of his AFC buddies.

"Stellar," I muttered. "Because I haven't spent enough time this morning wrangling with a bumbling nitwit who considers me incompetent."

"Be fair, Xan," Diver said, resting an arm lightly around my shoulders. "mar'Odrea didn't start bumbling until you lit a fire under his ass today. But," he conceded, leaning into me, flashing a sly smile and a wink, "then he started bumbling with the best of them. Topnotch bumbling, really. You've a knack."

"Great. All I have to do is drive him completely up a wall and when he snaps, maybe the rest will stop listening to him and join the light side of the Force."

"Don't worry, fireball. I have every confidence in your ability to drive people completely barking baffy."

I blinked at him. "*How* do you manage to make that sound like a compliment?"

"I meant it as one." His smile turned into a wicked grin. "It so happens I'm something of a connoisseur of that particular skill set."

I eyed him wryly. "Yeah, it shows."

Chapter Twenty-Three

Diver and I caught up to Captain Chui. She stood talking to Katya, who had come to relieve Anton of his shift. And, I noticed with some exasperation, she carried with her a nutrient-bar. *I guess it's for the best. I may not get a chance for lunch.*

"Captain Chui," I said softly, as I stopped near her.

She took the nutrient-bar from Katya and turned to hand it to me. "If you're going to try to talk your way out of this—"

I shook my head. "Marco said that Major Douglas wants to see us in his office."

"Of course he does," Captain Chui said, with far too much patience. "I suppose we had best do as he asks. Diver, why don't you go get some lunch?"

Diver glanced at me. Though the words hadn't been couched as an order, he had to know they were meant as one. After all, he hadn't been invited. Yet he hesitated, gaze sweeping my face in a way that turned me pink around the edges. I managed a small smile and nodded, even though I didn't want him to go. He made me feel better. *Hold it together, Xan. Your day is far from over.*

Finally Diver nodded at Captain Chui and took off down the hall, catching up to the tail end of the crowd. I fell into step beside the captain, with Katya trailing behind us, alert as always. As we walked, I unwrapped my nutrient-bar and broke off a piece, which I thrust rather pointedly in Captain Chui's direction. She took it from me, one feathery eyebrow rising.

"Didn't you say just this morning that you'd never force someone to eat these?"

"I'm not forcing you to do anything, ma'am," I said innocently. I took a bite, chewed and swallowed, and added, "I just knew you'd want to make sure you ate something too. After all, as the captain, it's your job to set an example."

Behind us, Katya broke into a small coughing fit. Captain Chui sighed.

"For someone who has to practice her subterfuge in front of a mirror, you can be alarmingly devious, child."

I said nothing, just chewed on my nutrient-bar. I could've sworn Captain Chui rolled her eyes before biting into her portion, but her expressions were always so subtle, I could've been imagining it.

I finished by the time we reached the major's office. Two AFC soldiers stood outside the door, and Katya took up position with them as one of them leaned in for a brief, rapping knock. The major called for us to come in, and the same soldier pushed the door open to admit us. Captain Chui went first and I followed behind. She fell naturally into parade rest as she stopped in front of the major's desk, so I did the same.

The office the Anmerilli had given him was quite fine, but then, he'd been assigned here for some time. The dark wood of his desk gleamed, uncluttered, and the floor shone as if it had been freshly polished mere moments before. A wide window behind him showed a view of the ocean. Lucky bastard.

"You asked to see me, Major?"

Major Douglas straightened in his chair and gestured for us both to take a seat. "Indeed. I confess, Captain, I was a bit dismayed to find myself blindsided by this... compromise of yours."

"I'm sorry, Major. But considering some of the impasses we've come up against during these negotiations, I thought it best to keep our plans quiet until we had a firmer grip on what we intended to do."

Huh. I hadn't thought of it like that, but it was a good point. Perhaps Captain Chui wouldn't have wanted me to mention it to Marco, after all. The less people knew, the less chance it would reach the ears of someone like mar'Odrea ahead of time. That he'd had no time to prepare a sound defense against it worked to our advantage. *Captain Chui might say she's a soldier, not a politician, but she's hella clever.*

"Understandable, I suppose, given the circumstances," Major Douglas mused, rubbing his chin. "But try to keep me apprised as much as possible in the future."

"Of course."

"Whether parliament will support this idea, that I'm less sure of."

210

"I think they will," I said quietly, drawing the major's attention to me. I tapped my hands against my thighs, nervous under his gaze. "They want—*need*—this weapon, and they especially need to keep it away from the Zechak. If a compromise will do the trick, it would be foolish to reject it. And if—if you and the AFC add your voices to ours, the argument for this compromise will be stronger."

"That's an interesting—young lady, *please* quiet your hands," the major said sternly. As I flushed and tucked my hands under my thighs, he continued, "An interesting point. But the Anmerilli's attachment to their weapons will be a sticking point. What did you have in mind there?"

I glanced at Captain Chui, my nerves shot from the major's scolding. She nodded once, a small, firm gesture that gave me back the smallest spark of confidence. "More compromise. We will require that all weapons be graded, and those deemed inappropriate for civilian use may be wielded only by the military.

"For now, civilians will be allowed to keep any weapons not deemed military-grade. This should give them at least a taste of lesser gun violence. If, at the end of five standard years, when the temporary membership is done, the Anmerilli are amenable to giving up their civilian weapons, they'll be invited to hold full Member status. If not, we'll negotiate a new special membership, with an eye to extending gun control to permits and the like."

I let out a breath, shocked that I'd managed to say all that with Major Douglas' stare burning through me. And he *kept* staring, his eyebrows up skeptically, his lips pursed in a way that I was pretty sure meant disapproval, though it was—as always—possible I had it wrong. I dropped my gaze to the surface of his desk and pushed down on my hands with my thighs, willing them to stillness.

"And you mean to say that *you* came up with this idea *on your own?*"

His incredulous words brought my head up sharply. Already in pain from forcing my body to a form of *propriety* that didn't suit it, I almost snapped at him. Instead I bit my lip, hard, and let Captain Chui speak for me.

"Xandri has a particular knack for viewing things—even things she disagrees with—from someone else's point of view. A...tactic for defense, call it," Captain Chui said. "She believes that the Anmerilli need a slower introduction to change and, as something of an expert in that need," here she smiled gently in my direction, "she was indeed the one to come up with the finer details of this plan."

"I see," Major Douglas said, though he still didn't look convinced. "Well, if you believe it will work, Captain, I'll stand behind it as well. Perhaps between us we can get parliament moving. Certainly I don't think they'll disagree with allowing the Anmerilli a taste of our healthcare. Though. . . " He paused, looking thoughtful. "Five standard years doesn't give them a chance to truly get much benefit out of life-ex, especially since it won't settle in their DNA for some generations yet. Perhaps we should also offer them access to PGE."

I froze. PGE—prenatal genetic engineering—was the process my parents *hadn't* undergone for me. After that span of years in which I—and others with various divergences or disabilities—had been born, parliament ruled it illegal to have children without proper PGE. It was freely available even to the poorest of families. No more little oopsies; no people like me among any Alliance species.

"That. . . seems a bit excessive. . . " I murmured.

"Nonsense! Five years without a single defect among their children? Who wouldn't want that?" Major Douglas said. "Captain Chui, I want that included in the compromise. Call it my contribution to the work."

A tick of silence, then Captain Chui nodded. I knew she couldn't refuse, not if we were going to get Major Douglas' help pushing this through parliament—and we needed it. Even so, I thought that nutrient-bar might come around for a second visit.

"As to your ideas about gun control," Major Douglas went on, gazing directly at Captain Chui.

"*Xandri's* ideas," she interrupted sharply.

The major smiled indulgently. "I appreciate your desire to give your crew members individual credit, Captain, but I've done enough reading to know that understanding the feelings and motivations of others isn't something she can—"

I shot up out of my chair; the clatter and scrape of it drowned out the major's words. *Of course you think that! You've never had to learn to be something entirely other than yourself. You never had to study your own species to understand them, to be like them, to defend yourself*

212

from them. If you didn't think I was capable of that, why did you call me here? Why do you think Captain Chui keeps me on? But I didn't say any of that, couldn't say it. Instead I spun and headed for the door.

"Young lady, I didn't dismiss you."

I half turned. "No, but then, you're not my boss. Captain, may I go now?"

"Of course, Ms. Corelel. Dismissed."

"There, see?" I smiled with a sweetness I didn't feel. "Now if you'll excuse me, Major, this *defect* has a job to do."

I left before he could say another word, shutting the door behind me with a bit more force than was, perhaps, strictly necessary. Abuzz with a tangle of anger and hurt, I stormed down the hall, forcing Katya to hustle to keep up with me. All I wanted to do was make this alliance succeed in a way that left both parties happy. What did I get for my trouble? Sabotage and a bunch of people who thought I had all the competence and sapience of a juvenile Nafta.

"Xandri? Hey, Xan, what's wrong?" Katya asked as she caught up to me.

"Nothing," I snapped. Nothing I wanted to talk about, anyway.

God, what a joke. Why had I even been invited along, if no one thought I was capable of the job? Did people honestly think Captain Chui gave me credit for things I didn't do? *Why? How would that even make sense?* And then I'd gone and lost control of my tongue in front of Major Douglas like a spoiled little child. Damnit. I sighed and toggled the controls for our private comm.

"*I hope I didn't fuck things up too much,*" I said, when Captain Chui picked up.

"*Not to worry, Xandri. It'll take more than a few sharp words to put a dent in Douglas' sense of moral superiority,*" Captain Chui returned. A pause, then, "*Do you want your name on this proposal? I know how you feel about being exposed to parliament, but...*"

I sighed. "*Do it. Anything to shut up Major Pain-in-the-Ass. And— and maybe they won't even realize...*"

Maybe they wouldn't, indeed. There'd been so many things they had never cared enough to notice, after all.

"I'm sorry, Kat," I said, as I clicked off the comm channel. "I didn't mean to snap at you."

"Eh, don't worry about it, kiddo," she said, putting an arm around my shoulders in a way that made me think she was spending too much time with Anton. She leaned in and whispered, "Major Douchebag makes me snappy, too."

I giggled, relieved. Though it seemed like I *finally* had more allies than enemies here, I knew I couldn't afford to lose a single one.

I was sitting on my bed, flipping through thumbnails of Cochingan flora and fauna, when someone knocked on my door. I paused, my fingertip hovering over the thumbnail of a creature that *might* have looked like an elephant—were it not for its fox-like size, three stout trunks, and the sharply pointed ears that stuck straight out from the sides of its head. Seriously, I was getting pretty positive there wasn't a single creature on this planet without something pointy on it.

"Yes?" I called.

The door creaked open and Kiri peered inside, followed by Diver, both of them peeking around the edge of the door like kids looking for mischief. I rolled my eyes, trying to fight my amusement, and waved them in.

"Studying?" Kiri said, plopping down on my bed. "After a long day of meetings? Don't you ever kick back and relax?"

Before I could answer, Diver flopped down behind her and said, "Kiri, for our fireball, this *is* relaxation."

I scowled at him—largely because he was right—and clicked off my wristlet's holo-display. Diver leaned against the wall next to the bed, lounging with the grace and indolence of a large cat. Kiri settled against him with much the same casual elegance, her head braced against his shoulder. My heart stuttered at the sight, an awful feeling of desire mixed with jealousy coming over me. Were they...?

"Don't look so distraught, starshine," Kiri murmured, a playful smile on her face. "It's not like that. I mean, not that I'd mind, but it's a little too soon for me." She tilted her head. "Though I might change my mind if you joined us."

"Stop teasing her, you temptress."

I looked down as the two of them chuckled. *Am I that obvious about it?* I tried never to let that sort of thing show, but Kiri—Kiri read people, even me, like we were all open books.

My heart pounded so hard, my whole body seemed to vibrate. I wanted to cross that short distance between us, crawl across the bed and drape myself across Kiri's lap, feel Diver's hands stroke my hair and maybe—maybe other places. I wanted it so much, but at the same time I didn't dare. I couldn't let people into my life that way; I simply couldn't.

All the same, I almost did it. I almost went to them, almost coiled myself into that tangle of limbs and warm bodies. Another knock on my door stopped me. Caught between relief and frustration, I called out for the knocker to come in.

"You're Miss Popular tonight," Kiri teased, as the door swung open to admit Marco.

He halted when he saw us all on the bed. "Oh. Um...I didn't mean to—"

"Ignore them," I said, waving a hand at Kiri and Diver as if they were flies to be shooed away. "They're just here to get on my nerves."

"Yep," Diver agreed.

Marco grinned, rolled his eyes and shook his head; I knew the feeling. He grabbed a seat from the table in the middle of my room and dragged it closer. Though he sat, his feet jittered restlessly. *Well, it's been a hectic day.* Sure, the second meeting had gone shockingly well. Many of the Anmerilli seemed quite taken with the idea of compromise, and even some of the staunchest gun proponents hadn't flinched from the idea of new regulations. But it would still be stressful until we had their agreement to the alliance.

"Well, I didn't come here to intrude on your free time," Marco said. "I just wanted to let you know that the World Council has called a halt to the meetings until we hear back from parliament on your special membership plan."

"Oh, thank god," Kiri groaned. "I haven't even been to all the meetings, and I'm sick of them."

And probably looking forward to at least a full day, if not several, of digging deeper into the Anmerilli security system. If both she and Diver worked on it together for a couple of days, they'd probably crack it.

"Yeah, I thought a break would sound agreeable," Marco said with a smile. "Especially for you, Xandri. You've been here more than two planetary weeks and barely gotten to see much of the building you're in. I thought I could show you some of my favorite places tomorrow, if you'd like."

I brightened. "That sounds like a great idea! Will there be animals? I want to see more of the local fauna."

"Oh, sweet lord," Diver grumbled. "No offense, man, but I hope you weren't intending to invite me, too. She has *no* off button where alien life forms are concerned and frankly, I still have a headache from today's meeting."

Under other circumstances I might be insulted, but I figured Diver was making an excuse for himself ahead of time, so he could get out of the trip without it looking suspicious.

Okay, I was a *little* insulted.

"Ah, well..." Marco smiled at me. "I hope you won't take this the wrong way, Xandri, but since I'd already figured I'd show you the menagerie, I wasn't planning on inviting your friends for this particular trip. I thought they might prefer to be—spared."

Kiri laughed. "I can see why the AFC hired you. You got brains."

"Can my team come too?" I asked, too excited to be offended. A menagerie full of Cochingan wildlife! I fought the urge to bounce and wriggle with excitement; Mother had always scolded me for that.

"I asked them, but they didn't seem up to it tomorrow," Marco said. "But it could take several days to hear back from parliament, right? Maybe we'll have a chance to all go together."

Huh. Odd. My team was usually always up for engaging with new alien life forms. We weren't called Xeno-liaisons for nothing. *Then again, considering the xenos we've been liaisoning with lately, I guess I could see why they might want a break.* And their last experience with the local fauna *had* gone a bit tits up, truth be told. Though it did concern me that Christa would have an entire day to plot with mar'Odrea, if that was indeed what she was up to.

"If you'd rather wait..."

I shook my head, perhaps a tad more vigorously than necessary. "No, I want to go. I'm not sure I can get out of bringing a bodyguard, though."

For a moment, a frown flickered across Marco's face. *No. I just imagined that.* He looked as open and warm as he always did. With people like mar'Odrea breathing down my neck, I was seeing negativity everywhere, that was all.

"Well, maybe we'll get them some earplugs to bring along," Marco joked. "Just in case your friend Diver is right about you not having an off button."

"Oh, I am."

I sighed. I didn't *mean* to carry on like I did; I just got so excited, and I wanted to share that with others. Especially people like Diver and Kiri, and even Anton and Katya. Even though I'd learned that it annoyed people, sometimes my enthusiasm just bubbled over. I'd have to try to be on my best behavior tomorrow.

Chapter Twenty-Four

Over-enthusiastic babbling: 5

Xandri's Best Behavior: 0

"I'm sorry," I said with a wince. "But I was reading about baksha last night and they're just so fascinating up close."

Marco laughed and ruffled my hair. "Don't worry, I was prepared for this. And you know, I've been here six years and I never knew that about their digestive systems."

"Wish I still didn't," Anton remarked, sounding queasy. "Tell me the next one won't be so gross."

I glanced at the holo-map I'd downloaded into my wristlet. "Kooyagi next," I said, unable to resist the spread of a wicked grin. "Just wait until you hear how they give birth, Anton. Their birth canal actually runs up through their—"

"How about I just hang back a little while you two take a look, huh?" Anton interrupted.

I pursed my lips tight to hold my laughter in check and led the way to the kooyagi enclosure. Marco had brought me to the menagerie early, so there weren't many people there, but even if there had been the animals would've stolen my attention away from the crowds and the noise.

The kooyagi alone was fascinating enough for an entire herd of xenozoologists. As I approached the enclosure, I searched the tree branches, as the holo-pamphlet instructed. It took a long moment but finally I spotted it, stretched along a tree branch, its grayish brown fur causing it to blend. Miraculous that a snake-thin, nearly four-meter-long mammal-like creature could blend with anything, but there you had it. *I wonder which part of it is the pointy part.*

"That was mean-spirited," Marco said, though he sounded amused even to my ears. "You and I both know it lays eggs."

"Well, yes," I said, trying—and failing—to suppress a grin. "Though it *does* incubate them by swallowing them and then regurgitating them when they're ready to hatch. Besides, Anton teases me all the time; I was just getting my own back."

I leaned against the glass—real glass—around the enclosure and peered in. Either this kooyagi was a male or it was a female out of season; there was no sign of the slight bulge it would get when its special sac was full of incubating eggs. *Darn. That would've been so stellar.* Well, I'd look it up later.

"I didn't know about the regurgitation part," Marco confessed, frowning. "That's gross."

"It's amazing," I argued. "A brilliant bit of evolution. Most animals you'll find on most planets aren't equipped for that—insides are a really good spot for digestive organs, and those are generally full of acids and the like to break organics down. But the kooyagi evolved this special sac that has no acids and can safely hold the eggs.

"That means it never has to build a nest or leave its eggs unprotected. The females can stay in the trees, camouflaged against predators, and their mates bring them food until the eggs are ready. Then—oh. I'm doing it again, aren't I?"

"Just a little bit, yes."

I flushed and looked away. No wonder people thought I sounded like a child. I cleared my throat, glancing at my holo-map. *Haputo next. Haputo, haputo, that sounds familiar... ah!* Right, the little fox-sized three-trunked elephant thing I'd been looking at last night. Technically the trunks were nostrils, but perhaps it would be prudent to keep that to myself. Also prudent to stand back—there was no glass on this enclosure and that thing *could* sneeze out of all three nostrils.

"So what do you think?" Marco asked, and I was primed to leap into another diatribe when he added, "Any chance we'll have heard back from parliament by tonight?"

"Doubtful," I said, as we strolled along, Anton sticking close enough to protect me but not so close that he'd have to hear about digestion and regurgitation. "With any luck they'll move faster than usual, but even so, expecting them to get a decision made in less than a few days is like expecting a Nafta to leave your ship vents without bribes."

"Well, I hope they'll agree to this. I wouldn't mind a new assignment after all these years."

"Something a little easier, I take it?"

Marco chuckled and leaned against the railing surrounding the haputo's enclosure. I leaned next to him, watching two of the creatures frolic in the dark depths of a pond. One of them launched itself out of the water, its webbed feet landing with loud *splats* on the rock, its tail flicking droplets back and forth. A small, pealing giggle escaped me before I could stop it, as I watched the creature waggle water from its ears.

"Easier would be nice," Marco agreed, drawing back to avoid water—or possibly haputo snot. "This whole thing has been—well. I'm just hoping it works. That parliament agrees and the Anmerilli sign."

"Well, if they don't, we try something else."

"That's right, I've heard all about the *Carpathia's* efficiency. You guys must have *at least* one backup plan."

Yeah, hacking into the Anmerilli's military database and stealing their plans for the graser. I doubted Marco was on the clearance list to know that, though. If Christa really *was* working against us for some reason, and parliament agreed to the special membership, would she spill what she knew? Of course, maybe she already had and mar'Odrea was simply waiting for a suitably dramatic moment to reveal it. That would be just like the bastard.

"Xandri?"

"Sorry," I said, forcing a smile. "Hey, look! Their ears flex upwards. Well, I guess that makes sense for a semi-aquatic animal."

"Oh... I'm sorry if talking about work bothers you," Marco said, gesturing to the next enclosure. "I guess I just want to be prepared to help you in whatever way I can, whatever comes next."

"Well, we'll probably just go back to the drawing board, you know? Maybe try to tweak the special membership so it'll be acceptable. Perhaps you can help with ideas for that—hey, look!" Pretty certain I was doing a horrible job of lying, I made a lunge toward the next area, trying to hide my failure in eagerness. "A kourai! They're related to carouas!"

They in fact looked like tiny versions of carouas, with smaller horns and clawed feet suited for moving about in the trees. *Focus on them. Don't let him get a good look at your face.* It wasn't even that difficult; the damn things were so cute.

220

"Well, if you need any help with your plans, you know I've got your back."

"Of course, Marco. You'll be the first person I'll go to if I end up needing to," I said, praying I sounded convincing. "But you know, I have a good feeling about this compromise. I think you'll be on that new assignment before you know it."

I perhaps spent longer in the menagerie than Marco had really intended, but it was huge and there was *so much* to see. There'd even been the Cochingan equivalent of a petting zoo, where I got to cuddle with something that looked suspiciously like a cross between a miniature mountain goat and an angora rabbit. I'd forgotten myself, giggling and rolling happily in the spiky Cochingan grass as it tickled me with its whiskers.

Anton was slightly less impressed, as his slobbered and snotted all over him.

On the other hand, our tour of the Cochingan Military History Museum made him feel a lot better. Heavy gunners, so predictable.

The museum, more crowded than the menagerie, wore me down and we spent some time afterward in a small, secluded cove by the beach. While we were there, while I calmed down under the soothing fingers of the sea breeze and the relative quiet, Anton wandered down to the water and plunged his hands in. He yelped a bit—I imagined it wasn't too warm—but that didn't stop him from scrubbing.

"What are you doing?" I called down to him.

"You have to ask?" he shot back. "I'm still covered in fluffy goat-thing snot!"

For some reason I laughed so hard, I toppled off the rock I was sitting on, landing with a thump in the sand and scaring the bejeezus out of my poor, tough, fluffy goat-thing snot-covered bodyguard.

"Really, Xandri, it's fine. It was my treat."

"But the *Carpathia* has funds for things like this," I protested, as Marco and I strolled down a breezeway in the general direction of my room. "I can't let you pay for *everything*."

As our day wound to an end, Marco had taken Anton and I out to dinner, to a place that served remarkably good noodles. If there was one thing that seemed to be nearly universal among sapients, it was noodles. Most cultures I'd encountered found a way to create their own variety—even the Shar had noodles made entirely from vegetable matter. The Anmerilli version was made out of some tuber or other, but had a consistency similar to egg noodles.

Marco laughed, a sound full of merriment and energy. "Really, it's fine. You can get the tab next time, if it'll make you feel better."

"I guess so," I said, stifling a yawn. No idea where he got his energy from. "But the AFC is paying, right? I mean—"

"Stop worrying so much! I said it was fine, didn't I?"

I blinked, startled by his tone. I reached up to rub my eyes, and when I glanced at his face, he was smiling. *Oh. I'm hearing things wrong because I'm tired.* That happened. I'd gained a lot of ability to recognize non-verbal language—and to control my own—but being tired or stressed made it more difficult. Things came out of my mouth in ways I didn't intend, and people's tone of voice became harder to decode.

"Um," I began.

"Whoa, hey..." Marco reached out and gently touched my arm. "I think I wore you out more than I intended."

"I'm all right. Just hoping I don't have to work tomorrow." I managed a grin. "Besides, it was fun."

"Fun? *Fun?*" Anton demanded. "Do you know, I can *still* feel that goat snot? It's like it's stuck in my pores."

"Maybe it's a defense mechanism," I said with a giggle.

"What's a defense mechanism?" demanded a new voice. I looked up to see Katya strolling down the hall towards us. "What'd you put poor Mulroney through?"

"It was really quite horrific," Marco said, as straight-faced and serious as I'd ever seen him.

"Quite the attack," I agreed, focusing on my tone to keep it flat.

"Worst case I've ever seen, in fact. I've never seen a—a—what was it called again, Xandri?"

"A long-haired pygmy ragoait. Remember? About yay-big," I held a hand down to knee height, "covered in fluff and made out of weaponized cute."

"Right, yes. It *sneezed* on him."

"It was the stuff of nightmares, Kat," I said, unable to stifle my laughter this time.

"Oh yeah, laugh it up, all of you," Anton grumbled.

"Come on, Mulroney," Katya said, grinning and patting him on the back. "Surely you can handle a small, cute animal or two."

"Look, I've been covered in *a lot* of alien slime since I got this job, but this was hands down the worst. It like, coats the skin. And it feels like that cold nutrient-gel they got the nerve to call food. And it *won't come off.*"

Katya wrinkled her nose. "That does sound pretty awful." She gave Anton another pat on the back and turned to Marco and I. "Hey, Mr. Antilles. It's my shift anyway, so I figured I'd come take them off your hands. Let you go get some rest."

"Oh. Well, I'm not that tired..." Marco began, rubbing the back of his neck. "But hey, there's probably some paperwork or other needs doing. Always is."

"Not for much longer," I reminded him. "Just hang in there another day or two."

He smiled, though it looked a bit strained. *I guess when you've been stuck in a place for six years, it gets hard to believe you'll ever see the light at the end of the tunnel.* I waved, then turned back to Katya and Anton, who were doing their usual flirting routine. Figuring Anton had had a rough enough day, I decided to leave them to it, without any little sister-esque comments from the peanut gallery. Besides, they were awful cute together.

"Poor Anton," Katya cooed, taking his hand in hers. "Oh, wow, I can feel it. That's disgusting. We'll have to see if the doc has anything that might help."

"Why Kat, it almost sounds like you care."

"Of course I care, you big lunk. That's your shooting hand."

"Oh, it's more than just my shooting hand, and you better believe it, darling."

I was doing my best to tune it out—unfortunately for me that was like trying to block out a cicada perched on your ear, chirping away—so I didn't notice when Katya went as still as death. Not at first.

Then she spun, moving in a fast, fluid motion that carried her the very short distance to me in a flash. She grabbed my arm, spinning me away from the center of the breezeway. Something loud cracked nearby, a sound that felt sharp and hard against my skin. I grunted as I went down, shoved to the floor under the shelter of the breezeway's low wall.

"Stay down!" Katya commanded as she crouched beside me, her gun out. "Anton, opposite wall! We could have shooters on both sides!"

Shooters!? My heart stuttered. I huddled low, wishing I'd brought my own guns with me. *Fucking breezeways, we're so exposed out here!* As Katya took a few crouched steps away and peeked cautiously over the wall, I tapped on my wristlet. No doubt she and Anton both had already contacted Captain Chui, but gunfights weren't like they showed in vids. They went down fast, and this place was fucking huge.

Crack. Crack. Katya snarled at the sound of gunshots, popped up, and fired. A howl in the distance told us she'd hit her target, though perhaps not fatally.

"I've got at least two or three over here," she shouted to Anton.

"Same on this side, and they're trying to close in."

"Like fuck they will," Katya growled.

"*Captain Chui,*" I sub-vocalized, as soon as the comm channel opened.

"*I know, Xandri. Keep your head down and only move if you have to. We're on our way.*"

I could do that. I huddled in a ball, my legs under me so I could spring up if I had to, and kept my eyes on Kat. She shifted, moving on the balls of her feet despite her crouched position, and sprang up again to shoot. I yanked my hood up, activating the sound-dampeners, but with both Katya and Anton shooting so close, the sound was still so loud. I squeezed my eyes shut, praying for Captain Chui to arrive soon.

I should've kept my eyes open, my ears uncovered. Both Katya and Anton were too busy to notice; *I* should've been on the alert too. But I wasn't.

An arm grabbed me around the waist, jerking me backwards. Before I could scream, a hand clamped down over my mouth. I kicked desperately, but I couldn't stop myself from being dragged down the breezeway, away from my bodyguards. Bodyguards who were, based on the muffled sounds of gunfire, in great danger of being overwhelmed by our attackers.

Chapter Twenty-Five

I had to do something. Katya and Anton couldn't afford to worry about getting me away from my assailant, not when the gunmen were moving in. Not that they weren't trying. Katya had spotted us and was creeping along towards us, the muzzle of her sidearm pointed at the floor.

I grabbed at the hand over my mouth, trying to pull. Whoever my assailant was, they were strong, way too strong for me to get free, especially when I couldn't get my feet under me. I kept trying anyway, remembering something Captain Chui had told me once. Getting away from the enemy wasn't necessarily about brute force. I didn't need to get my attacker off me completely; I just needed to get at a soft, tender bit.

Happily for me, one was close by. I ignored my fear, shoved it down deep, and yanked until the hand over my mouth slid down just enough, exposing the tender flesh between thumb and forefinger to my teeth. Without hesitation, I bit down as hard as I could, closing my jaws like an angry pit bull and refusing to let go. My assailant yowled in agony but still I hung on, tasting the horrible, coppery flood of blood in my mouth. Finally, with a chorus of swears, my attacker released me, tossing me away and into Kat.

She caught me by the back of the tunic and hauled me up into a more balanced crouch. As I raised a hand to wipe the blood away, trying not to gag, I saw my assailant—male and human, dressed in an AFC uniform. Shock froze me in place.

He lunged suddenly, bloody hand grabbing for my leg.

"Xandri!"

Katya had raised her gun, but the shot came from somewhere else. I screamed as the man's head blew apart, spattering bits and gobs along the pristine wall. Hot blood sprayed, soaking through the fabric of my cargo pants; several gobbets of brain landed on my legs. I kicked away, my feet slipping in the mess on the floor. Katya hauled me up, shifted me behind her, and readied her gun as two more AFC soldiers came at us.

Another of them went down with a large hole in his chest, and I caught a glimpse of Marco hauling ass down the breezeway, gun raised, heedless of danger. I'd never seen such fury as that which twisted his face as he caught up to the third AFC soldier. Marco grabbed the man by the sleeve of his uniform, yanked him around, and smacked him across the face with his gun.

Then I lost sight of him as the chaos escalated. Anmerilli gunmen came leaping over the walls of the breezeway, their landings drowned out by the pounding of soldiers' boots. One landed in front of Katya and I, and slipped in the blood and gore from the dead AFC soldier. Katya grabbed him while he was off balance, jerking his arm back and forcing him face down onto the floor.

"Take them alive!" Captain Chui's voice boomed down the hallway.

Oh, thank god. The cavalry. A hand came down on my shoulder and I twisted around. I wasn't a fighter, far from it—and Diver had chided me more than once for my lack of hand-to-hand abilities—but I was scared, pissed, and covered in gooey bits. So when I saw the Anmerillis, her gun raised to my forehead, I launched myself at her like a rabid baenil. My hands closed around her wrist, yanking her gun aside, and my weight, slight though it was, threw her to the floor.

She lost her grip on the gun as her skull cracked against the hard, seashell tile. I grabbed the gun for myself, even though I was unfamiliar with it, and pointed it at her face. She gazed up at me, eyes swimming and woozy, and held her hands up in limp surrender.

A flash of movement at the corner of my eye. I half-turned, gun still aimed at my prisoner—in time to see Diver grab the Anmerillis who was making a beeline for me. He spun the man around and disarmed him in a move so fast, I couldn't follow it. A solid punch to the face laid the Anmerillis out on the floor. Diver carried a gun, sure, but no matter how many times Captain Chui yelled at him for it, he still tended to wade into gunfights fists first.

My captive bucked beneath me, making a sudden wild grab for the gun. *Fuck. This. Noise.* I spun the weapon and smacked her in the forehead with the butt of the gun, knocking her out. Oh, sure, later I'd probably turn into a sobbing, blubbering mess, but that's what sedatives were for.

Diver caught me around the waist and pulled me up, sheltering me against his body as we barreled through the chaos. His hand struck my back, pushing me into a more sheltered corridor. Someone grabbed my wrist; I shoved my disheveled hair out of my face and caught sight of Kiri before she pulled me behind her. Though she didn't fight often, she was one heck of a shot, and now she stood poised and ready, gun aimed into the crowd.

I raised my own purloined weapon, and Diver stood beside me, all three of us alert for anything. Fortunately, we didn't need to remain alert long.

Captain Chui alone took down two Anmerilli, creeping up behind them, knocking them out and then binding their hands and feet with snap-wire. Of the eight that had attacked us, seven were taken alive, Katya and Anton netting one each. It took me a moment to realize one of those captures was technically mine, and a prickle of pride broke through my exhaustion and fear.

As the pandemonium died down, Captain Chui's voice cracked through the air like a whip: "Mr. Antilles, that is *quite* enough!"

I stared in shock. Captain Chui snapped her fingers and two of our soldiers lunged forward, grabbing Marco by the arms and hauling him off the corpse of the AFC soldier. What was left of it. Marco had pummeled the soldier's face to a pulp with his gun, and even now, as our own tried to calm him, he fought like a man possessed. I broke away from Diver and Kiri, heading for him against all sense.

"Marco! Marco, stop!"

He froze at the sound of my voice. Blinked once, slowly. "Xandri?"

"Yeah. I'm fine. Well..." I glanced down at my blood spattered clothing. "As fine as I can be, all things considered."

"You're safe," he breathed, his eyes drifting shut. "Thank god. When I heard the gunshots..."

"I'm safe," I agreed. "You...maybe you should—"

"What is going on here?" roared the familiar—and unwelcome—voice of Councilor Nish mar'Odrea.

I reached over and handed my purloined gun to the nearest *Carpathia* soldier, a casual move that I hoped gave no sign of my desire to raise it and shoot mar'Odrea in the face. *What's going on here? As if you don't know!* He had to be behind this somehow. Though I wouldn't mind knowing how the fuck he got several AFC soldiers into the mix. That one was hell of a trick.

Hands rested on my shoulders: Kiri and Diver. I let them pull me back, away towards our sheltering place, as the arguing began. Captain Chui spoke firmly but quietly, never raising her voice to match mar'Odrea's shouting. And before long more Council members were showing up, more people in general, crowding the breezeway, making noise until I wanted to scream.

"I want answers," mar'Odrea was saying, "and I want them now! Think you that I'll just allow you to slink off to lick your wounds?"

"I thought nothing of the sort," Captain Chui said. "However, some of my people are in need of care, as you can no doubt see."

"She," he began, jabbing a finger in my direction.

"Is also in need of care, and will be receiving it before I ask anything else of her. That is *final*, Councilor. The rest of us will, of course, do as you ask." Before mar'Odrea could protest further, Captain Chui added, "Private Mulroney, get the injured to Doctor Marsten. Kiri, Diver, help Xandri get cleaned up. The rest of you will come with me and help question these... people."

She shot a look of disgust at our assailants. It wasn't that simple, of course—there were bodies to take care of, among other things. But I wouldn't need to worry about any of that. Captain Chui wouldn't allow it.

Starting to feel sick, I leaned into Kiri and Diver as they helped me down the hall. I didn't care how it made me look to slink away from this; I was flat out done.

We made it to the corridor where our rooms were; there we found my Xeno-liaisons team, hovering in a cloud of worried murmuring. Kirrick and Marla spotted me first. Their dark skin—his more brown, hers more black—had taken on vaguely grayish tones. Even Christa was so pale, she seemed almost translucent. I immediately felt guilty for making them worry. *Which is ridiculous, Xandri. You didn't* ask *for someone to attempt to assassinate you.*

"Xandri, are you all—" Christa began, then stopped when she noticed the state of my clothes. "Never mind."

"Christa," Sho murmured, "I have some tea to settle the stomach..."

"Yes! Go brew some, please," she said. "Xandri, why don't you get in the shower? We'll keep watch out here, make sure no one disturbs you."

"Thanks, Christa. I—I appreciate that a lot."

She smiled gently, and I began to wonder why I'd ever thought she would betray us. Surely the saboteur had to be someone else, but who? *Ugh,* I thought, as Diver and Kiri helped me into my room. *There's just no fucking way I can sort this out right now.* What I needed was to get out of my gore spattered clothes before I started screaming. No one could think straight like that.

I didn't care what anyone would think of me for it: I spent a full hour under the hot spray of water, until my skin was red and my fingertips wrinkled. Even afterwards I still felt dirty, as if the blood-soaked material still clung to my skin. I sat, wrapped in a towel, and drank the tea Sho had left for me—usually for the sickness he got from shuttle drops—and it *did* make me feel a bit better. Well enough to change into fresh clothes and leave my room, though I still planned to get a sedative from Doctor Marsten later.

When I stepped out into the hall they were all still there, my team and Diver and Kiri. Anton had joined them. He immediately put an arm around my shoulders and gave me a squeeze; it said something about my emotional state that I really didn't mind.

"Captain Chui called while you were in the shower," Christa told me. "You're wanted in the meeting room."

"And we're coming with you," Marla added.

"And you're not going to argue," Kiri put in.

"No, no I'm not," I agreed. "Let's go."

We must've made a strange entourage, walking the halls of the World Council building. Guards—Anmerilli and human both—had been posted everywhere, alert to the possibility of a second attack. Not that I thought there'd be another.

We arrived at the meeting room to find all the Councilors in attendance. The Anmerilli assailants were there, bound to chairs and gagged for the moment. All eyes turned to us as we came through the door, curious eyes, a few accusing; mar'Odrea and his cronies sneered at me, in my worn tunic, with my hair, still damp, left free around my shoulders. I was too tired to care.

"Oh, *look* who deigned to show her face," mar'Odrea said.

"I'm sorry," I said, taking a seat next to Captain Chui. "Considering I was covered in a man's *brains*, I confess your circus wasn't the first thing on my mind."

"*Excuse* me?"

"You heard me, Councilor." I turned to Captain Chui. "Let me guess. These Anmerilli, upon questioning, insisted that *I* was somehow behind this attack. That it was all a ploy on my part and I was never in any real danger."

The corners of Captain Chui's mouth curled slightly. "Why, either you've developed prescience recently, or you have a pretty good idea what's going on here."

"Of course she does," mar'Odrea said, his eyes agleam. "You may think you're clever, young lady, but we are not fools."

"Indeed, we are not," Kinima Mal agreed, her voice laconic but her eyes narrowed on mar'Odrea in a way that could only be described as dangerous. "Yet someone here seems to think we are, and I'm not convinced that it's Ms. Corelel."

Whoa. I looked around the table. Many of the World Council members—not just the ones who were already on my side—were gazing at mar'Odrea with suspicion and distrust. He stared back at them, his eyes popping slightly, his body language radiating astonishment so clearly it was almost as if he were screaming in my face.

"But—but the attackers confessed," mar'Odrea protested. "They—"

"—most certainly did," Major Douglas agreed, his voice loud and stern. "Very quickly, I might add. In all my years of military service—and they have been many, Councilor—I have never seen anyone confess so quickly. It was quite odd."

Okay, so probably the major also didn't think I was competent enough to plan such subterfuge on my own, but whatever. In this case, I much preferred having him on my side. Though I wasn't entirely sure it was needful.

"I have no military experience," Councilor Ashil put in, "but I *do* recall that just yesterday morning you, mar'Odrea, were insistent that something like this would happen. That is what *I* find suspicious."

A murmuring chorus of agreement rippled around the table. Surprise and, strange though it sounded, pride welled up in my throat. *I haven't been giving these people enough credit. They're not as self-centered as they seem.* All the bickering over the past few weeks had made it seem like they would believe whatever suited them, but they had limits, that much was clear. There was a line, and I had a feeling mar'Odrea had just crossed it.

"Oh, but you don't find it suspicious that several of *their own people* were involved?" mar'Odrea retorted.

"We find that highly *concerning*," Major Douglas interrupted again. "First thing in the morning, Marco Antilles will begin an investigation into the matter." Here he turned to Captain Chui. "He was quite distraught over the danger Ms. Corelel was in tonight, so I ordered him sedated and sent to bed. He was terrified for her life."

"That makes two of us," I muttered, warmed by Marco's concern. Even if I was still a bit freaked out by the way he'd, well, freaked out.

"And that is the part *I* find most suspicious," Councilor Maru spoke up. "I can't fathom Ms. Corelel putting her life in so much danger for this, not when many of us were already considering agreeing to this compromise anyway."

A round of agreeing nods went around the table.

"And it *would* have put her life in danger," Captain Chui said. "The assailants attacked from both sides, exposing Ms. Corelel to crossfire. Had she not been shot then, she could have been killed when they closed in. A ploy that would do our mission more harm than good, but has numerous ways to work to the advantage of someone who doesn't want this alliance."

"I've been with the *Carpathia* for four years," I said, finally speaking up. "I'd know better than to plan a fake assassination attempt that could end with me actually getting killed. But you know what, Councilor? It doesn't matter whether *you* believe me."

I stood up, barely sure what I was doing. Even mar'Odrea's bright-eyed, slightly unhinged stare couldn't make me flinch right now. *Fucking douchebag. I got brains splattered all over me and I had to brush my teeth about five thousand times to rid myself of the taste of a man's blood. You think you're intimidating?* Fuck him. There was a sedative with my name on it and I wasn't going to be delayed from getting it because this bastard couldn't let go.

"I haven't been here as long as Marco Antilles, that's true," I said. "But I've been here long enough. I've felt no need for such convoluted plots because, first of all, I don't believe your people are so foolish as to fall for them, and second of all, I honestly believe this Council does want what's best for your people, in the end.

"If this compromise falls through, I'll find another one. If that one falls through, I'll find a third. I *will* find a way to satisfy as many people as possible, and I don't need tricks to do it. In fact, the only thing I need right now is sleep. I've had a long day, and I see no reason any of us should be held here all night over this. There will be an investigation, and I have no doubt the *real* culprit will be found."

"Oh, yes. And how *convenient* for you that those of your own people who were involved are *dead*," mar'Odrea hissed.

"With all due respect to the AFC, they are *not* my people."

"And as I already said," Major Douglas cut in, sounding furious now, "that will be investigated. Thoroughly. Until it has been, there is no point accusing people based on the highly suspicious testimonies of a handful of wannabe assassins."

"Agreed!" Mal said enthusiastically. "My leg is still healing and I'd very much like to return to my bed."

Mumbles of agreement, many of them sleepy in tone, rustled through the room. I glanced at mar'Odrea, even though looking at him directly hurt so much. The glower he gave me sent a shiver down my spine, but I lifted my chin as if I was not moved in the slightest. *If only you'd been a bit more subtle, you might have succeeded.* He had been succeeding, had been making me look bad, until he pushed too hard. The fool.

I was starting to get too tired to even notice the noise and the press as chairs scraped back and people started to leave. Someone caught my elbow—I glanced over and saw Kiri, her eyes dark with worry. Diver appeared at her side, and then there was my team, and all of them seemed concerned. A sense of warmth came over me and I let them surround me like a wall of protective flesh as we exited the meeting hall.

"I want to talk to Captain Chui," Christa said, breaking off from the group as we walked. "I have a thought on what we can do if parliament doesn't agree to the special membership. Sho and Kimi, come with me?"

I nodded when they both looked to me. "Anything that might help is a good thing. And Kirrick and Marla deserve some sleep, with all the work they've been doing."

"*You* deserve some sleep," Kiri said, still holding onto my arm. "I'm taking you to Doctor Marsten. She'll give you something that'll keep the nightmares at bay."

"Sounds good."

"Looks like mar'Odrea underestimated you, fireball," Diver remarked, sticking close to my other side.

I shook my head and tilted it in the direction of the retreating Anmerilli. "No. He underestimated them."

Chapter Twenty-Six

Kiri and I brought Diver with us to Doctor Marsten's makeshift office. Not that I wanted to be carried around *again*, but the sedative I'd be getting was strong. Strong enough that it would dampen my usual nightly cavalcade of weird ass dreams.

I rarely dreamed of things related to my current reality. I doubted I'd dream about a man's brains soaking into my pants, so you'd think I wouldn't be too worried. But knowing my brain, my dreams would set me down on some alien planet, where the plants pulled up their roots and chased me with gnashing, hungry teeth-petals and I had to get away by surfing, all while struggling to keep up with the incorporeal Ancient Earth mountain goat that was acting as my spirit guide. Not exactly restful, that.

"Here we are," Kiri said, pausing outside Doctor Marsten's door and reaching for the chime. "You hanging in there?"

Mainly I was hanging from Diver, trying desperately to maintain my footing. "Not really. I just want to go to bed."

"Well, I'm sure the doc—ah."

The door slid back to reveal Doctor Marsten, looking a bit worn around the eyes and a bit rumpled everywhere else. A little blood spattered her fresh white coat; the sight of it jogged me out of my torpor for a moment.

"Is everyone all right?"

She smiled. "Nothing some nanobots can't fix," she assured me. "What about you? Are you okay?"

"Depends on your definition of okay," I admitted. "I'm here for a sedative. Preferably the strongest one you've got."

She nodded and gestured for us to come in. Whoever else had been in here, there was no trace of them now; everything was spotless and in its proper place. Paper-thin plastic crinkled as Doctor Marsten drew a fresh sheet down over the medical bed. With Diver's help I reached the bed and plopped down on it, my exhaustion returning in a rush.

"Whoa," Diver murmured, his breath a warm tickle against my neck. "Easy there, Xan."

"Diver, keep a hand on her," Doctor Marsten called from the small table where she sorted through her sedatives. "This will hit her fast and hard."

"All right by me," Diver said, and I could hear the grin in his voice.

Kiri reached over to poke him in the ribs. "Selfish!"

I was too tired for desire or embarrassment or amusement. I slumped on the bed, waiting patiently while Doctor Marsten dosed out the sedative. Satisfied, she approached the bed where I sat and one quick pulse of the hypospray later, the sedative was chugging through my veins like a hell bent starship. I relaxed, my muscles loosening, and slouched back against Diver.

"There we go," Doctor Marsten said. "Get her back to her room. If either of you need anything, you know where to find me."

I barely heard Diver's and Kiri's responses through the rapid rising of sedative-induced blur. My eyes drifted shut and I leaned back farther, into the warmth and strength of Diver. *Got through it,* I thought muzzily, as Diver scooped me up in his arms. *And with any luck, all of this is almost over.* The smell of soap and grease and Diver curled around me as I let my head loll against his chest. *Finally almost over.*

The sun was high when I finally awoke. I rolled over slowly, stretching beneath the covers, feeling more well-rested than I had since this mission began. Sure, I ached from head to toe after the fight last night, but I was getting used to that. *Funny,* I thought as I pushed the covers aside and slid my legs over the edge of the bed. *Normally I only get battered around this much on planets* without *sapient species.* My own personal, low-grade healing 'bots would take care of the bruises soon enough, but for the moment, my legs looked a bit like the hide of a paint horse.

I moved with care as I dressed, slipping into a burnt ochre tunic of the long-sleeved, non-work variety. I sighed in pleasure as the thin, soft cotton settled down on my skin, and let the sleeves flop down past my hands.

Coffee waited for me in a therma-pot, alongside a nutrient-bar. I settled down at my small table and filled a mug with coffee, using my thumb to turn on my wristlet at the same time. It pinged and vibrated softly, informing me of new messages and files. Sipping coffee and taking nibbles from my nutrient-bar, I sorted through everything that had been sent my way, truly relaxed for the first time since we set down on Cochinga.

When I finished, I opened our private comm channel, sending a ping directly to Christa's HUD.

"*You're awake,*" she answered, and I winced. Was I rubbing off on her?

"*Yeah,*" I said, sub-vocalizing even in the privacy of my borrowed room. "*I've looked over the notes you sent me, too.*"

"*Oh, good. I've had the team prying into it for a while, but we've only been able to get some information recently,*" Christa said. "*The Council members have been speaking with their constituents about the Alliance agreement. They were at it pretty much all day yesterday.*" She paused. "*Well, at least,* most *of them were.*"

"*Let me guess. mar'Odrea was conspicuously absent from those activities.*"

"*Got it in one.*"

I sighed and glanced at the holo-display again. In most regions of Cochinga, anti-gun sentiment was strong; in a few it was overwhelming; in a very few, it came only from a minority. I'd seen this before in history class, more than once. People reached a point in society where they got alarmed by how much they were dying, generally from bullet wounds. They started to worry about their children, started speaking out against gun ownership. Sometimes, politicians listened. Sometimes they only listened to the gun-toting loudmouths. *And then someone else pays the price...*

A shiver walked down my spine and I swallowed hard. That was how it started on Ancient Earth. Too many guns, too many shootings, and too many people declaring the shooters "mentally ill" or autistic, like me. I didn't know the truth of it—I didn't really want to. All I knew was that when the dust finally settled and the furor died down, people like me had been erased. My very existence was a fluke.

"*Xandri?*" Christa's voice echoed in my ears, snapping me back to the moment.

"*Sorry,*" I said. "*I had a rough night last night.*"

Her voice came through gentler this time. "*I know. Look, we can discuss this later, okay? Maybe you should take a walk or something, get some air.*"

"*You know, that sounds like a good idea, actually.*" And then, before I could stop myself, I blurted out, "*Why are you being so nice to me?*"

In the silence that followed, I had to fight the urge to whack my forehead against the table. *Damnit, Xandri,* what *is wrong with you?* I hadn't wanted to be mean—I was genuinely curious—but I was willing to bet the words had come out snappish and short-tempered. They'd sounded a bit like that to my ear, at least, and I was becoming a much better judge of my tone than I'd once been. The controlling it part, however, seemed to be lost on me.

"*I'm sorry,*" I said. "*I wasn't trying to—I mean, I didn't want—*"

To my surprise, Christa chuckled. "*You're in a better mood than I would be if I'd gotten someone's brains spattered all over me less than a day ago. Just go for that walk, okay? Clear your head.*"

"*Okay.*" I refrained from mentioning that my head was *never* clear, since my mouth had run amok enough for one day.

I signed off the comm channel and sat back with a sigh. *You're not dealing with politicians who don't listen to their people this time, Xan.* I pushed my chair back and stood, giving my sleeve-covered hands a shake. I couldn't let myself think negative thoughts. I needed to go elsewhere, look at other things, try to fill my mind's eye with images other than that man's head exploding, and my ears with sounds other than gunshots.

I drew my hood up and shoved my already covered hands in my kangaroo pouch, then used my elbow to open the door. No surprise, Katya stood just outside, on alert. Several extra weapons hung from her belt today, including a blade and a more heavy-duty gun.

"Well, look who decided to rejoin the living," she teased.

"Had to be done eventually." I shrugged. "And before you ask, yes, I ate my nutrient-bar."

"Good. Are you planning on heading somewhere?"

"Just for a walk. I need to—I don't know, clear my head, something."

"All right. I'll buzz Anton, then. Captain's got you on double guard whenever you leave your room."

After last night, I guess I couldn't be surprised. But I wondered how annoyed Anton would be, after all the times he'd been dragged out of bed to protect me.

Not at all, as it turned out. He took one look at me and swept me into a one armed hug, ruffling my hair with the other hand. A surprising glow of warmth spread through my chest. *I guess I don't want him to be annoyed with me and—and it feels good that he isn't.* I slipped an arm around his broad bulk and gave him a quick squeeze in return before slipping out of his grasp. His look of surprised gratitude almost made me laugh.

"No weapons?" he asked me as we started down the hall.

I shook my head. Right now, the idea of touching a gun gave me a cold feeling in the pit of my stomach. I knew I ought to carry them, and I knew I ought to learn how to defend myself without them, but I didn't want to think about it right now.

I listened to Katya and Anton tease and flirt as we walked, which was far more pleasant than being stuck in my own head. We took a slow, circuitous route, avoiding the breezeway where the ambush had taken place; I took that time to drink in the architecture, the glittering seashell and the swirling shapes. Wondering about the techniques they used also kept most of my brain focused on better things. There was always one thread at the back, carrying on about doom-and-gloom, but I could drown it out easier now.

"Xandri," Katya murmured.

I blinked. We'd entered another breezeway, and I was watching the scenery outside when Katya called my name. At first I thought she was alerting me to our location; then I saw Marco perched on the wide breezeway rail, hunching over his sketchpad.

His dark curls were more rumpled than usual and he wasn't in uniform. The sleeves of his simple, dark shirt were shoved up to his elbows, and pastel chalk stained his hands up to his wrists. I approached quietly, moving on the balls of my feet so I wouldn't disturb him. Nonetheless, something must have alerted him to my presence, because he looked up. Smudges like bruises hung beneath his eyes, but he smiled when he saw me.

"Xandri," he said, as I perched on the rail next to him. "How're you?"

I couldn't help a nervous glance over my shoulder, but the land around us was too flat and open for an ambush during the day.

"Better than I could be, but not as well as I'd like. What about you?" I tilted my head, studying his face. "I um...I heard you were really upset last night. That you needed a sedative."

"You could've been killed. What was I supposed to be, sunshine and rainbows?"

"Well, no. But...I've never seen you like that before."

I didn't elaborate on what 'that' was; we both knew. Marco sighed and ran his fingers through his hair, oblivious of the chalk all over them. While he was collecting his thoughts, I glanced at the drawing on the pad.

A woman's face gazed back at me. She wasn't beautiful, her features too simple and plain for beauty, but...the way Marco had drawn her, she seemed to radiate light. He'd shaded everything in yellow and orange and brown, creating a golden-bronze effect, like a glow that spilled from her pores. That glow haloed out around her face, so even though she wasn't quite smiling, brightness reflected in her eyes, making them alive with electric blue luminescence.

"That's amazing," I murmured. "Is she someone you know, or did you make her up?"

He stared at me. "Xandri. It's you."

"*Me*? I don't look like *that*." Did I?

"Not all the time, no. But you should've seen yourself at the menagerie yesterday. Sometimes you shone so bright, it was hard to look at you."

I looked away, my cheeks burning. To stop my hands from going, I shifted them under my thighs. Maybe I should be flattered, but instead a prickle of embarrassment crept up my throat. I knew I got intense—often more intense than most people could handle—and I tried so hard to keep it under wraps. People tended to look at me funny when I was practically bouncing in excitement over something they found only mild interesting.

"Don't—don't take it the wrong way," Marco said hastily. "I draw what's interesting to draw. It's not like some weird stalker thing."

"Why would I think that?" Maybe I was naive or something, but I honestly didn't have a clue.

"Well, after last night..."

"What *did* happen last night?" I asked, perhaps a bit more bluntly than was socially acceptable. Hooray, life as me. "I mean,

Marco…maybe you think I won't understand but—I kinda bit a chunk out of a guy just to get away from him. Do you know how many times I've had to brush my teeth? Sometimes, when we're desperate…"

"I was *scared*," Marco said hoarsely. "When I saw what was happening and that you were in danger, it terrified me. I don't—always react well in dangerous situations. Sometimes I fall back completely on my instincts."

I tipped my head, considering. On the one hand, his actions had been brutally violent. On the other hand, my own had been pretty violent for me—*shudder*—because I hadn't known what else to do. And as much as I hated it, I was *alive* now thanks to my actions, and the actions of those who had come to my rescue. Who was I to judge?

"Okay."

He blinked. "Okay? That's it? You're not…upset?"

"Of course I'm upset. Hello, how many times do I have to point out that I had some dude's brains all over me?" I tried a smile, and Marco grinned back, looking more like himself. "But I'm not upset at you. That would be hypocritical of me, right? Besides, from the looks of things, we're almost home free, and that's something to celebrate."

"Ah, yes. I heard about that. Who do you think you are, Jeanne d'Arc? A few weeks and you've changed everything?"

His teasing smile made me blush again. "I didn't change anything."

"What are you talking about? Before you got here, we couldn't get anywhere with the Anmerilli. You changed their minds."

I shook my head. "But that's just it, don't you see? What's happening now—it's proof that change was coming for them anyway. The Anmerilli people *wanted* a lot of this. If they hadn't, there would've been nothing I could do."

"I don't believe that."

"Well, nothing I would've *wanted* to do. Change is always best if it comes from the inside," I explained. "That's my philosophy. It has to be something people feel. If you force it on people from the outside, it just becomes a set of instructions they're following, not something that has meaning to them. They'll drop it the moment they get the chance, or corrupt it."

241

Marco shook his head and let out a small, incredulous laugh. "You really *do* have a good grasp on people."

I swung my legs, letting the movement carry me down off the railing. "People still think that when Darwin said 'survival of the fittest' he meant the strongest, the fastest, the smartest." I lifted a shoulder in a half shrug and smiled wryly. "But he didn't. He meant the most adaptable. Adapt to survive. That's the other half of my philosophy."

Our eyes met. Something flickered in Marco's gaze and I couldn't tell if it was pity or understanding. Maybe it was both. I tossed my hair back, wishing I'd put it in a braid, and forced myself to smile. My cheeks hurt from the effort and I doubted it was convincing, but I held it anyway.

"Are you feeling any better now?"

"Yeah," Marco said. "Thanks, Xandri."

"That's what friends are for." More like that's what I *believed* friends were for. Most of the ones I'd had in life hadn't felt that way. "I'd better get going, though. I have some business to attend to with my team."

Marco gave me a lazy salute that would've made Captain Chui's mouth twist like she was sucking a lemon. I returned a much sharper—though still bad—version and headed on my way. Anton and Katya had taken up positions on either end of the hall, doing the whole silent, invisible bodyguard thing. They converged on me now.

"Let's get out of here," Anton said. "These damn open hallways give me the creeps now."

"They're perfectly lovely when no one's trying to shoot me," I responded.

Katya shook her head. "No thanks. First storm comes in off the ocean and suddenly you're stuck inside your room unless you want to risk being blown away. Not what I call a fun time."

"Oh, you don't like being blown away, huh?"

Realizing they were about to go back into flirt mode, I tuned them out. As we passed out of the breezeway, I took one last look over my shoulder at Marco. He'd gone back to drawing, his fingers moving in swift, elegant strokes across the paper. Despite everything, a shiver went down my spine when I thought of the way he'd looked last night, beating that soldier to a pulp. *Stop being so squeamish, Xan. You're going to have to adjust to this stuff eventually.*

I was woken the next morning when my door flew open. Still half-asleep, I rolled out of bed and was reaching for my pistol before I realized that my entire team, plus Diver, Kiri and Marco, had filed into my room. My fingers closed around the grip as I came to my feet.

"Nice reaction time," Diver remarked.

"Nice PJs," Kiri teased.

I glanced down at myself and sighed. At least my shirt covered most of what it needed to. I dropped my arms, still gripping the pistol, and glared at the crowd that had overtaken my room. First fucking thing in the morning, at god-only-fucking-knows o'clock, and my personal space was being invaded.

"There had better be a good explanation for this," I said, "because if this is just a game of Spanish Inquisition, I'm going to have to open fire."

"Not a morning person, is she?" Marco faux-whispered to Diver.

"No, she is *not*," I snapped. "I haven't had my coffee yet, so someone start explaining or I start shooting." Not to kill, of course, but I had a stun setting on this thing that could make an elephant think twice.

Christa didn't even seem flustered by my attitude. "We heard back from parliament. They've agreed to your special membership and the Anmerilli will be voting on it tomorrow."

"Not to mention it looks like the vote will go in our favor," Marco added with a wide grin. "Xandri, you did it!"

"I really couldn't have had my coffee first?"

They all laughed like I'd said something hilarious. I stared at them, bemused. *I don't get it. Surely this could've waited five minutes.* I set my pistol down and glanced around my room. No breakfast had been left for me this time. I tried to hide my disappointment, since my companions seemed so excited, but damnit. Coffee. How was I supposed to be a living, sapient being without it?

"I think we should go out tonight," Marco said. "This calls for a celebration."

Everyone cheered.

"Cof-fee," I said, enunciating as clearly as I could.

A hand reached in through the doorway, passing a therma-pot to Diver. "Give this to her or she'll be moaning about brains before long."

I heaved a happy sigh as the smell reached my nose. Thank god for Anton. I could almost get used to this bodyguard business. Too bad he also passed Diver a nutrient-bar.

Chapter Twenty-Seven

I stared at my hair in the mirror, on the verge of finding a scissor and cutting it all off. It was on its worst behavior today; no matter what I did, it kept slipping out of my grasp so I couldn't get it braided. Maybe it was time to seriously consider hair 'bots. Though there was a limit to what they could do for hair *texture*; they were much more useful for hair *color*.

I tuned into our comm channel and wailed, out loud, "Kiri! My hair is driving me baffy!"

"This is why I 'loc mine," came back Kiri's voice, rich with the tone of a chuckle.

"Even if white girl 'locs didn't look hideous," I retorted, "we both know my hair would *never*. Not in a million years."

"All right, all right. I'll be there in a minute."

I ran my fingers through my hair again and let out a disgusted sigh. Since we were going out to celebrate, I'd dressed up—in my case, that meant the outfit I'd worn a couple weeks ago for the reception banquet. *Full circle, Xan. This is finally almost over.* It still bothered me a little that I'd been needed for this at all—that somehow the people working on it for years couldn't figure it out—but then again, everyone was shortsighted sometimes.

A knock on my door pulled me out of my thoughts. I turned to answer it. Kiri stood waiting for me, and I had to bite my lip to keep my jaw from hitting the floor. She looked like a nebula in a dress of swirling purples, pinks and reds, with a flare of orange and yellow over her eyes and black beads tipping off her 'locs. The dress was some kind of silk, with a corseted bodice and a dramatic skirt that swooped down to her ankle on one side, and exposed her leg up to the thigh on the other. I was too stunned to feel frumpy.

"That's a lovely color of red on you," she teased, laughing.

"Well, at least *something* about my wardrobe is lovely," I muttered.

"We could change that, you know," Kiri said, gesturing for me to take a seat on the bed. "I could help you design some things for occasions like this."

"Maybe. It's just...most of the time I don't deal with occasions like this. Usually I'm hiking through jungles or digging in mud or being chased by something abnormally hungry and aggressive."

I settled on the bed. Kiri gathered a comb and a bunch of hair pins from the table and sat behind me. I couldn't hold back a sigh of pleasure as her fingers ran through my hair, smoothing it gently away from my face. Warmth tingled along my nerves as her fingertips lightly brushed the curves of my ears. She leaned forward and her breath, hot and tickling and arousing, coursed over my neck.

"Who said you can't do those things with style?"

"Uh..."

"By the way," Kiri went on, her lips brushing my ear as she leaned closer, "no matter what, we're in the clear. Diver and I cracked it."

It took a second for my fuzzy brain to catch her meaning. My ears were sensitive and every word she spoke sent shivers of heat and pleasure through me. "The schematics?" I managed. "You've got them?"

"We've got everything the Anmerilli had," Kiri confirmed, keeping her voice low. "Diver suspects our scientists could sort out the missing pieces fairly quickly—quicker if the Anmerilli work with us. But either way, it's ours now."

I slumped, my relief so intense it almost knocked me to the floor. The graser was in our hands and even if everything went to hell and the Zechak ended up with it too, we wouldn't be defenseless. The *people of the universe* wouldn't be defenseless. With any luck, we wouldn't see another incident like the Nīpa Diaspora. *I won't let it happen again. If I have to fight every Zechak off with my bare hands, I won't let it happen again.*

"It's all right now, starshine. Everything will be all right."

I let her words flow through me and her touch relax me, feeling truly confident for the first time in weeks.

The pink-colored drink smelled fruity and enticing, even to someone who didn't care much for alcohol. I leaned in and took a curious sniff. *Mmm.* I glanced at Diver, who had already had two of them. *What the hell? Can't hurt to try.*

One cautious sip later and I was drinking in large gulps. It tasted mainly of berries and sunlight, or perhaps more like the sensation of sunlight, warm on one's face. I couldn't taste the sting of alcohol and the drink slid smoothly down the throat, as refreshing as lemonade on a hot day. A hand closed around my wrist as I drank, and pulled the glass away.

"Easy there," Diver said. "This stuff is a lot stronger than it tastes."

"Oh, give her a break," Marco chimed in from my other side. He grinned his charming, boyish grin at me. "Anyone else would've been driven to drink weeks ago. At least let her celebrate."

"Celebrating is all well and good, but I think she should stick to teetotaler levels of celebration."

Here's a better idea. How about you both shut up and let me make my own decisions? Maybe if I'd already had more to drink, I would've lost control and said it out loud. I didn't, but I *did* take another long, defiant gulp of my beverage.

The restaurant Marco had brought us to was quite unlike anything I'd seen before. Though the walls still seemed to be crafted of seashell, it was a dark shell, almost black with iridescent shimmers of purple and green. The walls also sloped, at the base and at the top, curving so it felt like the place had no edges, a feeling almost similar to being in space. Both the ceiling and the floor were made of a see-through material somewhere between glass and plastic; above us was a sky filled with stars and below us, dark, loamy earth.

To me, the most fascinating part was the tables. Made from that same material as the floor and ceiling, they were built with sloped edges, and water fell through the insides, cascading down. At the sides the water flowed through tubes, right into the benches underneath us. I kept poking—surreptitiously, I hoped—at the tabletop with my finger, half expecting it to dip into liquid.

"—and besides, it's on me." Marco's words reached me as I went in for another poke.

"That's...quite generous." Captain Chui, across the table and a short distance down, raised her eyebrows at Marco. "Please excuse my indiscretion but...can you afford that on your salary? The *Carpathia* does have funds, Mr. Antilles."

Marco's laugh came out clarion bright, stinging my eyes. *Space-fried synesthesia.*

"So I've been told, but really, it's fine. You lot have gotten me off this spiky rock. This is the least I can do." He raised a hand and snapped his fingers, catching the attention of a passing waiter. "Another drink for our heroine, I think. She's earned it."

"Oh, that's all right. You don't have to—"

"It's my honor, Xandri," Marco assured me, his eyes almost as unbearably bright as his laugh. "Especially after everything you've done."

His voice sounded odd to my ears, but then, I was sitting at a crowded table in a crowded restaurant, and only the fascinating table in front of me helped me tune out the sheer *presence* of all the people surrounding me. I reached for my drink again. Maybe if I drank enough to relax, I'd hear things properly. *It's just the stress getting to me,* I thought, ignoring the frown Diver sent my way. *Everything is so bright and loud and I can't quite grasp it all properly.*

Below me the tabletop clouded over suddenly, blocking out the view of the water. A moment later writing appeared, in an Anmerilli dialect with a Trade Common translation underneath. Which helped very little, in the grand scheme of things.

"Want some help?"

I jumped a little and glanced up. Marco leaned close to me and nodded in the direction of my menu.

"Please," I said. "Anything so I don't have to stuff another nutrient-bar down my poor, abused gullet."

He let out another too-bright laugh and started in on my menu, describing the foods he thought I might like. I continued to sip my drink and soon moved onto my second, ignoring the glances thrown my way by my fellow *Carpathia* members. Even Katya and Anton were eyeing me funny. *Like I'm a child who should never be allowed to make her own choices.* Well, screw them.

It wasn't like they didn't drink their fair share with dinner. In fact, the entire table grew louder and more raucous as the evening progressed and the alcohol flowed, especially the soldiers. Even

Captain Chui had a slight pink flush to her cheeks, though she drank far less than anyone else.

"Hey Xan!" Anton's voice boomed across the table. "Do that trick you do."

I looked up from my—whatever it was—and stared at him. "Trick?"

"You know, the thing with the names and the colors."

Katya elbowed him. "That's not a trick, you lunk. It's how her brain works."

"Aw, c'mon, it's fucking cool. Do it, Xandri, please?"

I sighed. I noticed Marco eyeing me curiously and explained, "I'm synesthetic. It—it basically means my senses are kind of mixed up. Like I can see sounds, and names and words have colors, and all sorts of things like that. Um, like, Diver is blue with a bit of gray mixed in, and Kiri is yellow, and—"

"Me! What about me?" Anton demanded.

"Red," I said flatly, since I'd told him about a thousand times. "And Kat is yellow too, but there's some red in there."

"You've never told me mine," Captain Chui commented.

I reached for my—third? fourth?—glass and took a sip. "It's a bit odd. Chui is sort of...yellowish-white? Or perhaps whiteish-yellow. Shan is orange-red and Fung is...grayish? I can't always tell," I explained to Marco.

"What about me?" he asked. "What about my name?"

With the drink coursing through my veins, relaxing me, I almost just blurted out the answer. Something stopped me before I could answer, could tell him that his name, the sense of *him*, passed behind my eyes as pure black. People often didn't quite understand that I had no control over what associations my mind made. I'd found that people with black names tended to take offense, thinking there was somehow some deeper meaning to it when there wasn't.

"Blue," I said instead.

"Do me next!" called a soldier from down the table.

"Why sir," I replied, laughing slightly, "I don't even know your name!"

The double-sided joke brought a roar of laughter down around me, and the warmth of alcohol in my veins made me grin instead of flinch. Laughing and flushing a little beneath the teasing of his fellows, the soldier hollered his name down the table to me: Emin.

"Green," I told him. There was a hint of black in there, but I was afraid to mention it, lest Marco catch on. It was the M that did it.

Soon I found myself giving out colors to every member of our table, and a few from the tables around us. Sometimes I couldn't quite define the color; a few slipped through my grasp like my hair tended to, and some were colors that humans had no name for. Those I had to describe to the best of my ability.

Maybe it was the drink, or maybe it was the fact that we'd succeeded at last, but for once the game was fun, rather than just another round of curious neurotypicals poking at my brain meats.

"Whoa! Easy there."

I giggled as Marco caught me around the shoulders and pulled me upright. Not that it was funny, I just couldn't help giggling. The damn crushed seashell paths were *not* working for me. They seemed to swim under my feet as I tried to walk.

"She okay?" Anton called. He trailed behind us while Katya walked in front, giving us just enough distance for privacy.

"I'm fine," I said indignantly. "It's not my fault the ground is being all squishy and wriggly. It ought to stop moving."

"Agreed," Marco joked. "That's horribly impolite of it."

I laughed like it was the funniest thing I'd heard in ages. Marco laughed with me, the sound lower and throatier than my high-pitched, almost hysterical chortles. I should probably quiet down. I knew the others were not that far away, strung out across the path back to the Council building some short distances behind and in front of us, and they could probably hear me. But I felt so light and free for once.

"Okay, maybe I shouldn't have bought you that final drink," Marco conceded, still chuckling.

"I'm *fine*," I insisted. "It's not the alcohol, it's the relief."

"Glad you'll be going back to your normal job?"

"Mmmhmm. But mostly just glad no one's going to be blown to kingdom come." I slapped a hand over my mouth and giggled through my fingers. "Whoops. Wasn't supposed to say that."

Silence met my giggles. Marco kept walking. I glanced at him, trying desperately to read his face in the moonlight. *God, Xandri, what the fuck is wrong with you? You've done it now!* I hadn't meant to say it, I really hadn't. But it had been haunting me, occupying the back of my mind for so long, and I couldn't really talk about it. Now it wouldn't happen. I'd stopped it from happening without threats or violence or trickery.

"What do you mean by that?" Marco asked quietly.

I shook my head.

"It's all right, Xandri. I'm not going to tell on you." He caught my hand in his and gave it a squeeze. "I've been with the AFC long enough to know that sometimes, there's unpleasant things going on behind the scenes. I guess I'm just worried. It sounds like you've been holding onto a burden for a while now."

"It's losTavina," I blurted out, relieved at finally being able to speak the words. Thank god I had the good sense to keep my voice down. "I knew he was planning something when I heard that the entire fleet of Malevolence-class ships were in port, but..."

As we walked, the words flowed out of me like venom being drawn from a snakebite. Marco listened without comment, though from time to time he gave my hand a gentle squeeze. I outlined losTavina's actions at Halcyon during the Second Zechak War and how we'd come to our suspicions about what he was planning to do with the Malevolence ships. By the time it was all out, the lights of the Council building had appeared in the near distance.

"Captain Chui doesn't believe Admiral losTavina would do more than threaten the Anmerilli," I said around a hiccup. "And maybe he wouldn't, I don't know. But I would never let it happen either way."

"Xandri..."

"I mean it! If I had to blow the whistle on him, even if it meant I'd get thrown in jail for it, I'd do everything in my power to stop him from going through with it."

"I know you would," Marco said softly. "But hey... you don't have to, right? The problem is solved, the agreement will most likely be signed, and the Anmerilli will be none the wiser."

"And *I* can go back to what I prefer to do," I agreed. "I hate all this sneakiness and subterfuge. I hate having to keep secrets, especially from my friends."

Marco leaned over and kissed my temple. "No hard feelings, Xan. I get it. That's not the sort of thing that should ever get out. We get that in the AFC, too; it's just a thing that happens when sapients are involved, I guess."

"And people wonder why I prefer animals," I muttered.

"Oh, I don't wonder at all."

I ran a hand over my face. "I shouldn't have told you this..."

"You shouldn't have had to hold it in like that. I wish I'd known; maybe I could've found more ways to help you."

"You've helped me plenty. I doubt I would've gotten through all this without you. I really didn't even want to come," I admitted, "but when we figured out losTavina's plan, I knew I had to. We all had to."

The Council building loomed above us now. Marco helped me up the slightly sloping path, to where Katya waited by the doorway. I knew Anton would close the distance soon. Marco leaned in close to me, his voice a mere whisper now.

"Like I've said before, your secrets are safe with me. *You* will always be safe with me," he said.

I sighed, a contented sound, and warmth filled me despite the slight chill blowing in from the ocean. The last thing I had expected was to make friends on Cochinga, but it seemed I'd made at least one. *Maybe more than one.* I looked up into the tired but happy faces of Katya and Anton, and for the first time in my life, thought that maybe I was fitting in with the people around me.

My elation came crashing down as we all stepped into the back chamber of the building and I found Christa waiting for me, her arms folded, one foot tapping impatiently. *Oh, stellar.* On the bright side, seeing her was like being drenched under a tall wave of arctic water, leaving me feeling stone cold sober.

"She still doesn't trust me, I take it," Marco murmured.

"Either that, or I did something else to piss her off," I whispered back. "Maybe even both. Damnit, and things were going so well between us."

"I'm sure you can clear things up," he said, patting my shoulder. "And try to get some sleep tonight, yeah? You'll need to be present at the vote tomorrow."

I nodded. *Hopefully I won't be too hungover.*

Marco said his goodnights to Anton and Katya. As he passed Christa, he nodded cordially to her, which seemed to loosen the tension in her somewhat. Marco shoved his hands in the pockets of his neat, military style trousers and headed off into the breezeway, whistling. *Good to see he's in a better mood.*

Me though...I glanced at Christa and sighed. *I* had to face the music.

Chapter Twenty-Eight

"You still don't trust him, do you?" I said, intending to get the jump on Christa.

She looked startled. *Oh shit, I put my foot in it again.* I buried my face in my hands, knowing I should apologize but suddenly too exhausted to get the words out. What I needed was to be back on *Carpathia*, closed in my room with only my birds and books for company. Oh, how I missed Marbles and Cake. It would be so good to finally see them again.

"I... I didn't intend it to come off that way," Christa said. "I guess it comes out whether I want it to or not."

"That must be a total nightmare," I said, in the driest, most deadpan tone I could manage.

I started walking, heading towards the breezeway Marco had passed through. I needed to get back to my room and get some sleep. Even though the voting wouldn't start until afternoon, I'd need plenty of time to shake off those delicious—but clearly not Xandri-safe—drinks.

"I'm not here to talk about Marco, though," Christa went on, following me. Apparently she'd had enough to drink that she didn't care about my rudeness. "I really don't know why I still have a problem with him. Especially after the good advice he gave me. Yeah, it seemed suspicious at first, but it worked out."

"Advice?"

"Yeah, you know. It was his idea for me to spend so much time with Councilor mar'Odrea. I thought it seemed weird at first, since mar'Odrea *clearly* isn't on our side, but if I hadn't, I wouldn't have known what he was up to that night with the baenil skin."

Wait, what? *That doesn't sound right somehow...* My brain was foggy from drink and exhaustion, which made it harder to spool backwards through the Rolodex-like structure of my memories. I flipped through it determinedly anyway, hardly hearing Christa's words as she carried on. Something was *wrong* and instinct lashed me onward, forcing me to focus on figuring out what.

"No, this isn't about Marco. It's about you. Xandri...you're our leader."

Hadn't Marco said that *he* would work on mar'Odrea, that he would, at the least, keep the man in check? And—and hadn't he said he didn't know anything about the time Christa was spending with the Councilor? Yes, yes I was quite sure he had; the memory was like a moving picture in my head, complete with scents and sounds and the non sequitur observations that had been traveling through my head.

"And you—you need to set a good example. Someone in your position really shouldn't drink so much in public like that."

"Hey, give her a break," Anton cut in. "She's not a politician or a diplomat. She shouldn't have to be some fucking paragon."

"This is not our usual mission, Mr. Mulroney," Christa snapped. "She can't just act out like some teenager rebelling against her parents."

Any other time the remark would've sent me right through the roof, but my mind was too busy spinning and spinning around my current problem, trying to put it into focus even as I careened dizzily around it. Surely it couldn't be. Surely there had just been some misunderstanding somewhere. None of this made sense.

"Xandri, are you listening to me?" Christa demanded.

"What?" I gave my head a shake. "Look, Christa, can we talk about this some other time? I need to get some sleep."

She gaped at me. I stormed past her as she froze to the spot, too astonished to know quite what to say. Anton and Katya hurried to keep up with me as I wound my way back to my room, lost in the cloud of my thoughts. Marco was my friend. He'd tried to stop the hunt for me. He'd pointed me in the direction of allies. He'd listened to me just now with patience and understanding, and sworn he wouldn't tell my secrets. This *had* to be a misunderstanding.

"You all right, Xan?" Katya asked me as I reached for the door. "You seem upset."

I kept my eyes on the door. "I'm really tired. It hit me very suddenly and—and I just want to go to sleep."

"All right. Well, I've got first shift, and Anton will be out in around five or six hours. If you need anything, just let us know."

I nodded and pushed my door open. As soon as it was shut and locked behind me, I made a beeline for my balcony. I needed the cold ocean air to clear my head and help me think straight. Salt tang rushed over me, burning through my nose and down my throat, as I leaned on the balcony railing.

I remembered just a moment too late. *Don't worry, your secret is safe with me.* The words reverberated in my mind, as clear as if I was hearing them just now. I straightened. Something landed behind me, so quiet I barely heard it, and then a hand clamped over my mouth. I opened my mouth to bite and something acrid burned down my throat and up into my nose. Snarling, I fought against the hold on me, trying to get teeth around flesh, thinking my filter-implant would save me. But I was wrong.

Oh shi—

My eyelids felt so heavy. *No, not heavy, precisely.* I couldn't seem to open them, but it was more like my eyelashes were glued together. My head throbbed in time with my pulse and my mouth tasted worse than it did after a filter rinse. I seemed to be lying on something really hard, something that made my bones aches. And for some reason I couldn't move my arms very well, not even to do something about the white hot slashes of pain across my wrists.

Okay, Xandri, I know *you didn't get this drunk last night, so sort it out.* Where was I and how had I ended up—

Memories slammed into me suddenly. Me spilling my guts to Marco. Christa telling me that the time she spent with mar'Odrea had been Marco's idea. Me remembering that Marco had told me he knew nothing about it. I had just been starting to put the pieces together when—when—*the balcony.* Marco was the only one who knew I liked to stand out on the balcony to think.

A rustle sounded, followed by a series of soft, hurried sounds. With a great force of will, I got my eyes open. Something showered down from my eyelashes, leaving bits of crusty gunk at the corners of my eyes that I desperately wanted to brush away. I tried to raise my arms to do just that, and found my wrists bound by thick, vaguely elastic plastotape. My wristlet was gone. My pulse quickened. *Xandri, you've really done it this time.*

More movement. I kept my eyelashes swept downward, sliding my eyes around in an attempt to make out my surroundings. I couldn't see much aside from plain walls and Marco's back. He stood across from me, setting up some kind of computer. So it *had* been him on the balcony. But why?

Panic started to close my throat. I squeezed my eyes shut and forced myself to take a deep, long breath. I might want to curl up and scream and cry—might feel on the verge of doing so—but I absolutely *could not*. I had to figure this out. I was tied up god only knew where and my wristlet was gone. If I wanted any chance of sorting this out and escaping, I had to be clever about it. So I forced myself to keep breathing, slow and deep, and kept my eyes closed so that Marco would think I was still unconscious if he looked over.

But none of this makes any *sense! Why would Marco kidnap me?* I could think of only one reason: To keep me away from tomorrow's—today's?—vote. Or possibly to keep me from cleaning up the mess I'd made by blurting out Admiral losTavina's plan. *Knowing your luck, Xan, it's going to be both.* But *why*? To sabotage the alliance? He was a member of the AFC. He had no reason to want to sabotage this alliance—every reason to help it along, in fact—and the AFC would *never* do this. So why—

My eyes flew open and I let out a gasp before I could stop myself. There were two groups of people in the universe who would *love* to sabotage this alliance.

Marco dropped what he was doing and spun around. *Damnit.* No hiding that I was awake now. Struggling to hold in my fear—I had no idea what he'd do to me—I blinked at him with as much grogginess as I could manage. He approached me and, with gentleness that shocked me, helped me up into a sitting position. I leaned back against the wall, letting my bound arms drop to my lap.

"Good," he said, laying a hand across my forehead. "You're awake, and no ill effects as far as I can tell. Sorry I had to dose you with something so strong, but I had to make sure it would get past your filter. Don't worry, we'll get you rinsed out once we're safe."

"Safe?" I managed to croak. I was in a tiny room with bare walls and a complicated looking lock on the single door; my hands were bound and my only means of communication was gone; and I'd been kidnapped by a man who was working for the Zechak or the Last Hope for Humanity, or both. Clearly Marco and I did *not* share a definition here.

"Yes, safe," he said in reassuring tones. "Now that the Anmerilli know what the Alliance was planning to do to them if they refused to sign, it's not safe for you here. They're furious, and they're extra furious that you didn't show up for the vote. But don't worry. I'll protect you from those monkey-tailed bastards and your so-called Alliance."

I couldn't help a moan of despair. I'd ruined *everything*. I let my head fall back against the wall. Maybe I *should* just curl up and cry. What else was I good for? I'd been sent to do one thing, one simple thing, and I'd fucked it up but good. If only I'd been smarter, if only I'd talked to my team more and confronted Christa about mar'Odrea, if I hadn't trusted this man, hadn't believed he was my friend. Hadn't I had enough false friends already to know better?

But his words kept niggling at my brain despite my anguish. *Fight it, Xan. You can meltdown later.* Because no matter how much his betrayal hurt—and it cut through me like a hot knife—his words told me what I was dealing with. The Zechak might be imperialist bastards, but I'd only heard terms like "so-called Alliance" from LHFHers.

How? Why? Okay, why was obvious: The LHFH hated other species and didn't want humanity allying with any of them. This, though, this was new. If Marco was really a member of the LHFH, then he'd worked damn hard to infiltrate the AFC, going so far as to successfully complete diplomatic missions to earn promotions. I'd never heard of the LHFH involved in that kind of subterfuge. They were little more than dangerous but low grade terrorists, as far as I knew.

"Xandri?"

I blinked. Marco was staring at me, his expression concerned. "Sorry," I murmured. "Whatever you used is still... still getting to me a little." I let my eyelids droop, in the hopes that it would make it harder for my eyes to give me away. "And I'm so thirsty."

"I'll get you some water, okay?"

I nodded as if I was too weak to put up much fuss, a fakery not that hard to pull off. Everything inside me shook with fear and horror. If only I could understand what was going on.

258

As Marco got to his feet and headed back to the computer—and the bag sitting beside it—I tried scanning back through my memories. There were things that looked a lot more suspicious now, things perhaps I should have seen. He *had* said he would handle mar'Odrea for me, had said he would stop the hunt when he saw how much I didn't want to go, and yet it had gone forward anyway. If he really had mar'Odrea's ear, he could have stopped it—unless he had other reasons for wanting it to go through. And the night with the baenil skin. I'd thought Christa might have been the one to reveal my weakness, but Marco had seen me too, that night on the balcony when I cried my eyes out.

At least now I knew how he'd made those jumps on and off the balcony. The LHFH were big fans of military-grade gene-jumping.

"Here we go." Marco knelt again and held a bottle of water to my lips. "Sorry about the bonds, but that's how it has to be for now."

I nodded and opened my mouth, even though such compliance made my stomach churn and my brain try to release a barrage of unpleasant memories. As the water slid down my throat, I spooled my memory back further and further, ignoring all the things I *should* have seen and aiming for that first day. There was something there, something important, something I'd brushed away as my autistic brain playing tricks on me.

When it came to me, I gasped. The sound was drowned out in a series of coughs as water went down the wrong pipe. Marco drew the bottle away.

"Whoa, easy there," he soothed. "They said I could take you with me, but you're my responsibility, so be careful."

Not... cough... *gonna even try...* cough... *to figure that out yet.* Besides, I had the memory I needed. Marco coming through the door at our debriefing. The look on his face, just a flicker of expression, when he saw the Psittacans. I'd thought it was, at most, a bit of surprise at seeing a species so new to the Alliance. But now I recognized it for what it was: a slip. He'd be good at hiding his feelings about other species—he'd have to be—but he'd probably never seen a Psittacan before. They'd only been in the Alliance for four standard years; he'd been on Cochinga for six. Now I was *certain* he was with the LHFH.

Okay. Okay, that's not bad. You at least have some idea what's going

259

on here. Now you need to find a way out. My wristlet sat next to Marco's computer. My legs might not be bound, but even if I could somehow get up, there was simply no way to reach my wristlet before Marco stopped me. I had no way to communicate, only my wrist implant—

My wrist implant. Of course!

"Well, that cleared up fast," Marco said. I let out a small cough for good measure. "Want another sip?"

I shook my head. "Throat's still raw."

"Then I'm going to finish getting this thing set up." He put the cap back on the bottle and rose again. "God forbid they could've sent better instructions. But I'm close, and we'll be safely away from here before you know it."

I didn't ask any questions, not yet. Instead, I waited until his back was to me and carefully crooked my arms upwards. My wrist implant wasn't quite as fine a piece of chroming as Kiri's fingertip data transfers, but it was no slouch, either. It had its own memory, and it could record and broadcast over short distances. Normally it worked to boost my wristlet, but now...now I'd have to see what it could do on its own.

The problem? It needed to be voice activated. Very little of my already marginal chroming could be activated neurally. My brain tended to be a tangle of unmanageable pathways that weren't ideal for neural connections. One wrong word or a moment of distraction, and my brain would have my wristlet blaring out a lecture on the breeding habits of naba eels in the middle of an important debriefing.

So, with a bit of wriggling, I got my wrist right up against my mouth and breathed the words, "Activate internal wrist implant."

It buzzed to life and I winced. No one else could see it, no one could hear it, but I could feel it, and it made it seem like my bones were rattling. But Marco, to my relief, had noticed nothing. He was too focused on the computer.

"Access and broadcast to all available comm channels in the widest possible range," I went on. "Override code: Now hear this."

Marco turned. I pressed my mouth hard against my arm and coughed, letting my body shake with the motion. Beneath my lips I felt the slight vibration as my wrist implant—hopefully—did what I told it to.

"Looks like I got the thing running," he said, crouching again to face me. "With any luck, it won't take them too long to get here."

"The LHFH, you mean."

He chuckled. "Clever girl. I knew you'd figure it out eventually."

"I don't think I *have* figured it out. I don't understand at all. Why are you doing this, Marco?"

"What, do you think I'm going to spill my guts like some villain in a cheesy vid? Give me some credit, Xandri."

"I don't think you're a villain," I said quietly, staring down at my bound hands.

Like fuck I didn't. He was a traitorous bastard, and I wanted to claw his eyes out, but that was out of the question at the moment. So instead I tried to make him talk. Even if I couldn't get him to talk about his plans, it would give my people time to find me. I didn't know where my composure had come from or how long it would last, so I needed them, and soon.

"Of course you do. You've been brainwashed your entire life into believing the LHFH are villains and terrorists. But once you're in good hands, you'll see the truth. I'm going to take you away from these people. They're only using you."

I couldn't help but look up at *that*. Marco gazed back at me, his eyes fervently bright, and with a sinking feeling I realized he believed every word he was saying. Desperate tears stung my eyes, and I let them flow. Maybe the common conception of autistics as childlike and helpless could be of use to me now.

"Using me?" I hiccupped around a sob, even though that was *far* from what I wanted to say. I didn't think "Fuck you, you back-stabbing son of a Zechak" would get him on my side.

"Oh, Xandri. I know it will be hard to hear, but it's for the best, in the end. These people don't care about you. They never have and they never will. That's just how they treat people like you."

"Like me?" The tears stopped. What the hell was he on about?

"Think about it. Here they are, bending over backwards to get a bunch of alien freaks to ally with them, but how many of them ever spent this much time trying to help *you*? Trying to reach *you*?" Marco asked. "They're more accepting of beasts running their military and flying their starships than they are of their own. You and I both know that."

I ran my tongue over suddenly dry lips. "We—we do?"

261

"They erased us once, and they'd do it again if they could find the files on how. How is that right? Embracing aliens but hating us, their own kind, because we're a little different. It's bullshit, Xandri, and you know it."

The tears were back. My heart had sped up, slamming against my ribs with such ferocity that I was sure it would be heard through my wrist implant. There were so few people like me in the universe, so few neurodivergents, that I'd never met another before. Yet Marco's words... was he really saying what I thought he was saying?

"Yes, Xandri," Marco murmured, leaning forward to cup my tear-streaked face. "We're not so different, you and I."

"W-we're not?"

"I was part of the first wave, of course," he said. "And I wasn't diagnosed very young. Not with anything more than 'behavioral problems,' at least. But I know what you've been through."

"You're... autistic?" I whispered.

He shook his head. "Bipolar. I still understand. Tell me, sweetheart... did they abuse your body, too, or just your heart and soul?"

Oh. My. Fucking. God.

Chapter Twenty-Nine

The tears came faster now, and a keening whimper rose in my throat. I closed my teeth on it. *No. Hold on. You have to hold on just a little longer.* But fear made me shake like a shuttle in turbulence. How much did Marco know? How much *could* he know? Were all my secrets about to be spilled to everyone listening in? I had no idea what I'd do if I was found out.

"Did you think I wouldn't see the signs?" Marco asked softly. "I know what to look for. But I can't tell if you flinch so much from the emotional abuse, or the physical abuse." He stood, looming above me. "They used electric shocks on me from the time I was five. To teach me better behavior, they said. Did they do that to you, too?"

I shook my head. Bile rose in my throat. Electric shocks? On a *child*? Bad enough the way they'd pinned my hands down to keep them still. Bad enough how they coaxed and cajoled, treating me kindly only when I looked them in the eyes or let them do as they wanted, until I believed that complacency was the only form of acceptance. Bad enough that Mother had looked right at me, called me a liar and worse, before forcing me to hug the uncle who liked to corner me when no one was around, to grab my budding breasts or rub my hand against the crotch of his pants.

If I hadn't folded, if I hadn't complied, would they have used electric shocks on me, too?

"How—how could they do that?" My voice didn't seem to want to come out louder than a whisper.

"Because they're scared of us, Xandri. They resent us and hate us because we're not the way we're "supposed" to be. We look like them, but we're different, and that terrifies them more than six-legged sloth bear freaks."

I admit it, he almost had me. Because his words rang true to me; my parents had always looked at me like I wasn't *their* child. Or perhaps like they thought *their* child was in there somewhere, and if they just put me through enough therapy, this alien shell covering me would disappear and they'd have the child they'd wanted all along. But speaking that way about the Ongkoarrat...big fucking mistake. Akcharrch was one of the first people to treat me like I was worthwhile, one of the first who didn't want to scratch away at the autistic surface as if there was a "real" person underneath.

My heart ached to know that Marco had been through what I'd been through, but that didn't make his actions right.

"So—so the LHFH..." I let my eyes go big and round, let the tears shimmer in them as I gazed up at him. I focused on my hope, the hope that rescue would come soon, and tried to let it shine through my eyes. "They—they're better to you? They don't treat you like—like you're inhuman?"

"Oh, Xandri." He reached down, caught me beneath the arms and gently lifted me to my feet. "More than that, so much more. They gave me a whole new life. All I had was endless days of medication that rotted my brain. If I refused to take it, I got a shock. I wasn't allowed to go to school or make friends. I was kept inside all day and if the LHFH hadn't found me, I'd still be there. Rotting inside a room that might as well be a cell."

Pain cut through me, stabbing sharp through my heart. Panic and claustrophobia closed in on me as I remembered similar days, watching the world pass me by from my barred window.

"Don't worry. The LHFH gave me a new life and a new purpose. They accept me, and they'll accept you too," Marco said. "You'll see. I'm going to save you from all this and take you someplace people will really care."

Except I didn't believe it. Maybe the LHFH had found a use for Marco; he was certainly charismatic and charming. And they'd gotten him brainwashed but good. *They're using him. They have to be. If this goes wrong for him, they'll leave him here to rot.* Sure, they'd take the credit, but they wouldn't make an effort to rescue him. They believed in "pure" humans, unblemished not only by alien taint but anything else, as well. To them, people like Marco and I weren't *true* humans.

But Marco believed it with his whole heart. He gazed at me in this glowing way and I *knew* he believed he was saving me.

"I...don't quite understand," I said. "The ambush the other night...why would you set that up if—"

"That wasn't me!" He slashed the air with a hand as if he cut could my words right out of existence. "I *told* him to wait. I told him! If he'd just given me a little more time I could've come up with something, some better way, but he acted without my permission. He even used some of *my* soldiers. Xandri, I *swear* to you, I would never, ever hurt you like that."

"But what about the baenil skin?" I blurted out. "You set that up, didn't you?"

"I...I reported that it would probably...that you would break-down in some way if you had to touch it. I didn't *want* to, but it's my job. By then—I knew, when I saw you crying that night, that I had to do something. Before that..."

"Damnit, Xandri, you were supposed to fail. I spent six years working to make sure the Anmerilli would never sign. I pointed you in the direction of all the wrong allies, spread rumors about your attitudes towards Anmerilli tradition, put you in situations where you were sure to offend people and yet you—you just—I'm not even sure what you did or how. I set you up for a fall and yet you refused to stay down. It made me realize: You're much too special to be torn apart like that."

"I'm *not* special! I just bumbled my way through all that the best I could, that's all. And I *thought* I was succeeding because you were helping me."

"Don't you see? I *am* helping you. Helping you escape those people."

He gazed at me with such certainty. My sense of betrayal and my anger warred with intense confusion. If he understood, if he was like me, how could he have done this to me? And how could the LHFH have done this to *him*? How could anyone use a man who'd been tortured—genuinely *tortured*—throughout his entire childhood?

I struggled with an overwhelming mix of emotions, trying to keep them down and keep my head in the game. The pieces were falling into place, after all. Hadn't I been told that Marco had recommended a large number of AFC soldiers, especially the ones here on Cochinga? Then the ones who'd attacked that night had probably been LHFHers themselves. And Marco—Marco had made sure they wound up dead so they couldn't talk. The Anmerilli would remain loyal to whoever hired them, but LHFHers were known to be fanatics who loved to take credit for their deeds.

"Okay," I murmured. "You—you want to help me escape. I get that. I really do and—and I appreciate how much you care." I took a deep breath. As long as Marco was determined to save me, I could maintain control of the situation. "I guess I just wish you hadn't told the Anmerilli about losTavina's plan. We weren't even sure it was true, you know, it was just a worry we had, and we came to make sure it *wouldn't* happen even so."

"How else could I stop the monkey-tails from joining the Alliance? Sure, it would have offended them if you missed the vote, but I couldn't be sure it would change their minds."

"But I worked so hard..."

"And so did we. Six years of work, Xandri. Six years that you almost destroyed in two weeks."

I tipped my head, considering. "But I'm not the only one who almost destroyed it, am I? That ambush—whoever set it up was trying to frame me, but it backfired. It was an Anmerilli, wasn't it? Someone who had a stake in keeping this alliance from going through."

Marco's expression shifted, twisting with the first ugly vestiges of anger. *Oh shit.* I'd stepped too far, too soon. He loomed over me, and I pressed my back hard into the wall, wishing I could push myself right through it. Fear shot up from my belly as Marco's hands slammed into the wall on either side of me. Self-hatred flooded my heart as I whimpered and shrank in on myself, unable to stop my reaction.

"Nice try," Marco snapped. "But I'm not so easily played. If you think I'm going to tell you all my secrets, you're wrong. And even if I did, what good would it do you? Suppose you got away somehow; then what? You'll tell everyone what I told you?" He sneered. "We both know no one will believe you. Most people barely think you're competent enough to walk and breathe at the same time. You—"

And that was when the door flew open, thank fucking god.

I expected soldiers. Instead, a flurry of brightly-feathered figures rushed through the open doorway. Marco jerked away from me and stumbled back, reaching for his gun, as four angry Psittacans charged at him. Most people took one look at the Psittacans' feet and decided they were slow; but like the parrots they were named for, their feet were well adapted for movement in trees *and*

266

on land, and the Psittacans moved at a dizzying speed. They had Marco pinned up against the far wall before he knew what hit him.

"All right, Xandri-bird?"

"Many!" I cried, as Many Kills came towards me, his crest up in clear agitation.

Another figure appeared in the doorway, and I grinned when I recognized Kiri, dressed in light battle armor, carrying her own pistols and mine, and my extra belt of ammo. She lifted her hand and wiggled her fingers at me.

"Told you there was no lock that could keep me out."

I laughed, giddy with relief. "Captain Chui sure knows how to send in the cavalry."

"Hold out your hands, Xandri-bird," Many instructed. "As far apart as you can get them."

I obeyed, stretching my wrists as far from one another as the plastotape would allow. Many let his staff drop, catching it with one foot and propping himself partially on it, as he leaned in towards me. I tried not to wince as he bent his head and closed the tip of his enormous beak around the plastotape. I heard Marco—half smothered by feathers—gasp as Many's beak cut through the tape easily, freeing my wrists.

"Is it bad out there?" I asked, as Kiri tossed me my gun belt.

"Almost all of the so-called AFC soldiers," she shot a venomous look at Marco, "started attacking when your broadcast came through. There are some Anmerilli fighting with them as well. Captain Chui sent us to find you while she and the platoon hold them off."

" 'Us?' "

"The Captain smuggled us down by shuttle as soon as she found out you were missing," Many Kills explained. "There are several others with us as well, guarding the hall."

At his words, a familiar dark face peeked around the door and gave me a thumbs-up. Anton. I got my gun belt settled in place, then reached out and caught the ammo belt. It had to be pretty bad if someone thought I needed extra ammo. Usually my guns—really monster pistols in size—carried a decent enough amount of shots to get me through most situations. *It's not over yet. You're going to have to hold it together a bit longer.*

"All right, let's go," Kiri said. She gestured to the Psittacans. "Bring him."

Day Dawns Red jabbed at Marco with her staff. "Move."

"Great. I'm being bossed around by a giant chicken," Marco sneered.

"And we're herding a tailless monkey," Shadows Beneath Sunlight retorted, giving him a second jab. "We're even. Now *move*."

She clacked her beak for emphasis, and Marco started walking. Hard to believe sometimes that Sunlight had been considered so beautiful that her people had thought she would never be a warrior. She marched behind Marco with her crest up and her beak close to his neck, looking awfully threatening for a creature supposedly too beautiful to fight.

I stopped and grabbed my wristlet before following the others out. Having it back on my wrist—something about its comforting weight gave me back a little of the strength that had drained out of me through this ordeal.

As I stepped into the hallway—relieved to see we were, apparently, still in the Council building and not god only knew where—my eyes went immediately to Diver, waiting for us along with Anton, Katya, and several other soldiers. His gaze caught mine. I waited, expecting disgust or pity or both, but he just smiled, as if he was glad to see me.

"All right," Katya said, "Captain Chui wants us to regroup with her, but *carefully*. Mulroney, take point. I want Xandri in the middle with the prisoner, and Kiri and Diver, you flank her. Nazaryan, you've got our six. Everyone else on our flanks and stick together."

I recognized Emin from last night. He flashed me a broad grin before falling back to take the rear. I glanced around—we were in one of the closed hallways—and took a deep breath. As we all fell into position I noticed Diver eyeing me, but I still couldn't read his expression. *I wonder how mad everyone is...* They were being nice enough now, but when the chaos died down, what then?

We started down the hall, moving with care, Anton leading the way. I kept a pistol out and hoped I could shoot with my hands trembling.

The hallway led into a medium size chamber. I wasn't exactly sure which part of the building we were in, but this looked like one of the smaller meeting rooms, emptied for the moment. The soldiers around us turned in slow circles as we passed through the room, watching the doorways. Anton tilted his head and made a quick, snapping gesture, indicating in complete silence the door we were headed through. Several soldiers went first, while we hung back out of the way of any potential fire.

Anton signaled the all clear and we filed through, Silence In The Night walking backward to keep his staff pointed at Marco's chest. They fought mostly hand to hand with their staves, but the weapons carried some powerful rounds of fire in them, too.

We were halfway down the breezeway when the firing began. Immediately Diver reached over and shoved me down. The world burst into chaos, the gunshots so loud my eyes watered from the sound. A few feathers drifted through the air as the Psittacans, assaulted from the outside by the shooters, and by Marco from within, were forced to scatter; two of them went down but were, to my relief, quickly up again.

"He's escaping!" someone shouted.

I wrenched my head up, wincing as my neck protested. Marco shoved Many Kills out of his way and pelted down the breezeway. Many staggered; Lightning took flight, running hell for leather after Marco. But he had to zigzag to avoid the bullets, which cut into his speed. Marco ran unhindered, for no one took aim at him. I made to lurch upward, to follow myself, but a strong hand on my back kept me pinned, belly to the floor.

"He's getting away!" I cried.

Strong arms closed around me, and I found myself sheltered by a hard muscled body. I didn't know if I wanted to chase Marco because I wanted to stop him, or to get myself away from the noise. But Diver—and I knew it was Diver, I could smell grease and soap—seemed to understand. His hands covered my ears, muffling the sound of gunshots. I huddled beneath his warmth and protection, praying this would be over soon.

"There's too many!" Katya called over the din. "Mulroney, we gotta move 'em outta here!"

"Get your gun ready," Diver said against my ear. "Get ready to move, and stay low."

He eased up and off me, grabbing my elbow to help me up into a crouch. With a few quick flicks of my thumb, I turned the settings on my pistol to a good, forceful stun. There was too much discord for me to even feel much fear at the moment; I just moved along with the flow of events.

Moving as a close knot, crouched low to avoid the worst of the fire, we began to proceed down the remaining half of the breezeway. I mostly kept low and let the soldiers do the shooting, but when Emin cried out, when a small hole opened in the shoulder of his armor, I bounded up and took aim, firing three quick bursts into the mixed array of AFC soldiers and Anmerilli who were shooting at us. As I dropped back into my crouch, three of our assailants went down.

"All right, Nazaryan?"

"Nothing that can't be patched up."

"Good. Mulroney, get the door."

Soon we were through another room and making our way down another hall, our attackers in hot pursuit. Now fear reached me again, because there were so few of us and we couldn't move fast enough. I twisted around, firing over the shoulders of my companions from time to time, but it was hard to aim on the move and if this kept up, we *would* be overwhelmed.

"Keep moving!" Katya roared in a command voice that would make Gunnery Sergeant Huff proud. "Move, move, move!"

I was no soldier and I felt it now as I struggled to keep up. *Can't be much farther. We have to reach Captain Chui soon.* The noise, the pace, the recoil of my pistol slamming back against my hand, the bodies crowding around me—it was all getting too much. This had to be, hands down, one of the worst days of my life, and that was saying something.

We made it through the next breezeway and came out into one of the segue chambers. And that was really where it all came to shit. I found myself jostled back and forth as soldiers closed in around me suddenly, forcing me to a halt. I wobbled, trying to peek between their bodies. Only the Psittacans broke away from our group, flocking to stand with Swifter Than Lightning, who stood in the middle of the room, his staff aimed at Marco.

Marco, who stood with guns out, his hair rumpled and his clothes disheveled. Marco, who was flanked by a dozen AFC soldiers, all armed and blocking our way forward. And of course there were the attackers behind us, cutting off our retreat.

"Well, Xandri," Marco said, breathing hard, "what clever little plan will you come up with to get out of this one?"

Chapter Thirty

"It's all right," I murmured, pushing gently on my protectors. "Let me handle this."

A strange feeling had settled on me, a calm I couldn't quite understand. Calm—and determination. I had made this mess, and I was going to clean up as much of it as I could. Even if I couldn't salvage the alliance, I could damn well stop Marco and his fellow LHFHers. No matter how much pity I felt for him, he *had* to be stopped.

"No way," Diver said. "You're not going anywhere near that—"

"It's fine," I insisted. "Just please...trust me."

He glanced at Katya. She studied my face for a very long moment, then glanced back at the soldiers and Anmerilli blocking our way. She knew we needed to do something, even if it was just to buy ourselves some time. If she realized I had a plan, it didn't show.

"All right," she said at last. "But if I see so much as a trigger finger twitch, you're going on the floor. Got that?"

"You know," I replied, as my protectors parted like a curtain, "I'm going to suggest that Captain Chui promote you when this is over."

Despite the danger we were in, Katya grinned and the other soldiers chuckled. As I started forward, Diver caught my hand. I glanced back. Both he and Kiri watched me with worried expressions, but I knew they wouldn't stop me. I entwined my fingers with Diver's for a moment, giving his hand a reassuring squeeze. Something passed across his face, something I didn't have the time or wherewithal to examine.

I turned and headed towards the Psittacans. As I walked, I clucked my tongue as sharply as I could. All five of them straightened, bringing their staves up, bracing them against the floor and letting them slant across their chests. I placed myself between Many Kills and Day Dawns Red, staring straight at Marco, even though it hurt now. I held my gun loosely by my side, but Marco kept his pointed at me.

"Enough, Marco," I said. "This is over. Surrender now, and no one has to get hurt."

All around us, our assailants laughed. Marco stared at me for a moment, his eyes wide in disbelief. Then he laughed too.

"What are you going to do? Sic your overgrown chickens on me?"

"Funny you should mention chickens," I said.

"Oh shit," Katya said behind me. "Everyone, down!"

I heard them hit the floor as I held out my hand and snapped my fingers, once and as loudly as I could. It might have been soft, but it was a decent approximation of the Psittacan signal for 'charge.' Then I hit the floor too.

Guns were ideal for long range combat, but they were ill-suited to these sorts of close quarters. The Psittacans, having evolved in the thick jungles of Psittaca, had no such disadvantage. I heard the rustle of feathers and the scratch of claws as they scattered in all directions, moving faster than the human eye—even gene-jumped—could easily follow. Oh sure, their weapons likely had tracking computers, at least some of them, but that wouldn't help them now.

"No!" Marco shouted as the first shot fired. "Don't shoot! Don't shoot!"

And this is what happens when you stuff a bunch of xenophobic burnt-brains in a room with a sapient species they don't know and have no clue how to deal with. The air of panic in the room was palpable, helped along with the ring of gunshots and the sound of screams. I huddled on the floor, listening to people die around me, torn between horror and a vague sense of smugness.

At one point I raised my head, in time to see Many Kills launch himself into an impressive leap. A panicked AFC soldier aimed, trying to track the Psittacan as he rose a good three meters, but the man's fear threw him off target. He howled as Many landed on his chest, strong, clever toes seeking out weak spots in his armor, two sets of ten centimeter long talons digging through and into flesh. As the soldier went down, Many shifted a foot to his throat, opening his jugular with a quick flick of a toe.

I glanced around, sick and fascinated at the same time. It was like something out of an Ancient Earth dinosaur monster movie, only with a more appropriate amount of feathers.

Soldiers and Anmerilli alike tried to flee. I heard more shouts, more gunshots, and voices screaming surrender. The flurry died almost as quickly as it had started, as soldiers—*Carpathia* soldiers—filed through all four doorways, marching the few captured survivors in front of them. The Psittacans backed off, claws and beaks bloodied, and stood at attention as Captain Chui appeared in the doorway behind Marco.

Marco himself stood slowly, his face pale and his expression dazed. I rose too, and heard my companions doing the same behind me. Captain Chui raised her own pistol, aiming it directly at Marco. He let his gun fall and lifted his empty hands in a gesture of surrender, but anger was still deeply etched in his features.

"Let that be a lesson to you, Mr. Antilles," Captain Chui said, straight-faced and dry-voiced. "Never bring a gun to a Psittacan fight."

The Psittacans clacked their beaks in approval and amusement. Marco's anger burned hotter and he made a small, jerking motion in their direction. I raised my gun, not entirely sure who I was protecting; unarmed, Marco wouldn't stand a chance in hell against Many Kills and his team. All around me other weapons were raised, every gun muzzle aiming at Marco. I lifted me free hand.

"I can handle this," I said, loud enough for everyone to hear.

I didn't need to look to know that all eyes turned to Captain Chui. She nodded and lowered her weapon, signaling for everyone else to do the same. Not that I thought Marco would get past her now that she was holstering her pistol. You had to be space-fried to think Chui Shan Fung was less dangerous simply because she no longer had a weapon in her hand.

"So." Marco spoke between heavy, panting breaths. His disheveled hair hung in his eyes. "You going to shoot me to protect these monsters?"

"*Monsters?*" I might feel for Marco, but I was pissed at him too, and he was getting on my last nerve. "They're my *friends*. They're risking their lives, coming down here to save me from *you*."

"Look at what they did! They tore my men apart like savages, Xandri! With their claws and—"

"Oh, right, because it's so much more civilized to shoot someone. How naive of me. *Of course* the only *proper* way to kill is to put a bullet through someone's brain."

I would *not* stand for this. The Psittacans had killed to protect me and themselves. They knew enough about the LHFH to know what would happen to them if they *didn't* strike to kill. In truth, it went against Psittacan beliefs to kill in battle. It was, to their minds, more honorable and a greater challenge to capture their enemies. Many Kills had gotten his name from his hunting prowess, not his skill as a warrior.

Although admittedly we did tend to let people draw their own conclusions about his name.

"Xandri," Marco began again, his voice quavering despite his attempts at a reasonable tone, "we talked about this. You might think it means something that these people showed up to help you, but in the end, you'll be the scapegoat. The LHFH—"

"Will leave you to rot, too," I interrupted. "You're not pure enough for them, Marco. Now that the truth is out about you, they'll have no use for you."

He took a step towards me, furious. I aimed my pistol at his head. A smile curled his lips, a mockery of his usual sweet, boyish grin.

"You're not going to shoot me, Xandri. You're too soft-hearted."

My pistol wavered. I didn't want to hurt anyone. There'd been enough death here already; the smell of blood hung in the air, the scent sharp and sticky rather than coppery, as it was always described. I let my gun droop and Marco's grin widened in response.

Sudden anger flared in my gut. This man had pretended to be my friend, pretended to help me, all while doing his damnedest to sabotage my efforts. He put me in a situation where I had to go hunting, tried to get me to have a meltdown in front of the entire World Council, probably lost me my job *and* he kidnapped me. Now he had the nerve to laugh at me? I flicked several settings on my weapon, raised it, and fired at his knee.

He went down with an agonized howl, clutching at the precision hole I'd blasted through his patella.

"Looks like my heart is still harder than your kneecap," I said quietly.

Laughter echoed around me. I flinched. *No. I won't feel guilty for this. Look what he did to me!* But it would be one hell of a struggle.

275

"Bring him along," Captain Chui said. "Along with any other survivors. Major Douglas and the Anmerilli ought to see what's been hiding in their midst for so long."

I lowered my pistol and slid it back into the holster as soldiers moved to follow Captain Chui's orders. Marco glared at up me from the floor, his eyes filled with hurt and betrayal. *How? He's the one who betrayed me!* I turned away—and found myself staring up at Diver. I wanted to throw myself into his arms, needing something that felt good and comforting against my skin, but I didn't. I remained frozen to the spot until Diver slipped an arm around my shoulder and steered me towards the door.

We ended up next to Captain Chui, with Anton and Katya just behind us, and Kiri close to them. I glanced over my shoulder once, to see the Psittacans surrounding Marco. His hands had been bound with plastotape and with this many soldiers around, it was unlikely he'd escape again. *So it's over. I don't know whether to be grateful or scared.*

"Xandri." Captain Chui's voice, grim and stern, brought me to attention.

"Oh god, I know," I blurted out, suddenly on the verge of tears. "I messed up completely, I know. I don't even know what to—"

"Hush, child. It's not you I'm angry with."

I blinked. "It's not?"

"You made a mistake, yes, and there will be a price to pay," Captain Chui said. "But it was a mistake that would be a good deal less grievous were it not for the many, many mistakes the AFC had already made. This should *never* have happened."

That didn't make me feel even the slightest bit better. If anything, I felt worse. *You'll be the scapegoat,* Marco had said. I wrapped my arms around myself and leaned into Diver, suddenly cold. The AFC wouldn't want this to get out, wouldn't want the universe to know just how severely they'd screwed up.

"Don't worry," Diver murmured. "Captain Chui won't let them."

"How do you always know?"

I felt his shoulders move in a shrug. "You ain't so hard to read, you know. Not to me. It's...kinda more like reading an obscure dialect of Trade Common than another language. Once you get used to it, it's easy."

"Oh."

He leaned in even closer, his lips near my ear. "How're you holding up? Captain's taking us straight to the shuttles. Already had your stuff packed and everything."

"What? But what about the Anmerilli? We have to—"

"Easy, fireball. Take it easy." Diver's hold on me tightened. "We ain't giving up. Captain just wants the Anmerilli to have some time to cool down, and she thinks you'll be safer on the *Carpathia* while they do."

My head ached, my thoughts spinning. I let myself be led through the labyrinthine Council building, letting my eyes unfocus as we walked so I wouldn't see too much of the carnage left by the rest of the fighting.

We were close to the entry chamber when every comm unit— including my wristlet—buzzed, warning us of an incoming signal from *Carpathia*. My heart jumped into my throat. An attempt like that, to reach *anyone*, could only mean extreme danger. Under most circumstances, Lieutenant Zubairi would only try to reach the Captain first; if she was reaching out to all of us, she had a message that had to get through *no matter what*.

Captain Chui wasted no time in answering. "Chui speaking." A pause. "There's a *what*? A mothership? How far out is it? All right, listen to me, Lieutenant. Contact the *Devil's Love Song* and tell them Major Douglas has given orders for them to move three or more of their ships insystem now. They're to head straight for the mothership. Do you understand?" Another pause. "I know. *I* will take responsibility. Oh, I'm aware of that. As far as I'm concerned, Major Douglas can go hang. Now get it done. Chui out."

She disconnected and turned to us. "The *Carpathia's* sensors have detected a Zechak mothership in the system."

"Well, this day just keeps getting better and better," I muttered. "What's next? The Hand of God? A few lightning bolts, maybe an earthquake or a tornado?"

"Always looking on the bright side," Diver said, his voice gently teasing.

"Can the Malevolence-class ships reach it before it reaches us?" I asked, ignoring Diver. My mind was still racing, this time with an idea. It was a risk, a big one, but if it would save lives. . .

"*If* they follow orders, then yes, they most certainly can," Captain Chui answered.

"Then…then tell Kha—Lieutenant Zubairi that if they refuse, she should have *Carpathia* contact the *Hellfire Requiem*."

Captain Chui studied me for a moment, and then her voice came through over my private comm, sub-vocalized, "*Are you certain?*"

"*They're warships, Captain. They believe in their duty to protect people. They deserve the right to have a say, too.*"

She nodded and turned away, contacting Khalida sub-vocally this time. I prayed I'd made the right judgment.

Finally, we reached the entry chamber. Waiting for us there was Councilor mar'Shen, flanked by yet more Anmerilli soldiers. Major Douglas stood with him, only a few AFC soldiers behind him. I might've felt bad for the man—he looked pale and shell-shocked—but I'd had one hell of a day and he was, in some ways, at least partially responsible for that. *So fuck him. He should've made sure those background checks were deeper than the Marianas Trench.*

"Captain Chui," he said immediately. "What is going on here?"

"A good question, Major," the captain replied, coming to a halt. Every soldier following her stopped on a dime. "One I myself would very much like an answer to. Unfortunately, at the moment there isn't time for discussion."

"There will be no more discussion with *you*," mar'Shen cut in. A heavy rifle hung over his shoulder, the length of the barrel indicating a gun that wasn't to be trifled with. "You thought we were a bunch of fools, didn't you? Well, we know about your plan, about your ships, and we—"

"Will be quite lucky if they arrive before the Zechak mothership does," Captain Chui finished for him.

"Zechak mothership?" Major Douglas repeated, going paler beneath his military tan.

mar'Shen's lips twisted in a sneer. "As if we're going to believe anymore of your lies."

"Believe what you wish, Councilor. I'm not here to argue with you. Major Douglas, I suggest you join us on the *Carpathia*. It is *your* job to sort out these prisoners, after all." Captain Chui gestured to the captured humans and Anmerilli we'd brought with us. "Though I suppose I'd best leave your people with you, Councilor."

"And the girl," mar'Shen said. "She must face judgment for her crimes against us."

"And what crimes would those be, Councilor? Trying to forge an alliance with you? Saving the life of one of your Council members? Bending over backwards to plan a special membership acceptable to your people? Exposing the man who's been sabotaging our alliance with you for six years?" When mar'Shen didn't answer, Captain Chui nodded as if that was exactly what she expected, and turned toward the entry doors. "Then we'll be leaving. Soldiers, leave the Councilor's people with him."

She didn't wait to see if her orders would be followed, and I couldn't help envying her confidence as she strode to the door. And sure enough, our soldiers released the captive Anmerilli into mar'Shen's custody, though they didn't remove the plastotape binding the prisoners. I wasn't sure this was the best idea, but on the other hand, I could barely think straight. I just followed Captain Chui, trying to tune out the chatter of both Major Douglas and mar'Shen as they pursued us, protesting.

Once outside, a gust of fresh ocean air woke me up a little. I glanced over my shoulder. Having mar'Shen behind us, carrying that absurd looking rifle, made my skin crawl. I couldn't wait to be in the shuttle, lifting off from Cochinga, Zechak mothership or no.

"Captain Chui!" Major Douglas called, hurrying to keep up with the captain's swift strides. "The World Council is deliberating *right now*. If we want any chance to salvage this operation—"

I tried to focus on the crunching of seashells beneath my feet rather than Major Douglas. *I can't handle any of this now, I can't, I can't—*

And then the sky above us seemed to break open, as if an enormous hand had torn a gash in it. In truth it was light, a blaze that streaked through space, an explosion so large and fierce that it penetrated through the Cochingan atmosphere like a streak of lightning. Instinctively I clapped a hand over my eyes, protecting them from the sudden flash of brightness. The air around me filled with a chorus of gasps and even a few frightened shrieks, and then it was over.

"Well," Captain Chui said, not the least bit phased, "looks like the cavalry arrived in time."

I opened my eyes carefully. The light was quickly fading and Captain Chui had started moving again, as if we hadn't just seen the fallout of a Zechak mothership being blown to smithereens practically right above our heads. The motherships were excellent sneaks, creeping up on planets with systems dampened, making them difficult to detect. If *Carpathia's* sensors had been just a tiny bit later in detecting the ship, this would've turned into a disaster.

Diver, who had remained beside me, though he'd kept quiet, giving me space, nudged me now and said, "Motherfuckers, huh?"

"Motherfuckers," I agreed with a nod and a grin.

And then something slammed into me from behind, and a sound like thunder cracked through the air. As I fell, my brain began a gibbering stream of ultra-pedantic nonsense: *That's impossible, that explosion happened in space, there wouldn't be any atmosphere to carry sound, we can't have heard*— Gravelly bits of shell dug into my skin as I skidded across the road. More cracks of thunder went off as someone grabbed me by the wrists, hauling me farther away, while twisting me around to face up.

I scrambled to get my feet under me. My cheek stung where bits of shell had cut it, but when I saw what was happening, I forgot the pain.

"Stay down!" Diver shouted in my ear.

As if I could do anything else. I'd frozen in shock. mar'Shen had opened fire with that gun of his, and what had looked like a particularly large hunting rifle turned out to have an alarming rate of fire. Three of our soldiers were down, including Katya, who lay where I had stood, a puddle of blood rapidly pooling around her from a roughly three centimeter hole in her abdomen. A scream rose from my belly and stuck in my throat. I tried to lunge for Katya, but Diver held me back, pinning me down as shots rang out on both sides.

I lay belly down in the gravel, watching in horror. We had more troops, but the weapons the Anmerilli carried were powerful. Major Douglas, for all I couldn't stand the man, had grabbed the nearest Anmerilli and wrestled him to the ground, fighting to wrest the gun from him. The only spot of stillness in the chaos was Anton, leaning over Katya's prone form.

Suddenly he let out a bellow, leapt to his feet, and charged across the battlefield at mar'Shen, his weapon forgotten.

"Mulroney!" Captain Chui shouted.

mar'Shen raised his weapon. The moment seemed to slow, as if we were caught on the time-dilating edge of a black hole, and that was when I saw what no one else had seen. The Psittacans had fallen behind the entire group and now they came up on mar'Shen and his fellow Anmerilli. Four of them crept slowly, but Silence In The Night sped across the gravel without making a sound. His wing-arms flared as he jumped, launching himself like a caroua and landing on mar'Shen's shoulders. The Anmerillis' shot went wild as he fell back, Silence's beak digging into his neck.

Then the other four were there, staves at the ready, choosing to disable their opponents rather than kill them this time.

"Cease fire and hit the deck!" Captain Chui bellowed.

All around me soldiers—and the civilians they were protecting—hit the ground. Free of friendly fire, the Psittacans cut through the panicking Anmerilli like a hot knife through butter. A few shots went off; one of them must've hit, because Shadows Beneath Sunlight shrieked in pain and dropped her staff. The Anmerilli who'd shot her went down in a heap, his head no doubt dented in by the blow from Many Kills' staff. Sunlight scampered away from the fight, her injured wing-arm pinned tight to her side.

And then, just like the earlier fight, it was over. I continued to lay there as our people rose to face the aftermath. This last—what, half hour?—however long it had been, it felt like we'd been running and fighting for days. And now—now…

Someone rolled Katya over. Her personal 'bots had tried, but they couldn't stop the bleeding. For a moment I stared at her open, blank eyes, until someone—it was Anton, I realized now—gently closed them. That was when it all finally hit me, colliding with my stomach like a gut punch. Katya, who laughed and joked so easily, would never laugh again, because there were people in this universe so obsessed with getting their way, they would do *anything* to achieve it. Because those people had targeted the force put in place to fight them: Me.

I didn't remember getting to my feet. Something inside me had snapped, but instead of tears or screaming or sorrow, all I felt was cold. Not the kind of cold that made one shiver; the kind that wrapped around one like armor, deep and thick and impenetrable. It seemed almost astonishing that my breath didn't turn to mist with every exhale.

I'd had enough.

Chapter Thirty-One

While I waited for my wristlet's computer to finish scanning for all the files I'd told it to find, I visited with the Psittacans. The gun that had been fired at Sunlight had been less vicious than the one that—than the one belonging to Councilor mar'Shen, and it wouldn't take nanobots long to heal the hole in her wing. Relieved, I made several clicking sounds with my tongue—as close an approximation of sincerest thanks as I could manage—and left them be.

Doctor Marsten had returned from the shuttle where she'd been waiting and was helping to get things organized, instructing soldiers on how to help their injured fellows. Katya and the two other dead soldiers lay beneath sheets for the moment. The Anmerilli were bound, and mar'Shen lay where he'd fallen. If it weren't for that feeling of cold, I would have been angry enough to spit on him.

Instead, I headed for where Diver and Kiri sat together, both of them looking a bit stunned and scraped up, but not too bad, considering.

"Hey, Diver?" I said as I reached them.

"What's up, fireball?"

"I need a couple of things. Do you have a holo-projector with you? One with bigger capacity than my wristlet, preferably."

He nodded. "In my bag, in the shuttle. I can get it for you, if you'd like."

"Please," I said. "Bring it to the main meeting chamber. And... " I hesitated, looking back and forth between them. "Could I have the graser schematics? I won't use them if I don't need them, but... "

They exchanged a look. Not angry, not disappointed, not disgusted—a long, considering look, tinged with a hint of sadness. Maybe they thought they knew what I was about to do; maybe they weren't even that far off. All I knew was that I had to attempt to salvage something from this mess, and I didn't think waiting for the Anmerilli to "cool down" would do the trick. Not if I was going to have any chance at undoing six years of Marco's lies.

"All right," Kiri said at last. "I'll get them sent to your wristlet."

I nodded. As Diver rose to retrieve the holo-projector and Kiri tipped her head to focus on pulling up the data I'd asked for, I glanced over in Marco's direction. He and the other LHFHers sat in the grass beside the pathway, their ankles bound now as well as their wrists. All of them were unusually subdued for zealots, none of them more so than Marco. He stared at the ground, looking more shell-shocked and horrified than anyone else here.

"Here," Kiri said, reaching up and closing her hand around my wrist.

"Thanks." As the data transferred, I added, "Could—could I ask one more favor? There's no one else aboard ship that would be able to do it."

"You want me to find information on Marco." It wasn't a question.

"If you can."

"I'll be honest, starshine. I don't get it. But…I'll try." Kiri grinned. "Now you go kick some politician ass, yeah?"

I managed a small smile in return and turned. Taking determined strides, I started across the scene of the battle. People turned to stare at me, and Captain Chui rose from where she was crouched, studying one of her injured soldiers. As I headed past the Psittacans, I held a hand out in their direction.

"Many," I said, "staff."

He didn't hesitate. He dropped his staff down to his clawed foot and, with a surprisingly strong jerk of his leg, flung it to me. Without pausing, I grabbed the staff out of midair, a move of such exquisite coordination that it would have, under any other circumstances, sent me into fits of squealing joy and pride. Right now I felt only cold.

"Ms. Corelel," Captain Chui called. "Where are you going?"

I didn't bother to look back. "To pull some weeds."

I walked into a meeting hall nearly as chaotic as a battlefield, with all forty-three—*forty-two, now*—World Council members trying to speak at once. Even Secretary Shinda had given up on trying to achieve order and sat slumped in his chair, his staff across his lap. The Council was so consumed by their argument, they didn't notice me come storming in, despite the torn state of my clothes, the bloody scratches on my face, and the tangled mess of hair I'd thrown into a low, sloppy ponytail.

Enough of this.

I approached the table, raised the staff, and brought it down on the floor as hard as I could, the reinforced metal end slamming loudly into the hard seashell. At the same time, doing my best to channel women like Captain Chui and Gunnery Sergeant Huff, I bellowed, "Silence!" I must've startled them, for they all went silent at once, forty-plus heads swiveling around to stare at me in shock.

"Now sit down and be quiet!" I added.

Most of them dropped like rocks, still too stunned to know what else to do. Others sank slower, and Kinima Mal, laboring with her half healed leg, sat down slowest of all. Only Nish mar'Odrea remained on his feet. The look he gave me was the ugliest I'd ever seen, his cheek ridges and bulbous forehead giving his features a monstrous cast. Yet I was beyond it all. I glared at him and swiveled the staff around, setting it comfortably between my arm and body and pointing it at him.

"Have you come back to answer for your crimes or—"

"I said, sit down and *shut up.*"

"I will *not* be ordered around by a—"

His words cut off as I flicked a button on the staff and the clear sound of it charging up reached his ears. "Did I stutter?"

mar'Odrea sank into his chair, his expression never changing. Whatever. I didn't care. I gazed around the table, daring anyone to challenge me. As I stood there, Diver came in and reached over to set the holo-projector on the table, where I could reach it. Captain Chui, Kiri, the Psittacans and several soldiers huddled in the doorway, watching but not interfering. *Well, this is supposed to be my job, after all.*

"Now," I said, as I leaned over to turn on the holo-projector, "we're going to talk about this like reasonable adults. And when I say "like reasonable adults" I mean *I* am going to talk and *you* are going to listen."

"Where is Councilor mar'Shen?" mar'Odrea demanded, ignoring my orders.

"Dead," I said flatly.

He paled. "Dead?"

"Yes. Just like the three members of our crew that he murdered in cold blood."

"I will not stand for these lies and neither will the rest of us!" mar'Odrea protested.

Kinima Mal snorted. "Oh, please, Nish. We all know you sent him out there with soldiers and a gun. One would almost think you wanted Ms. Corelel dead, and once one starts thinking down those lines, one might start to wonder *why* that is." The fact that several of her fellows murmured agreement told me everything I needed to know.

"I cannot believe you're all swallowing more of her lies!" mar'Odrea exclaimed, outraged. "*Her* people brought in that lying Antilles. *Her* people brought in soldiers that could have killed us in our sleep. *Her* people planned to destroy our entire planet with their special ships. She—"

"Is telling the truth, Councilor," Major Douglas said wearily from the doorway. "mar'Shen attacked us."

"And we will discuss all this, I promise," I added. "But right now you're going to listen because, Councilor, this," I tapped the staff, "has a stun feature, and I'm not afraid to use it.

"Now, I'd like to draw your attention to the holo-display," using my wristlet, I transferred the first bit of data I wanted them to see, "and this. This is a Zechak." One of the creatures we called orcs seemed to spring right out of the table, fully three-dimensional and life-sized. Huge and hulking, with feet hoofed like a goat's and a somewhat piggish face—right down to its snout and tusks and floppy pig ears—it looked like something out of an Ancient Earth fantasy novel. Hence: orcs. "The males can grow to be nearly three meters in height. They are brutal, cunning, and utterly ruthless, and if you're not lucky enough to be killed when they attack, they'll probably enslave you.

"This," and the holo-display changed again, showing a truly odd-looking ship, long height-wise rather like an office building, "is a Zechak mothership. They tend to carry upwards of a thousand fighters per ship, depending on class, and one was just blown to

285

bits not far above your planet by those "special ships" you were just complaining about."

mar'Odrea opened his mouth, probably for more complaining. Several other Council members shot him a look that quieted him. Whatever else they might feel about me and the Alliance, they seemed to be out of patience for mar'Odrea.

I reached for the holo-display. With quick, experienced fingers I divided the display into sizable screens, flicking each finished screen down the table in one direction or another, until every Council member had a good view. Then I called up a new image: A bipedal creature of roughly a meter in height, with about seventy centimeters of thin, whip-like tail. To the untrained eye it resembled a rodent with two blunt-looking, slightly curved horns on its forehead, but I recognized the wideness of its face, the opposable thumbs on its hands and the set of its pelvis that spoke of an entirely different creature.

"These are the Nīpa, and this is what the Zechak did to them." I changed the image on the screens, allowing vid footage of the carnage—piles of dead Nīpa; Nīpa chained together, being marched onto ships; Nīpa fleeing from the ruins of their homes. "Marco Antilles is a member of the Last Hope for Humanity, a xenophobic group of zealots that want to stop humanity and other sapient species from allying with each other. He kept all of this from you—the knowledge of what we're trying to protect you, to protect the entire universe, from.

"The Zechak wanted the Nīpa's homeworld for their own. The knowledge of a sapient species living there did nothing to deter them. If it hadn't been for the Nīpa's ingenuity, they'd be extinct now. As it is, the children of the Nīpa Diaspora live spread out across the universe. They have no homeworld anymore; the Zechak destroyed it. And they're the lucky ones."

I gave that time to sink in, letting the images flash across the holo-display in a continuous cycle. If it hadn't been for that cold feeling, the imagery would have made me sick. Shots of mutilated Nīpa slaves, their tails bobbed off or their horns broken, were some of the worst—especially since so many of them were children. I took a deep breath and switched the screens, continuing on.

"These are the only two species to ever ally with the Zechak," I said. "The Attana and the Sheerat. They had assets to offer the

286

Zechak too. The Attana lived on a mineral rich planet and the Sheerat were some of the best fighters, on land and in space, in the known universe.

"The Sheerat were too good." I changed the screens again: Burning towns, screaming mothers clutching dead young, more piles of corpses, many of them mutilated by Zechak tusks. "In the end, the fighting prowess of the Sheerat was such that the Zechak didn't even dare turn them into slaves. They hunted them down, every last one they could find. If there are any left alive in the universe, no sapient being today knows of them. But again—you *might* say they were the lucky ones."

Many of the Council members were leaning back in their chairs, as if they could escape the images flashing before their eyes. Xenophobic they might be, and alien the Sheerat might look—but there was nothing alien in what they suffered. Nothing alien in the mother curled around her dead children, half her head missing and an enormous hole torn in her back. Nothing alien in the terrified screams and desperate shouts as Zechak tore families apart and killed them.

"Technically the Attana are still around," I went on, merciless. They *had* to see, had to know. "A planet with that much on it to mine needs someone to mine it. And why bother relocating slaves there when there are people already planetside? What reports get through tell us that few Attana live more than thirty or forty standard space years, and that's *with* life-ex in their DNA. That's how poor their living conditions are."

Now I brought up images of the Attana, the ones a few brave individuals had collected over the years. The Attana lived in huts that wallowed in mud from all the ecological destruction the mining had done to their planet. Their emaciated forms were covered with open sores and flies buzzed around those sores. Feeling a small prickle of mercy, I chose not to mention that what looked like flies were actually more mosquito-like and tended to carry deadly parasites. Though if they proved stubborn, I might.

I let them look for a while. Despite their horror, some murmurs broke out here and there. Others remained silent, but reactions showed in their faces and I noticed an awful lot of tails drooping in dismay. They had really never seen any of this before.

"I'm showing you these things," I said, "because often, words aren't enough. Among humans there is sometimes a—a taboo

287

about showing these kinds of images, especially of the dead. I used to believe in that taboo, too...until I learned how easily people can deny the truth of the words they hear. But footage like this... it speaks loudly.

"This—*this*—is what Admiral losTavina is so desperate to prevent that he's willing to threaten your planet with destruction. My superiors don't believe the admiral would actually destroy Cochinga, but that doesn't matter. I don't want him to even threaten you. I want to stop *all* of this, and that's why I'm here. Because honestly? I'm not the right person for the job."

I had no idea where all these words were coming from and why they flowed so smoothly, but I had to keep pushing on. Soon I would run out of cope and that would be the end of this. I had to finish it.

"I'm not a diplomat, not even close," I admitted. "I have no idea what I'm doing. But I don't want to see another Diaspora, I don't want to see more people killed or enslaved, and I don't want to see anyone threatened. That's why I'm here, when really, someone more skilled should have been chosen. Someone who would have seen through Marco Antilles. Hell, one of my own people *did* see through him, and I didn't listen to her. I've made a lot of mistakes. But the biggest mistake I made was trusting someone I shouldn't have."

I looked straight at mar'Odrea as I spoke the next words, even though it hurt. "Maybe you, Councilors, need to ask yourself if you've been trusting someone you shouldn't, as well."

More murmurs stirred around the table. I reached over and turned off the holo-projector; the screens blinked out of existence. Weariness started to settle on me, melting the ice that had been protecting me. Katya was dead, Marco was a traitor, and I had screwed up big time. I couldn't take much more of this.

"What if," Councilor Ashil began, "we choose to ally with neither you nor the Zechak?"

"Then we'll still do what we can to protect you from them," I answered with a shrug. "It's what the Alliance does. The Nīpa Diaspora taught us that we can't simply sit back and let the Zechak do whatever they want."

"So you serve your own interests?"

"Who doesn't?" I shot back. "It's those interest of yours that allowed Marco Antilles so much room to manipulate you. He used

288

them against you. The Last Hope for Humanity is another threat we can help protect you from, though. They'd want to destroy you, too. For all we know, they were working with the Zechak." They wouldn't be the first fanatics to use weapons they technically didn't believe in.

"Oh, and a great job you've done protecting us," mar'Odrea growled. "That man lived among us for *six years*, "manipulating" us as you say. And your *Alliance* just let him walk right in and do it."

"It's funny, though," Kinima Mal said, "that not a single one of us, in all of those years, discovered what he was up to." She shot mar'Odrea a look. "Especially you, Nish, since the two of you were such close friends."

Everyone at the table turned to stare at mar'Odrea. No matter what else they might think, they *knew* the truth behind Mal's words. They'd been here to see the friendship between mar'Odrea and Marco. Hell, *I* should've seen it, though Marco had clearly worked to keep it hidden from me. I had no doubt that mar'Odrea was the accomplice Marco had talked about, the one who'd planned the assassination attempt on me. Too bad there was no good excuse to set the Psittacans loose on him.

"Stop and think for a moment," mar'Odrea snapped, clearly keen to change the subject. "After everything they've done—they sent ships to threaten and perhaps destroy us!—you're still listening to her. She's only being generous now because they still want our weapon."

"No," I said.

They turned to me. I held up my arm and tapped my wristlet, calling up the largest holo-display it could manage. I heard a few gasps around the table, confirming that what I had was indeed what it looked like: The Anmerilli's full schematics for the graser. There was a reason I packed half a dozen books on a shuttle drop and always had extra underwear stuffed into my bag regardless of where I was going; it really never hurt to be as prepared as feasibly possible.

"The *Carpathia* has a lot of crew members who are very good at their jobs," I said. "We don't need you to give us your weapon, because we have it. And though we might complete it quicker with your help, we can do it without. We have what we came here for,

289

Councilors, and yet still I stand here offering you an alliance. A choice."

"What kind of *choice* is this?" mar'Odrea demanded, his voice gone notably shrill.

"It *does* seem you can force our hand now," Councilor Sendil admitted.

"It does. But we won't. If you don't wish to ally with us, then fine; we'll still protect you from the Zechak. You'll only be our enemies if you ally with them. Moreover, we won't demand that you sign for full membership. The offer of a special membership still stands." Okay, I was taking liberties with that bit, but if my superiors didn't want to uphold their offer, *they* could be the ones to explain why. I didn't think they'd withdraw it though, and so I held up the schematics for all to see. "I show you this as proof. *We offer you a choice.*

"What kind of choice, Councilor Nish mar'Odrea? An *actual* choice. The Zechak won't give you that, and if you don't believe me after everything I've shown you, then you are such fools the likes of which not even divine intervention could save."

Chapter Thirty-Two

Three days. The Anmerilli seemed to like that particular time period. *At least I don't have to wait too long.* By the end of three days, one way or another, we would have their decision.

I stopped outside the door to my rooms, my shoulders sagging. I might just have pulled it out of the fire. Something in what I'd said had evidently struck a chord with them, if they were still willing to discuss the possibility of signing. I just hoped *enough* of them were still interested. With mar'Shen dead, we would need thirty-one votes instead of thirty.

Of course, I hadn't found any of this out until I'd stirred awake on the shuttle back up to the *Carpathia.* I had left the meeting room as soon as I'd finished, ostensibly to give my exit the most non-vocal impact I could. In truth, I hadn't gotten far down the corridor before I'd collapsed, exhaustion finally overwhelming everything else. And even though I'd dozed a fair bit on the shuttle, I still felt worn to the bone, like the last day had been more like a week.

I sighed and slapped my palm to the door lock. As the door slid back, a pair of parrot voices greeted me. A small smile curved my lips despite my weariness. I dropped my pack just inside the doorway and made a beeline for the cages, commanding them open as I walked.

As soon as I reached my hands out to the open doors, Cake and Marbles climbed down from their perches to greet me. Marbles emerged first, clambering onto my hand and up my arm to my shoulder. Normally I discouraged her from sitting there, as she was large enough that her beak could cause damage if she was startled, but for now I let it slide. As I reached up to scritch her, Cake made his way up to my other shoulder. He made a distinctly disapproving sound and began pulling tangled strands from my ponytail to preen.

"Sweet Mother Universe, I missed you two."

"Marbles loves mommy," Marbles chirped.

"Aww. I love you too, Marbs." I leaned into her and she rubbed her soft, feathery head against my cheek. "Mommy's gonna hit the shower. You guys want a bath?"

Cake ruffled his feathers and continued preening me. Marbles rocked back, tilting her head to eye me in a way that looked rather skeptical. Well, no surprise there. Millennia of domestication and aviculture had raised the intelligence of these already astounding birds, and Marbles was too smart for anyone's good, especially her own.

"Well, you're getting one anyway." I headed to the bathroom and turned on the sink. "Don't think I don't know how much trouble you gave the Psittacans while I was gone. I got the full report."

"Bah!"

"Cranky puss," I chided, as I lifted them down off my shoulders and set them on the sink.

I stripped out of my dirty, tattered clothes and dropped them in the recycling chute. Bruises and scrapes covered my body; the worst cuts had been sprayed over with water-proof flexi-bandaging. Only a few spots stung as I stepped under the hot water, and those were shallow enough that my personal 'bots were already closing them up.

As I scrubbed myself, and Marbles and Cake splashed in the sink beside me, I began to feel like things could return to normal, in time. At least, as normal as the *Carpathia* ever got.

I got to eat real food, recognizable food, for the first time in weeks. That should have made me feel better. But as I sat down to eat, the first files came in from Kiri. I blinked at my wristlet in surprise. *That was fast.* Of course, she'd had criteria to go by, but even so, I figured there had to be some electronic breaking and entering involved. On the other hand, I'd noticed times in the past when Kiri worked to keep her mind off other things; maybe this was her way of coping with everything that had happened.

I forced myself to eat my sandwich first. I'd had our chef stack it up with vat-grown turkey and some of the genuine cheese the *Carpathia* carried in her stores; between that and the hearty bread, no one could argue that I needed a nutrient-bar. Marbles and Cake sat with me on the bed, their feathers dry, and occasionally I fed them bits of bread crust.

Finally, although part of me didn't want to, I drew out a reading screen from my holo-display and got to work.

The first thing Kiri had sent me was the information she could scrape together about the neurodivergence known as bipolar disorder. I tried to take it with a grain of salt, as I knew from experience that the knowledge from Ancient Earth about my own disorder didn't always match up with what I felt. Still, it explained a few things, like the way I'd seen him jittering, his restlessness, the time he was out at night for a jog; the swings in his mood that had begun to manifest as time went on; the extravagant way he'd insisted on paying for things his salary couldn't possibly afford.

More files came in as I read. I kept on, even as my eyes began to sting, because I had to know. Some of what I read made my shiver, for it seemed perhaps Marco truly *had* believed he was doing the right thing, that he was protecting me and rescuing me from people who meant me harm. I had no clue how to feel about that.

When I leaned back to take I break, to glance at the time, I saw I'd been at it for hours. Night—by the ship's clock, anyway—had fallen. I rose, stiff joints creaking in protest, to put Marbles and Cake back in their cages. They mumbled protests at me, but I knew they were getting tired; Cake even cracked a yawn as I set him on his favorite perch. Once they were safely away, I covered their cages and dimmed the light.

As I settled on the bed again, uncertain what to do, my comm pinged. *Kiri.* I hesitated a moment, before I realized just how nice it would be to hear her voice. I let the call come through.

"How're you holding up, starshine?" she asked.

"About as well as can be expected, I guess." I shrugged, even though she couldn't see it. "I've been looking at the files you sent me."

"I just sent the last few I found. Try not to read *all* of it tonight?"

I murmured something that could, if one wanted, be mistaken for assent. "How'd you find it all so easily? The AFC never found anything in their background check."

"Well, I knew there was something to look *for*," Kiri pointed out. "I used everything you told me and what little else we could find out as search criteria. Military medical records and the like might be classified, and all, but we know civilian records are a bit less...sacred." I could almost see her making air quotes around the last word. "Especially...well, the First Wave, as they're sometimes called, were highly publicized."

"Until parents got so embarrassed they started hiding it instead," I muttered.

"I'd like to believe that at least *some* of them wanted to keep their children away from prying journalists. Though that might just be my optimism talking."

"Probably."

Kiri sighed. "Xandri...I sent you the most likely candidates. I marked one of them that fit the criteria the best and...be careful when you read it, okay? It's pretty ugly. If that's who Marco really was, it's no wonder the LHFH was able to manipulate them the way they did and I...well, it made me wonder. About you."

Something inside me shook. *Not now. Not after everything. I'm just not ready.* Doubtless Kiri wasn't the only one wondering. Others had to have heard what Marco had said to me; surely some of them wondered what abuses I'd suffered. But even if I thought I could trust anyone with the knowledge of who I was and what I'd been through, I wasn't ready to.

"It's okay," Kiri said softly. "I understand. But if you ever decide you *do* want to talk about it, I'll always be there for you."

"But I didn't even say—"

"You didn't have to. Try to rest up, yeah?"

By the time I signed off, I felt a little dazed. So many people had gone in and out of my life, most of them leaving faster than they came, some of them staying longer because they'd found a convenient doormat. Until I came aboard the *Carpathia*, I'd never met people like Diver and Kiri and Aki, who seemed to get me.

I can't think about this right now. As I reached to turn on the holo-display again, I noticed my hands were shaking.

I almost shot through the hull of the ship when my door chimed. Who the hell would even be here right now? And did I want to find out? I sat frozen on my bed, staring at—or more like through—the holo-display, trying to figure out what to do. Maybe if I didn't answer they would assume I was asleep and go away.

Instead, the door comm chimed, because I was never that lucky.

"Xandri? It's Christa. Can I come in?"

I said nothing. Thoughts flitted through my head like moths, moving too fast and erratically for me to catch. All I could do was sit, wondering if she'd go away. Why would she even be here right now, anyway?

The door slid open, and if I had been able to move, I would've slapped my palm against my forehead; why had I forgotten to lock it? Christa stood in the doorway, probably trying to adjust to the dimmer lighting in my room. I continued to stare, the bluish glow of the holo-display blurring before my eyes. Somewhere deep inside I sensed the reason she was here, even if my brain couldn't quite call it up, and it terrified me.

"What are you doing? Why aren't you dressed?"

Dressed?

"You can't go to the funeral in that ratty old thing."

Oh god. My stomach knotted, hard as a rock, and my throat closed around any words I might say. I'd been to one funeral in my time here, though there had been several others. That one was more than enough; I never went to another one again. I couldn't quite explain it, but the feeling I got at them—everything inside me was numb and still while all around me people grieved, and it felt so strange.

"Xandri? Hello? The least you could do is look at me when I'm talking to you."

But I can't move! The words were there in my mind, but they simply wouldn't come out of my mouth.

"What the hell is wrong with you? Wasn't Katya your friend? Don't you want to say good-bye?"

Good-bye? She's already gone! There wasn't a chance to say good-bye. What good would it do now?

"I can't believe this! How can you be so cold?"

Is that what I am?

"Say something!"

But I really can't! I wanted to wail the words at the top of my lungs, but they just wouldn't come out. My jaw stayed locked shut and my eyes stayed on the holo-display, and inside I felt—odd. I had gone so still and I ought to have been able to figure out my own emotions, but they looked nothing like what I'd seen in other people.

"Ugh! Fine. Be that way. *I* am going to pay my respects to the woman who saved your life."

I cringed as the door slid shut. For long moments afterwards I stared at the holo-display, until my eyes began to water. Not tears, though. Shouldn't I be crying? Someone I cared about was dead. What should I be feeling? *What is* wrong *with me?* My hands were still shaking. I reached out and accessed more of the files Kiri had sent me, because I didn't know what else to do.

Maybe it would have been better if I'd gone to the funeral after all. I tried to shove the worst of my feelings away and focus on the work I intended to do, so I wouldn't have to think of Katya's blank eyes and the hole that had been torn through her. But reading the file Kiri had marked—the one on the person she suspected had been Marco—brought up other memories. My mother's voice kept speaking in the back of my mind, demanding to know why I didn't love her—but I'd never said I didn't.

Sometime in the night, I turned off my wristlet, took it off, and sat on my bed, the lights dimmed near to darkness around me. I clutched my knees against my chest and stared into the shadows, my eyes burning from sheer, baffling dryness. When my door slid open without my permission for the second time that night, I didn't move, didn't even turn my head. I did nothing, just sat there; felt nothing, not even annoyance at the scrape of claws that announced my uninvited guest.

My bed creaked as a considerable weight climbed up onto it. Two sets of limbs wrapped around me, dragging me against a warm, furred body.

"That's enough of that," Aki said, her voice rumbling near my ear. "Let go now, Xandri. It's safe."

At her words, something inside me crumbled. I turned into her, pressing my cheek against the extra soft fur of her belly, and then the tears came, wracking sobs that hurt as they traveled through my chest and up my throat. Aki's claws stroked gently through my hair, but at the moment the motion couldn't soothe me. Everything was just so fucked up and I was not equipped to deal with it.

I don't know how long I carried on, but Aki stayed the whole time. Even after my tears quieted she remained, making a rumbling sound in her chest similar to a cat's purr. I lay against her, exhausted, my eyes closed, letting the sound soothe my battered nerves.

I woke up with stiff, crusty eyes and a sore throat, but in a lot of ways, I felt much better. I went to the bathroom first, to wipe my face clean; the cool water helped shake off the last dregs of sleep. Waiting for me when I returned to the main room was a cup of coffee, sending up steam and delicious aroma. I scooped it up off the table as I headed towards Marbles' and Cake's cages.

"Thanks, *Carpathia*," I said into the empty air. She didn't answer, but I knew some part of her had heard.

Cake and Marbles greeted me enthusiastically as I drew the covers off their cages, and I couldn't help but smile. I opened their cages and, sipping my coffee, headed back to the tiny kitchen to fetch them some breakfast. Ideas swirled in my head, and though all those thoughts made me feel a bit dizzy, I thought it was a good thing. It made it harder for me to think about things that would only drag me down.

"Got a lot of work to do today, guys," I called to my birds as I prepared the mix of seeds and fresh veggies for them. "Next couple of days are gonna be busy ones, I think."

First thing was first: I needed a couple favors. *I just hope Diver will be willing to be help me.* He'd never actually turned me down before, but when he found out what I was asking for, I had a feeling he'd be pissed.

Chapter Thirty-Three

"You didn't have to come with me, you know," I said. "He's under heavy guard. I'll be fine."

"I don't care if he's in a full body straitjacket and has a graser pointed at his head," Diver grumbled. "You're not going in alone, and that's final."

I clutched the tablet to my chest and tried not to sigh. Diver had *not* been pleased with my request, not at all, but for some reason he'd done it anyway. And it had only taken him a day—though I suppose it was easier than most of the things he usually did. Of course, when I'd arrived this morning to pick it up, he'd been waiting, hair a bit disheveled but clothing clean, to escort me to the cells. Which admittedly hadn't been part of the plan.

"I'm carrying my weapons," I said. "The guards will have weapons. I'm going to be in and out in no more than five minutes, just like I promised Captain Chui. I think a bodyguard might be a bit much, don't you?"

"I'm not here as your bodyguard, Xan. I'm here as your witness."

I blinked and turned my head to gaze at him, even as I struggled to keep up with his long, irritated strides.

"Think about it. After everything that happened, this isn't going to look good to the Powers That Be. I'll be able to vouch for you, to tell them you weren't, I don't know, plotting to take over the universe or something."

I snorted. "Because I'd want to take over the universe with the guy who kidnapped me. Give me some credit, Diver."

For a moment I thought he might say something scathing. The look on his face surprised me, so stern and at odds with his usual happy-go-lucky nature. Then he sighed and ran his fingers through his hair, rumpling the loose curls even further. I held back on the urge to reach up and push a few of the soft-looking strands from his eyes.

"So who *would* you take over the universe with?"

I grinned. "Well, you and Kiri, of course. And Aki, because she's the best pilot there is. Really, all of *Carpathia.*"

Diver chuckled, and some of the tension around us dissipated. His stride slowed a bit, and together we reached the small prisoner area where Marco Antilles and the other surviving LHFHers were being held. A transport ship was on its way, but until then, the Alliance had requested we keep the prisoners here. God forbid they be allowed on the Alliance's precious ambassadorial ship.

Soldiers stood outside the doors in the small corridor, two to each door, all of them armed with rams and smaller pistols as well, plus a tranq gun. Diver and I walked down to the end of the hallway, where a double set of guards flanked the door. One of them, I noticed, was Anton. He glanced at me once as we approached, then looked away.

A soldier I didn't know looked us up and down. "State your name and business."

Eep. "Xandri Corelel, Head of Xeno-liaisons," I said, clutching the tablet tighter. "I'm here to see the prisoner. Captain Chui has already sent ahead permission."

"Diver. Part of R&D...well, sort of." He shrugged. "I'm just here as an escort. And to punch the prisoner in the face if he gets out of line."

The soldier unhooked the tranq gun from his belt and handed it to Diver. "Looks a bit better in the press if you use one of these." He gestured, and the other soldiers spread out a bit farther. "Go on in."

"Thank you," I said, even though he was just following orders.

The room beyond was small and empty, except for a bed, a tiny bathroom behind a curtain, and a line of bars separating it in half. Marco Antilles sat on the bed, dressed in a prisoner's plain white, his gazed focus on the wall as if he could see through it if he just stared hard and long enough. I didn't need much skill at reading body language to see the melancholy and despair radiating from him.

He turned his head as we entered. His expression, normally so controlled, changed to astonishment when he saw us. After a moment he closed his mouth and tried to sneer, though it seemed half-hearted at best.

"Well, if it isn't my favorite sacrificial lamb," he said, without nearly the bite I'd heard in his voice before.

Diver made a soft growling sound and took a step forward. I rolled my eyes, flinging out an arm to block his path.

"Look, boys, I don't have time for this. Diver, if you want to be the macho alpha, do it on your own time," I said. I regarded Marco. "I'm not staying. I just came to bring you something."

"Why the hell would you do that?"

"See, that's what I keep asking," Diver said.

"Both of you, shut up." I crossed the room and slid the tablet through the bars, handing it to Marco. "Here."

He took it, though his eyes remained on me. I gazed over his shoulder. It hurt to look at him, not just his eyes but his face in general. I wondered if he noticed that. He dropped his gaze to the tablet, to the sleek casing. It wouldn't matter where he looked; he'd find no way to open it without destroying it completely. That had been one of the conditions it had to meet before Captain Chui would approve of it.

"What is it?" Marco asked at last.

Diver made a sound oddly reminiscent of Aki's chuffing. "For a smart guy, there sure ain't a lot going on up there. It's a computer, ding-brain."

"Oh, really? I thought it was a toaster. No, you puffed-up asshole, what does it *do*?"

"You know, I'm sensing a bit of hostility here. Maybe the criminal needs a nappy."

"Okay," I cut in, "for the last time, Diver: Shut. Up. Marco, you shut up too." They were, after all, getting on my nerves about equally. "Look, it's simple. There's games on there, music, books... a drawing program."

Marco remained silent.

"There's no connection to any kind of communication whatsoever, so don't get any ideas. And you can't fiddle with it, as you can already see, and if you think you're capable of hacking past Kiri's protections, you're space-fried. It's for entertainment purposes only. You're going to serve the time you've earned."

"Not if my people come for me," he retorted.

"But they probably won't," I said. "And even if they do, it'll take them time. You and I both know you'll go stir crazy before then without something to do."

"Why the hell do you care what happens to me?"

I looked down. "There's a lot of cruelty in the universe. I prefer not to be a part of it if I can help it."

"In other words, she's too nice for her own good," Diver put in. "C'mon, Xan. Our time is up. We need to go."

I nodded and turned away. These days I was feeling so many things, *questioning* so many things. I wasn't even sure I should be doing this, but after everything I'd read, it felt wrong to leave Marco without even something to distract his brain from the way it was guaranteed to treat him as the days wore on. I knew far too well what it was like, having your own brain treat you like a lost cause, and it always succeeded best when you had nothing else to do.

"Xandri," Marco called as I started through the doorway.

I paused but didn't look back.

"Thank you."

I gave a tiny nod. Then Diver and I left the room and started down the hall again, after Diver handed the tranq gun back to the soldier outside Marco's door.

"I really don't get it," Diver said, not for the first time. "Why are you showing him any kindness, after what he did? He's the bad guy, Xan."

"Is he?" I tilted my head. "Maybe he is. But he was also tortured as a child, and the LHFH exploited that. The person Marco is now wasn't created in a vacuum. What he's been through doesn't excuse his behavior, but does that mean we should let the other people who shaped him go free of any responsibility?"

Diver went silent. I couldn't even begin to guess what he was thinking, but it didn't matter; I knew what *I* thought. If I hadn't met Captain Chui, if she hadn't pulled me out of that gambling den and onto the *Carpathia*, I could've ended up just like Marco someday. There was nothing about me that was inherently kinder or better than him; the only real difference was our circumstances. Knowing that, I'd had to do *something* for him.

The comm on my wristlet pinged, startling me out of my thoughts. Without really thinking, I tapped it on.

"Xandri," I said as the link opened.

"Ms. Corelel, Mr. Diver," came back Captain Chui's voice. "I need both of you in my office. On the double."

We ran.

We slowed as we hit the corridor where Captain Chui's office was, to regain our breath. I also made an effort to tidy my hair, until Diver—whose own hair was sticking up in flyaway waves—gave me an amused look. *Yeah, I guess that is a lost cause.* I couldn't resist the urge to smooth down my tunic, though, as the office door slid open.

I froze inside the doorway, my heart dropping like an anvil in vacuum; it was a miracle there wasn't a hole in the floor. Gathered in Captain Chui's office along with the captain herself was Magellan, Kiri, my entire Xeno-liaisons team, and Major Douglas. It was that last one that had me considering whether I should make a run for one of our emergency escape pods. Unfortunately, Diver put a hand on my back and nudged me gently inside before I could make up my mind.

"Thank you for joining us so quickly," Captain Chui said, her expression a study in the perfect poker face. "Please, both of you, take a seat."

Two empty chairs sat waiting for us. I stepped forward tentatively, Diver's hand still on my back, and slid into the chair next to Christa. Christa stared straight ahead, her cheeks turning slightly pink. We'd seen each other a few times since the night of the funeral, but she wouldn't even look at me.

"Well, Major Douglas, we're all here," Captain Chui said. "What was it you wanted to share with us?"

He straightened. "We've received word from then Anmerilli. They've agreed to sign."

Holy shit. A round of relieved laughter traveled through the room. I sat frozen in my chair, wishing I could get a better grasp on my own feelings. I was stunned, sure, and relieved, but beyond that—beyond that I didn't quite know. Had I really managed it after all? It had been a risk, and I wasn't fully happy with the way I'd achieved it, but surely that meant things could only improve from here.

Major Douglas held up a hand. "There *is* a condition."

Dread turned my blood to ice in my veins. All around me the room went silent and still, until the silence was a buzzing in my ears. *Sacrificial lamb...scapegoat...* I knew. Somehow, I *knew.*

"A condition?" Captain Chui raised her eyebrows. "Major Douglas, we have already agreed to *many* conditions."

"Yes, though those were before—well, they were before. Considering that you brought an alien species onto their planet, that the Anmerilli are willing to sign at all is quite generous."

"Two," I blurted out, which as *a lot* milder and more succinct than what I wanted to say.

Major Douglas looked startled. "Pardon?"

"We brought *two* alien species onto their planet," I said. *You supercilious ass.* "We brought ourselves as well."

"And considering I had to retrieve one of my own from the hands of Alliance traitors," Captain Chui put in, "it was a necessary decision."

"Perhaps the Anmerilli will be willing to see it that way, in the end. The fact remains that...well, we needed thirty-one votes. The final signature will come from Councilor Nish mar'Odrea if, and only if—"

"Absolutely not," Captain Chui said.

"You're in no position to argue, Captain," Major Douglas shot back. "Your actions were risky. It's only because I have generously chosen not to report you that you haven't been thrown in jail for giving orders in my name. The Alliance overlooks your many transgressions but they will not continue to be so lenient if this alliance falls through. Ms. Corelel has to go."

And there it was. Not that I had expected anything less from a man like Nish mar'Odrea. I'd embarrassed him in front of his peers, beaten him at his own game, and if he couldn't stop the alliance from happening, well, he would damn well ruin *me.* I wondered if mar'Odrea had agreed to keep the AFC's mishaps quiet. They'd love that. A successful alliance and no word breathed about their own mistakes, all for the price of my job. Of my entire life.

"Are you serious?" Diver demanded. "This alliance wouldn't even be happening if it wasn't for her! She saved your ungrateful asses, all of you."

"It was *your* mistake to begin with," Kiri added. "You're the ones who had an LHFH wingnut running lose in your ranks for years!"

Major Douglas drew himself up, indignant. "*We* are not the ones who spilled sensitive military plans to the enemy."

"I'd argue you've been doing that for a while," Diver growled, "what with having moles in your ranks."

To my surprise, Christa cut in too. "Shouldn't we be far more concerned with the behavior of the LHFH? Xandri believes, and I agree, that the LHFH chose to work with the Zechak on this."

"That's absurd!"

"No, it's not. What better way to cover their tracks after the alliance failed?" I jumped in, a bit of hope flickering at all the support I was getting. "We leave in failure, *they* leave with the graser plans, and then the Zechak move in and destroy Cochinga, so no one can ever track what happens. Probably the LHFH originally agreed to share the graser plans with the Zechak, but something clearly changed because—"

"Enough!" Major Douglas snapped. "Would you listen to yourself? Captain Chui, this would have happened eventually anyway. After the actions of Marco Antilles, parliament will be discussing quite seriously whether individuals such as Ms. Corelel ought to be allowed to have jobs such as this one. The danger—"

"Danger?" Diver was on his feet. "You can't be serious!"

"That's quite enough," Captain Chui barked. "Diver, sit down. Major Douglas, Ms. Corelel is one of my most valuable crew members."

"And if you refuse, you won't have a crew," the major said. "The Alliance will shut you down once and for all. Either she goes, or you go. *All* of you. As long as she stays, she's a danger to the Alliance and to the *Carpathia*."

I huddled in my chair, my arms wrapped around me. This was it. No matter what, Captain Chui couldn't risk the entirety of *Carpathia*. The work the crew did was too important, far more important than me. The same went for the alliance with the Anmerilli, although we did at least have the schematics for the graser. *And parliament will be discussing people like me. They think we're dangerous. That's what got us wiped out in the first place.*

After what Marco had done...I shivered. The noise in the room was increasing, turning into an incoherent buzz around me. I had to get out of there.

My chair fell back as I shot to my feet, quieting the room for a moment. Diver reached out, trying to catch me, but I dodged away from his hand and bolted for the door. I slammed my palm against the release and fled into the corridor, where I froze on the spot, too stunned to move. Where would I even go? I couldn't return to Wraith; I *refused*. But then where? *Maybe I could go to Psittaca? But I don't really know other Psittacans that well...*

Shouting echoed in the room behind me. I ought to move, ought to do something with myself, but I couldn't budge.

A moment later the door slid open again, and others poured out. People circled around me, crowding too close. *Go away! Please, just leave me alone!* I scrunched up tighter, wanting to jerk away from the hands resting on my shoulders. Their voices reached my ears as noise, noise I couldn't understand, and it threatened to overwhelm me.

Claws scraping the floor cut through the voices. I turned my head slightly, caught sight of Aki loping down the hall. Her six legs carried her down the corridor faster than her furry bulk implied, and she skidded to a halt next to the group surrounding me, letting her rump come to rest on the floor.

"Enough of this," she cut in, her voice like a low rumble of thunder. "Leave her be."

"But Aki," Diver said, "the Anmerilli want her fired!"

"I know. But you're not helping her, not like this." Aki heaved her bulk up off the floor and walked towards me. I reached down instinctively, wrapping my fingers in her fur. "Captain Chui would like to talk to you—all of you—when she's done with Major Douglas. I will help Xandri."

Help me? There's no helping me now. I tightened my fingers, letting them sink down into Aki's coarser underfur. I couldn't even understand what the people around me were saying. I just stood there, waiting, until Aki started walking, giving me a gentle nudge to get me moving. We were halfway down the hall before I spoke again.

"Where are we going?"

"Right now? To your room," Aki said.

"Aki... I don't have anywhere to go. And Captain Chui promised me she wouldn't make me go home."

Aki made a soft rumbling sound. "And so she won't. I'm taking you to *my* home. To Karrckchak."

Chapter Thirty-Four

I stood in my empty room, staring at the bare bookshelves, the tidy bed, the space against the wall where Cake's and Marbles' cages had once stood. Most of my bags were in the hall, and the travel cages were already loaded onto *Mr. Spock*, Aki's personal ship. I shouldered my small pack, which held some clothing and a few last books, and sighed.

Major Douglas had been under orders to remain aboard the *Carpathia* until I was gone. Until I left, the crew would be stuck with him. *Besides, I don't want to stay any longer than I have to.* Being here hurt. This had been my home for four years, the only place I could remember being happy, and now I had to leave. At least I wouldn't have to return to Wraith. Aki intended to get me a position as an *attoaong* on Karrckchak.

The only human attoaong *in Ongkoarrat history. I should be proud.*

I snorted and turned to leave the room. When I pressed my hand to the door, it didn't open. Surprised, I jerked back and opened my mouth to call for *Carpathia*.

"I wanted a moment to say good-bye," her voice echoed from my wristlet, before I had a chance to speak. "My friends are usually other ships, and I don't get to see them often. I will miss you."

Tears pricked my eyes. "I'll miss you too, *Carpathia*."

"But I *will* return for you in time," *Carpathia* said, her voice insistent. "You belong here. You will always be part of my crew and I will have you back."

I didn't want to tell her how impossible that was, now that the Alliance would be arguing my very right to exist. Instead I said, "Thank you. I—I look forward to that day."

"As do I."

The door released, allowing me into the hall. Diver waited for me outside, my bags hefted easily over his shoulder. My heart wrenched to look upon him. He looked so good, the warm red-brown of his skin and the bits of red-gold in his hair; the clear and

306

defined whipcord muscle under his T-shirt; the startling brightness of his eyes. *Will I ever see him again?*

"Captain Chui will find a way to get you back, you know," Diver said. "She's not going to just let parliament walk all over her."

"I'll miss you too," I said with a small, forced laugh.

His expression shifted. He took a step towards me, then another, and leaned in close. I inhaled deeply, wanting one last moment near his warmth and the smell of grease and soap and *him*. To my surprise, he leaned even closer, until the tip of his nose nearly touched mine. My heart sped up as his mouth brushed the corner of mine and slid over my cheek.

"I'm going to miss you too, fireball," he murmured. "But we *will* get you back."

He drew away and I swayed slightly. I wished I had the courage to put my arms around him, to kiss him as I'd been longing to for so long, but I didn't. Instead, I fell into step beside him as he started down the corridor. Sorrow made my heart feel like a stone in my chest, pressing heavy against my ribs. *If I'm supposed to feel so little emotion, if that's what makes me so dangerous, why do I hurt so damn much?*

We used the grav-tubes to get us down to the docking bay with the weight of my luggage to carry. I didn't know what I expected to find down there. I thought perhaps Captain Chui would come to see me off, because she was that kind of captain, but...

She was there, all right. As were Magellan, Kiri, Lieutenant Zubairi, the Psittacans and the Professor, several members I'd worked with in the anthropology division, Anton, and my—*the*—Xeno-liaisons team. Even Christa had showed up. I hesitated a few meters away. The horrible voice in the back of my mind insisted that they were happy to see me go. It shut up as the Psittacans half-buried me in feathery hugs.

Laughing, I managed to crawl out of their huddle, though not before getting a bit of dander up my nose. As I swiped an arm across my face, I noticed Major Douglas at the far back of the crowd. I briefly considered walking over and punching him—after all, what else could anyone do to me?—but I didn't feel like taking the risk. I might break something on his tremendously hard skull.

"Do hurry back, my dear," the Professor said as I made my way past him. "Those feathered monsters of yours run completely amok in my garden without you around."

I blinked. "They run amok in there even with me around."

"Well, yes, but at least they don't *eat* things anymore."

"Just spray the plants with something non-toxic but foul tasting," I suggested. "That'll stop them."

"Traitor," Many Kills hissed, flicking his crest in amusement.

I made my way down the line, mostly shaking hands. Kiri stopped me, hauling me into a tight hug. In front of everyone, she brushed a very light kiss over my lips; I turned so red and hot, I thought I might melt the floor under me. She grinned at me, and I shuffled onwards, trying to cool my flushing cheeks as I exchanged good-byes with the Xeno-liaisons team. I paused again in front of Christa.

"Look..." I began.

She peered up at me tentatively.

"I sent you a file. Read it, okay? It's really important."

"I will." She nodded and looked away again.

The words *hey, you've gotten what you always wanted: my job* bobbed up in my throat, but I swallowed them back down again. I wouldn't leave on that note. Even if I never came back—and I wasn't as convinced as Diver that there was a way to get me back—leaving on bitter terms seemed pointless.

And if I did come back, I didn't want to return to a shitstorm.

Finally, only Captain Chui and Magellan remained. I shook with Magellan, then turned to the Captain. Aki waited for me at the base of *Mr. Spock*.

"Don't say good-bye," Captain Chui said, as I opened my mouth to speak. "We'll come back for you, one way or another."

All I could manage was a nod.

"Consider this extended leave." She smiled and raised her hand for a salute.

Everyone along the line echoed her to the best of their ability— though the Professor and the Psittacans required much modified versions. Tears welled in my eyes as I returned the gesture. Then I spun away, quickly, and ran up the ramp into *Mr. Spock*. The small, spherical vehicle was typical of Ongkoarrat vessels, and at the moment, it was my refuge. I didn't want anyone to see my emotions getting away from me.

I busied myself inside the ship, adjusting the copilot's chair for a human body and ensuring that Cake's and Marble's travel cages were secured down, and that the mild sedative was taking effect. I heard the ramp come up and Aki's claws clicking on the floor as she trundled in. *Think about it, Xan. Captain Chui must mean it when she says she wants you back. She's sending her finest pilot to escort you to your new—temporary—home.* Aki could have just sent ahead to get me permission to land on Karrckchak, but she was taking me herself.

Once I was certain my birds were secure, I strapped myself into the copilot's chair. By then Aki was set up and ready to go, and the bay doors were opening. This was it. I was leaving the only true home I'd ever known.

Don't think about that now, I told myself, watching the stars as they seemed to flicker into life all around us. *Find something else to focus on.* My heart ached. I wanted to go back right now. I wanted to throw myself into Diver's arms and give him that kiss I was too afraid to give him a short time ago. I wanted to punch Major Douglas after all. But it was too late, so I did what I always did when I couldn't cope: I studied.

"It's not healthy to shove your emotions down like that," Aki said quietly.

I flicked through my holo-display. "I don't know what else to do with them. According to common knowledge, I'm not even supposed to have them."

"The problem with common knowledge is that it's far more common than it is knowledge," Aki said with a snort.

"Can't argue there. Hey, Aki..." I raised my head, frowning. "What do I—how do I call people on Karrchchak? I've always used 'she' for you but..."

The Ongkoarrat didn't have gender pronouns of any sort, really. They used the words *ongko* and *ongki*—respectively, and a bit roughly, baby-giver and baby-carrier—instead. There was little dimorphism in them, as well; they tended to be the same size, regardless of *ongko* or *ongki*, and coloration varied by individual. Only their voices were different. Aki's voice sounded more female to my ears—an evolutionary adaptation that, in the days before achieving sapience, had helped the Ongkoarrat find mates.

People had already been using 'she' and 'her' for Aki when I came aboard the *Carpathia*, and I'd fallen into the habit as well, though I knew better.

"Call me as you wish," Aki said. "Your words cannot change who I am."

"Wish I could feel that way."

She chuffed at the exasperation in my voice. "To be fair, my people have a great deal of practice at it. *Our* society never had much room for a concept like gender, and we don't have—how would you put it?—many fucks to give about how people see us."

I giggled.

"The—we'll call them the People of the Great Rock, to make it easy on you. They'll tell you their names, and if it comes to it, how they prefer to be called, though they likely won't care, as long as you do your job as *attoaong* well."

My kind of people. Maybe for once I wouldn't find myself constantly putting my foot in my damn mouth. I leaned back in the chair with a sigh. As soon as I took my mind off my work, everything inside me started to hurt again. I closed my eyes, breathed in deep, and reached for that feeling I got when I was angry, like I was made of ice. I envisioned it all around me, protecting me like armor, encasing my heart and numbing the pain. In, out, in, out. Breathe in the air, arctic air that cooled my insides, and breathe out the pain.

"Xandri."

I opened my eyes.

"We're about to make our sling."

"Already?" I blinked in surprise at the approaching star. "Sorry...I guess I drifted off or something."

"It's fine. It's not like either of us are very skilled at small talk. And besides, you should take whatever time you need, when you need it."

"Hey, Aki..."

She sighed. "Yes, I will give you a chance to try a sling during the trip. How many simulator hours do you have now?"

"I stopped keeping track in my head once I passed five-hundred, but it's in my wristlet somewhere."

An emotion penetrated the ice: Excitement. I hadn't gotten to try much actual piloting yet, let alone a sling, but Aki would let me.

I watched her—always a little in awe—as she shifted in her chair, and it swung around her, moving with the cradling sphere shape of the ship. All six limbs worked at once, steering, maneuvering, releasing the sling-grapples. She never missed a single cue; was never even the tiniest bit slow.

"Wheeeeeee!" Marbles cheered behind me as we launched into the sling.

"When you *do* finally come back to the *Carpathia*," Aki said mildly, "and you will, you have got to stop letting Private Jensen watch those birds."

"I'm dearly afraid that she picked that up on her own."

"Wheeeeee!"

"Silly bird," Cake chirped.

Aki started to chuff. I buried my face in my hands, shaking with laughter and a few tears as well. I still had Marbles and Cake. I still had Aki. Maybe, if I was lucky, I still had Diver and Kiri too. I didn't know how long it would be until I saw them again but... *But I've made it through worse. I can get through this too. I have to.*

I'd come through too much to give up now.

About the Author

Kaia Sønderby is an American currently residing in Sweden with her Danish husband. She hopes to eventually escape to a warmer country that actually sees the sun for more than one month out of every year. Her hobbies include reading, playing video games, various and sundry art projects—usually involving far too much glitter—and being a feminist killjoy, and her interests vary from history to the paranormal to maritime disasters. She is also the proud momma of a continually expanding array of rodents (expanding in numbers, not just expanding outwards, though they're doing that too).

Want More?

At The Kraken Collective, we know how frustrating it can be to reach the end of a book and want more. Within the following pages, you'll find books with a similar feel to help you scratch that reading itch and why we're recommending them.
We hope our suggestions will help you find your next favourite read!

City of Strife

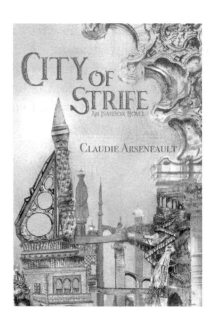

If you're looking for more political back and forth underpinned by deeply personal stories, check out *City of Strife* from Claudie Arseneault! *City of Strife* is a mosaical, epic novel with a large and majorly queer cast, a web of political intrigue and personal narratives, and a heart of gold. In it, an elven noble's attempt to stop imperialist wizards from taking over his city will have repercussion on its inhabitants, from its richest towers to the homeless shelter at its bottom. Fans of elves, magic, and crisscrossing storylines will find everything they want within this story.

Cheerleaders from Planet X

If you're looking for more science fiction with aliens, check out *Cheerleaders from Planet X*. Laura Clark thought she was just your average college freshman—until the day she saw a cheerleader on a skateboard get into a superhuman brawl with a lightning-wielding stranger in a trenchcoat. And the only person who saw it is the beautiful, standoffish Shailene, one of the possibly superpowered cheerleaders of her Laura's rival school. Fun and fast-paced, *Cheerleaders from Planet X* is a perfect blend of old tropes and fresh twists wrapped around a romance that might just be ... out of this world.

Made in the USA
Middletown, DE
20 August 2020